D0053521

PRAISE FOR BETH K. VOGT

"Beth Vogt has long been a favorite for romance, but she finds her true niche with her first women's fiction entry, *Things I Never Told You*. Engaging, sympathetic, and almost painfully honest, this story of buried family secrets and hidden trauma will stay with you long after the last page is turned. I'm impatiently awaiting the other titles in this series."

CARLA LAUREANO, AUTHOR OF *FIVE DAYS IN SKYE* AND *THE SATURDAY NIGHT SUPPER CLUB*

"Questions, regrets, and memories hang over all our lives. *Things I Never Told You* authentically explores past and present hurts in a way that will take readers deeper into the heart. Beth's story will give real hope to anyone struggling with fractured relationships."

CHRIS FABRY, CHRISTY AWARD–WINNING AUTHOR OF *DOGWOOD* AND *THE PROMISE OF JESSE WOODS*

"Talented author Beth Vogt brings her storytelling to a new level in this women's fiction debut by tackling the messiness and beautiful bond of families in *Things I Never Told You*. Told through the voices of sisters, Vogt uses a clever twist in this tale of love and forgiveness. Readers will savor this one."

RACHEL HAUCK, *NEW YORK TIMES* BESTSELLING AUTHOR

"Once again Vogt's beautiful writing captures the struggles and hopes of her broken characters, this time with a cast of sisters who find themselves forced to confront their pasts, their fears, and the healing power of forgiveness. Powerful, moving, and redemptive. Everything I hope for in a Beth Vogt novel."

SUSAN MAY WARREN, *USA TODAY* BESTSELLING, CHRISTY AWARD–WINNING AUTHOR

"Earnest. Emotional. Hope-filled and complex . . . With the characteristic depth and heart readers have come to expect from a Beth Vogt novel, *Things I Never Told You* marks the author's memorable entry into contemporary women's fiction. Whether sister, mother, daughter, or friend . . . each will find shades of herself in this redemption story. It is a must-read, must-share novel!"

KRISTY CAMBRON, BESTSELLING AUTHOR OF THE LOST CASTLE AND HIDDEN MASTERPIECE SERIES

"*Things I Never Told You* is a poignant, emotionally moving story that pulled me in from the opening chapter. Compelling threads of past hurts and present fears, long-kept secrets and complex family dynamics, kept me turning pages. Beth Vogt's latest book, complete with a soul-stirring faith journey, is one that will stick with you long after the end."

MELISSA TAGG, AUTHOR OF THE WALKER FAMILY SERIES AND THE ENCHANTED CHRISTMAS COLLECTION

"Beth Vogt is one of those authors who legitimizes the depth of story hidden in dramas not unlike our own. In *Things I Never Told You*, she tugs the reader through the pages as a child might plead, 'Come and see.' Before the book's end, the characters have become the reader's extended family, their pain and joys our own. Another story well-told."

CYNTHIA RUCHTI, AUTHOR OF *A FRAGILE HOPE* AND *AS MY PARENTS AGE*

"In *Things I Never Told You*, Beth K. Vogt deftly explores family dynamics, the push and pull between sisters, the pain of loss, the journey of grief, the beauty of forgiveness, and so much more. I rejoiced and wept with these characters and was sorry to let them go when I reached the end. Highly recommended!"

ROBIN LEE HATCHER, RITA AND CHRISTY AWARD–WINNING AUTHOR

"This beautifully told story tugged me into the lives of three sisters separated by tragedy and time. The book is a beautiful tale of redemption and hope in the midst of darkness and fear. It is filled with characters that will stick with you long after you read the final line."

CARA PUTMAN, AWARD-WINNING AUTHOR OF *SHADOWED BY GRACE* AND *IMPERFECT JUSTICE*

"Rich with spiritual truths, emotionally compelling and endearing characters, *Things I Never Told You* peels back layers of the soul, exposing the dangers of secrets kept, and the freedom found when light shines through the darkness as the truth is told. A beautiful reading experience not to be missed."

CATHERINE WEST, AUTHOR OF *THE MEMORY OF YOU*

"Beth Vogt has an ability to draw her readers more deeply into a story, revealing secrets only when necessary, and never tell all until the end. Women's fiction at its finest."

HANNAH ALEXANDER, AUTHOR OF *THE WEDDING KISS* AND THE HALLOWED HALLS SERIES

"A book this good is a double-edged sword. It's a wonderful reading experience and the ultimate frustration because it's over far too soon. Beth Vogt is truly one of the great ones. She's established herself as a consummate storyteller and a grand master of her craft."

EDIE MELSON, DIRECTOR OF THE BLUE RIDGE MOUNTAINS CHRISTIAN WRITERS CONFERENCE

Things I Never Told You

a Thatcher Sisters novel

BETH K. VOGT

Tyndale House Publishers, Inc.
Carol Stream, Illinois

Visit Tyndale online at www.tyndale.com.

Visit Beth K. Vogt's website at www.bethvogt.com.

TYNDALE and Tyndale's quill logo are registered trademarks of Tyndale House Publishers, Inc.

Things I Never Told You

Designed by Julie Chen

Edited by Sarah Mason Rische

Published in association with the literary agency of Books & Such Literary Management, 52 Mission Circle, Suite 122, PMB 170, Santa Rosa, CA 95409.

Things I Never Told You is a work of fiction. Where real people, events, establishments, organizations, or locales appear, they are used fictitiously. All other elements of the novel are drawn from the author's imagination.

For information about special discounts for bulk purchases, please contact Tyndale House Publishers at csresponse@tyndale.com, or call 1-800-323-9400.

Library of Congress Cataloging-in-Publication Data
Names: Vogt, Beth K., author.
Title: Things I never told you / Beth K. Vogt.
Description: Carol Stream, Illinois : Tyndale House Publishers, Inc., [2018] | "Thatcher Sisters."
Identifiers: LCCN 2017049669| ISBN 9781496427236 (hardcover) | ISBN 9781496427243 (softcover)
Subjects: LCSH: Family secrets—Fiction. | Sisters--Fiction. | Domestic fiction.
Classification: LCC PS3622.O362 T48 2018 | DDC 813/.6—dc23 LC record available at https://lccn.loc.gov/2017049669

Printed in the United States of America

24	23	22	21	20	19	18
7	6	5	4	3	2	1

To my daughters, Katie Beth, Amy, and Christa:
You define sisters *beautifully. And for that, I am thankful.*

THE WHAT-IFS TAUNTED ME every time I visited my parents, but any hope of beginning again had vanished years ago—if there'd ever been one.

What would have happened if my parents had gone through with selling the house in Colorado Springs my sisters and I had grown up in? If they'd labeled and taped up all the boxes—the clothes, the books, the dishes, the photographs, the awards, and the trophies—and unpacked them in a different house?

A change of location. A chance to start over.

But unexpected loss held my parents captive.

For the most part, our family seemed unchanged. The

kitchen clock—a porcelain plate decorated with bright red-and-yellow flowers but lacking any numerals to designate the passing of time—hung in the same place it had since a dozen Mother's Days ago. The same white wooden shutters hid the bay windows in the breakfast nook. The same worn round table in the middle, surrounded by four chairs adorned with nondescript blue cushions our mother changed out every few years—whenever Johanna reminded her to do so.

I pushed the Start button on the once-new dishwasher. My parents had installed it at the Realtor's recommendation when they'd planned to move into the larger house that offered a coveted view of Pikes Peak.

Time to focus on the cheesecakes—the engagement party dessert finale. The hum of the dishwasher blended with garbled conversation as the door between the kitchen and dining room opened, the sound of Jillian's fiancé's booming laughter sneaking in. Geoff and his corny jokes.

"Just getting the dessert, Kim—"

"I'm not your timekeeper, little sister." Johanna's no-nonsense voice interrupted my concentration.

I stiffened, gripping the handles of the fridge. Why hadn't I posted a Do Not Enter sign on the door? Maybe I should have caved to Nash's insistence to attend the party, even though tonight was more work than play for me. Why not have my boyfriend act as bouncer outside the kitchen? Flex his muscles and run interference?

I had no time for my oldest sister. Any minute now,

Kimberlee would return from setting up the silver carafes of coffee and hot water for tea, along with cream, sugar, spoons, and other necessities. She'd expect the trio of cheesecakes to be arranged on their individual stands—my job tonight, since we'd only had the caterers deliver the food for such a small gathering.

"Do you need something, Johanna?" I pulled the first cheesecake from the fridge, my mouth watering at the thought of key lime and dollops of whipped cream. Being the party planner for tonight meant I'd had no chance to indulge in the hors d'oeuvres or cocktails, despite this being my other sister's engagement party. And vegan or not, I could appreciate a decadent dessert—and postpone interacting with Johanna.

"You and Kimberlee are pretty good at this event-planning business." Johanna leaned against the kitchen counter.

"Mom and Jillian seem happy. That's the important thing." I settled the cheesecake on its stand, the plastic wrap clinging to my fingers as I uncovered it. "It's all about finding out what people want and then making it happen."

"Festivities is making enough to pay the bills, apparently."

"Yes."

Not that I was going to produce an Excel spreadsheet of our accounts payable and receivable for my oldest sister.

"You two didn't charge Mom and Dad full price—"

"Really, Johanna?" Not sparing my sister a glance, I shoved the fridge door closed with my hip, a turtle cheesecake balanced in my hands.

"Oh, don't get in a huff, Payton. Honestly, how do you manage your customers if you're so touchy?"

And this . . . this was yet another reason why I didn't come home unless absolutely necessary. I concentrated on transporting the second cheesecake from the fridge to the island, refusing to square off with my sister. Best to change the subject and prep the desserts.

"Jillian and Geoff seem perfect for one another, don't they?"

Johanna took the bait. "Of course they do. They enjoy the same foods. The same movies. He makes her laugh. They're content with a typical version of happily ever after."

And now my question had set Johanna's sights on Jillian. Should I ignore the unspoken criticism or not? "You don't approve of Geoff?"

"I wouldn't marry him. They remind me of that old nursery rhyme. 'Jack Sprat could eat no fat, his wife could eat no lean . . .'"

"And I suppose one of the reasons you're marrying Beckett is because you make such a good-looking couple?"

"You've got to admit he's easy on the eyes."

Easy on the eyes? Who said stuff like that anymore? "Not that he's around very often for anyone to get a look at him."

"If I don't mind being in a long-distance relationship, I don't see why you should be so critical." Johanna's stilettos tapped a sharp staccato on the wood floor, her platinum-blonde hair caught up in a tight ponytail that swished down between her shoulder blades.

"I'm not criticizing. Just mentioning that Beckett plays the role of the Invisible Man quite well."

"You're almost as funny as Geoff." Ice frosted Johanna's words.

Time to change the subject again unless I wanted a full-blown argument with one sister during my other sister's party. Not that I could think of a topic Johanna and I agreed on. "Isn't it odd? You and Beckett have been engaged for over two years now. Shouldn't we be planning your wedding so Jillian and Geoff don't beat you two down the aisle?"

"It's not a race. Beckett's stationed in Wyoming and I don't want to give up my job to move there—"

"Did I know Beckett was in Wyoming?"

"Honestly, Payton, he's been there for a year." Johanna sniffed. "But then, it's not like we chat every other day, is it? You and Pepper were the close ones—"

Heat flushed my neck. My face. "There's no need to bring Pepper into the conversation, is there?"

"Why, after all this time, are you still so sensitive about talking about her?"

"I'm not sensitive. I just don't see why you had to mention Pepper when we were talking about you and Beckett—"

The sound of voices rose once again as the kitchen door opened. Poor Kimberlee. She didn't know she'd have to assume Jillian's usual position as the neutral zone between Johanna and me.

"Have you seen Jillian?"

Not Kimberlee. Mom, who was also an expert human buffer.

"Isn't she with Geoff?" I removed the cling wrap from the cheesecake.

"She was a few moments ago, but now I can't find her." Mom circled the island as if she expected to find her middle daughter crouching down hiding from her. "Isn't it almost time for dessert? And aren't we supposed to open gifts after that? They certainly received a lot of presents, didn't they?"

"Yes. It's a great turnout." If only the kitchen didn't feel like a revolving three-ring circus. How would Johanna like it if our family showed up at the hospital pharmacy where she was in charge?

Before I could say anything else, Kimberlee, the one person I'd been waiting for, joined the crowd. "Are we all set in here, Payton?"

"Just about." I swallowed back the words *if people would stay out of my kitchen.* This wasn't my kitchen. And family or not, Mom was a client, at least for tonight, and needed to be treated like one. And I'd been dealing with Johanna for years. If I wanted tonight to be a success, the less said, the better.

"Mom, why don't you and Johanna join the guests?" I removed the classic cheesecake from the fridge. "I'll find Jillian while Kimberlee makes the announcement about dessert and Jillian and Geoff opening their gifts."

As Johanna and Mom left, I faced my business partner, shook my head, and sighed. "Family. And before that, a longtime family friend wandered in, asking for the crab dip recipe."

"It comes with working for relatives." Kimberlee took the cheesecake from me, the eclectic assortment of rings on her fingers sparkling under the kitchen lights. "But honestly, everything has gone beautifully. There's hardly any food left."

"That's because I know how to plan portions."

"It's because we know how to throw a good party."

"Well, let's keep things going and get this dessert set up."

Once the trio of cheesecakes was arranged on the table in my parents' dining room, I nodded to Kimberlee. "I've got to go find our bride-to-be."

"No problem. I can handle this." Kimberlee smoothed a wrinkle from the white tablecloth and repositioned the vase filled with bright-red poppies, my mother's favorite flowers.

"It's not like she wandered far. She's probably in the bathroom touching up her makeup."

Not that Jillian was a "refresh her makeup" kind of gal. Mascara and a little bit of basic eyeliner was her usual routine. Lipstick was reserved for fancier affairs. She'd probably be cajoled by the photographer into wearing some on her wedding day.

The upstairs bathroom was empty, lit only by the flickering flame of a cinnamon-scented candle. Where could Jillian be? A thin band of light shone out from beneath the door of Johanna and Jillian's former bedroom at the far end of the darkened hallway. Why would my sister be in there? As

I moved past my old bedroom, my fingertips brushed the doorknob for a second. I pulled my hand away, balling my fingers into a fist.

I paused outside the bedroom and then rapped my knuckles against the door. "Jillian?"

Nothing . . . and then, "Payton? Do you need me for something?"

Just for her party. I eased the door open, stepping inside. "What are you doing up here? It's time to open your gifts."

What had once been Johanna and Jillian's room was now a generic guest room. At the moment, the only light came from the slender glass lamp on the bedside table. My sisters' beds had been replaced by a single larger bed covered in a gray-and-white paisley comforter. An idyllic outdoor scene adorned the wall across from the dark oak dresser.

Jillian, who'd been hunched over on the corner of the bed, straightened her shoulders. "I, um, got a phone call and decided to take it in here away from all the noise."

"Is everything okay?"

"Yes. Absolutely." Jillian's smile seemed to wobble for the briefest second. "Did you need me for something?"

"Your engagement party? It's time to dismantle that Jenga tower of gifts in the family room." I shook my head. "*Tsk.* And after all the hard work I put in arranging it."

"Right." Jillian smoothed her yellow empire-waist sundress down over her hips. "It's been a wonderful party, Payton."

"Thank you for saying so, but it's not over yet." I touched Jillian's shoulder. "You're really okay?"

She nodded so that the ends of her hair brushed against the back of my hand. "Yes. Nothing that won't wait until Monday."

I didn't know why I'd asked. It wasn't like Jillian would confide in me. We weren't the "Will you keep a secret?" kind of sisters. "All right then. Why don't you go find Geoff and I'll bring you both some dessert? Do you want key lime, classic, or turtle cheesecake?"

Now it was my sister's turn to shake her head. "I should skip it altogether. We're going wedding dress shopping soon enough, and I know I'm going to look awful—"

"Oh, stop! Don't become a weight-conscious bridezilla." My comment earned the ghost of a laugh from my sister. "What's wrong?"

"You know Mrs. Kenton?"

"Of course—the family friend who can get away with saying, 'Oh, Payton, I knew you when . . .' and does. Every time she sees me. She pull that on you tonight?"

Red stained my sister's face. "No. She just said—in the nicest way possible, of course—that she hoped I'd lose a few pounds before the wedding."

"And what did you say?"

"Nothing."

Of course she didn't. "Jillian—"

She waved away my words. "Forget I said anything."

"It was rude." And Mrs. Kenton, family friend or not, could forget about ever seeing the recipe she'd requested. "How about I bring you a small slice of each cheesecake? Calories don't count at engagement parties, you know."

"Really small slices?"

"I promise. This is a celebration. Your one and only engagement party."

"You're right." Jillian stood, brushing her straight hair away from her face. "Tonight, we celebrate. Tomorrow . . . well, we're not thinking about that, are we?"

"No, because tomorrow means playing catch-up for me. And prepping for next week."

And Saturday morning breakfast with my family.

Something else I wasn't thinking about.

⌐

Breakfast at my parents' always required drinking at least three cups of coffee.

I retrieved the glass coffeepot from the kitchen and brought it to the table, pouring a steady stream of dark liquid fortitude into the Dallas Starbucks mug from one of Dad's business trips. A trip equaled a coffee mug. Just like everything in the kitchen, the coffeemaker was outdated. Maybe I could convince my sisters to buy our parents a Keurig for Christmas. "Anyone else need a refill?"

Only Dad nodded, moving his faded orange-and-blue Broncos mug closer to me so I could add coffee, the roasted aroma filling the air. After returning the pot to its proper place, I slid into my chair across from Johanna and began sweetening my coffee.

"Three sugars? What is that, your second cup of coffee?"

Johanna wrinkled her nose. "Have you ever heard of Splenda or Stevia?"

"My third. And I prefer the real stuff. I like my caffeine with a jolt of sugar." I stirred the overabundance of sugar, my spoon clinking against the rim.

"I'm surprised your teeth haven't rotted out of your head."

My fingers tightened around the handle of my mug. "Well, if they did, I'd be the one paying my dental bills—"

"Really, girls, it's barely ten o'clock in the morning," Mom interrupted the exchange. "And you're both adults. Stop bickering."

"Weren't we discussing the bridal shower?" Dad's tone was even.

"We've discussed the basics." Johanna scanned the list she'd made on her iPad. "With the wedding in April, we could wait until February for the shower. Or we could do something sooner, say November, and let your friends and coworkers host another shower closer to the wedding date. As maid of honor, I'll be hosting this party, of course, with Payton and Kimberlee's company catering it."

"As long as Jillian's happy with all that." I resisted the urge to toss a fourth spoonful of sugar into my coffee. I could either hassle my oldest sister or drink my much-needed eye-opener in peace.

"I'm sorry—what?" Jillian yawned and moved leftover scrambled eggs around her plate with her fork.

"I just said Kimberlee and I are happy to cater the bridal shower so long as you're good with that."

"Oh . . . of course. I loved all the appetizers you served."

"The bison sliders were awesome." Geoff spoke around a bite of bacon.

"I wouldn't want anyone else to do my bridal shower." Jillian smiled when Geoff reached over and squeezed her hand. "But, Payton, could you work something out so you can attend the party, too? I hardly saw you last night."

"I was there when you opened gifts—well, most of them." I pressed my fingertips into the knots at the base of my neck. The consequence of setup, cleanup, and loading supplies into the business van Kimberlee drove back to North Denver last night. "I'll see if we can arrange things so I can be around for more of the actual bridal shower. We can always bring in other people to help."

Johanna added something to her list. "I'll get together more specifics about a theme, food, and decor and e-mail you, Payton. And then Jillian just needs to let us know a preferred date."

"That'll be fine." I glanced up from a text from Nash asking when I'd be getting home. Let Johanna take the lead and relegate me to the background. That was easiest. "If we're done here, I'll finish my coffee and hit the road . . ."

Mom shifted in her chair. "There is one more thing we need to talk about."

"There is?"

"Yes. I, um, got a phone call—" Mom made eye contact

with everyone at the table but me—"from Pepper's high
school volleyball coach. Your coach."

My phone slipped from my hand, bouncing off the edge
of the table and tumbling to the faux Persian carpet with a
soft thud. "Coach Sydney? Why would she call you?"

Now Mom looked at me, then concentrated on setting
her silverware on her empty plate, one piece at a time. "Well,
she wanted to tell me the high school is honoring some of
their former outstanding athletes. And Pepper is included
because of all the school records she set. They plan on retiring
her jersey number and displaying it in the gym."

My hands gripped my jeans-covered knees, and I willed
myself to remain still as Mom talked. It was no surprise the
school would honor a star athlete like Pepper. Several college
coaches had been keeping track of her statistics by the time
she was a sophomore.

Mom twisted a strand of her brown hair that was threaded
through with gray. "Remember how they called you and
Pepper—?"

"Double Trouble." I whispered the nickname given us by
some of our opponents because Pepper and I were identical
twins, and we both played middle.

"That's right. It was always fun to read that in the paper."
Even all these years later, Mom seemed to relish the memory.
"Anyway, Sydney was trying to get in touch with you because
she hopes you'll say something about Pepper at the ceremony."

Mom's request might as well have been a well-aimed dump
by a setter—and me, one of the unsuspecting defenders on

the other side of the volleyball net. "What? No. Surely they can do this ceremony without me being a part of it."

"Pepper was your twin sister, Payton. She was closer to you than anyone else."

"Mom, please!" I shoved my chair back, stumbling to my feet, almost stepping on my phone.

"Honey, it's been ten years since Pepper died—"

"I know how long it's been, Mom. That doesn't mean I want to talk about Pepper in front of a bunch of people I don't know or haven't seen in years."

"What is wrong with you?" And now Johanna had to join the conversation. "This is a chance to honor Pepper's memory. Why don't you want to be a part of it? Everyone else is on board."

"Am I the last one to know about this?" I forced myself to face my family instead of walking out of the room. Out of the house.

"Well, you don't visit that often, do you?" Johanna managed to twist the conversation away from honoring Pepper to skewering me. "Or call. This is the first chance we've had to talk with you about the ceremony."

I'd deal with today's unexpected issue and ignore Johanna's typical attack. "And you're all okay with this idea?"

"Payton, we're talking about one evening. A couple of hours at most." Dad's words were low. Steady. Ever the voice of reason. "We'll all be there together. Have a chance to remember Pepper and something that was important to her. And you, too. So yes, we all think this is a good idea."

"I don't have a choice?" Did anyone else think I sounded like a sulky adolescent?

"Of course you have a choice." Mom's smile held the hint of an apology. "We're not going to force you to participate—"

"But think of how it would look if we all attended and you didn't."

"Thank you so much for not forcing me, Johanna."

"Be an adult, Payton. Stop making this about you."

"But I'm the one expected to be up front, talking . . . about Pepper." I swallowed a sudden tightness in my throat.

I should have skipped breakfast and driven straight home. Coming home was like trying to step into a faded family photograph—one that had been partially torn so that the image was incomplete. "When is this event taking place?"

"Sydney said it was scheduled for the middle of September." Mom twisted her napkin. "I have her phone number if you want to talk to her . . ."

Maybe surrender was my best option for dealing with this ambush—at least for now.

"Fine. I'll call her and get the details."

"You'll do it?"

I bent to retrieve my phone, trying to ignore the hope in Mom's voice. At least my overnight bag and purse were already by the front door. "I said I'd talk to her. I need to think about this more before I say yes. *If* I say yes. I need to make sure Kimberlee and I don't have a competing commitment." Maybe, just maybe, I'd get that lucky. "Text me her number, please. I need to head home. Nash is hoping to spend part of the day together—maybe catch a movie."

"Tell him we missed seeing him." Dad half rose from his chair.

"Of course." I came close enough for a quick hug, following that up with a similar duck and hug with Mom. "No need to walk me out. We'll talk soon."

As I backed up, I nodded to everyone else at the table, hoping a smile would suffice for a good-bye. "Have fun getting all that loot back to your apartment, Jillian."

"We will, but it's going to Geoff's house. He's got more room."

"Sounds like a plan."

Johanna didn't even look up from her iPad. "I'll be e-mailing you about the bridal shower, Payton."

"Fine." Another nod and then more distance.

Welcomed distance.

2

She'd given up being particular about her clothes a long time ago, but a thin pink paper top was the worst excuse for a cover-up she'd ever seen. Or worn.

Sweat formed along the waistband of Jillian's navy-blue pants. The astringent scent of alcohol lingered in the room. How long had she been waiting for Dr. Sartwell? She eyed her large teal purse sitting on top of her neatly folded blazer, blouse, and bra in the chair against the wall. Should she hop down and retrieve her cell phone? Scan her e-mails while she waited? Maybe pull up the e-book she was reading?

Jillian shifted on the edge of the exam table, causing the strip of protective paper to crinkle beneath her legs at the same time the top threatened to slip off her left shoulder.

17

No. She would not be traipsing around in this one-size-doesn't-fit-all medical fashion statement.

A sharp knock on the door signaled Dr. Sartwell's arrival.

"Come in." With one hand holding the front of the top closed, Jillian used the other to finger-comb her hair into place. Not that her attempt mattered all that much.

"Good afternoon, Jillian." Dr. Sartwell entered the room, her thin frame covered by a starched white lab coat, her black cat's-eye glasses crowning her salt-and-pepper hair. She paused, head tilting to one side. "Oh. You're in an exam gown."

Jillian nodded. "Your medical assistant told me to change into this."

"I'm not planning on doing an exam—unless there's something about the biopsy site you want me to look at."

"No, it's fine."

"Well, I believe if we're just talking, and if I get to have clothes on, then you get to have clothes on, too."

"Oh, that's all right—"

"It's only fair. I kept you waiting, so I can wait while you change." The doctor backed up. "I'll give you a few minutes, okay?"

"Okay."

In less than five minutes, Jillian sat across from her family doctor, fully clothed, the flimsy paper top tossed in the trash.

"Better?" Dr. Sartwell set her laptop on the small desk to her side, slid her glasses down, and tapped in her password to open Jillian's chart before turning to face her again.

"Much better, at least as far as my selection of clothing goes."

"Well, yes. But you're not here to discuss that."

"No." Her short burst of laughter sounded too high. "I need you to help me figure out what's going on. What do I do about the biopsy?"

"Like I told you on Friday night, the biopsy shows cancer."

Cancer.

In a repeat of Friday night's conversation, it was as if time slowed for a few moments . . . as if her hearing dulled, and she had to mentally repeat the word to process the truth.

She had cancer.

She still hadn't spoken the two-syllable word out loud. Still hadn't told Geoff about the phone call. Or that she'd even had a biopsy after her supposed-to-be-routine annual physical ten days ago. As long as she didn't say anything to anyone else, she maintained a thin veneer of control on her life.

"But I'm only thirty-two. And there's no history of breast cancer in my family—"

"I understand that, Jillian. I know that after you hear the word *cancer* applied to you, your brain shuts down. But we need to talk about the next steps for you to take." Dr. Sartwell paused and then reached out and touched Jillian's hand, her fingertips cool against her skin. "I know you didn't expect me to find a lump during a routine breast exam. It's a shock—and I'm sorry."

Jillian pressed her lips together, her chin quivering. *No crying.* If she cried, her face would get all blotchy and people would stare at her when she left the office. She averted her gaze and blinked, once, twice, then refocused on her physician, who had the answers to her questions. "What do I do now?"

"The mammogram shows a one-centimeter lesion, which is about the size of a small grape." Dr. Sartwell held the invisible grape between her thumb and forefinger. "I'm optimistic we caught this early. Now comes a variety of things. Blood work. A more thorough physical exam. Then we need to schedule you an appointment with a breast surgeon, who will probably recommend an MRI—"

Jillian scrambled to process everything, but one question trumped all the others. "How soon can we get this done?"

"We've already done your annual exam, and I can recheck a few more things today—like listening to your heart and lungs again. Then I'll order your blood work. You can have that drawn here." Dr. Sartwell typed something into her laptop. "I already discussed your case with Dr. Williamson, one of the top breast surgeons in town. I highly recommend her, but she's out of town for the rest of the week, speaking at a medical conference. The soonest she could see you is a week from this Wednesday."

Nine days.

"Is it okay to wait that long?"

"Breast cancer is not generally aggressive, and as I said, based on the initial findings, I believe we've caught this early. So yes, it's fine to wait. But if you prefer, I could recommend someone else who might be able to see you sooner."

Jillian ran her fingertips along the premade crease in her pants. "I don't need to shop around. I trust your recommendation."

"Fine. I'll make sure you have Dr. Williamson's information before you leave today so you can schedule your appointment. Is your fiancé with you? Does he have any questions to ask me?"

"I . . . I haven't told Geoff anything yet." Jillian twisted the material of her pants between her fingers.

Dr. Sartwell's eyebrows rose over the rim of her glasses. "Why not?"

"Because there's nothing to tell. Not really."

"Jillian, we do know that you have cancer—"

"You said we caught it early. We'll confirm that it's not that serious and then I'll tell Geoff. No sense in worrying him."

"You might want to take someone with you when you have your initial appointment with Dr. Williamson." Dr. Sartwell's calm voice soothed Jillian's frayed emotions. "It helps to have someone else there to hear everything that's said. Maybe even take notes and help you process all the information. And if Dr. Williamson recommends a lumpectomy—"

"Dr. Sartwell, I can only focus on realities, no *ifs* or *maybe*s. And I realize you might handle this differently if you were the patient, but for now, I prefer to keep this to myself. I don't want to have to worry about everyone else's reactions. Does that make sense?"

"Yes. But at some point, your family and your fiancé need to know—"

"I understand." Jillian straightened her shoulders. "I just need to decide when to tell them."

There was time to make that decision later. For now, she'd finish this appointment. And maybe some of Dr. Sartwell's calm assurance would transfer over to her so that she could get through everything without breaking down.

⌒

Should she take someone with her when she met with Dr. Williamson—or shouldn't she?

Jillian flipped Dr. Sartwell's business card over, reading the information her family practice doctor had scrawled on the back, as if she'd find the answer to her question hidden within the surgeon's name and office phone number.

She was an adult. She'd been going to doctors' appointments by herself for years. She'd take careful notes just in case she didn't remember everything Dr. Williamson said. Because yes, she'd have to tell Geoff and her family. And then she'd have to answer all their questions.

She turned the card over again. If she did ask someone to go with her, who would it be?

Geoff? No, she wouldn't ask him. He was swamped with helping a company recover from a malicious malware attack that took down their computer system. The man didn't need something else to worry about. And maybe she was old-fashioned, but being her fiancé didn't mean he had to sit in on a discussion with a breast surgeon.

Harper? As much as she might want to confide in her best

friend, she couldn't. Geoff would be hurt that Harper had known something before he did.

Her mother? Definitely not. Just asking her mother to come to a doctor's appointment would prompt questions she didn't want to answer like "Why?" and "What kind of appointment?" Besides, most thirty-two-year-old women didn't ask their mothers to take them to the doctor.

And there was no asking her father, either. He was good for watching Broncos games with, for grilling her steak just the way she liked it, and for still tweaking a strand of her dark-blonde hair and calling her "Jilly." But she couldn't tell him that she had cancer and ask him not to tell her mother.

Johanna? No, not if she wanted to retain some control of this situation. If she asked, Johanna would throw on her big sister cape, do extensive research, and come prepared with all sorts of questions. Then Johanna would do all the talking as if she were the one facing cancer, relegating Jillian to the role of spectator.

Payton? Jillian closed her eyes, unable to stop the quick huff of laughter. The thought was an off-key bit of comic relief in the midst of too much seriousness. Her relationship with Payton was distant at best, the last decade choked with so many things unsaid. And now she was going to call her sister, pull her into her confidence, and ask her to come to a medical appointment?

No.

Her cell phone rang from within the depths of her purse—what Geoff called a "suitcase"—and Jillian dug past her wallet, keys, change purse, and various tubes of ChapStick and packs of gum before rescuing it.

"Hello?"

"Am I speaking to the future Mrs. Hennessey?"

Geoff's question caused her to giggle, scattering her internal debate. "Why, yes, you are. And who is this?"

"This is Mr. Hennessey, your future husband. I'm also the guy who missed having lunch with you today."

"I doubt that. You've been so busy lately, we haven't had time for lunch dates." Jillian pulled a cold can of soda from the fridge. "Besides, won't I be seeing you in less than an hour? With deep-dish pizza?"

"I did notice we missed lunch together because I had no reason to take a break." Geoff paused. "And I called to say I can't make it tonight."

"What?" Jillian pressed the can against her heart. "Why not?"

"We ran into some additional problems and I have to work late."

"Geoff, really? You've been putting in so much overtime as it is."

"I know. I know. But this project is my responsibility. Besides, what with the engagement party this past weekend, I wasn't around as much as I should have been."

She shouldn't complain. One thing she loved about Geoff was his determination and commitment. Yes, he liked to laugh and joke, but he worked hard. "I understand."

"You know I'd rather be there with you, right?"

"Yes."

"Once we help the company recover from this incident, my hours will be back to normal." His voice lowered. "And besides, in nine months, we'll be married and coming home to each other."

"Now that's a nice thought."

"Yes, it is. I think about that a lot. You sure you don't want to skip all this wedding stuff and just elope?"

Jillian set her soda on the counter and went in search of a bag of white cheddar popcorn. "How many times are you going to ask me that? I'm beginning to think you're not joking."

"Hey, I'd elope with you tonight."

"Now I know you're joking. You'd never elope in the middle of something like this."

Geoff's burst of laughter warmed her, dissipating the shadow that had lurked alongside her all day. "You know me so well."

"I do. And you understand I want a fun wedding to celebrate with our friends and family."

Or was a big wedding the chance to prove to so many doubters how wrong they'd been about her chance of ever getting married?

"All right. No more talk of eloping. We'll do this getting-married thing up right—and then party all night long."

"I like the sound of that. But first, you get back to work."

"And what are you going to do?"

"Me? I'm going to relax. Maybe read a good book."

"I'll call you later."

"Only if you have time."

"I'll make time."

Jillian's apartment was too quiet after she ended her phone call with Geoff. Her secret hung suspended in unspoken words between their hello and good-bye.

Should she have told Geoff? Shifted the weight of her diagnosis off her shoulders onto his?

No. Not yet. Geoff was already worn-out with work. It was just over a week until she saw Dr. Williamson and confirmed Dr. Sartwell's optimistic outlook. It was worth waiting to be able to tell him and her family there was nothing to worry about.

Jillian stuck the business card to her fridge door, holding it in place with a colorful fish magnet her parents had brought her from their last vacation to Mexico.

It was a doctor's appointment, not an inquisition. If anything, she'd be the one asking questions. She knew how to listen, how to take notes. More than likely, they'd hand her a pamphlet to take home. The surgeon would confirm what Dr. Sartwell said about the cancer being caught early and then outline what needed to be done. Jillian would have one more appointment before she had to tell anyone else. One more appointment before she had to admit that, yes, she had cancer.

Before she had to help everyone else be okay.

My cluttered desk and Kimberlee's even messier one greeted me as I flicked on the overhead light in the back office. Coming to work was like a walk back in time—straight to our college days, when we shared a small, disorganized apartment. Except we'd abandoned the white twinkly lights, beanbag chairs, and textbooks in exchange for a messy but more businesslike decor that included file cabinets, desks, rolling chairs, and a full-size fridge.

Did I ever wish that my workplace was a gym—on a volleyball court with a team?

I'd made my decision about that question a long time ago.

Dumping my purse on the floor beside my desk, I stocked

the fridge with coconut milk yogurts and fruit and stashed the reusable cloth bag in the supply closet. It took less than two minutes to make a cup of coffee, thanks to the office Keurig, and the caffeine and jolt of sugar would shove away the last remnants of sleep. Despite seeing me on Sunday, Nash had insisted on coming over last night, too, and then stayed too late, despite my not-so-subtle hints to leave.

Almost as if on cue, my phone buzzed.

Nash. He wouldn't appreciate how his phone call brought up similar feelings to my family interrupting me while I worked Jillian's engagement party four days ago.

I pushed the Speaker button to leave my hands free and powered up my computer. "Hello?"

"And good morning to you." He dropped his voice to a sexy whisper, although the effect was ruined with his voice amplified through the phone. "Did you sleep well?"

"Why, yes, I did. Thank you for asking."

"I did, too, although someone kicked me out instead of letting me stay."

My skin warmed as if someone else had heard his comment. "*Tsk.* Sounds heartless."

"You know, if we lived together, we wouldn't be having this conversation—"

"And we are not having this conversation now, Nash." I typed in my password. "I'm at work. You should be getting ready for work, too."

"Well then, how about if we continue talking over dinner tonight? And I'll use my most persuasive powers to convince you it's time to take our relationship to the next level."

A smile was woven through his words. I was tempted to admit his suggestion tugged at my heart. I could imagine how his brown eyes darkened—the way they did right before he kissed me. But what I couldn't imagine was Nash moving in. Getting that close. He already stayed too many nights at my town house, his toiletries crowding my bathroom shelves. Clothes lingering in my closet.

"You are distracting me, sir." His laugh came across the phone line, just as I knew it would. Teasing always worked when I needed to distract Nash. To put him in his place. "And while dinner sounds nice, I can't tonight."

"What can I do to convince you?"

Maybe he could just take no for an answer? "There's no convincing me. I'm sorry, but I've got some things to catch up on, so I'm going to be working late—and so is Kimberlee."

"Lunch?"

"Nash!" I softened my tone with a quick laugh. "You are persistent, but it has to be no. No lunch. No dinner."

"This is what I get for dating someone so dedicated to her job."

"You say that like it's a bad thing." Before he could reply, I moved the conversation on. "I really do need to get to work. Please."

"I understand. I love you, Payton."

"Mmm-hmm. Even if I am a little too dedicated to my job, right?" With a laugh, I ended the call.

I should have said I loved him, too. But maybe the bantering tone to our conversation had covered up my omission. It wasn't that I hadn't ever told Nash I loved him. But each time I said those three not-so-little words, I committed more of myself to him.

Did I want to keep moving toward a deeper commitment with Nash? After dating him for eight months, I still wasn't sure. Not in the same way he was ready to commit.

Kimberlee breezed in forty-five minutes later, her blue-streaked blonde hair flying about her face, begging forgiveness and bribing me with a half-dozen homemade doughnuts. "Is Bianca here yet?"

"Of course. She's sorting through the mail and listening to the phone messages."

"I'll let her choose one or two of these and then come back so we can start talking about the day."

"Sounds perfect. I should have my in-box under control by then. And grab the to-do list I asked Bianca to print off, will you? We can look over that when you get back." I selected a doughnut, plopping it onto a napkin on my desk. "When did you have time to make these?"

"I like to bake. It's no big deal."

Homemade glazed yeast doughnuts. No big deal. Right.

I logged out of our bank account just as Kimberlee returned, balancing the box of doughnuts in one hand and carrying the list in the other. "Someone's here to talk to you."

"What? I checked and we don't have an appointment until after lunch."

"He's not here to talk to *us*. He's here to talk to *you*." Kimberlee tossed me a wink. "And if you weren't dating Nash, I'd mention he's kind of handsome in an outdoorsy way."

"Well then, I know you're not really interested in him. The most time you spend outdoors is walking back and forth to your car. Who is he?"

"He introduced himself as Zachary Gaines and asked if you were available to talk."

"I don't know . . ."

Zachary Gaines.

"Payton? What's wrong?"

The way I'd frozen behind my desk in a half-standing, half-sitting posture must have alerted Kimberlee that something was off.

"I just remembered how I know Zach Gaines."

"Is there a problem? Do you want me to tell him you can't talk right now?"

"We . . . we went to high school together." I rounded the desk, wiping my sticky fingers on a napkin, the sugary sweetness of the doughnut congealing in the back of my throat. "I'll see what he wants. Maybe he's planning a wedding or a birthday party and heard about Festivities—"

"More than likely that's it."

"Go ahead and look over the week's schedule. We've got Mrs. Anderson's very posh eightieth birthday party on Thursday and the Morrison wedding on Saturday. And some consultations—"

"I've got it, Payton. Don't keep the guy waiting."

Keep him waiting? I could have lived my whole life without ever seeing Zachary Gaines again.

Zachary was chatting with Bianca when I entered the reception area. Could I say I would have recognized him anywhere? No, not really. Gone was the eighteen-year-old boy who'd been a high school cross-country standout with dark hair and an alluring smile. The guy who seemed to always be surrounded by a joking, laughing group of friends and who attracted the attention of quite a few of the teen girls. In his place stood a wiry man with a weathered face and eyes that seemed to shift between shadow and sunlight.

And now I was waxing poetic about a man I didn't want to talk to.

"Hey, Payton."

There was just a hint of the smile I remembered. "Zach. I wasn't expecting to see you here."

"I wasn't sure you would . . . would have time to talk to me." Zach shifted his feet, his hands tucked in the pockets of jeans that were worn at the knees.

"What do you want?" Even with my voice lowered, my words sounded harsh, but surely he wasn't expecting me to welcome him with a hug and a "What have you been up to since I last saw you?"

"I was hoping we could talk. I know you're working, but this was the only way I knew how to find you."

Why did he need to find me?

"Payton?" Bianca spoke behind me.

"Yes?"

"I have some things to work on in the back." She pushed her chair away from the semicircular desk. "I'll take any phone calls back there, too."

"That's fine, Bianca. Thank you." I motioned for Zach to follow me to the alcove where Kimberlee and I talked with clients. "Well, she staged a convenient exit, didn't she?"

"Yeah." Zach settled into the cloth chair covered with bright, multicolored polka dots, a small tempered-glass table between us. He picked up one of the pens resting on top of a pad of paper decorated with our company name, rolling it between the palms of his hands. "So this is your business?"

"Yes. Kimberlee and I plan events for people. Birthday parties. Wedding receptions. Showers. Whatever." Maybe my initial hope was correct. "Did you come here because you wanted us to help you plan something?"

"No." Zach glanced away, hesitating for a moment. "I wanted to talk to you about Pepper."

Below the table, I clenched my hands into fists. "Pepper?"

"I know it's been a long time—"

"Ten years."

"Ten years. Right." His Adam's apple bobbed up and down. "I got a call about this event the high school is doing to honor some of the former athletes . . ."

Again with the ceremony. My mom had said they were honoring various athletes. Zach Gaines had broken numerous school cross-country records. Jaunted off to college on a four-year scholarship months after my sister died. It only made sense he would be included in the group of students the school would be celebrating.

"Congratulations. But I still don't know why you needed to see me after all these years."

"I asked my coach who else was on the list. He said they were retiring Pepper's jersey number, so I figured your family was going to be there." When I didn't say anything, Zach continued, "And that got me wondering . . . hoping . . . I could finally make things right."

Everything Zach said made sense until those last three words. *Make things right.* I didn't like that he was here. Didn't like what he was saying. But at least I understood him until then.

"What did you just say?"

Zach rubbed his hand down his face. Small black letters were tattooed on several of his fingers. "I mean . . . I know I can't make things right. But I thought maybe I could finally apologize to you . . . to your family . . . for the accident."

"You want to talk with my family?" I flexed my fingers, but they fisted closed again.

"Yes. Look, I'm not proud of that night . . . of the five years of my life after. But I'm also not that messed-up kid anymore. I've changed . . . a lot . . . in the past few years. I'm not drinking or doing drugs . . . I've gotten myself straight with God—"

Zach Gaines could stop right there. Because just as much as I didn't want to talk to him about Pepper, I had no desire to talk with the guy about any god he might have stumbled across, drunk or sober. "What is this? Some sort of religious thing?"

"It's not a 'religious thing.' I've been in AA and I'm a Christian now. I want to make things right—"

Make things right. There was that insulting phrase again.

"And you think saying, 'I'm sorry' to me and my family is going to make things right?" I gripped the edge of the table to stop myself from leaning across. Getting in his face. "You'll feel better, won't you? Make your apology and go away, patting yourself on the back—but things still won't be right, will they? Because Pepper will still be dead."

"This isn't about making myself feel better, Payton."

"It isn't? I'm not so sure."

"I am sorry for what happened that night."

"I'm sure you are. And are your parents sorry they covered up the fact they'd been serving alcohol at a party where there were underage kids?"

Zach recoiled as if I'd slapped him.

"It's nice to have influential parents, isn't it? Keeps certain facts out of the papers."

"Look, Payton, I didn't come here to rehash what happened that night."

"Sounds to me like you only want to talk about selective details." In an instant, my sister's sixteen-year-old face flashed through my mind. *No.* I couldn't think about Pepper. "I didn't come to work this morning expecting you to show up here with some sort of self-righteous agenda—"

"Payton, I admit I had a couple of beers the night of the

crash. I'll even admit it to your parents. But Pepper was the one who caused the accident—"

"Oh, you don't want to rehash what happened, but you're okay with passing the blame? You think the crash wouldn't have happened if someone else had been driving the snowmobile? If I'd been driving—?"

"That's not what I'm saying!"

"I don't know why you're here." I stood, shoving the table away, causing the pens to roll over the edge and onto the carpeted floor. "You can't just show up and start talking to me about the night my sister died!"

Zach rose to his feet. "Payton, I'm sorry. I didn't want to upset you—"

"What did you think, Zach? That we'd have a nice chat about Pepper and the night you killed her?"

That shut him up.

Zach stood in front of me with his head bowed, staring at the carpet. Maybe he'd forget this whole idea of talking to my parents.

He ran a hand through his black hair, a sigh shifting his shoulders beneath the jean jacket covering his plain cotton T-shirt. When he looked at me again, the shadows had reappeared in his gray eyes. "I imagined this conversation for years. Prayed about it. And I never thought it would be an easy one."

"I'll give you credit for that." I didn't even attempt to hold back the sharp words.

"I've never forgotten that night." He held up his hand,

fending off my reply. "I'm not comparing my pain to yours, Payton. I just wanted the chance to talk to you. To your family. The chance to say I'm sorry."

"Well, you've talked to me. That's going to have to be enough."

He straightened his shoulders. Took a deep breath. "Won't you at least think about telling your parents that I'd like to see them?"

"I don't think so."

"Will they be at the ceremony?"

"If they are, I don't want you anywhere near them." I backed away from this unwelcome visitor from my past. "Now if you'll excuse me, I have to get back to work."

"If you change your mind and want to get in touch with me, I'm on Facebook—"

"I won't."

Zach nodded.

If he expected me to say something like "Thank you for coming," or "Have a good life," that wasn't going to happen. I escaped into the back room without even saying good-bye, holding my breath until I heard the soft chime indicating the front door had opened and Zach had left.

Both Bianca and Kimberlee tried to act as if they hadn't been waiting for my return. I restacked a pile of invoices on my desk and shook my head. "Don't ask. Not work-related."

"Are you okay?" Kimberlee seemed ready to come give me a hug, so I slipped into my chair and rolled it close to my desk.

No, I wasn't okay. I hadn't been okay for years. What would she say if I admitted that?

"I'm fine. An unexpected interruption. We've all dealt with those."

"Nash doesn't have some unknown competition he should be worrying about then?" Kimberlee waggled her eyebrows.

"Hardly." Zach hadn't been my type in high school, and we had nothing in common now.

Except for the night my twin sister died . . . something that would forever link our lives together.

JILLIAN LEANED AWAY from the table as the waitress set a plate in front of her. Strawberry-vanilla stuffed French toast. *Yum.* Her blood sugar would skyrocket and the scale would groan, but her agenda for today's family breakfast warranted good old-fashioned comfort food.

Just because she had to be a grown-up today didn't mean she couldn't enjoy the kind of breakfast she'd indulged in as a kid.

The table became a veritable advertisement for IHOP as the waitress served the rest of the family. Geoff, who loved breakfast more than any other meal, had chosen the sampler. Her parents split a pancake and egg combo. Payton requested more coffee and would probably pick at her bowl of oatmeal with almonds and walnuts or let Nash eat it when he finished his scramble. And Johanna, ever vigilant about her calories, had opted for a veggie omelet and fruit.

If her yet-unspoken announcement hadn't been lurking in the back of her mind, Jillian could have gotten lost in comparing this morning to childhood weekend visits to IHOP to celebrate report cards. Or a sports victory. Or just because their parents thought breakfast at a restaurant sounded fun.

As she reached for her glass of orange juice, her engagement ring, set off by her French manicure, caught her eye—a sure sign she wasn't just the middle Thatcher daughter anymore. In less than a year, she'd be Jillian Hennessey, a married woman. If choosing to say, "I do" to forever with someone didn't mean you were grown up, facing a cancer diagnosis did.

Of course, cancer had nothing to do with age. Children battled cancer every day.

"Jill." The sound of Geoff's voice brought Jillian's focus back to the present. "Honey, your mom asked if we wanted to talk about the wedding."

"Oh, sorry. My thoughts wandered for a moment."

"I imagine between work and planning a wedding, you've got a lot on your mind." Her mother transferred some of the scrambled eggs from the plate in front of her father to a smaller plate, adding a slice of crisp bacon.

"Yes." Beneath the table, Geoff clasped her hand in his, intertwining their fingers and caressing her skin with his thumb. She was tempted to scoot closer to him and rest her head on his shoulder. Savor his closeness.

How was it that when she was with him, she didn't think about her weight? It wasn't that she felt beautiful. No. She didn't know if she'd ever feel beautiful. But Geoff loved her. That she did know. When he looked at her, he didn't compare her to other women. He never looked at other women when they were together. She was enough for him.

The only other man who had accepted her so completely was her dad.

"One day, Jilly . . . One day a guy is going to look at you and say, 'You are exactly what I want in a woman.' And you'll believe him."

Every time her father had told her that when she was growing up, she'd thought he said it because, well, a dad had to say those kinds of things to his daughter. But when she met Geoff, she was finally able to tell her dad that he'd been right all those years.

With Geoff next to her, she could face her family and say what she needed to say. Telling him about her cancer ahead of this family get-together meant at least one person would remain calm when she revealed her secret. Why wait until after breakfast to share her news?

"I'll admit juggling work and the wedding is interesting." Jillian paused. Sweat slicked her palms, but she refused to let go of Geoff's hand. Her pulse beat at the base of her throat and her words seemed to tumble over one another. "And then something else came up that has added a bit more pressure."

Now she had everyone's attention. She'd practiced what she wanted to say, talking it through with Geoff—once he'd recovered from the shock of her news himself. Once he'd understood why she hadn't told him sooner about her diagnosis. He'd had no hesitation in taking time away from work for Sunday breakfast. She'd even rehearsed the words in her head as they drove to the restaurant.

Quick, like swallowing bad-tasting medicine. That was best.

"I've been diagnosed with breast cancer."

Her father stilled, his brow furrowing. Her mother's mouth formed a silent O, even as her eyes filled much too fast with tears. Payton's spoon clinked against her mug, shattering the sudden silence that shrouded their table, as Nash put his arm around her. Johanna seemed to assess everyone else, her face a mask against her emotions.

Johanna spoke first. "When did you find this out, Jillian?"

"I got the initial diagnosis the night of my engagement party."

"What?" Her mother's gasp was laden with tears. "And you didn't tell us?"

"There was nothing to say, Mom. I met with Dr. Sartwell that Monday and got more information—"

"What do you know?" Again, Johanna spoke.

"My doctor is optimistic we've caught this early."

"When do you have your next appointment?"

"I've already seen the breast surgeon Dr. Sartwell recommended."

"Jillian!" Her mother's fork clattered against her plate. "Why didn't you say anything before now?"

"I wanted to have something specific to tell you."

Geoff drew her closer as if the physical action would remind her that she wasn't facing her family alone. "If it makes you feel any better, Mrs. Thatcher, Jillian didn't tell me anything until after she'd had her preliminary visit with the breast surgeon five days ago."

Had she ever heard Geoff sound so serious?

"Like Geoff said, I met with Dr. Williamson last Wednesday. Dr. Sartwell said she's one of the top surgeons in town." Jillian forced herself to slow down. "We discussed what needs to happen next. I'm scheduled to have an MRI this Tuesday morning—"

"You mean . . . the day after tomorrow?" Her mother's voice quavered.

"Yes. And then I'll wait for results. Like I said, Dr. Sartwell is optimistic." Jillian infused her voice with confidence. Maybe if she kept repeating the word *optimistic*, her family would finally hear it. "The lesion was only the size of a grape—a small grape."

"When will you have the complete results?" Johanna had abandoned her breakfast and taken on the role of interrogator.

"I'll see Dr. Williamson the following Monday." In some ways, Johanna was making this easier. All Jillian had to do was answer her sister's questions. "Mom . . . Dad . . . I'm going to be okay."

"You don't know that." Her mother's tortured whisper

scraped Jillian's nerves raw. "I can't . . . I can't lose another daughter."

Across the table, Payton's face whitened, but she remained silent.

Her father wrapped his arm around her mother's shoulders. "Jillian said the doctor has given her a good prognosis, Heather—"

"I know that's what she said, but we don't know . . ."

Maybe her decision to share this with her family without more positive information had been wrong. "I'm sorry. Maybe I should have waited—"

"Don't be ridiculous, Jillian." Johanna negated Jillian's apology. "Of course you had to tell us. We're your family. Did you do any research on this Dr. Williamson?"

"No. I trust Dr. Sartwell's recommendation."

"Really? Don't you know anything about taking charge of your health care?"

"It's her choice, Johanna." At last, Payton spoke up, but only to take on Johanna. Of course.

"I'm just saying she should have gotten a second opinion—"

Payton's response was quick and sharp. "Let it be, will you? Please?"

Nash leaned over and whispered something into Payton's ear, causing her to wrap her hands around her mug of coffee and look away.

Jillian stared down at her plate of food, the whipped cream collapsing and puddling into the syrup covering her French toast. How was she supposed to fix this? Johanna and Payton were on the verge of another quarrel, and typical or not, she wasn't up for it. Her mother was about to fall apart at the thought of her dying like Pepper. And her father was once again going to have to reassure everyone. So much for the idea of choosing a public place and maintaining some sort of control over the situation. She'd been fooling herself.

She'd known her announcement would upset her family. But was it wrong to want someone to ask her how she was doing? For her sisters to stop fighting and focus on her for once? To see her? To not want her mother to compare her cancer to losing Pepper, but just let this moment be about her?

Was it so wrong to need her family?

"Jill, is it all right with you if I say something?" Geoff lowered his voice so only she could hear his question.

"I guess so." Jillian pressed her fingertips against the pressure building behind her forehead. She closed her eyes, blocking the sight of the breakfast in front of her, the rich confection unsettling her stomach.

Geoff slipped his hand from hers, but only so he could place his arm around her waist and pull her even closer. "I'm certain we all have our opinions about how we would have handled this situation. But Jillian did what she thought was right."

Jillian wanted to twist and stare at her boisterous fiancé who had gone so somber on her, but she remained still. Maybe Geoff could handle her family. She certainly couldn't.

"I admit I would have liked Jillian to tell me about everything sooner. I hate the thought of her going to the biopsy
appointment by herself." Geoff paused for a moment. "But
like I said, that was her choice. We all know now. The most
important thing is that we support Jillian however she wants
us to."

Geoff's words helped Jillian straighten up and face her
family again. She had to remember she wasn't alone in this.

"You're right, Geoff." Her father nodded. "We're all just a
bit shocked by this news."

"I know, sir. I was, too. I wish there'd been some way to prepare you better, but there's really no good way to say this . . ."

"Well, it's been said. Now we have to deal with it." Her
father offered her a smile. "We're here for you, Jilly."

His words caused tears to threaten. Instead, she forced
herself to smile in return. "I know you are, Dad. I promise
to let you all know as soon as I have the MRI results."

"Do you want me to go with you? I can take off work."
Johanna was already pulling up her calendar on her phone.

"Thank you for the offer, Johanna, but there's no need for
anyone to take me to the appointment."

"I wanted to be there with her, but Jillian insisted I not
miss work because of the deadline we're dealing with."

"The appointment's scheduled first thing in the morning,
so I'll be back at work almost on time."

"If you change your mind, you know any one of us would
go with you." Her mother offered an almost-normal smile.

Jillian shifted away from Geoff, picking up her knife and

fork and slicing into her French toast. If she took small bites, maybe she could stomach the too-sweet dish. "I appreciate that. Now that everyone knows, maybe we can get back to our breakfast?"

"But I think we should discuss some things—" Johanna raised her voice enough that several people at nearby tables glanced at her.

Jillian gathered her strength to respond to her sister, but Geoff spoke first. "There's really nothing to discuss until after we get the final report from the surgeon. What Jillian wanted to do this morning was to inform you of her diagnosis and tell you about her upcoming appointment. Why don't we talk about something more pleasant, like the wedding, okay?"

And just like that, Geoff had done it again and come to her rescue. That was sweeter and more comforting than any amount of French toast topped with a lavish amount of strawberries and whipped cream could ever be.

I was almost alone. Almost. Just a few more steps and I would be inside my town house. By myself. Able to begin processing Jillian's startling announcement earlier this morning.

"Nash, please, just go home." I leaned against the frame of the front door, which seemed to be the only thing holding me upright.

"But I'm worried about you." Instead of leaving, Nash snaked an arm around my waist and pulled me close. "You've been so quiet all day."

"I just found out my sister has cancer. What do you expect?" I rested the palm of my hand against his chest. "I'm trying to process all of this."

"Let me help you process." He pressed his lips to mine, lingering for a moment. He was too close. The scent of his aftershave too heavy.

"I don't think 'processing' is what you really have in mind." Nash's kisses, usually so enticing, sparked no response from me. Well, not the kind of response he was hoping for.

"You can talk . . . I can listen. I could even run you a bubble bath . . ."

I couldn't help but laugh. "A bubble bath? Me?"

"Just trying to help you unwind. Would you like a back rub maybe?"

When he kissed my neck, his breath hot against my skin, I shrugged out of his arms. What part of "not interested" did the man not understand? I didn't want to talk . . . or do anything else. I'd already let him convince me to go see some sci-fi movie I didn't care about, followed by an early dinner at a Mexican restaurant. I didn't remember how the movie ended or what I'd eaten.

"I just want some time to myself." There. That was as plain as I could say it, other than my "just go home" statement, which he'd already ignored. "It's been a long day. I'll probably go to bed early so I'm ready for work tomorrow."

Nash backed off. *Finally.* If I didn't look in his eyes, I wouldn't see how hurt he was to be kicked out. Not that I'd even let him in the door tonight. It wasn't his fault he wanted more of me than I was able to give him. How did I explain that it wasn't him, it was me? A romantic cliché that had ended all of my adult relationships, yes. *It's not you, it's me.* But just because I'd said those five words over and over again in one form or another didn't make them any less true.

My capacity to love, to be close to someone else, had been wounded ten years ago and never healed.

But how was Nash supposed to know that when I barely mentioned Pepper to him or to anyone else? A decade after my sister's death, most people didn't even know I had a twin.

My life was easier that way.

Blunt and nonresponsive worked. Nash left, but not before he promised to call later, his shoulders down, his steps slow.

Let the man sulk.

I escaped into my house, closing the door on the late-summer twilight and my stubborn boyfriend.

I kicked off my wedges, leaving them in the foyer beside several other pairs of sandals, and dead-bolted the door. What had my parents always said when they left Pepper and me alone in the house when we were younger?

"Nobody in. Nobody out."

That was just the kind of evening I had planned.

My town house was a multiroom replica of Festivities's back room. A small neglected living room, with my laptop perched on one end of the couch. One of these days I'd buy a coffee table. Various white cotton ankle socks—a preference developed during my volleyball days—were tossed about the carpet, along with empty plates and glasses stacked near the couch, waiting to be taken to the kitchen. That room was not much better than the living room, although I could hide the dirty dishes in the dishwasher, which I always forgot to start until no clean dishes remained in the cupboards.

I changed into a loose-fitting T-shirt and black yoga pants left over from a brief phase that ended when a too-ambitious attempt to do the crow pose earned me two black eyes and a swollen nose.

As I pushed my hair back with a thin black headband, my cell phone rang. Somehow, I knew who it would be.

"Yes, Johanna?"

"What? No hello?"

"Hello, Johanna. What can I do for you?" As I waited for Johanna's reply, I ransacked my freezer for a small container of ice cream. I might not indulge in a bubble bath, but Ben & Jerry's vegan Chocolate Fudge Brownie was always an option.

"I've been thinking . . ."

Uh-oh. Not a surprise and never a good thing. "Yes?"

"We need to convince Jillian to move up her wedding date."

"What?" I almost dropped my spoon. "Why?"

"I've been on the computer all afternoon doing some research."

Was I surprised? No. My sister—the woman who researched. Who controlled. Who told other people what to do.

"Jillian didn't ask you to do any research—"

"I'm the one with a medical background. I know where

to look for up-to-date information. Jillian said her doctor thinks they caught her cancer early, but what if they didn't?"

"Way to be positive—"

Johanna ignored my comment. "She and Geoff are planning on getting married next April. But what if the prognosis isn't good? Why not get married sooner so they can enjoy their wedding and honeymoon before she has to have chemo or radiation? Then she's not alone while she's going through treatment. It just seems like the best—"

"It seems like the best idea to you, Johanna. *To you.*" I tore the lid off the ice cream container. "But it's not what Jillian wants to do."

"That's why I'm going to call her and suggest moving up her wedding. And then you can call her and suggest she change the date, too. If we both talk to her—"

"You're jumping to conclusions. I'm not going to call her."

"Payton—"

"Johanna. Stop. I mean it. Keep your research and your recommendations to yourself. Jillian and Geoff will figure this out. They need our support, not our unwelcome advice."

"Researching and offering advice is how I support them."

"No." I paced the kitchen, my ice cream left on the counter. "It's bossing them around, like you're the parent and they're children. This is their wedding. They'll decide if there's any change to the date because of her . . . her diagnosis. If they want anybody else's opinion, they'll ask." Was it possible to turn the focus from one sister to the other? "Shouldn't you be planning your own wedding?"

Johanna paused for half a second before responding. "I already know what kind of wedding I want."

"Don't you mean what kind of wedding you and Beckett want?"

"Yes, that's what I meant. Stop twisting my words."

"Have the two of you even set a date?"

"We've tossed around some possible dates."

"Just possible dates? You've been together for seven years. Why are you waiting?"

"Beckett has the choice to deploy overseas for a year and then have a three-year follow-on assignment to Colorado, and then he could retire."

"Well, why don't you attend to your own life?" I rushed ahead before Johanna could respond, not that I understood all the military talk about Beckett's career choices. "Let's wait for Jillian's update after she has the MRI. That's what she asked us to do, after all."

I chose to take my sister's silence as agreement and said a quick good-bye.

I'd lost my appetite. Some people assumed I was naturally thin, but I was one of those women whose appetite fled at the first sign of stress. I tossed the carton into the trash and added the spoon to the dishwasher, which overflowed with dirty dishes. Then I curled up on my couch, pulling a multicolored quilt made from old volleyball T-shirts over my body. I'd close my eyes for a few minutes before updating Festivities's Facebook page.

"Payton."

That voice. It was so much like my own, except it sounded younger. Lighter.

"Hey, Payton."

Was that . . . Pepper?

I turned around, my tennis shoes squeaking on the cement floor. Where was I?

Humid. Dimly lit. An odor of . . . what? Sweat and soap.

Rows of blue lockers filled the room.

What was I doing in my high school's girls locker room?

My sister sat astride one of the long wooden benches positioned between the rows of lockers. She wore gray sweatpants and a white team T-shirt, her long auburn hair in a single braid. She could be heading into volleyball practice.

I stopped at the end of the row. "What are you doing here?"

"Waiting for you." Pepper leaned forward, her hands resting on the bench.

"Waiting for me?"

"Yeah. I wanted to talk to you."

"Why?"

"I was wondering how you were doing."

"What?"

A smile curved her lips, lighting her eyes, the blue eyes that hinted at turquoise just like mine did. "You've got to admit it's been a long time since we've talked, Pay."

Was that supposed to be some sort of joke? I forced the words past my dry throat. "But you don't look any different."

"I know." Pepper tilted her head, her braid swishing to the side. "You do, though. You're all grown up. So that's what I'd look like, huh?"

Her carefree giggle caused my chest to ache even as I touched the ends of my hair that lay tangled against my shoulders. "If you went shorter and opted for layers and blonde highlights, yeah."

"I like it. We always had long hair."

"The volleyball girl look, right?"

"So people said." Pepper pulled her knees up to her chest and wrapped her arms around them. "Are you still playing volleyball? Coaching? That was your plan."

"No. I couldn't . . . Not after you . . . It was too hard. I own a party-planning company with a friend."

"Huh. I never would've figured that."

"I like it." I hadn't lied to her. I did like my job, so long as Kimberlee was the "party" part of the business and I was the "planner" part of the business.

"What kinds of parties?"

"You name it. Wedding receptions. Birthday parties. Would you believe we just catered Jillian's engagement party?"

"Jillian's getting married? Wow. Is he cute?"

I'd never really thought about that. "Jillian thinks so. Remember how we used to watch those old black-and-white Dick Van Dyke TV shows with Mom?"

"Yeah."

"I think Geoff—that's Jillian's fiancé—kind of looks like a

young Dick Van Dyke. And he's got the crazy sense of humor, too."

"Well, good for her. What about you and Johanna?"

I'd focus on Johanna's love life. "Johanna's engaged to Beckett. He's in the Air Force."

Pepper leaned forward. "Pay?"

"Yeah?"

"I miss you."

My throat tightened. "I miss you, too. Every day . . ."

Pepper didn't respond. Instead, she stood, casting a long shadow against the wall, and walked right past me.

Where was she going?

"Pepper—" My voice was a whisper. I couldn't move. Couldn't turn around.

The locker room went dark.

"Pepper? Where are you?"

"Where are you? Where are you?" I woke myself up yelling the question into my dark living room.

Early on after my twin sister died, I'd had dreams—nightmares—where I stood in the dark and screamed her name. Over and over again. Pepper never appeared. And I was thankful when the medications prescribed by the psychiatrist ended months of disturbed sleep.

I didn't need nightmares to know I'd never see my sister again.

And now . . . now she'd shown up in a dream. Just to talk. To find out how I was doing. How Johanna and Jillian were doing.

I found my cell phone tangled up in the quilt. Almost nine o'clock. I gathered the quilt around my shoulders again. Maybe I should have given in to Nash's advances and let him stay. I could always call him. He'd come back. But every night he stayed over weakened my argument against him moving in with me. . . .

I pulled my knees up to my chest, pressing my forehead against them. This dream was some sort of emotional fluke caused by Jillian's unexpected announcement earlier in the day. Did I want to start something *more* with Nash because of an unsettling dream?

I abandoned the couch and the warmth of the quilt and reached for my laptop. I'd do some work. Maybe even search online for new recipes. Peruse Pinterest for ideas for Jillian's bridal shower. Why did I have to wait for Johanna's marching orders to plan things? As the oldest sister, she was the maid of honor by default, but that didn't make her the boss of me.

Would my older sister ever realize that? Or years from now would we be two gray-haired old ladies in an ongoing power struggle? Maybe my work on Jillian's shower and wedding would help her learn the lesson that I was a capable adult a little sooner.

I opened my laptop, powering it up so that the familiar view of the Festivities logo appeared on the screen. For now, I'd focus on work. Reality. And forget about seeing my twin sister again—even if only in a dream.

5

"WHAT'S THE PLAN FOR TONIGHT?" Harper slipped into one of the chairs in front of Jillian's desk, kicking off her floral high heels and running her fingers through her black hair. "Do you want to go have dinner? Or do you want to try that paint-it-yourself place? Wine and arts and crafts could be fun."

Jillian started to twist her hands together, then settled them in her lap, out of sight. "I wanted to talk to you about something before we headed out. . . ."

"Wedding stuff?" Her friend leaned forward. "You know I totally understand about Johanna being your maid of honor, right? Sisters and all."

"Yes. You've been great about that." Jillian turned her

THINGS I NEVER TOLD YOU

engagement ring around and around her finger. She'd never suspected that something so beautiful would be mistreated whenever her stress levels increased. "And no, this isn't about the wedding."

"Is it work-related?"

"No." Harper needed to stop. No matter how many guesses she made, her friend would never figure out what she wanted to talk about. "I went to the doctor and—"

"Oh, my gosh! You're pregnant!" Harper fell back against the chair, her expression almost comical. Almost.

"No! No, I'm not pregnant. I can't even believe you'd think that." At least she'd been smart enough to close her office door. "I . . . I have cancer."

There. She'd said it.

Harper gasped, her brown eyes widening and then filling with tears. "Wait. What?"

"I said—"

"I heard you. But you can't have cancer. . . . You can't . . ."

"That's exactly what I thought when the doctor told me. *I can't have cancer.* But I do." Jillian exhaled a shuddery breath. "Breast cancer."

Harper bolted from her chair, coming around the desk and kneeling on the carpet beside Jillian as she grabbed her hand. "How?"

It took only a few moments to explain everything to Harper, as silent tears streamed down her friend's face. Harper clung to her hand. Never interrupted. Just let Jillian tell the stark details. The horrible truth.

"How are you?" Harper's question filled the silence between them when Jillian had nothing left to say.

"I'm . . . scared." No sense denying it—and her friend would know anyway. "But I trust my doctor. And the surgeon. So I'm hopeful, too."

"And Geoff?"

"He's been great. I can't imagine facing this without him."

"You've told your family?"

"Yesterday."

"How did that go? No, don't tell me. Johanna try to boss you around?"

"She means well. And Payton . . . well, she didn't say much. I think it's just too hard for her . . . you know."

"Your parents?"

"My dad was composed as always." Jillian shifted, pressing the palm of her hand against her forehead, as Harper settled on the floor. "I'm worried about my mom."

"You have to take care of yourself, Jillian. Your family should be helping you—"

"But this is hard on them, too."

"I get that, but you're the one with . . . with cancer, not them. Let them support you." Harper squeezed her hand. "Now tell me what I can do for you."

Jillian pressed her lips together, blinking back tears. Why was such a simple request enough to make her cry?

Harper leaned up, wrapping her in a hug. "What is it?"

"Nothing. I'm just so thankful you're my friend. And I don't know what I need right now. . . . Just be my friend.

Okay? You're really good at that. And I think that's what I'm going to need most of all."

"Friends for always."

Harper's whispered words echoed of friendships forged in middle school. If only she'd had a friend like Harper back then. "Friends forever."

"Nothing—absolutely nothing—is going to change that." Harper squeezed her tighter. "Cancer picked the wrong person. Nobody messes with my best friend."

⌒

"You haven't heard a word I said, have you?"

Kimberlee's question interrupted the replay of Sunday's dream. Every day this week my emotions had balanced on the edge of an invisible precipice as I invented ways to stay busy so I could avoid going home. Avoid going to sleep and possibly dreaming of my twin sister. Avoid longing to see Pepper again, even as the ache lingered.

"I'm listening." I tilted my mug to my lips only to find it empty, the faint aroma of coffee still inside. When had I finished that cup?

"Do you want to tell me what I just said?" Kimberlee leaned back in her chair, crossing her arms. Waiting.

"I'm not playing that game with you." I retreated to the coffeemaker. "You want another cup?"

"I'm good." Kimberlee waved away my offer, picking up several sheets of paper off her desk. "We—or rather *I* was discussing Evangeline Forsythe's wedding reception. And the long list of must-have items she faxed over this morning. Did you read this?"

"Yes. Nice of her to alphabetize it."

"An elevated dance floor . . . jeweled seating cards . . . topiary tree arrangements . . . colored glassware . . . and I haven't even gotten to the menu additions. Are we really going to put up with her demands?"

"The real question is, are we really going to turn away such a huge event?" I tilted my head, trying—and failing—to raise my eyebrow. Sometimes a girl just needed to be able to arch her eyebrow to make a point, but I lacked that particular skill. "We've done everything else she's asked of us. Why are you balking now?"

"Because we're less than five weeks out from the wedding and the woman is giving me a headache." Kimberlee dropped the list and the papers scattered across her desk. Closing her eyes, she pressed her fingers to her temples. "Honestly, she's going to cause my blue highlights to fade."

"At least there are no animal attendants involved in this ceremony, right?"

"True, true. No need to set up a separate table for canine members of the wedding party or order three courses of doggy delicacies. So we're saying yes to all this?"

"And calling in a few favors while we charge the appropriate fee."

"And crossing our fingers we get a glowing endorsement. And lots of referrals."

"Exactly. We can only hope her friends won't be quite so

demanding." I set my mug on the counter and retrieved a yogurt from the fridge. "You want one?"

"No, thanks. Switching gears. Have you got any details for your sister's bridal shower?"

"No. I don't even know if she wants the early date or the later date, but I keep expecting Johanna to call or fax me at least a preliminary list. She's such a control freak. So far, it's been quiet. Surprising, since Johanna thinks Jillian and Geoff should move the wedding date up."

"Why?"

And now I had to explain things to my business partner, who was also my friend. There was no easy way to say it. "Jillian's been diagnosed with breast cancer."

Speaking the words out loud created an ache in the back of my throat.

Kimberlee's gaze locked on mine. "What? When?"

"In a case of horrible timing, she received the call the night of the engagement party. That's why we couldn't find her when it was time to open gifts."

"You're kidding." Kimberlee shook her head. "Forget I said that. Of course you're not kidding."

"Jillian had an MRI on Tuesday. She's seeing the surgeon again next Monday." I paused to catch my breath as if I'd been running around the office, not talking about my sister's cancer diagnosis. "Her family practice doctor is optimistic that her case isn't advanced."

"Then I don't understand why Johanna thinks Jillian should change the wedding date."

"Johanna always has an opinion about how things should be done. She thinks Jillian should get married sooner just in case the prognosis is worse than expected. Ever the optimist, right?" I retreated to my desk. "She wants me to help her convince Jillian to do it—as if I had any real influence with her."

"Do you think Johanna said anything to her?"

"Not yet. At least, I hope she hasn't. Jillian has enough to worry about without our big sister swooping in and telling her when to get married."

"Johanna wouldn't pressure her, would she?"

"You're talking about someone who would come home from college and hide the snacks in her bedroom closet because she thought Pepper and I were eating too much of them. Johanna would stash the potato chips and the Goldfish crackers on the top shelf—and then fill her own bowl whenever she wanted some."

"Oh, come on. . . ."

"Aren't you glad you don't have a big sister?"

"Sure. I just had a little brother I had to babysit for free, and all his friends had crushes on me—"

"And you never liked any of these younger guys?"

"Well, there was this one guy, Frankie—"

The ring of my cell interrupted Kimberlee's confession. "Let me get this and then you can tell me more about Frankie."

I didn't recognize the number, but maybe it was a potential client. Then again, why wouldn't they have called the main business number?

"Hello, this is Payton Thatcher with Festivities."

"Payton . . . hi. It's Geoff."

"Geoff . . . Jillian's Geoff?"

"Yes. I got your number from her cell phone."

I swiveled my chair so I faced away from Kimberlee. "What's wrong?" Silence greeted my question. "Geoff?"

Geoff cleared his throat. "The surgeon called about the MRI results. It appears this may be a larger tumor than they first suspected."

No. No. No.

"What . . . what does that mean?"

"Dr. Williamson said we'll discuss the options on Monday." Even though Geoff tried to keep his voice businesslike, his words were laced with a tremor.

I needed to say something in response to Geoff's announcement. To at least thank him for calling me. "Can I talk to Jillian?"

"She just finished talking to the doctor and wanted everyone to know because you've all been waiting for news, too. But she's not up to talking to anyone right now, so she asked me to call everyone. Your parents. Johanna. Harper."

"I understand."

What would I say to my sister? Offer her words of comfort? How was I supposed to bridge the years of silence and come up with just the right thing to say now that she needed support? Was I supposed to tell her not to be scared? She had every right to be scared.

"How bad is it, Geoff?" My voice had pitched so low I almost couldn't hear my question. Would he?

"I don't know. This isn't what we were expecting. . . ." He stopped. "We'll just have to wait until Monday."

I ended the phone call with a brief "Thanks for calling and telling me." I should have said something more. Something comforting. Something that would have defused the emotional bomb that had just been handed to Jillian. To Geoff. To our entire family.

Turning, I confronted Kimberlee, who still sat at her desk, her gaze trained on me. "What's wrong?"

"That was Jillian's fiancé." I fought to focus through the internal echo of my conversation with Geoff. "The MRI results are worse than they expected."

"Oh, Payton, no."

"We still have to wait until Monday before we know what's going on." I scooted my chair up to my desk. "Time to get back to work."

"Are you going to call her?"

"No. Jillian doesn't want to talk to anyone right now. I'll wait until Monday."

"Tell her I'm sending her good thoughts, will you?"

"Sure."

Good thoughts. What else did I have to give my sister?

You can beat this thing, Jillian.

I'm pulling for you, Jillian.

You've got this, Jillian.

I sounded like some sort of cheerleader on the sidelines of my sister's life.

I love you, Jillian.

That was true, wasn't it? But when was the last time I'd told her?

Jillian huddled beneath her comforter, the bedroom door closed so she couldn't hear Geoff phoning everyone to give them the update.

She'd left her clothes—shoes, pants, blouse—in a pile on her closet floor and pulled on her soft, roomy robe. The one that swallowed up her curves and extra pounds like a warm hug instead of the sharp rebuke some of the other items hanging in her closet always gave her body.

Then she'd pulled back her pale-blue down comforter, crawled underneath, and buried her face in her pillow—and waited to cry.

But no tears came.

Instead, the doctor's words echoed in her head over and over again.

"It appears the cancer has extended beyond what we saw in the mammogram. . . ."

Surely the promise of happily ever after should last at least until she and Geoff said, "I do."

But cancer had lousy timing. It had no sense of timing at all. And it didn't seem to care about her hopes for future happiness. That she was planning a wedding. That so many people never even expected her to get married. Oh, sure, they never quite came out and said so to her face. But hidden behind all of the "You'd be so pretty if only you lost forty pounds" statements was the unspoken belief that no man was going to look at her, much less date her . . . much less propose to her.

Some of those same people hadn't even tried to hide their surprise when the improbable happened.

And now . . . this. This *thing* invading her body, storming past Dr. Sartwell's assurance that they'd caught the cancer early and taking control of her timetable. Her plans.

Her life.

Jillian twisted beneath the weight of the comforter, rolling onto her back to stare at the stark white ceiling. Was she a coward, not making the phone calls herself? Or was she just reserving her strength for what lay ahead?

She moved her arm so that her hand rested against her breast, her fingers sliding over the skin that covered the tumor lurking inside her body.

What was she facing? Chemo? Radiation? A mastectomy?

Her brain seemed to stutter over the last word. Four syllables denoting such horrible mutilation of her body . . . to save her life. A shiver coursed through her, and Jillian's hand fell back against the mattress . . . away from the body that had betrayed her. The body that had never lived up to her expectations. That she'd never felt comfortable in. That she'd only begun to accept, thanks to Geoff.

But Geoff hadn't planned on marrying a woman scarred by cancer, had he?

She stiffened, closing her eyes, as the bedroom door opened.

Geoff whispered, "Jillian? You asleep?"

For the briefest of moments, she considered keeping her eyes closed, evening her breathing out, and feigning sleep. Geoff would press a kiss to her forehead, tuck the blanket up around her shoulders, and leave her in peace—not that there was an ounce of peace anywhere inside her. Cancer had stolen that, too.

But she opened her eyes, rolling over to face the door, not bothering to fake a smile. "I'm awake."

"Do you need anything?" Geoff sat on the edge of the bed, his hand curling around hers where it lay against the pillow. "Are you hungry?"

No, she wasn't hungry. For once, she wasn't hungry.

"No. Thank you."

Geoff caressed each of her fingers with his thumb. "I called everyone."

"Thank you."

"Your parents are concerned about you."

"I know."

"Of course Johanna wanted to talk to you." He ended the comment with a faint laugh.

Of course.

"And Payton asked to talk to you, too."

"Payton?"

"Yes, but I explained you were resting. Should I have let her talk to you?"

"No. Maybe tomorrow."

"Maybe I should go and let you get some rest . . ." The mattress shifted as he moved.

"Don't leave. Please." She clutched his hand.

"Okay. Do you want some hot tea? Maybe we could watch a movie?"

A movie. Numb her emotions with a chick flick that came with the kind of happy ending that was slipping through her fingers? Or assault her already-bruised mind with a Jason Bourne thriller that Geoff liked to watch sometimes? The only kind of movie she felt up to was a Disney film, but even watching something with magical adventures and singing animals seemed like too much.

"Would you . . . would you just hold me?"

"Here?" Geoff's eyes widened behind his glasses. "I mean, do you want to come out to the living room . . . to the couch . . . ?"

His nervousness was endearing and understandable. She'd been beyond modest with him. Hesitant when it came to his advances. Not that she didn't welcome them, but at first she couldn't believe he found her attractive enough to want to kiss her—or anything else.

"Yes." She scooted over, allowing him access to the bed. "Here is fine. I just need you to hold me."

Jillian waited as Geoff slid off his shoes, turning and lying down beside her, slipping his arm beneath her head. As he moved closer, she rolled to her side, curling her knees to her chest as he curved his body to hers.

"I love you, Jilly." His voice was low in her ear.

"I know." She spoke against the tightening of her throat. It was silly to cry when he'd told her that he loved her so many times already. "I love you, too."

"We'll get through this. It's going to be okay."

Jillian squeezed her eyes shut. Forced her breathing to remain even. Of course Geoff would say that.

But Dr. Sartwell had been wrong.

"I know it will be."

The words were nothing more than the proper blend of consonants and vowels. She didn't know anything anymore. And the unanswered questions—the possible ways her life could career even further off course—scared her most of all.

6

JILLIAN SAT ON THE EDGE OF HER BED, her damp hair wrapped in a towel, her robe belted around her waist. If she didn't get moving and blow-dry her hair and get dressed, she'd be late for work. The first time ever.

She remained sitting, the soles of her feet rubbing back and forth on the soft carpeting.

It wasn't as if anyone would reprimand her. Or ask why. Or even think for one second her fiancé had stayed at her apartment until three o'clock in the morning—fully clothed and sound asleep, holding her as she stared into the darkness.

Not the well-behaved, punctual, and pleasant Jillian Thatcher.

And if someone asked, "Are you okay?" she'd say yes. Nothing more, nothing less. She wasn't prepared to invite more people into this new reality. Wasn't ready to deal with their reactions. To watch them struggle to say the right thing. Or to listen to their advice. What their mother or sister or grandmother or second-aunt-twice-removed did or didn't do when she had breast cancer.

Everyone had a story. Fine. She was stuck in this un-expected chapter of *her* story. She'd thought she was living in a romance, only to discover she was in the middle of a medical drama.

Somebody needed to hand her a copy of the story of her life so she could read ahead. Find out what came next.

If she lived or died.

Jillian stood, jerking her robe open and advancing on her closet, only to be stopped by the ring of her cell phone where it lay on the bed.

"Hello?"

"Hello, Jillian. Did I catch you on your way to work?"

Johanna.

Her sister's voice was like a splash of cold water to her face. "No. I'm still getting dressed."

"Running a bit late this morning, aren't you?"

"Yes." Jillian grabbed a simple black shift dress from the closet, tossing it on the bed and putting her phone on speaker. "Go ahead and keep talking. I can listen while I finish up."

"First, thank you for having Geoff call about the MRI results. I told Mom and Dad that I'd . . ." Johanna's voice became muffled as Jillian pulled on her dress. "So how are you?"

"Fine. Waiting to talk to Dr. Williamson on Monday. That's all I can do."

"I was online last night—"

"I don't have time for that this morning." Jillian grabbed a pair of gray leather boots from the closet. A paisley scarf in blues and whites from the rack hanging over the back of her door.

A moment of silence and then, "I understand."

More like Johanna was tabling that conversation until later. What else did she want?

"Have you thought about when you want to have your bridal shower? Before the holidays or early next year?"

Now Johanna was back to her timetable. She'd always been about keeping her calendar organized. In high school, she'd color-coded her classes and after-school activities and job schedule, using Sharpies and highlighters and markers. Jillian was the one who loved the rhyme and rhythm of numbers, but even today her calendar was a bit helter-skelter, the front of her fridge covered with a maze of magnets that pinned down appointment reminders and coupons and last year's photo Christmas cards.

And today she didn't want to be squeezed into her sister's timetable.

"Johanna, I really haven't had time to think about this. Do we have to decide now?"

"You know we could simplify things."

"What are you talking about?"

"Why don't we forget about having the wedding in April and plan something much smaller—but just as nice—in about five weeks?"

"Forget about having the wedding in April."

The words stung somewhere deep inside her.

"Are you crazy? We can't have a wedding in five weeks—"

"Hear me out, Sis. We can still have the things that are most important to you. The flowers. The colors. Maybe even the location if we move fast. The style of dress you want. A small wedding can be so intimate and lovely."

"But I've always wanted a spring wedding. . . ."

"I know. But this way you and Geoff would be married before . . . before you start any sort of treatment."

Johanna had it all thought out. As far as she was concerned, abandoning all of Jillian's plans was the right, best thing.

Jillian dropped the boots to the floor beside the bed, causing the small stack of bridal magazines to topple over. Should she fight Johanna? Or was her sister right?

"There's no way we can plan a wedding in five weeks—"

"With Payton's help we can."

"You talked to Payton about this?"

"Yes."

She couldn't deal with a cancer diagnosis and fight both her sisters. "I don't know . . ."

"Why don't you talk to your doctor on Monday? See what she thinks?"

Ask Dr. Williamson on Monday about getting married to Geoff in five weeks while they discussed her cancer.

Ridiculous.

"No. No more ideas, Johanna."

Would her sister even listen to her? It seemed Johanna would never hear the voice inside Jillian's head demanding, *Listen to me! Look at me!* Maybe one day Jillian would actually say it out loud.

"Why don't you think about it for a few more days—?"

"I'm getting married in the spring like I've always wanted to. Just like Mom and Dad did."

"Then we stay with April." Johanna's voice was subdued. "The way you planned it."

Jillian's shoulders relaxed. Argument won. This was Johanna, the sister she'd been closest to growing up. They'd shared a bedroom and a love of Disney princesses—Ariel for Johanna and Belle for her—and bonded as "the other Thatcher sisters" once the twins were born. How often had she called out, "Johanna, wait for me!" while she ran for the school bus or got ready to go outside and play?

And her big sister always waited for her.

"Thank you for understanding."

After saying good-bye, Jillian settled back on the edge of her bed, reaching for one of the magazines on the floor. She flipped through the pages, past images of serene brides. Grooms lingered in the background, like some sort of nuptial secret agent. Handsome. Sexy. Just a bit dangerous. Nothing marred their make-believe wedding days.

She'd thought she had all the time in the world to make her plans. To daydream her way through Pinterest and create her haphazard wish list. Plan a wedding that blew her budget and then be realistic and make everything just the way she wanted.

But this was her life . . . and welcome to it.

Who would want it?

She didn't. Not this way.

It was as if someone had taken a paintbrush, dipped it in red paint, and splattered the word *CANCER* across some perfect bridal layout.

Jillian tossed the magazine to the floor. It was time to finish getting dressed and go to work. Do something easy, like read through loan applications. Maybe she could make someone else's dream come true.

I paced my galley kitchen, tapping my cell phone against my chin, the black-and-white tiles cool against my bare feet. A row of appliances on one side—step, step, step all the way to the cozy breakfast nook at the end. Turn around and step, step, step to the archway leading to my living room. And repeat. For once, I'd remembered to start the dishwasher, the mechanical rumble echoing my mood.

Just make the phone call already. How hard could it be? It wasn't as if I was facing . . . what Jillian was dealing with.

Stop. I couldn't think about yesterday's conversation with my sister's fiancé.

Calling my former high school volleyball coach and talking to her about the upcoming awards ceremony didn't mean I was going to the event. We'd say hello. Have a conversation. Catch up. Talk about Pepper.

Pace. Turn. Pace. Turn.

And then I'd say, "Thank you for wanting to include me in honoring my sister, but I can't attend because I have a previous commitment. With my job."

A lie, yes. But a cowardly lie was better than standing up in front of a room full of people—my family included—and reminiscing about Pepper.

I started to put Coach Sydney's number in my keypad. Stopped. What was I doing? This was her old phone number—the one from a decade ago. Would it still work? Funny how I still remembered it all these years later. But then again, maybe not so odd, what with all the times Pepper and I texted her about practices and games and tournaments and summer camps.

I found the phone number Mom had given me in my notes app as I settled on the couch. Might as well be comfortable if I was going to do this. And what could Sydney do when I said no? She wasn't my coach anymore, so she couldn't make me run laps or do wall sits or conditioning exercises. Or bench me.

But then Sydney said hello, her voice sounding so much the same. For a moment I was sixteen again. Pepper should be here with me, waiting to interrupt the conversation with her own questions and funny comments until I gave in and handed her the phone.

How silly. I only saw my sister in my dreams these days.

I shook my head, dispelling the thought. Silence loomed on both sides of the phone.

"Hey, Coach . . . Sydney . . ." What did I call her now? "This is Payton Thatcher."

"Payton! I'm so glad you called. How are you?"

"I'm fine. Good. How are you?" I pulled the T-shirt quilt up over my legs. So many T-shirts from clubs and tournaments around the country. So many memories of volleyball, all stitched together.

"Exhausted all the time, if you want to know the truth. But that's what I get for being a mom and running a volleyball club." She laughed, the sound of the TV playing in the background. "I love my life."

"How many kids do you have?"

"Two—a boy and a girl. My husband and I are debating whether we go for a third or not. What about you?"

Me?

And just like that, Sydney turned the attention away from herself. She'd always been more concerned about the team. Her girls. Our goals. Our high school struggles and romances. Our plans for the future.

"Um, no kids. Still single. Busy with my job."

"What are you doing these days? I think your mom mentioned you're an event planner?"

"Right. I own a company with a college friend." I traced the outline of a volleyball in one of the quilt squares. "We specialize in social events. Wedding receptions. Anniversary and birthday celebrations. Those kinds of things."

"Party all the time. Sounds like fun. Can I find you on Facebook?"

"Yes. Festivities—that's our company. One of my responsibilities is to keep all the social media updated with photos from our events. I love doing that." I twisted the end of my hair. Did I sound too happy, as if I was trying to convince her that my life was good—really good? "I'm not too active on my personal page."

"I found that out. That's why I had to track you down through your parents. I'd just about given up on you."

"I'm sorry I didn't call sooner." I forced myself to talk slower. Just say what needed to be said. "About the awards ceremony—"

"You probably want details."

No. I didn't want details. I wanted to say no.

"Your mom gave you the date, right? Saturday, September 16, from seven to nine o'clock. So far, we're expecting about seventy-five to one hundred people. Someone from the local news might cover it. We're still not sure about that."

News coverage?

"We're having light hors d'oeuvres and putting together a slide show. Your mom told you that we're retiring Pepper's jersey, right?"

"Yes." Should I say something more? "Pepper would like that."

"I thought so, too. That's when I'd like you to say something. I'll present the jersey and I thought you could share a memory or two about Pepper. Five minutes, tops."

As Sydney detailed the verbal black-and-white about the ceremony, I pressed my hand against my chest, trying to stop a dull ache from building inside me.

One hundred people.

A reporter.

My family.

Was I hesitant because I didn't want to get up in front of all those people? Or was I jealous that even ten years after her death I would be standing in the shadows while the light shone on Pepper's memory?

I'd been proud of Pepper's success all those years ago. Why would I be jealous now?

"What do you think, Payton?" Sydney's voice interrupted my internal debate. "Can I count on you?"

Could she?

My sister couldn't count on me.

I'd failed her ten years ago. Speaking at the awards ceremony would never atone for my mistake, but at least I would be doing the right thing now. For one evening. Two hours—or less, if I arrived late and left early.

"Absolutely, Sydney." I forced the words past my tight throat. "I'm happy to do it."

A lie. Not the lie I'd planned on, but a lie, nonetheless.

And my appearance at the event in a few weeks would be pure pretense as I faked my way through the evening.

But then, hadn't I been faking things for the past ten years?

SOCIAL MEDIA—the introvert's answer to networking without having to talk to people face-to-face.

I settled in one corner of my couch, my laptop close by, tuned to a favorite Spotify playlist of country songs. I'd already opened the tab for Festivities's Pinterest account, ready to add pins to our event boards. But first, I'd add some photos to our Instagram account.

Our "Paint the Town Red" bachelorette party several weeks ago had thrilled the bride-to-be. The red Hummer limo where the guests enjoyed Sweet Eves cocktails—a red twist on champagne. Guests wearing red dresses receiving gift bags containing bright-red lipstick, nail polish, faux ruby gemstone rings, and feather boas. And a Celtic Woman concert at Red Rocks Amphitheatre, complete with backstage passes.

Not my idea of fun, but Kimberlee loved the idea. Even Bianca joined in, suggesting the faux jewelry and feather boas. And now to post photos, anticipate people's reactions, and reply to their comments. Hope we attracted future customers, enabling Kimberlee's dream to grow even bigger. If my business "superpower" was keeping up our social media presence, so be it.

Saturday evening spent behind the scenes? Easy. And satisfying, especially since I knew how happy Kimberlee would be when I showed her all the updates on Monday.

Wait a minute. Was someone knocking at my front door? I muted my playlist right as Keith Urban was crooning, "I'll be the fighter." Sure enough, two rapid knocks sounded. Should I ignore it, assuming someone was selling candy or cookies or something else I didn't need? But I needed to refresh my coffee anyway, so I'd check the door and then grab a refill before getting back to work.

I opened the door, expecting to see some adolescent asking for a donation to their band program in exchange for a chocolate candy bar. Instead, Nash stood there, holding a huge brown paper sack.

"Surprise! I brought you dinner." He smiled his most disarming smile as he moved past me, the aroma of Thai food causing my mouth to water.

"Nash, I told you I was working."

"But a girl's got to eat, right? And I know you. You won't take time to make yourself dinner." Nash continued up the short flight of stairs to my kitchen. "You'll get all caught up in doing whatever it is you've got to do and suddenly it will be midnight and you'll be starving."

After so many months together, the guy knew me. And I should appreciate his surprise appearance with food—most likely Thai curry for me. Nash was being kind. Loving. So why did his showing up on my doorstep feel more like an intrusion?

"You want to grab dishes while I unpack all this food?"

"Sure."

What had Johanna said about Beckett? He was "easy on the eyes"? So was Nash. He had brown eyes—my favorite. Black hair, just like I preferred. Had a standing monthly appointment with his hairstylist. Spent enough time at the gym to be muscular without being over-the-top about his workouts or his abs or arms. Always smelled good and dressed nice, too.

In so many ways, he was everything I wanted in a guy. What was wrong with me?

Now was not the time to answer that question.

After filling our plates while Nash poured us each a glass of wine, I moved my computer so Nash could join me on the couch.

"Do you want to put in a movie while we eat?"

"You go ahead and watch a movie if you want. I'll probably eat some and then get back to work."

"Can't you relax just for tonight? We haven't had a date in a while."

"That is not all my fault. Work has been busy for both of us. And you were traveling—"

"I'm just saying I miss you."

All of our conversations eventually came to this. Nash said he missed me. I said I missed him. But I didn't. He complained he didn't see me enough. And I was fine not seeing him at all.

As I struggled to say what Nash wanted to hear, he'd moved closer to me on the couch, hemming me in. Making it even more difficult to be who he wanted me to be.

I couldn't fake what I didn't feel.

Wait. That was wrong. Yes, I could. I'd been doing it for years.

I didn't want to pretend that I loved Nash. But I also didn't have the energy to break up with him tonight, in the middle of an impromptu dinner.

I was a liar and a coward.

If I couldn't say I missed him, could I at least act like I'd missed him?

"Listen, I'm glad you stopped by, and not because you brought me dinner. I meant to talk to you about this sooner." I shoveled a bit of Thai curry into my mouth. Chewed. "There's a ceremony in a few weeks. It's at my old high school. Honoring star athletes—"

"Are you going to be honored?"

"No. Not me. Pepper. She was the one who set all the

school records." I set my plate on the floor, wiping my hands on a napkin. "Anyway, my family is going, of course, and I was asked to talk about Pepper. Nothing too elaborate. I was hoping you'd go with me."

"I'd love to go with you, Payton." Nash took my hand in his. "I know this might be hard for you."

I broke contact by retrieving my dinner. "It's fine. No big deal."

What was one more person? I told him the date and time, trying to ignore how pleased he looked to be included.

He was all about supporting me, and I was all about fulfilling an obligation. This was the death knell of my relationships—the word *obligation*. And by inviting Nash, I had to go to the event. No backing out now.

"How about if I put in *The Italian Job*?"

"Sure." One of the action DVDs Nash brought over months ago and left here.

Juggling my plate, I closed my laptop. Stayed close to Nash when he sat beside me. There'd be no more work tonight.

At least I'd made him happy . . . for the moment.

DR. WILLIAMSON'S EXAM ROOM had a split personality.

One wall was decorated with a large photograph of a trio of waterfalls cascading over a broken bank, exposing the rough roots of trees, into placid water below. All forest greens and browns and foaming white and even teal blue where the photographer had captured what was below the surface of the water.

Serenity in a picture frame.

On the opposite wall hung a full-color, side-view drawing of the inside of a woman's breast. A poster detailing how to do a monthly breast exam. Another titled "101 Breast Cancer Facts."

"You okay, Jillian?" Geoff's question distracted her from the too-small-to-read list of facts.

"Yes. I just wish Dr. Williamson would get here. I know she's busy, but—"

"First patient of the day, and we still have to wait. Crazy, huh?"

"Yes." She'd keep her attention on the waterfalls.

"How are you doing?"

She could be honest with Geoff. Go past the "fine" answer she said to everyone else. "It's like I'm on some sort of horrible game show. I know I picked the wrong box . . . or the wrong door. I know it's bad. I just don't know how bad."

Her heart rate seemed to slow down the longer they waited for the doctor. Every beat seemed harder. Louder. Would her heart stop? Would she keel over in the office before Dr. Williamson showed up?

No. She couldn't do that. Couldn't scare Geoff like that. This was her life and she had to face whatever truth she'd hear this morning.

Just as the door to the exam room opened, her phone pinged with a text from Harper.

Be aware of the good.

Be aware of the good? What was good about cancer?

Jillian scrambled to think of something—anything—good about her situation.

Having Dr. Sartwell and Dr. Williamson on her side was good.

Having Geoff with her was good.

Having some sort of medical coverage was good.

There. That was the best she could do right now. She knew how to be okay, no matter what was happening. The middle child. Not the oldest. Not one of the athletic, attention-attracting twin daughters. She was just Jillian—and her claim to fame was cancer.

Dr. Williamson sat down in front of them. Said good morning. Apologized for being late, offered a brief smile. But she never lost her "I'm the doctor, you're the patient" demeanor.

Maybe that was how Jillian could get through this appointment. By being businesslike. She knew how to do that, too. She'd had to deny loans to clients. Had to talk to them about foreclosures. And she'd been caring, but professional.

"I assume this is your fiancé, Jillian?"

"Yes, this is Geoff. He wanted to be with me this morning."

"I think that's wise." The two shook hands. "Do either of you have any questions for me before I talk to you about the MRI findings?"

"No." Jillian spoke first as Geoff nodded for her to continue. "No, I think we'd like you to tell us more about the MRI."

"Technology has pros and cons, but we're glad we can image things better now. It helps us plan the surgery more accurately rather than changing things in the operating room."

Dr. Williamson inserted a disc into her computer, turning the screen toward Jillian and Geoff. Once the image appeared, she began orienting them. "Although this looks like shadows, I can point out the density and which is the cancer. . . ." She paused. "Maybe this will help you. Do you know why it's called cancer?"

Geoff answered. "No, ma'am."

"Decades ago, when people first looked at cancer in the body, they said it looked like a crab—a central body with appendages. Some people called it cancer, after the astrological sign." She turned back to the MRI. "You can see the central mass, but there are tendrils spreading out from it. Unfortunately, doing a lumpectomy like we had originally planned isn't sufficient. We need to get as much of the cancer cells as possible so that chemotherapy will be effective. The less cancer your immune system has to kill off, the more likely it is to be successful."

The words *mass* and *tendrils* and *chemotherapy* swirled in Jillian's brain, even as the room seemed to sway around her. Someone might as well have come up behind her while she'd been standing on the edge of a cliff and shoved her off.

When she remained silent, Geoff spoke up. "What are you recommending Jillian do?"

"We need to do a unilateral mastectomy."

A mastectomy? Even as she resisted the urge to move her hand up to shield her breast, Jillian found her voice. "That's one side, right?"

"Yes."

For some reason, she noticed the time on the clock: 8:37 in the morning. The moment she learned what was behind the door.

"How soon?"

"This is not an emergency, but the sooner the better. I recommend scheduling surgery next week. We still need to do other tests."

One week. Seven days.

"Like what?"

"Blood work and a CAT scan." Dr. Williamson turned the screen back toward herself. "This is your decision, Jillian. You're welcome to get a second opinion. And if you'd like me to talk to your family, I'm available to do that, too."

"I don't know. I do want to talk to Dr. Sartwell, but there's no need for you to talk to my family."

"I've already spoken to Dr. Sartwell, but I'm certain she's expecting a phone call from you."

Jillian didn't remember saying good-bye. Checking out at the billing desk. One minute she was talking about dates for surgery, the next she was sitting in the passenger seat of Geoff's car.

"What do you want to do, honey? We can go get breakfast—"

"I want to go to work." Jillian set her purse at her feet and clicked her seat belt into place, staring straight ahead at the other cars in the parking lot.

"Jillian—"

"I want to go to work." She didn't mean to sound harsh. She wasn't angry with Geoff. She wasn't angry with anyone. "I'm not hungry right now. And you need to get into work, too."

"Do you want me to call anyone for you?"

"I'll call Dr. Sartwell on the way. You're driving."

"What about your family?"

"I'll call Johanna. And my parents. And Payton."

Geoff rested his hand over hers. "You don't have to do all that. I can call them when we get to the bank. And my parents, too."

"It's fine, Geoff. I'll call my family and you can call your parents later. Right now just go ahead and drive."

As Geoff directed the car into traffic, another text appeared on her phone from Harper. **What did the doctor say?** And then a meme with the words *No negative thoughts*.

A sharp laugh stalled in the back of her throat. Negative thoughts? It was hard to think anything at all when she was in a free fall emotionally, a silent scream welling up inside her. Would she ever reach bottom?

She scrabbled for some semblance of a businesslike front as she called Johanna. Maybe her sister wouldn't answer. What was the proper thing to do if she got voice mail?

"Jillian? I was debating calling you."

"Hi, Joey." She slipped back into her sister's childhood nickname. Hadn't used it in years. "I wanted to tell you what the surgeon said."

"Okay."

Jillian blinked away the burn of tears. Businesslike. This was her practice phone call. If—when—she got through this call, she'd do better talking to the rest of her family. "Because of the size of the mass, the surgeon recommended a unilateral mastectomy."

"I see." She might have surprised her sister, but Johanna's voice remained level. "You're getting a second opinion, right?"

"She recommended that, too. I'm talking to my family physician, but I went ahead and scheduled the surgery for next week."

"I really think you should wait—"

Jillian gripped her seat belt. "Please, I can't talk about this right now. I called to tell you what the doctor said. That's all."

"Do you want me to call everyone else?"

"No. I can do that. Geoff's driving me to work."

"Is there anything I can do?"

Was there?

"No. I just wanted to tell you. I need to call Mom and Dad. And Payton."

"Okay." There was a moment's silence. "Love you, Jill."

The words were as odd as Jillian calling Johanna by her nickname. "Love you, too."

The exchange threatened to crumble her impersonal facade, even as she tucked the words close to her heart. She took a deep breath and prepared to finish calling her family. And then she'd call Dr. Sartwell. She'd focus on one thing—one person—at a time and get through the task of being the bearer of her bad news.

I'D NEVER SEEN a hospital room set up as a mini waiting room before. Then again, I shouldn't be surprised at what Johanna could pull off because of her position at the hospital.

The standard bed had been pushed up against the far wall. A round table surrounded by four plastic chairs stood in the middle of the room. Someone had even thought to put a small glass vase of white and red carnations in the center of the table. A compact lounge chair—probably used when a family member slept over—sat at the foot of the bed. The TV, mounted in the upper corner farthest from the door, had been turned on, tuned to a morning news show, and muted.

"I talked to the hospital administrator," Johanna had

announced as she ushered us past the surgical waiting room. "I thought it would be nice to have some privacy, and he agreed to let us use an empty room while we wait for Jillian to get out of surgery."

She said everything with such a gracious air, I didn't dare protest or tell her the room seemed claustrophobic. That I preferred the regular waiting room, even with all the strangers coming and going, the background noise of the TV, the scattered magazines and newspapers, the coffee cups and soda cans.

"Mom, Jillian asked to see you." Johanna stood in the doorway. "The nurse said I could bring you back to the pre-op area."

"Is that okay, Don? Should I go? Would you rather go?" Even as she asked the trio of questions, Mom was moving toward the door.

"Of course, Heather. Go with Johanna."

Mom disappeared, ushered away in the cloud of my older sister's kindness.

Which was fine. I wouldn't know what to say to Jillian beyond the text I'd managed to send her late last night.

Try to get some sleep. You've got a good surgeon. We'll all be waiting for you. I'm bringing the Warheads.

I blamed the last sentence on seeing a bag of Warheads candies at the grocery store earlier in the week. And then remembering a family vacation to the beach when Pepper and I were ten years old. Jillian was sixteen and Johanna was eighteen—getting ready to head off to college. We'd discovered Warheads in a local drugstore—beyond-sour candies in flavors of lemon, blue raspberry, watermelon, black cherry, and apple. For the rest of the vacation, we challenged one another to see who could suck on a Warhead the longest, sometimes even daring to try two or three at a time.

I'd bought the candy on a whim—and then stuck them in my purse last night after I texted Jillian. What was I going to do? Offer her one in the recovery room?

"You want me to go find coffee, Dad?"

"No, thanks. I'm good for now." He settled in the lounge chair, glancing at the TV. He looked so calm. How did he do that? He rubbed the palm of one hand against the back of his other hand—the only giveaway that he was anxious. Other than that, he could have been sitting in his recliner at home, preparing to watch the Broncos take on the Cowboys.

Outside the hospital window, the sun shone in a clear blue sky on a normal Wednesday morning before Labor Day. Normal for so many other people who were battling traffic on their way to work. Taking their kids to school. Debating whether to drive through Starbucks or not.

Was it wrong to wish that it was still dark outside? That it was even earlier in the morning and that Jillian had been the first patient wheeled into surgery, instead of having to wait her turn in line? That would be a silly thing to complain about.

I wanted to say something encouraging. Something positive. But the longer I was in the hospital, the more I fought memories of the night Pepper died.

"*This clinic is so small. . . . Why aren't they taking her to a bigger hospital? . . . Somebody tell me something. . . . Let me see her. . . . When are my parents going to get here? . . . Why can't I talk to the doctor or a nurse? . . . Somebody . . . Mom! Dad! Let me go back with you. . . . Please . . . please . . . I need to see Pepper. . . .*"

My father took my hands in his. Was he encouraging me to hang on to him? Or was he hanging on to me?

"*Payton—*" *my name was guttural as if it came from the depths of a broken heart—*"your sister didn't survive the accident.*"

"*No—*"

"*I'm sorry. . . .*" *My father pulled me into his arms, sobbing as if Pepper's death were his fault.* "*I'm sorry. . . .*"

He had nothing to be sorry for.

Geoff opened the door to the improvised waiting room, ushering Mom in with a flourish and an "After you."

His arrival prevented the memories of that night from overtaking the reality of today.

"How's Jilly?" Dad rose from his chair, going over to Mom and hugging her.

Mom took his hand in hers, intertwining their fingers. Was her action because she needed to feel close to him or because she knew of his nervous habit, too? If I noticed the action, certainly she did.

"My future wife is absolutely amazing." Geoff beamed as he boasted about my sister. "She was so relaxed. So nice to everyone else."

My father nodded. "That sounds like Jilly."

"Everyone knew Johanna, of course." Mom perched on

the arm of the lounge chair. "I think that's why people were being so extra nice to Jill."

"I would hope the hospital treats all their patients well—not just family members."

"Oh, Payton, you know what I mean. Even a chaplain stopped by and offered to pray with us. Wasn't that nice?"

I turned away from my family, facing the window again. Traffic continued along the roadway outside.

Nice, yes, but unnecessary. So far, my family had gotten through life without any sort of god. What did the Thatcher family have faith in? Getting up each morning and trying again, I guessed. That life was worth it all, for some reason.

But what was the reason?

We'd been taught to play fair. To share. To be good sports. To do our best. Because those were the right things to do.

But why? What was the big gold ring we were reaching for?

And was believing life was worth it all how my parents got through Pepper's death? Was choosing to get up each morning and try again how they were going to get through today while another daughter underwent major surgery in an effort to save her life?

"Everybody doing okay?" Johanna entered the room as if she owned the hospital. All business. "I talked with Dr. Williamson right before Jillian's surgery started, and she said someone will come and update us about halfway through."

"Oh, how wonderful. Thank you so much." Mom hugged my older sister as if she'd accomplished some miraculous task.

All I could see was Johanna grandstanding on the morning

our sister was having a mastectomy. Still finding a way to make today about her.

Was I overreacting? Maybe it was fine for Johanna to use her influence to benefit our family. After all, this was "her" hospital and Jillian was family.

As she stepped away from our mom, Johanna sniffled and blinked.

Tears? Would I ever figure my oldest sister out?

It didn't matter. Jillian would get through today. Life would get back to normal. And I could retreat to my safe place, away from so much togetherness with my sisters.

Again, the door opened. For a private waiting room, we were getting a lot of traffic.

"I'm so sorry I'm late!" Harper backed into the room, carrying not one, but two drink carriers. "How is she? Has the surgery started? I got coffee. Jillian told me everyone's favorites."

That was so like Jillian.

"How on earth did you manage?" Mom took one of the carriers.

"I'm just thankful for automatic doors and helpful people."

As Harper handed Geoff his drink, she also slipped him a few bills and some loose change. I'd sent my sister a text and told her I was bringing a bag of Warheads. Meanwhile, her best friend treated everyone to coffee.

I guessed this was one of those "something is better than nothing" moments.

I thanked Harper for my coffee and eased toward the door.

"Where are you going, Payton?" Johanna's question stopped me from exiting the room.

"For a walk."

"Why?"

"It's going to be a while before we hear anything about the surgery." I took a quick sip of my coffee, sweetened just the way I liked, the hot liquid scalding my tongue. "I want to take a walk. Do I have to explain myself to you?"

Dad set aside his cup of coffee, rubbing the back of one hand with the other again. Was it because he was anxious about Jillian—or because Johanna and I were bickering?

"You don't have to always argue with Johanna, you know."

The whisper of Pepper's voice almost caused me to drop my cup. How many times had she told me that when we were growing up?

"Just ignore her, Payton. It doesn't matter what she says."

But I could never ignore Johanna. What she said always mattered to me.

Not today. Today I'd be quiet. For my parents' sake. For Jillian's sake. For Geoff's and Harper's sake.

"I think a walk will help me calm down. I'll be back in a little bit." I slipped out the door, closing it on any further protests from Johanna.

10

Why was I having such a difficult time sleeping?

It wasn't as if I'd had surgery. No, Jillian was the one recovering from a mastectomy. So why was I lying awake, tossing and turning, mentally begging my body to relax . . . and then dragging myself into work the next morning, exhausted and still half-asleep?

It had been a week since Jillian's surgery, and this was turning out to be another sleepless night.

Retrieving my cell phone from my bedside table, I noticed a text from Johanna from ten o'clock. Two hours ago. How had I missed that?

The first week is behind us. Spent the day with Jillian.

She says the pain is decreasing. Still limited to sponge baths until her drains are removed. Mom will stay with her starting next week.

Johanna's texts had started within minutes of Jillian arriving in the recovery room with a **Heard from the anesthesiologist that Jillian did well** message and continued several times a day since then. I kept telling myself she meant well, that this was the simplest way to keep us all updated and included.

But for some reason I felt excluded. Unneeded. Harper and Johanna helped Jillian the first week after surgery, and then Mom would be with her. After that, Jillian planned to go back to work.

What was I complaining about—even if only to myself? Wasn't I the one who always demanded distance?

This was what too little sleep did for me. I overthought my life—the life I'd worked so hard to attain. To perfect.

Of course, I could always call and check on Jillian if I wanted to. See if she needed anything.

But not at midnight.

I dragged myself out of bed, taking my comforter and pillow with me, and made my way through the darkened town house to the couch. Maybe a change of location would do the trick. If my mother were here, she'd recommend a glass of warm milk flavored with honey. But even though I was still awake, I didn't have enough energy to make an updated version of my mother's remedy using almond milk and maple syrup.

I tossed my phone to the end of the couch. Grabbed the

remote and channel surfed until I found some inane Disney Channel rerun certain to put me to sleep. I snuggled beneath the comforter, punched my pillow into shape, and stared at the TV screen, muttering, "Go to sleep, go to sleep, go to sleep."

The dock moved beneath my feet, my flip-flops sounding a dull thud against the weathered boards. I shaded my eyes against the sunlight streaming across the water that stretched out in front of me. The air carried the scent of salt. Of humidity. Of summer.

"I love this place."

I stumbled to a halt, not noticing Pepper seated on the edge of the dock until she spoke. She wore a yellow tank top and a pair of cutoff jean shorts.

Pepper patted the space beside her, staring straight ahead, her bare feet dangling over the edge of the dock. "Sit down."

I slipped off my flip-flops and sat beside my sister, our bare arms touching. "I haven't been back here since—"

"Summer vacation when we were ten. I know. So many good memories, right?"

"From that summer, yes."

"I never expected you to be such a cynic, Pay."

"I grew up, Pepper."

How odd to say that when I was sitting next to my sister in a dream, and she was still sixteen.

"Is it so bad, growing up?"

What kind of question was that?

"It's not what I expected. You're gone . . . and I've never had much of a relationship with Jillian and Johanna."

"Then change things."

"It's not that easy."

"Sometimes you just have to forget all the other stuff and remember we're sisters."

"What?" Something buzzed around my ear and I swatted it away. More buzzing. *"What do you mean?"*

I woke up to the sound of buzzing and struggled to sit upright. What was that sound? My neck ached when I turned my head. I was going to regret my night on the couch.

Digging through the folds of the comforter, I found my cell phone, alarm blaring. Six o'clock in the morning? Here I'd been worried about going back to sleep and having another odd dream—and it was time to get ready for work.

What had the dream been about? What had Pepper said? I shoved my hair out of my face, rubbing at my dry eyes. But trying to remember the dream was like dropping a piece of fragile parchment paper into the ocean and then trying to retrieve it. The words blurred . . . it disintegrated . . . and disappeared with the tides.

I was wasting my time.

All I could do was get ready for work—and make good on my late-night decision to call Jillian and see how she was doing.

With her mother in the kitchen making lunch, Jillian could talk to Harper undisturbed. Even so, she slunk a little lower on the couch, thankful the sound of the TV added another buffer to their conversation.

"You know you don't have to keep checking up on me,

right?" She switched off speaker mode and put the phone to her ear. At least her friend didn't hear her soft hiss of pain at the movement. "My mom is here this week."

"I'm not calling you because I have to, Jill. I'm doing this because I want to. How are you feeling today?"

"I feel like I'm about four years old again."

"What? Why?"

"My mom is helping me get dressed. Fussing about what I'm eating. Reminding me to do my arm exercises. She's even asking if I've gone to the bathroom."

"So? Johanna and I did that when we stayed with you—"

"You never once asked me about going to the bathroom."

"Okay, that's true."

"And I could tell you to leave me alone."

"Like you ever did that."

"No . . . but I could." Jillian shifted her position again, trying to check over her shoulder to make certain her mother was still in the kitchen. "I'm sorry I'm such a grouch."

"I understand. How's your pain level?"

"Not as bad as last week. I might try to start going off some of the pain meds."

"Just do what the doctor said. You've still got the drains in. Why don't you wait until your first post-op appointment?"

"You're right. I know you're right. I just hate feeling sleepy all the time."

"Sleepy is better than hurting."

"Right again."

"What's your positive thought for today?"

"I don't know. I haven't read it."

"Come on, pick one from the jar. That's what it's for."

"It's in the bedroom, Harper." Now she sounded like a bratty kid.

"So? Go get the jar. I'm waiting."

Jillian pulled herself up from the couch, grumbling the entire way down the hall so that her friend could hear her. Harper's laughter sounded back through the phone.

The simple glass jar filled with multicolored pieces of paper sat on her dresser, the silver lid beside it among a jumble of receipts, earrings, and bracelets.

"Pick one already!" Harper raised her voice to be heard.

"All right!" Jillian dipped her hand into the papers, swirling her fingertips, and selected a bright-purple one as she cradled the phone against her shoulder. The twinge of pain was worth it to keep her friend happy. "I got one."

"What's it say?"

"'When I smile, I feel better.'"

"Okay. Look in the mirror and smile."

"Are you kidding me?"

"Do it."

Harper would badger her until she smiled at her reflection, so Jillian tilted her head, met her own gaze, and smiled. It was forced. But it was a smile.

"Feel better?"

"I feel ridiculous—and that's better than grouchy, right?"

"Right. I know this is tough, but you're no quitter." Harper's tone softened. "I love you."

"I love you, too. Get back to work. And thanks for calling."

Jillian tucked the purple slip of paper into her jeans pocket as she headed back to the living room. Sometimes this whole "positive thinking" idea seemed like an exercise in futility. She would read the line—*Think positive thoughts and positive things will happen*, or *Believe you can*—and try to hold on to it. But it seemed to float away, to burst . . . like the rainbow-tinted bubbles her mother used to blow for her and her sisters in the backyard. She'd chase after them, hands reaching, and then they'd pop.

Maybe she'd do better once she was off the narcotics for pain. Once she was sleeping better.

As she sat on the couch, her arm brushed her chest . . . where her breast should be . . . causing her to catch her breath at the pain.

Maybe she'd do better once she got used to her body again.

It had only been a week. Both Dr. Williamson and Dr. Sartwell had said she needed to give herself time to adjust.

One of the first positive thoughts she'd pulled from the jar was *Your attitude determines your direction*.

She wanted to go forward. Wanted to heal. But she was going slowly.

Her mother appeared, carrying two plates. "Lunch is ready. Are you hungry?"

"A little. Maybe we could watch TV?"

"Sounds perfect." Her mother set the plates on the coffee table. "I'll get our drinks. Hot tea sound good?"

"Yes."

By the time her mother returned, Jillian had tuned the TV to a rerun of *Property Brothers*. "Just some background noise."

"I've always liked the show."

"Really?"

"Yes. It intrigues me, I guess, because of the twin brothers. . . ."

"Did you like having twins, Mom?"

"I liked being a mom. Period. Having twins, well, it was a different kind of challenge. I mean, here I was, forty years old and coming home from the hospital with not one, but two babies."

"I imagine that was a bit of a shock."

"Yes, it was. Everyone was making such a fuss over the twins, your father included. I was worried you and Johanna would get lost in all the excitement."

"It's kind of to be expected, isn't it?"

"You say that now, but it was a pretty big change for you and your sister."

"Ye-es, but I don't feel like I lost you after Payton and Pepper were born."

"Thank you for saying so."

They sat without talking, watching one of the twin brothers demolish a kitchen.

"I remember doing this when I was little."

"What? Renovating a house?"

"Very funny. No. Staying home from school when I was sick. You'd turn on the TV and let me watch daytime game shows." When her mother touched her hand, Jillian asked, "How are you doing, Mom?"

Her mother half turned to face her. "Me? I'm fine."

"No, really—how are you?"

"No mother wants to see her child sick . . . or hurt . . . or . . ." Her mother picked at the remains of her salad. "I'm glad I can be here to help you. I'm thankful you've got good doctors. I believe you're going to be okay, Jillian. I really do."

For a moment, her mother had been vulnerable. Shared some of her fears. But how could she believe that Jillian would be okay? Pepper had died. Maybe her mother thought losing one daughter exempted her from losing another one.

Or maybe her mom survived on positive thoughts, too. Taking it one day, one crisis, at a time. Believing tomorrow would be better. Easier.

Jillian didn't know. They never talked about it. Pepper died . . . and they all somehow adjusted to one less Thatcher sister in their own way. Now, years later, they were here. Facing her diagnosis. And they just did what needed to be done.

Her mother's choice to get up and live the next day . . . and the next . . . and the next had been enough when Pepper died. Choosing to do so again would be enough now. For all of them.

From elementary school to halfway through my junior year of high school, I could crawl into bed, put my head on the pillow, and not remember anything until morning came, the sound of my mother's voice or of the alarm clock dragging me from blissful oblivion.

And then Pepper died. A nuclear bomb of emotions detonated inside me, one that doctors tried to calm with medications.

At times memories of Pepper overwhelmed me. Guilt threatened to strangle me. Despair haunted me day and night. Sleep evaded me. I wrote desperate thoughts in my journal, as if the reckless flow of words might somehow fill the void in my life.

THINGS I NEVER TOLD YOU

I would not become that girl again.

But sleeplessness taunted me. I'd taken to moving back and forth between the couch and my bed, hoping changing my location would stop Pepper from finding me while I slept. But as if she knew the importance of the upcoming evening, she'd invaded the moments in between my waking and sleeping.

Last night's dream returned as I finished applying my makeup—a little blush to feign color in my skin.

"Heading back to high school tonight, huh?"

Pepper. I turned around, trying to get my bearings. She leaned against a locker—her high school locker. Mine was right next to hers, decorated with a white construction-paper volleyball with my jersey number on it.

"Yes."

"Looking forward to it?"

"Sure."

"Oh, come on, Pay. I know you better than that. You don't want to go."

"Fine. I don't want to go. But I'll do it."

"Thanks." Pepper straightened. "Tell me something?"

"Sure."

"What's with the vegan thing?"

"It's not a 'thing,' Pepper. I've been vegan for years."

"Why?"

"I feel better eating that way. Healthier."

"O-kay. Then it's not some sort of social statement—"

"It's a personal choice."

"Why don't you have a dog? Or a cat?"

"Really? We're talking about pets now?"

"Do you want to talk about Nash?"

As Pepper moved down the hallway, I fell into step beside her. "No, I don't want to talk about Nash—"

"Come on, Payton, we used to talk about everything."

"That was before—"

"What? Before I died?"

"No. Before you changed."

Pepper stilled. Stared at me. "Everybody changes, Payton. You did."

"I did not."

"Yes. Yes, you did. If you'd just told the truth, things would be different—"

"It's too late for that now."

"Is it?" And then she turned her back on me and disappeared into the hallway that was now filled with other students.

Tell the truth. How easy for some dream-Pepper to suggest I tell the truth all these years later. That things would be different. Better.

If I could ask Pepper a question, it would be why she decided to show up now—and when she was going to leave me alone.

My cell phone rang, and despite seeing that it was Johanna, I answered. If I didn't, she would call back until I picked up.

"Hey, Johanna."

"You're still coming tonight, right?"

"Just getting ready to walk out the door."

"Good. It starts at seven. No need to be late."

"I've got plenty of time."

"You know how important this is to Mom and Dad—"

"I'll see you there," I interrupted my sister, ending the call without a good-bye. If I let her, Johanna would hunt me down tonight and critique whatever I said about Pepper.

My phone buzzed again, but this time with a text message from Nash.

I'm here. I'm coming up.

I scrambled to text him back, almost knocking my makeup bag onto the bathroom floor. **I'm on my way down.**

Within moments, I slid into the passenger seat of his sports car, accepting his kiss before adjusting my seat belt.

"You look nice."

"Thanks." No need to tell him how many outfits I'd left tossed all over my bed before deciding on a pair of slim dark jeans and a patterned blouse paired with low-heeled purple leather boots.

"How are you feeling?" Nash reached over and clasped my hand in his.

"Fine. I'm good." I resisted the urge to shake off his touch.

"Are you nervous?"

"I'm not nervous."

"Did you write down what you're going to say? Do you want to practice—?"

"No." *Keep holding his hand. The man means well.* "I—I've gone over it enough. I don't want it to be too perfect, you know? Besides, it's only four minutes. How badly can I flub it?"

"Pepper would be proud—"

"Red light." I pulled my hand from Nash's, bracing myself against the dashboard.

"Relax, babe."

"Is it okay if I put on some music?" I turned on his radio, satisfied with whatever station was playing.

"Sure. Listen, do you want to go out to dinner after the ceremony?"

All I wanted was for Nash to stop talking. "I don't know. Maybe. Why don't we see how it goes?"

"I'll mention it to your dad, okay?"

"Can we just get through this?" I didn't try to soften the sharp edge to my words.

"Fine."

I leaned back, closing my eyes to fend off any more conversation.

But the words of my presentation scrambled in my brain like train cars lined up out of order—caboose, passenger cars, engine, more passenger cars.

Was tonight going to be a train wreck?

I could do this. I could stand up and talk about Pepper for less than five minutes. Share a memory of playing volleyball together. Find it in myself to laugh about how we were called Double Trouble. Say how much Pepper would appreciate this honor . . .

Yeah. I could fake anything for that long.

It was the thought of all the small talk . . . the chit-chat . . . the "So what have you been doing since high school?" questions before and after that caused my throat to tighten.

What had I been doing since high school?

Avoiding all of this. Going forward, not backward. Pretending . . . no, not pretending. Reinventing myself and being true to who I was now.

"Babe?"

Nash's voice had me sitting upright. "What?"

"We'll be there in about ten minutes."

How had we gotten here so quickly? Had I fallen asleep?

"That was fast."

"For once, traffic from Denver was good."

"Great. Wouldn't want to be late."

That wasn't the truth. I didn't want to be there at all.

⌐

Zach folded the "Hello, my name is" tag in half and shoved it into the back pocket of his jeans. Bad manners, yes, but he'd always avoided the tacky squares that fell off within seconds or that he forgot to remove until hours later. If he wanted someone to know his name, he'd do it the old-fashioned way and introduce himself without relying on preprinted fluorescent-green letters. Refusing to wear the name tag wasn't going to hide his identity like Superman donning a pair of glasses and a suit and becoming Clark Kent. Not that he was a superhero.

Not a chance.

He stayed on the outskirts of the crowd, avoiding eye

contact with the others gathered for the ceremony. Some people clustered in groups, casting furtive glances at the name tags before engaging in "How have you been?" small talk. Others claimed seats at the tables covered with white-and-maroon tablecloths—the school colors—positioned around the gym, while photographs skimmed across the screen at the front of the room.

He had every right to be here. After all, he was one of the seven people being honored by the high school athletic department. His now-and-then duo of photographs rotated through the montage on the screen. He rubbed the letters tattooed on three of the fingers of his left hand—uneven black block letters. *R. U. N.* It was a good thing he hadn't been too drunk to figure out the word *runner* wouldn't fit on one hand. He wasn't a runner anymore, and he wasn't going to run away today.

As he stood in front of the table covered with punch-filled plastic cups, the Thatcher family took their seats at one of the tables up front. Payton's parents. Her older sister Johanna, looking as reserved as she had at Pepper's funeral. Jillian sat next to some guy—had she gotten married? Zach cracked his knuckles one by one. There they sat, unaware they were the jury, able to declare him guilty or, with a word, with an act of kindness, to pronounce him free from his past mistakes. But thanks to Payton, he couldn't even approach them.

He gulped down a glass of punch, reaching for a second. Tasted like the same stuff they'd served at every single awards banquet he'd ever attended. Payton entered the room at last, like some judge claiming her courtroom. She'd already refused to grant him a pardon. A man accompanied her, his arm around her waist drawing her close to his side. Zach knew by the way her posture stiffened, her steps slowed, exactly when she noticed him. He nodded, offering her a small salute, hoping it came off casual, not cocky.

Payton whispered something to the guy—Zach could only assume he was her boyfriend from the way he pressed a kiss to her lips—and then stepped toward Zach. This was what he wanted, right? A chance to plead his case again? Then why was his mind a blank? Where were all those carefully rehearsed words? He had to come up with something more than "Hello" and "How are you?" if he wanted to get the advantage of Payton Thatcher.

As Payton positioned herself in front of him, Pepper's photo—a quick reminder of what Payton had looked like in high school—flashed across the screen behind her, confirming he wasn't the only one who'd changed in ten years. Gone was the athletic girl who'd walked the hallways with her sister, their auburn hair hanging down their backs. In her place stood an achingly thin woman with dark circles under her eyes, her hair pulled back from her face by a thin headband, a few tendrils falling against the sharp curves of her cheekbones.

"Before you go and ask why I'm here, I'll remind you that I'm one of the honorees—"

"Where's your family?"

"I didn't tell them about tonight."

"What? Why not?"

"I kind of wrecked high school for me and my family—but I don't have to tell you that." Zach straightened his shoulders.

"Yes, well, since you are here, I'll remind you that I asked you to leave me and my family alone tonight. Please." She tacked on the last word as if forced to do the right thing—to use her nice words.

"I remember your decree, Payton." His choice of words caused her lips to form a thin line, her eyes flashing. Well, at least he had her attention, even if he did feel like a defendant about to represent himself with no preparation. "But I don't think I'm being unreasonable to ask for a chance to talk to your family—"

"This isn't about what you want, Zach. This is about you leaving my family alone today, tomorrow . . . forever. We've all made our peace with Pepper's death—" Payton swallowed as if even mentioning her sister was a struggle—"and your appearance will just be disruptive and painful."

"Be reasonable, Payton. I don't have to ask permission to talk to your parents. But I'm trying to be considerate of your feelings. You're not the only one who was hurt by Pepper's death—who needs healing. Closure."

"Don't come here and start talking to me about healing." Payton slashed the air with her open hand. "I'm fine. My family is fine. And we'll be fine if you stay away from us."

"If you were really fine, you'd let me talk to your parents—"

"So you say. Talking doesn't always help. Confession isn't

always good for the soul. Words don't always heal. Sometimes they . . . they . . ."

"Sometimes they what, Payton?"

"Sometimes words create more confusion . . . more hurt . . ." She stopped talking. "I don't know why I'm standing here having this conversation with you. All I wanted to do was remind you to stay away from my family. I'm done talking with you. I need to go sit down before the program starts."

So much for pleading his case. If anything, he'd lost ground with Payton. Zach could almost hear the strike of a gavel echoing through a courtroom. Had he mistaken God's prompting to seek out Payton Thatcher? Had he tried too hard to have his own way rather than waiting on God? He pressed his fist against his lips. He refused to believe this setback was permanent. He'd waited this long. He could wait longer. If there's one thing he'd learned since God had broken into his life, it was that He was always working in the waiting times.

12

EVERYONE ELSE IN THE GYM seemed happy to be here. A celebratory mood filled the room, the site of so many school plays, choir concerts, awards assemblies.

A new mural covered the left wall, an impressionistic blur of athletic figures representing football, basketball, track and cross-country, tennis—and yes, even volleyball—all against a backdrop of Pikes Peak. Up front, photos splashed across a video screen. A high school moment frozen in time paired with a current image of the same person. Some faces I only recognized because of the name written across the bottom of the picture.

Zachary Gaines appeared on the screen, all of seventeen or

eighteen, long-legged and lanky, coming around the curve during a cross-country meet, sweat matting his hair to his forehead, the barest hint of a smile curving his lips. And then a second photo of Zach today, a profile shot of him. Older. Weary. Worn.

A few more faces flashed by and then . . . one painfully familiar. Pepper, frozen in midair, arms raised as she blocked the opposing team's ball. No other photo. Just Pepper, forever sixteen.

That photo had been taken during our last high school volleyball season, Pepper and I rotating in and out of the game, but my sister was the one who racked up blocks and who was surrounded by news reporters afterward.

"Do you like the photo I selected of Pepper?" My former high school volleyball coach knelt beside my chair.

"That's when we won state." I forced myself to pin on the obligatory so-thrilled-to-be-here smile. "Pepper would be glad you chose that one, Coach."

"Coach? After all these years?" She leaned in to give me a hug. "Just call me Sydney."

"You'll always be Coach to me." I easily looked past the way the last decade had added a few lines around Sydney's eyes and saw the vivacious twentysomething woman who had influenced both Pepper and me in so many ways. "Love your blonde hair."

"Just having some fun." Sydney leaned back on her heels. "Thanks for being here."

"As if I could tell the woman who made me do wall sits and circuit training no."

"That was a long time ago." Her voice turned serious. "How are you?"

"Doing great."

"I know this is hard for you. I appreciate you being here."

"Like I said, can't say no to my high school coach." It was best to keep things light. "So I checked out your club online. Your eighteens team made it to nationals last year!"

"Yep. I was so proud of those girls. They earned that." Sydney's smile lit up her eyes. "Club Brio. My life is still all about volleyball—and now my husband and kids, of course. Let me know if you ever want to coach . . ."

Her words caused me to lean away, even as I tried to laugh them off. She couldn't be serious. I wasn't that girl anymore. I'd left those dreams behind years ago. Had no right to them. "I don't think so. Festivities keeps me busy enough, and I haven't been on a volleyball court since . . . since high school." Nash slipped his hand into mine, his presence a welcome diversion. "Sydney, this is Nash, my boyfriend."

"Nice to meet you." Sydney shook hands with Nash. "I left my husband home with the kids. Easier that way."

"Any future volleyball players in the family?" I had no problem talking about volleyball, so long as the topic wasn't focused on me.

"Of course. Dale—that's my husband—played soccer, so he's hoping for soccer players. Either way, we're a sports family." Sydney rose to her feet, smoothing her skirt. "You ready for the presentation?"

"Absolutely. A couple of minutes is all you wanted, right?"

"Right. Just come up front when I do, okay?"

"Will do."

As Sydney left, Zach Gaines glanced my way from where he patrolled the edge of the gym like some sort of self-appointed security guard. Was the guy going to pace around the room until it was time for him to accept his award? Did he think staring at me would get me to change my mind?

"Who were you talking to?" Johanna's sharp whisper jerked my attention away from Zach and back to my family. Were they all staring at me, waiting for an answer?

"You mean Coach Sydney?"

Johanna almost looked as if she wanted to roll her eyes at me. "No. The guy."

"Just someone I . . . someone Pepper and I knew in high school. He's another honoree today."

"He looks familiar. Do I know him?"

"Johanna, you graduated from high school years before we did. No, you don't know him."

I could only hope my reply prevented my sister from making the connection between Zach and the Gaines family and the spring break party ten years ago. The news coverage had been brief. My parents' overwhelming grief back then had kept them from placing blame on anyone. Pepper's death was a tragic accident—no one was to blame. Honoring her tonight might be enough to distract them from the past and present colliding, causing them to recognize Zach.

I ended the conversation by twisting away from her,

leaning across Nash, and focusing on Jillian. "How are you feeling?"

It was wrong to use Jillian as a diversionary tactic against Johanna—especially when she was only a couple of weeks postsurgery. And Jillian was probably tired of people asking how she felt. Her pale face and slow movements indicated her tiredness and pain. But Jillian being Jillian, she wouldn't admit it.

"I'm fine. A little sore, but the surgeon warned me about that."

"You could have stayed home. Everyone would have understood—"

"I'm fine, Payton. Besides, all I'm doing is sitting here. Once it's over, Geoff's taking me home. I wanted to be here." She leaned back into Geoff's embrace. "I know you'll do a good job up there."

And now Jillian was encouraging me, not even aware that I'd been using her, even if it had only been in a small way. It seemed I was destined to fail, over and over, at my relationships with my sisters.

But then again, just like Jillian, I'd shown up. I'd do what needed to be done and then retreat to the safety of my home until the next time family demanded something more of me, something that pulled me from the safety of the neutral zone.

⁓

I'd followed Sydney's instructions. Waited as the other former athletes were honored, including Zach Gaines. Waited for the brief slide show highlighting Pepper's volleyball accomplishments—all the records she'd set. Walked up as Coach Sydney came forward with a framed number 11 volleyball jersey—just like Pepper used to wear. Stood beside her as she announced the number would be retired and the jersey hung in the gym. And then, at last, I was alone in front of everyone.

All of them waiting for me to say something about my twin sister.

I gripped the sides of the podium, swallowing against the stinging dryness in my throat. I pressed my lips together, heat coursing up my neck. I needed water. Even more, I needed the words that had escaped from my mind. To my left, someone shifted in their seat—Nash, offering me a brief nod and a smile. Although I had my doubts about him, about our relationship, he was always there for me—even when I didn't want him to be.

"Good evening." My voice rasped in my ears. How awful that must sound magnified through a microphone. "I'm Payton Thatcher, Pepper's twin sister. . . ."

Wait. Sydney had already said that. Why was I repeating her?

I fought to calm my erratic breathing, opening and closing my hands to try to stop them from tingling. Had someone lowered the lights in the room?

"My family . . . my family wanted to say . . ." Again, motion in the room caught my attention. Who was walking around?

A tall, slender female paced the back of the room, her braid swishing against her back.

"Pepper . . ." The whisper of her name fell from my lips into the silence filling the room. My vision blurred and I blinked. That couldn't be Pepper. . . . I only saw her when I was sleeping. Was this just another dream?

No. I was awake. But when I tried to talk, to say the words I'd rehearsed, my throat closed up like it had the time Pepper and I both had strep and lived on Jell-O for a week. I shoved away from the podium, bumping against Sydney so that she almost dropped the framed jersey. "I'm sorry . . . sorry . . ."

I skirted around the tables, ignoring whoever called my name—most likely Johanna—and exited the gym. The hallway was empty, another entrance to the girls' locker room was nearby.

Where was she? If she'd come here, why hadn't she waited for me? I was wide-awake, ready to talk. To answer any of her questions.

My heels echoed on the tile floor in the hallway, and I slipped as I pushed into the darkened locker room, the wooden door crashing against the wall. "Pepper! Pepper, where are you?"

My voice ricocheted against the rows of lockers even as I slammed my hand against a mirror, my breathing uneven. I stumbled farther into the room, then dropped to the floor and crawled to one of the shower stalls, backing into a corner. Pulling my knees up against my chest, I wrapped my arms around my legs, trying to stop my body from shaking.

"Oh, God, oh, God . . ."

The words were useless. I didn't believe in God . . . any god. Didn't talk to any kind of deity or higher power who supposedly listened or cared or watched me from a distance. God was only good for children's songs and books . . . for fueling heated debate around the dinner table . . . for changing the people you thought you knew best . . .

I needed to get back to the ceremony, but I couldn't make my arms relax. Thoughts of *should* and *can't* collided in my head, causing me to press my body harder into the corner of the shower. The faint scent of ammonia surrounded me. At least the shower was clean. Surely someone would come looking for me. Sometime. Or maybe I could pull myself together. But when I opened my eyes, the room seemed to sway in front of me, causing me to drop my head to my knees.

"Payton? Where are you?"

Of course it would be Johanna who searched me out. I sat silent. She'd find me soon enough without any help.

Her steps echoed in the silence, growing louder as she came closer. At last the lights clicked on and the pointed tips of her black high heels appeared in front of me. "What are you doing in the shower?"

No "Are you okay?" or "How can I help you?" Johanna the Good, who probably fell asleep at night and slept in sweet, dreamless peace, stood in the opening to the shower, sounding as horrified as if she'd found me naked and soaking wet.

"I . . . I needed to get away—"

"Payton, you went completely mental out there. I didn't know if you were going to faint or start spouting off gibberish. What happened?"

"Nothing."

"Nothing? Everyone saw *something* happen."

"Do you expect me to go out and explain myself, Johanna? Is that why you're here?"

"No—"

"Well, I know you're not here because you're worried about me." I struggled to suck in a deep breath, my chest tight. "Let's not pretend this is anything more than you trying to control the situation again."

"Really, Payton? You're attacking me when you're the one who made Pepper's ceremony all about you?"

I struggled to my feet, my hand slipping against the tiled wall. If I was going to fend off my sister's attack, I needed to be upright, not tempted to curl up in a ball on the shower floor. "Right. That was my plan all along. Stage a breakdown and steal the attention—"

"And now you're going to argue with me—"

"Did I ask you to come in here?" I pushed away from the wall, Johanna's appearance balancing me on a teeter-totter of emotions. Reality still seemed tissue-paper thin, but Johanna's accusations sliced through me as sharp as a razor. "No."

I shoved past her, stumbling toward the exit.

"Where are you going?"

"As if you care." I yanked open the door, coming to a halt when I found Nash waiting on the other side.

"Payton, what on earth happened?"

I gripped his arm. "Just take me home. Please, Nash. Just take me home."

13

I NEEDED SPACE. Privacy.

I needed to get out of Nash's car and into my town house—without him following me.

"Payton, I'm worried about you." Nash leaned across the console, causing me to press farther into the passenger seat. Too close. He brushed the back of his hand against my cheek. "Talk to me."

He'd been kind enough to let me ride almost all the way home in silence, not even turning on the radio to search for mood music. What kind of *mood* was this, anyway? Near nervous breakdown? But now his desire to take care of me, to hover, had overtaken him, backing me into a corner.

"Nash, please . . ." I forced myself not to turn away from his touch.

"I love you. Let me help you."

"This isn't your issue. This . . . this is family stuff."

He tried to hold my hand and I couldn't hide how my fingers trembled. "Babe, you have to know that I want—"

"Please . . . I'm not up to talking." I twisted my hand away from his, searching for the keys in my purse. My front door was mere steps away. Behind it—silence. Darkness. Isolation.

And please, no Pepper.

"Why do you keep shoving me away?" Nash fell back against the seat, providing me a little extra room.

"We're doing this now?" I sucked in a breath, and the faint scent of ammonia stung my nose. Where was that odor coming from?

"I didn't know we had to 'do' anything." Nash leaned forward, his hands gripping the steering wheel. "I thought we were in a relationship—a relationship with a future. Something permanent."

"Did I ever say that?" I fumbled with the door handle.

"Payton, we're good together—you have to see that."

"What I see is you jumping to conclusions about us based on what you want. When have I indicated that I want more in our relationship?"

Why was he pushing me now? When he acted like this, he seemed no different from Johanna. Determined to get his way. Ignoring my feelings. Steamrolling over what I was saying because he knew better.

Why hadn't I seen this before? I thought Nash cared, really cared about me, but his words—the way they clutched and clawed for more—seemed to rake against my skin.

"Have you been listening to anything I've said the last few months?" Nash's voice rose as if he could convince me by talking louder, faster. "I'm not just fooling around here. . . ."

Now I almost wished Johanna were here. Talk about making a situation about himself. I pushed the door open, the smoky scent from someone's chimney wafting into the car. "Thank you for the ride home, Nash. And thank you for making it easy to say this. We're done."

"What?" Nash bolted out of the car, not bothering to close his door. "You don't mean that. You're just stressed—"

"Yes, I'm stressed—and if you really understood that, you wouldn't be talking about you . . . me . . . us—any of this." I hiked my purse over my shoulder, the keys cutting into the palm of my hand. "I'm done. And not just for tonight. We're done."

When Nash grabbed me by the arm, I whirled around, reeling off-balance for a moment as the ground rolled beneath my feet. In my brittle state, he might as well have slapped me. "Do not touch me. I said I was done and I meant it."

"You're being irrational."

"Fine. I'm irrational. And I still meant what I said. We're over." Nash would not touch me again. He was always grasping for more . . . always wanting things from me that I just couldn't give him.

My hands were shaking so badly that it took three tries to even get the key into the lock.

"Payton—"

I stumbled backward after slamming the door. Some people might say shutting the door on Nash was unfeeling, even harsh. Not true. It was more an act of desperation than one of cruelty, coupled with the hope that separating myself from him would also stop the tingling in my hands, the tightening in my throat.

The hope that my world would right itself again.

I kicked off my shoes, leaving them in front of the door. Threw my purse on the couch, causing a pillow to fall to the floor. Ignored how Nash pounded on the front door.

"I'm going to bed." The words, spoken out loud, tumbled into the darkness. "I'm going to bed—to sleep."

I marched up the stairs to my bedroom, into the continued shifting shadows caused by the play of streetlights and moonlight coming through the window. There was no need to turn on any lights. I knew my way around the house and had no fear of bumping into an end table or wall. As far as furniture was concerned, my house took minimalist to the level of Spartan. It wasn't about determining which things brought joy in life. I just didn't care, paring my belongings to the bare necessities.

If only I could maintain control of my emotions, but I couldn't seem to will myself to be okay. Instead, my thoughts careened into one another, knocking me off-balance.

I fell across the bed, curling my knees up to my chest,

pulling the corner of the blanket across my body, burrowing my face into the pillow. "Don't bother me, Pepper. I don't want to see you. I just want to sleep. . . ."

My words were muffled, but surely if my sister lurked nearby, she'd obey my demand and leave me alone.

"It looks nice, doesn't it?"

I turned in a half circle, trying to get my bearings. Why was I always trying to figure out where I was? Where Pepper was? "What? What looks nice?"

"The jersey. I like where they hung it."

Pepper stood, her back to me, hands on her hips, staring up at her framed volleyball jersey that now hung over a row of bleachers on the north side of the gym. "Me. Zachary Gaines. Pete Jenkins. Paula Ferrell . . . Who knew back then we'd all be celebrated by the high school? Of course, I'm the only one whose number was retired. Couldn't have gotten all those records without the team."

That was my sister. Somehow she could manage to sound humble even when she bragged on herself. I nudged her in the ribs. "Hey! You're wearing your jersey."

"So? This is a dream, right? They hang one up, I can still wear one."

"Um, okay. No one's ever told me the rules." Not that I ever anticipated the whole see-my-twin-sister-in-dreams scenario. "I'm sorry."

"What are you sorry for?"

So much . . . so much. "I'm sorry I didn't hold it together for the ceremony today."

"Oh, I know you were never the public speaker, Pay. It's okay."

"*I let you down.*"

"*I'm not mad.*"

"*You're not?*"

At last Pepper turned and faced me. "*I would say life is too short . . . but really, it's too long for me to stay mad at you. Johanna's the tally keeper, not me.*"

"*You saw all that in the locker room?*"

"*No—I'm not playing some sort of spiritual spying game on you. I just figured Johanna hasn't changed. Has she?*"

"*No. No, she hasn't.*"

"*But you have.*"

What was I supposed to say to that? "*Well, of course I have. I'm older and—*"

"*Wiser?*"

No. "*Why are you here, Pepper?*"

"*You know why.*"

"*If I knew the answer, I wouldn't be asking the question. Am I some female version of Scrooge?*"

"*A Christmas Carol? Really? You know I only liked the Muppet version of that story. And I never believed in ghosts.*"

"*I don't want to talk about what you believe in.*"

"*You don't?*"

"*Were you right?*"

"*Was I right about what?*"

"*Never mind . . . It doesn't matter.*"

"*But you asked. . . .*"

I asked, but did I really want to know? Did I want to get into who was right and who was wrong? "*Are you happy, Pepper?*"

"It's not about happiness, Payton. It's about truth."

"So are you happy because you knew the truth?"

My sister paced the gym floor. "You're not asking the right questions—"

"And you are? Asking me about why I don't have a dog or a cat? Why I'm vegan?"

"I'm just trying to catch up with you, that's all. To get to know you again."

"Maybe you're not asking the right questions, either." There. Two could play that game.

"Fair enough. What were you and Zachary Gaines talking about?"

Any question but that. "Nothing."

"Oh, Pay. Don't lie to me."

The look in her eyes stopped me short from uttering a flippant remark. "I don't want to talk about Zachary Gaines."

"What do you want to talk about?"

"Nothing. Really, nothing at all. It's been too long."

"There you go, lying to me again—"

"And what makes you such an expert on my life all of a sudden?" If only I could figure out how to walk out of this dream. "Ten years. Ten years I've been living all of this by myself. Figuring this out all by myself . . . I'm fine, Pepper. Fine. Just leave it alone, will you, please?"

"That's been working for you all these years?"

"Yes. Yes, it has."

"I don't believe you—and you don't either."

"Go away, Pepper. Just . . . go away."

THINGS I NEVER TOLD YOU

My eyes flared open and I stared into the darkness.

I'd done it. I'd ended the conversation. Walked away from my sister.

Victory carved a hollow space in my chest where my heart should have been, my breath seeming to whistle through my lungs. The last time I'd won an argument with my sister, I'd killed her.

MOST DAYS, work was my salvation. I lost myself in planning—keeping track of the calendar, calling suppliers, hunting down all the obscure things people wanted, finding bargains, managing social media—while Kimberlee was the perfect face of Festivities, interacting with clients and being more hands-on the day of the event. Kimberlee could calm a crowd or a distraught bride. She'd stood in for a DJ gone AWOL and a maid of honor who had one too many and couldn't stand up to toast the bride. That was my partner—a walking, talking life of the party.

But today, work was a clichéd necessary evil, dragging me from my bed after a night of little to no sleep following my meltdown and the dream of Pepper in her volleyball jersey, spouting cryptic statements and too many questions. I was more suited to be setting up for a funeral than a thirtieth birthday celebration. I'd even opted for slim-fitting black pants and a black top, softening it with a string of pearls. In my red flats, I looked like a vintage version of Mary Tyler Moore.

But today wasn't about "Woe is me." My concern was Addison, the birthday girl, who would arrive in a couple of hours for what she thought was a casual dinner with her friend Lena, only to be surprised by ten friends jumping out and shouting, "Surprise!" and welcoming her to a "Good-Bye to the Roaring Twenties!" themed birthday party.

Kimberlee had turned the birthday cake over to me after the bakery delivered it moments ago. My job? Remove the two-tiered confection from its box without smudging the pristine white frosting. After opening all the sides, I held my breath and slid the cake onto the kitchen counter. Gorgeous, it was absolutely gorgeous, topped with a glittery golden filigree number thirty. But even better was how both layers of the cake were adorned with "framed" color photographs of Addison growing up. An adorable newborn. A grinning toddler. A high school and college graduate. A bride kissing her husband.

Pepper and I had our photographs on our birthday cake on our sixteenth birthday—the last birthday we celebrated together nine months before she died. My photo on the left, her photo on the right, and the words *Happy Birthday, Payton and Pepper!* scripted in blue icing in the middle. Of course, we looked so identical my parents could have put a single photo on the cake.

But even more than the cake and the party with our friends—mostly our volleyball teammates—I remembered our conversation later that night.

Pepper rolled on her side, facing me from her bed across the room. "It was fun today, wasn't it, Pay?"

"Yeah. Hey, you want to sneak back downstairs for another piece of cake?"

"Absolutely." She was out of her bed before me, tossing her braid over her shoulder. "Come on!"

Within minutes, we were settled at the table in the breakfast nook, digging into huge slices of cake. Corner pieces, of course. Less cake, more icing.

"What happens if one of us passes the driving test and one of us doesn't?" I retrieved the milk from the fridge, lifting the plastic container and giving it a shake. "Want some?"

"Sure—and we're both going to pass, just like we're both going to the same college and playing volleyball." Pepper brought two glasses to the table.

"Well, you'll be playing volleyball, anyway."

"You will, too."

"Maybe. Maybe not. I'm not the one who already has coaches calling me." I refused to voice aloud my doubts about landing a scholarship like Pepper. I would be happy for her if she did. I just didn't know what I would do if I didn't. "You're the one the college scouts are looking at. Things just need to slow down—"

"You've got to think ahead. It's not like these are the best years of our lives. There are more important things than getting a driver's license or a college scholarship." Pepper played with her cake.

"What do you mean?"

"It's just that I've been talking to some friends, and they're helping me see that I should be thinking about things like what I believe about God—"

"What is it with these friends you're hanging with?" Why was Pepper talking about God again? I shoved a bite into my mouth, trying to savor the rich taste of chocolate cake and sugary icing. *"I don't get it. Why is God such a big deal all of a sudden?"*

Pepper's eyes lit up at my questions, even as her enthusiasm shut me down. "Alex and Scott and Tari are honest and open about what they believe. They don't push God down my throat or anything like that, but they've been answering my questions. They even gave me a Bible—"

"Why would you want a Bible?"

"So I could read it, of course. Learn more about God."

Pepper's blue eyes were shining, her just-a-bit-too-large mouth smiling, as she leaned forward. Staring at her had always been like looking in a mirror, but in the past weeks, Pepper had changed. Moved away from me in ways I didn't understand. Looking at her now, it was as if her reflection was blurring, shifting out of focus.

"That birthday cake turned out even better than I imagined." Kimberlee's words jarred me, causing me to grab the edge of the kitchen counter so that I didn't jump backward. "I love the photos."

"Um . . . me, too."

"Caught you daydreaming again, didn't I?" Kimberlee came to stand in front of me, leaning her hip against the counter, a smile softening her words.

"Nothing important." I blinked away the remnants of the memory.

"Are you okay, Payton? It's like you're only half here today."

"Just need more caffeine." I retrieved the carafe from the coffeemaker and refilled my mug.

"If I'm correct—and I have been keeping track—that's your sixth cup of coffee." Kimberlee's gaze heated my back as I spooned sugar into the black liquid. "What's wrong?"

Her question reminded me of sitting in Mr. Richardson's high school history class, half-asleep. And then being called upon to answer some obscure question, even though my mind was as blank as a newly scrubbed chalkboard. Unprepared. I had nothing.

"Just a bad night's sleep." The sugary scent of icing assaulted my senses, turning my stomach. The sooner I got this cake displayed, the better. "Yesterday evening was the high school ceremony honoring Pepper."

"What? Did I know about this?" Kimberlee's voice was a mixture of confusion and hurt.

"No . . . I guess with everything else going on with Jillian, I forgot to mention it."

"So?"

Kimberlee obviously cared more about an explanation

than she cared about getting things ready for the party. The question was, how could I keep things brief?

"The high school Pepper and I attended had a ceremony honoring outstanding athletes. Pepper was one of them. They retired her volleyball jersey. My coach contacted me and asked me to say a few words—" did this sound as garbled to Kimberlee as it sounded to me?—"and I did."

Kimberlee tried to make eye contact, but I focused on the cake again. "I imagine that had to be hard. How are you? What can I do?"

"Nothing. I'm fine. Just sleep-deprived." Images of my family . . . the crowd in the auditorium . . . Zach Gaines . . . flashed through my mind. How would I explain all of that to Kimberlee? Or explain Pepper showing up in my dreams? I was fine. We had a birthday party to coordinate.

But for the rest of the day, even though she never said anything, Kimberlee watched me. She'd morphed from my high school teacher to my parents, who'd kept me under not-so-covert surveillance for months after Pepper died. Every glance was a silent "What can we do to help you?"

There was nothing my parents could do. Nothing the doctors could do. Nothing anyone could do. And Kimberlee, good friend that she was, didn't even know the whole story, so there was nothing she could do now, either.

I focused on the numbered list I'd prepared for the day. It was my paper lifeline, the only thing that gave me a reason to think about something other than last night's events. Even if I wanted to, now was not the time to bare my heart to Kimberlee. And what good would it do, anyway?

When my cell phone buzzed, I was tempted to throw it in one of the kitchen drawers. Or the trash can. A quick glance revealed a text from Johanna this time. I should have kept a running tally of how many calls and texts I'd received from my family—and Nash—since last night.

They all might as well have been standing in the kitchen with me, just like they had during Jillian's engagement party. Couldn't they understand that if I didn't answer my phone or reply to a text the first time, I wasn't likely to reply the sixth time? Hearing the repeated muted buzzing indicating texts or phone calls wore my nerves down.

The phone vibrated again just as I went to stash it in my purse. Probably Johanna or my parents. But Jillian's name and face appeared on the display.

Jillian? She had enough going on in her own life. She didn't need to be worrying about me.

I turned my back on the kitchen to gain a little privacy. "Hello?"

"Payton? Oh, I'm so glad you answered. Are you okay?" Jillian's words were a rushed whisper.

"Yes, I'm fine." I stared out the French doors into the expansive backyard. "There's no need to check up on me, Jillian—"

"I'm worried about you, Payton. We all are."

I'm sure Jillian heard my loud snort of disbelief. "Johanna's just annoyed at my *act* last night."

"She's worried, too—in her own way."

I wasn't going to argue with Jillian, the sister who was always caught in between Johanna's and my arguments—the human Switzerland between two warring countries.

I softened my tone to match Jillian's. "I appreciate you calling. I'm okay. I'm sorry I haven't checked in, but I'm working today. Kimberlee and I are putting on a thirtieth birthday celebration. So, see? It's all good. If . . . when you talk to Mom and Dad, would you tell them I'm sorry about what happened?"

"We know yesterday was hard for you, Payton. We all understand. Really."

Nice words. But there was no way anyone could understand how yesterday seemed like another small chipping away at my mental stability. They thought my behavior had to do with the ceremony—but that was because they knew nothing about Pepper appearing in my dreams.

"Thanks." A few seconds of silence stretched between us. "Listen, I need to get back to work—"

"Of course."

"Don't worry about me, okay?"

"I won't."

"I'll call soon."

"Great."

We said our good-byes, each of us knowing that Jillian would worry and that I wouldn't call her anytime soon.

Later that night, I slipped into a corner of the living room and surveyed the party. Addison sat surrounded by her girlfriends, a smile stretching across her face, laughter ringing through the air. Unwrapped gifts were left sitting on the floor. Crumbs of the glorious photograph cake were left on glass plates on the table. But it was clear the greatest joy for Addison came from these women. Her friends.

A line of birthday cards staggered across the mantel. Addison must have treasured reading each one, be it funny or sentimental. When was the last time I'd sent anyone a birthday card? Most of the time I posted a brief *Happy birthday!* on Facebook, thankful for the automated reminder, or sent off a text with *Hope you're having a good day*. My parents and my sisters rated a phone call and, eventually, the required family get-together.

These women were here tonight because they loved Addison and wanted to celebrate her. I hadn't experienced that kind of camaraderie since the high school volleyball team. There was something about working out until you wanted to throw up and battling against bigger division schools who thought your team would be an easy win that created unity and strong bonds between people. We knew we had each other's backs both on and off the court.

But I'd walked away from the team—and those relationships—after Pepper died. Since then I'd survived by keeping people at a distance. No close friends—even Kimberlee was allowed only so close, but no closer. Romantic relationships? None had lasted more than a year. And my family? I preferred seeing them infrequently and for short amounts of time—kind of like going to the dentist or the gynecologist.

Maybe I hadn't been born a loner—that would have been impossible after spending nine months in the womb with a twin sister. But losing Pepper . . . that certainly made me prefer a solitary life.

I was late to work—or at least an hour and a half later than I usually showed up at Festivities. Bianca would be there, but odds were I'd still beat Kimberlee into the office. She'd never know, unless I confessed to her. Not that she'd care. We were partners, after all. Adults. We didn't keep track of each other's schedules.

The everyday mess of our office greeted me. The piles of papers and mugs half-filled with cold coffee and leftover decorations from past events might bother someone else, but the disorganization was familiar and, in an odd sense, comforting. No ghosts of mistakes past lingered here.

As I slipped my purse off my shoulder, Bianca appeared in the doorway that led to the reception area and remained standing between the front and back rooms. "Payton, I—"

The reality of what I'd forgotten zapped through me like someone had served a volleyball into the back of my head. "I am so sorry! I told you that I'd give you a rundown on how the birthday party went yesterday—especially since you sat in on the brainstorming session."

"It's okay—"

"And you wanted to see how I put together our upcoming events calendar."

"Payton. It's okay." Bianca tilted her head toward the front office. "I wanted to tell you that Zach Gaines is here to see you again."

I paused. "Did you say Zach Gaines is here? To see me?"

"That's exactly what I said."

"Bianca!"

"Payton!" Our receptionist's whisper mirrored my shocked tone.

I collapsed in my chair. "Couldn't you have told him I had an appointment this morning?"

"Hey, you're the boss. I do all sorts of things for you, even cleaning the fridge." Bianca crossed her arms. "But I don't lie for anybody. Never have, never will."

"You're right. I'm sorry." Zach Gaines was my problem, not Bianca's. "Tell him I'll be right there after I get a cup of coffee—"

"Um, you don't need to do that."

"Why not?"

"Just trust me." Bianca motioned toward the front. "He's in the alcove."

I hitched up my jeans as I moved toward Bianca. Wait a minute. I'd bought these jeans a month ago, falling in love with them in the dressing room because they fit just right. Was I losing weight? Not that it mattered right now, but new jeans were new jeans.

And obviously Zach Gaines didn't know how to take a

hint, much less a straight-up directive. He was worse than the guy in my college math class freshman year who kept asking me out for coffee, ignoring all the different ways I said, "No, thank you," "Not today," and just plain "No." But eventually that guy caught on when I moved to sit right in front of the professor.

Zach was where Bianca said he'd be—in the area reserved for clients. One of these days, he needed to show up requesting our help. Not that I wanted him to keep showing up. He wore his usual jean jacket over a dark T-shirt. For a moment, I imagined his closet containing a solitary jacket and an assortment of dark cotton shirts. Not that I cared what the man wore. Two insulated cups from the specialty coffee shop located a block away sat on the table in front of him, along with a small brown bag. Before I could even say a word, Zach started talking, motioning to the two cups of coffee.

"I'm hoping I can convince you to take one, because I'm not planning on drinking both of these." He opened the bag, dumping out a pile of white plastic containers of cream, a couple of black stir sticks, and white, yellow, pink, and blue packets. "I wasn't sure how you doctored your coffee—if you do drink the stuff—so I brought options."

"Thanks." I wasn't going to say something like *You didn't need to do that* because what I wanted to say was *What are you doing here? Again?* The less said, the better. I sifted through the pile, searching out the sugar packets. "You want any of these?"

"No, thanks. I drink my coffee black."

I took my time removing the lid from my cup and then emptying sugar packet after sugar packet into the black liquid, the rich aroma working its caffeinated magic on my sluggish brain cells. Bringing me coffee? This was something a friend would do—and Zach Gaines and I were not friends. The last time I'd seen him, we'd squared off as I'd redrawn the Do Not Cross This Line boundary for him. Seemed like Zach was just as stubborn as I was. I should respect that, but right now I focused on fixing my coffee.

"So I wanted to ask how you're doing." Zach wasted no time with small talk. "I can't stop thinking about you since the high school ceremony—"

I choked on my sip of coffee, sputtering and coughing and effectively silencing the man sitting across from me, at least for a few seconds.

"Th-that didn't come out the way I meant it." Zach's face was flushed a dull red.

I stared at the photographs filling the wall space over his head. Images of past Festivities events. *The Great Gatsby* themed birthday party. A barn wedding reception—because who wasn't in love with those? And stuck in the middle, a collection of photos from some of Kimberlee's earliest campus parties. The awkward silence stretched between us—and I wasn't going to be the one to ease the tension.

"Payton."

At the sound of my name, I made eye contact with Zach again.

A half smile curled his lips. "Now that I've removed my

foot from my mouth, let me try again to explain why I'm here."

Give the man credit for a quick recovery.

"I know you had a rough go the other night at the ceremony honoring Pepper—"

"A rough go. That's one way to put it." I began stacking packets of sweetener by color. Yellow. White. Pink. Blue. Repeat.

"And I wanted to see how you're doing."

His interest should feel intrusive, controlling—similar to when Johanna pried into my life, asking for details that were none of her business. But for some unknown reason, a part of me was tempted to relax. Not to confide in Zach exactly, but to answer his question rather than take evasive action like I would with Johanna.

Maybe it was the way he exuded the faint scent of a Colorado breeze. Crisp. Inviting. When was the last time I'd escaped work, escaped the city, and lost myself in the openness of a mountain trail or meadow? Blue skies, warm sunshine, fresh air . . .

"Did I lose you?"

"Hmm? Sorry. Just thinking." I took a sip of coffee to gain another moment. "I'm doing okay. What happened the other night . . . it was just some sort of odd emotional glitch. I—I'd been working a lot and had a couple of nights where I didn't sleep well—" that was the truth—"so it was just a bit of a meltdown. A very public meltdown. All better now."

"I'm glad to hear that—I mean, I'm glad to hear you're

better." Zach seemed ready to take my words at face value. Smart man. His concern caught me off guard, but I wasn't sure I was ready for cross-examination. "Do you have a busy week ahead of you?"

Small talk? I supposed I could manage a few minutes of small talk. After all, the man had bought me a cup of coffee. "Yes. Festivities has become quite popular in the past six months."

"And why is that?"

"Word of mouth, mostly. Thanks to one of Kimberlee's friends, we planned a function for a wealthy family in Denver, and that seemed to be the springboard to bigger and better things."

"Are you busy every night and weekends, too?"

"Our calendar varies. Certain seasons are busier than others, obviously. We can say yes or no, but right now it's a lot of saying yes." And now it was my turn to ask a question or two, just to be polite. "What about you? What do you do?"

"I work for a custom woodworking business."

"Woodworking? Like signs and things?"

"Um, no. I make custom cabinetry for homes."

"Oh."

"That reminds me of something I wanted to talk to you about." Zach focused on his cup of coffee. "I, um, made a bench a couple of years ago . . ."

"A bench?"

"Yes. I put a brass plaque on it to commemorate Pepper.

The bench sits on our property near . . . near the scene of the accident. I was wondering if you'd like to come up and see it."

He'd made a bench. In honor of my sister. Located it right where she'd been killed.

The air around me seemed heavy, pressing in, making it hard for me to breathe. Why did Zach have to be like every other guy in my life? We were sitting here, enjoying coffee together, and then he had to ask more from me than I could give. Was this a religious thing? Didn't AA talk about a higher power and making amends?

I moved my cup aside. The coffee would remain unfinished, and this conversation was over, too.

"I don't think so. Thanks for the invitation, though." There, that didn't sound rude. "Listen, I need to get ready for an appointment."

I eased away from the table, resisting the urge to tug at the waistband of my jeans again. Bianca might not be willing to lie, but that didn't mean I wouldn't.

"Oh, sure. I understand." Zach pulled his wallet out of his back pocket. "If you change your mind . . . about the bench . . . let me know."

I took the proffered business card without looking at it. "Thanks. And thanks for the coffee."

"Not a big deal." Zach paused for a moment as if he was going to say something and then nodded. "See you around, Payton."

"Good-bye, Zach."

I ran my thumb over the smooth surface of his business

card as Zach left. In high school volleyball, whichever team won three out of five sets took the match. As far as I was concerned, Zach had *lost* the last three times we'd met up. I could only hope he recognized that and realized the uselessness of continuing to contact me.

What had he expected? That he'd walk into Payton's office bearing coffee and expressing concern, and she'd suddenly be happy to see him? Even more, that she'd be open to his offer to come see the bench he'd built?

Sure. That sounded like Payton Thatcher, the walking, talking brick wall.

Of course, Pepper had been the more outgoing Thatcher sister in high school. The leader of the duo. The better athlete with the more competitive drive. But Payton had been friendly, too. Not that they ran in exactly the same circles, what with him being a year ahead of them in school. But their paths crossed enough that the Thatcher sisters ended up at the spring break party at his parents' cabin in Winter Park the night Pepper was killed.

"Hey, Zach, I heard the girls volleyball team is spending the week at the Snow Mountain Ranch Y. I invited some of them to your party. You okay with that?"

Zach grabbed his notebook and slammed his locker door shut, moving alongside his friend. "Sure. Anybody in particular?"

"I've got my eye on Payton Thatcher—so hands off, okay?"

Brice jostled against him in the crowded hallway. "Her sister will come too, of course. And a couple other girls."

"No problem, man. Payton Thatcher is all yours."

They'd laughed as they'd separated—never imagining how life-changing Brice's decision to invite girls from the volleyball team would be. For Pepper. For Payton. For Zach.

Zach tossed his empty coffee cup into a trash can on the corner outside Payton's office building.

I'm failing at this, God. No matter what I do, I run into one no after another from Payton.

He'd learned not to pray out loud—even whispered words—in public. Enough people thought he was crazy to toss aside logic and opt for faith. Not that choosing one meant ignoring the other.

What do I do now?

Wait.

God's answer seemed borne along on the breeze. A soft whisper to his soul.

Wait.

Okay, God. I've done everything else You've asked me to do. Payton knows what I want. She knows about the bench. She knows where to find me. I'll wait—but it won't be easy.

He'd wait . . . and he'd keep praying, too.

15

Girls' Night must go on, or so Harper had decreed.

They'd both agreed that something was better than nothing and that Jillian could call it an early night if she needed to. But getting together was an in-person form of positive thinking.

All Jillian could hope was that she'd make it to eight o'clock before admitting she needed to crawl into bed.

Harper held up her wine goblet, swishing the purple contents inside. "I've got to say I'm not a big fan of this."

"Really? And Geoff made that one special for tonight. Ever since he bought me that juicer, he's insisting I try all these fruit and veggie concoctions that are supposed to be healthy for me. I never know what color they're going to be or what they're going to taste like, either." Jillian raised her glass to her nose and sniffed the concentrated liquid. "I think this one has beets, strawberries, and blueberries—"

"Stop." Harper stood and held the glass away from her. "You lost me at beets. Would I be a terrible friend if I tossed this down the sink and poured myself a glass of wine? And maybe found some chocolate?"

"You could never be a terrible friend, but I probably am. Go ahead and see what you can find, but I don't have any wine or chocolate to offer you."

"What?"

"Sorry. I gave Geoff the two bottles I had, along with all my snack food. I'm trying to eat healthy."

"That explains the cardboard crackers. But the cheese is good." Her friend disappeared into the kitchen.

"And the grapes." Jillian raised her voice. "Just grab whatever you want to eat, okay?"

"I found a soda in the fridge." Cupboard doors opened and closed in rapid succession. "Aha! A half-full bag of Fritos that you somehow missed when you purged your cupboards! We're saved!"

All the special food Geoff was encouraging her to eat reminded Jillian of the different diets she'd gone on through the years. The time she'd sworn off sodas. The time she'd given up candy. Or carbs. The time she'd gone on that big diet before she started her junior year of high school. Chopped carrots and celery and eaten like a rabbit and drunk so much water she spent most of each day in the bathroom. Maybe, just maybe, she'd return to school looking like someone new. And maybe, just maybe, she'd be noticed. Invited to homecoming. But she showed up the first day of school all of ten pounds lighter. The same old Jillian Thatcher.

"So let's talk dresses." Harper sat across from her on the couch again, selecting one of the bridal magazines from the stack in front of them.

She'd found the magazines Jillian had left abandoned in her bedroom, brought them out to the living room, insisting they should browse through them and discuss possible wedding dresses.

Jillian winced as the skin around her incision strained when she shifted her shoulders. She needed to be patient with her body, to give herself time to heal. Chemotherapy started in one week. *Tick, tick, tick.* How was she supposed to plan all the details that went into a wedding? How was she supposed to look at gowns when she didn't know who she'd be the day of her wedding? What kind of body she'd have? Was she ready to look at all these posed, perfect happily-ever-after moments again?

Harper flipped through the pages of the magazine in her lap. "Well, let's get down to business. What kind of wedding dress do you want? You know me and my *Say Yes to the Dress* addiction."

"Yes, but is it for the dresses or the family drama?"

"Oh, the drama, girlfriend. The drama."

"Let's hope we can keep that to a minimum when I go shopping."

"All the more reason to know what you want. I'll back you

up. So what's your dream dress? Princess? Mermaid? Sheath? Empire waist?"

"I don't know, although I think we can rule out the whole princess style. That would only make me look shorter and fatter."

"No negative talk, Jill. Think positive, remember? Just say you don't like that style, okay? How about your budget? Have you and Geoff talked about that? It's always good to know your price point."

"Geoff and I budgeted for the wedding. We weren't planning anything lavish even before . . . before my diagnosis. No more than one hundred people. Late afternoon, so we can get by with a buffet and wedding cake."

"Sounds good."

"But now my parents are insisting they want to give us some money toward the wedding, too. They plan on doing the same for Johanna and Payton. Although Johanna's been dating Beckett for so long I don't know that she'll ever marry the guy."

"You're accepting the money from your parents, right?"

"Isn't that a bit old-fashioned? I mean, Geoff and I are both in our thirties. We can pay for our wedding."

"It's not about whether it's old-fashioned or not. It's that your parents offered to help. You say yes and thank you." Harper mimed accepting a check, holding it in both hands, and kissing it before turning serious. "There's not a lot your parents can do to help you through your treatment, Jillian. But they want to help with your wedding. Let them."

"To be honest, with everything going on, I find it hard to even think about planning a wedding. Johanna's called a couple of times about the bridal shower. And then she not-so-casually suggested Geoff and I move the wedding up, before I'm too far into chemo." Jillian set aside her juice. "You know how I've always felt lost in the middle of my sisters?"

"Yes. It's always made me glad I only had one younger brother."

"Well, it's like cancer is some unnamed, invisible sister that has shown up and shoved herself into my life. She's telling me to forget my dreams. Telling me it's all about her. I should be used to this by now—"

Harper shifted so that she was closer to Jillian, wrapping an arm around her shoulders. "That's just the tiredness talking. You're still in recovery mode. You're going to have the wedding you want, *when you want it.*"

As her friend talked, Jillian scanned the page of the open magazine in her lap. A headline snagged her attention.

Real Weddings.

Just how real would her wedding be? Would she be bald on her wedding day? Would she be able to find a dress that hid her mastectomy scar and the fact that she had to wait for reconstructive surgery until after her chemo and radiation? Would Geoff look at her differently when she walked down the aisle toward him? How would he react on their wedding night? She'd always worried about her weight . . . but now she'd face him with a scarred body and no hair. What if she lost her eyebrows and eyelashes, too?

A tear plopped onto the page.

"What is going on?" Harper's voice dropped to a whisper.

"Maybe . . . maybe Johanna's on to something." Jillian sniffled, swiping at her eyes.

"You think you should move the wedding up?"

"No. No, I think maybe we should postpone it. Maybe April isn't the right time. Maybe now isn't the right time to be planning a wedding. Geoff's so busy with work that we hardly see each other. Maybe I won't be able to do everything I need to do—"

"Okay, now you're talking crazy. You've got to go easy on yourself for a little while, Jill. You're tired. And you're eating a bunch of . . . of junk. I mean, I'm all for eating healthy—and bless Geoff for buying you a juicer. But find healthy food you like! There's no sense in wasting money on stuff you're not going to eat." Harper crumbled a handful of crackers onto her plate. "Geoff loves you, and he's not the kind of guy to change his mind about wanting to marry you because you have cancer. Sure, he's a bit of a goofball and he tells the corniest jokes I've ever heard, but the guy's steady like an atomic clock."

Once again, her best friend was being a much-needed voice of reason.

"Remember when you called me and asked, 'Why is Geoff Hennessey asking me out?' and I said, 'Because he likes you!' Was I right or was I right?"

"You were right." Even as Jillian gave a little laugh, she couldn't help but notice her friend's wedding band, the one

Harper refused to take off eight months after her husband had left her when he'd reconnected with his high school sweetheart on Facebook. Harper—the woman who refused to be anything but hopeful.

How could Jillian not dig deep into her own heart and find some sort of hope, too? For the time being, she'd just lean into her friend's endless wellspring of optimism.

"And remember, we're all here to help you. Me. Your mom. Payton. And yes, even Johanna in her own way. And I'm sure Geoff's mom wants to be included. I forget: does Geoff have any sisters?"

"No, he's an only child."

"Well, in some ways that simplifies things." Harper handed her another magazine. "We need to plan a day to go look at wedding dresses. It'll be fun. We should go before you start chemo. Shop and then do lunch. Or dinner. Maybe we can look at the calendar before I leave and text people with a possible day?"

"That would probably be good. I could try on different styles and at least get an idea, even if I don't find something."

"Oh, you never know. A lot of women find their dress the very first time they try something on. I did."

"How do you do that?"

"Do what?"

"Talk about your wedding after what Trent did?"

It was Harper's turn to flip through a magazine. One page. Another. Then she sighed and made eye contact with Jillian. "It's a choice. I waited a long time before I found someone I wanted to marry. And as crazy as it may sound, I still want to be married to Trent. I can either give up and give in to the anger—and believe he isn't the man I married—or I can believe we're going to get through all of this and he's going to get tired of that . . . that woman and come back to me."

"And you'd take him back?"

"Yes." Her friend clenched her fist, crumpling the corner of the page and then smoothing it out. "I would. If he realizes what he's doing is wrong . . . and with a lot of counseling . . . yes, I'd take him back."

"You're a better woman than I am."

"Oh, that's not what it's about—comparing ourselves to one another. We've stuck by each other through all sorts of challenges. Right now, life is throwing us both some major curveballs, but we'll help each other through it like we always have. Just realize I may decline any more of Geoff's health food juices."

"I promise to have something else for you to drink the next time we do Girls' Night."

Even as she joked with her friend, Jillian ran her fingers through her hair. It wasn't thick and luxurious like some model's—and it wasn't as if Geoff was marrying her for her airbrushed skin or thin body. He wouldn't be like Trent and decide to find someone else . . . someone prettier . . . healthier . . . than she was now or after chemo or radiation.

After Harper left, Jillian gathered up the magazines and piled them on the coffee table. She loaded the dishwasher with their glasses, plates, and silverware, glancing at the clock.

No call from Geoff yet, but it was early still. Just because he wasn't calling her as often, wasn't texting her as often, that didn't mean anything was wrong. He was busy with a very demanding project—nothing else. She could always call him, but she didn't want to hear him ask, "How are you?" and have to confess that she wasn't okay. Again.

She needed to get control of herself. Of her emotions. Her thoughts. Harper had presented her with an entire glass jar full of positive thoughts. She'd never really thought of herself as a negative person before, but since her diagnosis, she seemed to face a daily battle with her body and her mind.

Finding a roll of tape in a drawer in her office, Jillian returned to the pile of papers. She'd opened dozens of Harper's positive thoughts by now. Read them. Left the slips of paper in a pile on her dresser, unwilling to throw away something her friend had worked so hard on. She picked up a red slip—*One positive thought in the morning can change your whole day*. Using tape, she adhered it to the upper corner of the mirror over her dresser. Picked up a slip of blue paper that read, *Every day may not be good, but there's something good in every day.*

For twenty minutes, she covered part of her mirror with slips of colored paper, rereading the positive thoughts written out by her best friend. The last slip of paper she taped up said, *This too shall pass.*

Well, if nothing else was true, that one was.

And maybe it wasn't just about reading the thought each day, but remembering it.

One minute I was updating our Facebook page; the next moment Kimberlee loomed over my desk, casting a shadow across the papers scattered everywhere, her freshly high-lighted hair falling around her face.

"Did you eat breakfast?"

"Yes, I ate breakfast."

Although Kimberlee wouldn't count a partially eaten bowl of quinoa as breakfast.

"Lunch?" She tilted her head to the left.

"Are you asking me *to* lunch or asking if I *ate* lunch?"

"Did you *eat* lunch?"

"I don't know . . ."

"Are you losing weight?" Now she tilted her head to the right.

"Does it look like I'm losing weight?"

"Yes. Are you trying to lose weight?"

"Kimberlee, you sound like my mother." I pushed away from my computer. "And you never, ever sound like my mother. That's one of the reasons we work so well together."

"I'm worried about you."

That made two of us, but I wasn't about to admit that out loud.

"I've lost a little weight. I'm concerned about Jillian. That's normal, right?" I tried to laugh, refusing to tug at my pants on my way to get a cup of coffee. "The only problem is I need to buy myself some new clothes."

"Oooh. Shopping! When do you want to go?"

At least Kimberlee was distracted from my weight by the idea of a shopping trip. When my phone rang, Kimberlee picked it up off my desk and announced, "It's Jillian."

Jillian. That was just some kind of odd coincidence.

"Do you want me to answer it?"

"No. You can fix my coffee." I took my phone from her. "Please."

Jillian's "Hello" sounded the most normal it had in weeks. "I hope I'm not bothering you . . . interrupting anything . . ."

"No, I can talk. Is everything okay?"

How long would our phone calls be like this? Wondering if something was wrong? Even Kimberlee watched me as she stirred sugar into my coffee, wondering the same thing. Was my sister's life going to be overshadowed by cancer forever?

Calm down. Just keep talking with Jillian.

"I'm going to go look at wedding dresses this Saturday. I was hoping you'd come and join the fun."

"You want me to come wedding dress shopping with you?"

"I know it's last-minute—"

"That's okay. Let me check."

Kimberlee mouthed the words *"Go, go,"* even as I pulled up the calendar on my computer. "What time?"

"I have a four o'clock appointment and then we thought we'd go out for dinner afterward."

"We?"

"Me, you, Mom, Johanna, Harper, and Geoff's mom. It'll be fun."

Fun. Right. I'd be surrounded. But there was no abandoning Jillian. Johanna was not going to push her around while she tried on wedding gowns. Besides, this was what sisters did. They went wedding dress shopping with each other.

"I'd love to go. Thanks for inviting me."

"Great. I'll text you the name of the bridal salon. It's in south Denver."

"Perfect."

Kimberlee set my coffee down in front of me, along with a pumpkin muffin, as I disconnected the phone call. Coffee and calories. "Not very subtle."

"Just eat it, okay? What was the phone call about?"

"I'm going dress shopping. You heard me tell her yes." When my phone rang again, I held up it up so Kimberlee could read my older sister's name. "And this is why. I'm going to protect Jillian from Johanna."

I wasn't going to be some sort of silent, peacekeeping sister and stand by while Johanna ignored what Jillian wanted. No, I'd be more like a tank rolling in to defend one sister from the other—armed and ready to provide firepower if needed.

"No. You're going because it's the right thing to do." Kimberlee motioned toward my phone as it continued to ring. "Are you going to answer that?"

I bit into the muffin, shaking my head. "I don't have the patience for Johanna right now. She probably wants to map out some sort of game plan for Saturday. Besides, you and I need to talk. What are we going to do about the bar mitzvah on Saturday?"

"Bianca can help me."

"That's perfect! She's been wanting to learn about the business. Saturday is an ideal opportunity."

Kimberlee executed a small half bow. "Thank you. I thought so, too. Since we're using caterers to handle the big crowd, it's an ideal time for her to shadow us . . . I mean me."

"Only she'll be doing more than shadowing you. Maybe you should make sure she's available to help you on Saturday." I took another bite of the muffin. "And I'll go ahead and take this phone call from Johanna."

Kimberlee paused in the doorway leading to the front. "Is she calling you again?"

"No, but she will. I know my sister."

I had to give Johanna credit for allowing me to finish the muffin and my cup of coffee before she called a second time.

"Hello, Johanna. I've already talked to Jillian."

"Hello—what?"

"I said I've already talked to Jillian." I dropped the empty muffin wrapper and napkin into the trash can by my desk.

"Then you know about Saturday."

"Yes. And I plan on being there."

"You're not busy?"

"I'm adjusting my schedule. This is important." Did Johanna want me to be busy? "Is that why you were calling? To see if I was coming Saturday?"

"Yes. Are you coming to dinner, too?"

"Yes. Is that okay with you?"

"Don't be childish, Payton. I was hoping we could talk about the bridal shower during dinner—"

"Why don't you not try to plan things for a change? Jillian wants to shop for a wedding dress on Saturday. That may be all she's up for."

"But we need to make some plans—"

"At this point, let's plan on a bridal shower after December. Then we don't have to worry about anything else right now."

"But—"

"Seriously, Johanna. Saturday is about shopping and only shopping. There's no rush on the bridal shower, except according to your agenda."

"I'm just trying to make sure things are nice for Jillian."

For once, I wouldn't argue with her, choking back a snarky comment that would only prolong our phone call. "I know. I'll see you on Saturday."

Questions bombarded me after the phone call ended. Why did all of my conversations with Johanna seem to start in the middle of an argument? Was there ever a time when Johanna hadn't been angry with me? But what was she so angry about? What had I done—or not done—to make my sister dislike me so much?

SHE WAS GETTING HER LIFE BACK to some semblance of normal—her life postmastectomy—just in time for cancer to change things up again with chemotherapy sessions starting on Monday.

But she didn't want to think about that now. Tonight was one of those perfect Colorado September evenings—one of her favorite things. Even with the sun beginning its descent toward Pikes Peak, the air was still comfortable. Not too hot. Not too cool. Geoff had agreed to her suggestion for a walk— a short one—and she'd ignored his insistence she wear a light jacket. She'd also vetoed his suggestion to drive over to Palmer Park, opting to stay in her neighborhood—closer to home.

"I'm sorry we didn't get to go out for dinner tonight." Geoff sidestepped a low-hanging tree branch. "I tried to break away sooner—"

"I understand. Going for a walk is nice."

"Are you excited about shopping for your wedding dress tomorrow? My mom really appreciated you inviting her."

"It'll be fun, having both her and my mom there." Jillian kicked a pinecone so that it skittered ahead of them on the sidewalk. "Why don't you meet us for dinner later? I could ask my dad—"

"Tomorrow's a girls' day, Jill. You don't want me there."

But she did. Not while she tried on wedding dresses—she wanted to keep with the tradition of Geoff not seeing her in her gown until she walked down the aisle to him. And she could only hope breast cancer wouldn't wreak havoc with her determination to *feel* as beautiful as possible when she said, "I do" to Geoff.

Was her wedding going to be all about pretense?

"Besides, I haven't had a quiet Saturday in so long." Geoff grinned. "I'm looking forward to sleeping in late. Maybe going to the gym. Other than that, I'm not making any plans."

Jillian shrugged off the heaviness clinging to her as if someone had dropped a wool coat on her shoulders. Geoff wasn't saying no to her. Not really. He was just tired. The man deserved a day off. From life. From work. From her.

Their shoulders bumped, the backs of their hands brushing together.

And the fact that Geoff wasn't holding her hand while they walked? That didn't mean anything, either. He didn't have to hold her hand all the time to prove he loved her.

"So . . . work? How's that going?"

"More of the same—well, that's not true." Geoff huffed a humorless laugh. "This company had nothing but the most basic security set in place. The good news is they'll probably keep us on after we fix this mess they're in."

"That's great."

"Did I tell you that Rick's wife had her baby? He's cut back his hours some, which means I'm picking up the slack."

Of course he was.

Jillian wanted to say something positive, but instead she stayed silent. Here she was, stuck in the middle again. She should be used to this. Only this time she wasn't lost between her sisters. No, now cancer and Geoff's job closed in on her from both sides.

"Do you want to talk about the wedding?" Jillian inhaled the light scent of Geoff's aftershave. Familiar. Comforting. "Were you thinking about tuxes for the guys? Or suits?"

"Oh, honey, I haven't had time to think of that. Shouldn't we wait until you find your dress tomorrow?"

"I may not find my dress tomorrow—"

"With everyone's help? Sure you will." Geoff adjusted his steps to her slower pace. "And no matter what you wear, you'll be beautiful."

How like Geoff to say that. But she didn't want him to say the right thing just because it was the right thing—an automatic response just like he adjusted his pace to hers without thinking about what he was doing.

Jillian's steps slowed even more. "I think I'm ready to head back—"

"Sure." As they turned toward her apartment, putting their backs to the vivid oranges and golds of the sunset, Geoff took her hand in his. "I'm so proud of how well you're doing with all this, Jilly."

"Sometimes I wonder how I'll handle the chemo—"

Geoff squeezed her hand before drawing her close and slipping his arm around her waist. "You're a fighter. You're going to beat this."

Right. That's what Geoff kept telling her. Despite all of Harper's positive-thinking notes, did Jillian believe it? Was that even the right question? She *had* to believe it. Had to keep fighting. But with each passing day, it seemed as if she was fighting multiple battles.

All that was missing was the television camera crew. Oh, and the mandatory visit with a skilled makeup artist who would ensure she was primped and prepared to play the bride-to-be.

As she faced the door to the wedding salon, Jillian shook her head, dispelling the silly daydream, a figment of her overactive imagination. Thanks to Harper, she'd indulged in too many episodes of *Say Yes to the Dress*. She should have left the binge-watching to her best friend and caught up on her sleep. Maybe then she wouldn't find herself dozing off over mortgage loan applications every morning, with too much work left to do before she could go home and change into her pajamas and collapse on the couch. When Geoff made it over in the evening—which was rare—he usually found her asleep in front of the TV. But the man never complained. And she needed to be understanding about the demands of his job, not think—

"Daydreaming, Jillian?"

Johanna's voice drove her further into reality. "No, no. I was just . . . thinking."

"You did schedule an appointment, right?"

"Yes."

"Well then, why are we standing outside the shop?" Johanna stepped ahead and pulled the glass door open. "I'm sure they'd like us to be prompt."

If there was one thing Jillian had learned watching reality shows of brides shopping for their dream dress, it was that there was always one outspoken member of the group. Cue Johanna's entrance. Johanna disapproved of the shopping trip altogether, having made it clear she still thought Jillian should have changed her wedding date.

But if nothing else, Jillian could control her wedding. Well, some of it. She couldn't stop the . . . physical alterations that would be hidden beneath a veil and gown. With cancer, she fought an unseen, internal adversary. Come Monday, she'd be relegated to the sidelines as the oncologist waged a medical war with rounds of chemotherapy.

Her wedding wasn't going to become another unraveling in her life.

No cameras or lights or makeup artists or TV personalities waited for her inside the store. Just her mother. And Harper. And Geoff's mom. And Payton. But when the in-charge saleswoman approached their group and asked, "Who's the bride-to-be?" Jillian got to say, "I am," designating herself as the reason everyone else was here. The center of attention. And she didn't expect to be interviewed about her fiancé while she tried on different dresses, but still, this was her first and last time all rolled into one. After Monday, she'd have precious little time to go wedding dress shopping.

"You're planning an April wedding, correct?"

"Yes."

"She's considering changing the date—"

"No, she's not." Payton interrupted Johanna.

The older woman with straight salt-and-pepper hair that hung past her shoulders seemed stunned by the verbal grappling taking place between Jillian's sisters, her stylus poised above her iPad.

"The wedding date is April 14, as I told you over the phone. There's no change."

"Jillian—"

"Johanna, I'm here to look at dresses, not talk about whether you think we chose the right date or not. Geoff and I discussed your suggestion and decided we're fine with the original date."

The woman made a few notations on the screen. "I've got you all checked in then." Another woman, this one as slender as a runway model, approached them. "This is Brigitte. She'll be assisting you today."

Some of the magic of the day faded. Why hadn't Jillian realized she'd have to undress—over and over again—in front of some stranger who probably never struggled with her weight a day in her life? Someone who wore a size two and laughed at the idea of layering Spanx.

Brigitte ushered them to a dressing room area shrouded in rich blue velvet curtains. "The rest of you ladies are welcome to get comfortable while Jillian and I go talk about what kind of wedding gown she wants. Can I get any of you a bottle of water?"

Johanna ignored the small semicircle of chairs. "I'm the maid of honor, and I had some thoughts about what kind of gown Jillian should try on."

Brigitte nodded. "Of course. It's always good to hear suggestions."

"I'm sure my sister told you that she has breast cancer—"

Brigitte paled, her smile frozen in place. "Um, no. She hadn't mentioned that."

Jillian's mother stepped forward, placing an arm around her waist. "It's a recent diagnosis."

Why did Johanna have to discuss this in the middle of the store as if she was telling the woman, *"My sister has six fingers on her left hand"* or *"My sister has a third eye"*? Heat coursed through Jillian's body, seeming to pool at the scar on her chest. "I was going to talk with her before we tried on any dresses." She offered Brigitte a small smile. "I apologize. When I called to make the appointment, they just asked me for a time and how many would be coming. It was a very brief phone call."

"So . . . so what should I know in light of your . . . illness?"

"Nothing, really. I mean, there are certain designs I'll stay away from. Nothing too revealing or low-cut, but that's not my style anyway."

"She should probably look at something with sleeves." Johanna spoke up again. "And obviously nothing too form-fitting. Maybe an empire waist."

"Does anyone else have any thoughts about what kind of gown would look best on Jillian?" Brigitte's gaze encompassed the rest of the group. "Mrs. Thatcher, what would you like to see your daughter wear?"

"I think Jillian would look lovely in something with lace. Maybe a vintage look. Ivory, maybe? What do you think, Payton?"

"I think Jillian should get whatever she wants. Short. Strapless." She held up her hand as Johanna started to sputter. "Oh, I'm kidding, Jo. But let Jillian get what she wants."

By the time everyone had given their suggestions, Jillian was lost in the cross fire. She could have been eleven years old again, sitting at the family dinner table, her father having asked, "How was your day?" How was she supposed to join the conversational fray, the words and sentences tossed back and forth across the table between Payton and Pepper and

Johanna? How did she fight for her place—demand some space and declare it hers?

"Okay then. Why don't I take Jillian back to the dressing room and select a few styles, and we can start having some fun." Brigitte guided Jillian away from the group, motioning to a silver tray of small water bottles. "You all relax. Please, have some water. We'll be back in a few."

If Brigitte could make trying on wedding dresses fun, she was more magician than saleswoman.

The woman handed Jillian a blue satin robe, not unlike one she'd seen women wearing on *Say Yes to the Dress*. "Do you need any help getting undressed?"

"No. My surgery was just over three weeks ago. I'm fine."

"Great. I'll go find some dresses for you, then, and be back in just a few minutes."

Jillian didn't know who was more relieved when Brigitte left—the other woman or herself. She rubbed her palms against her jeans, blowing out a breath. There was no "if" she was getting undressed. She was here to try on dresses. This wasn't the time to hesitate.

She kicked her flats to the side, discarding her jeans and T-shirt on the chair positioned in one of the corners. Her reflection mimicked her hurried movements as she slipped into the cool satin robe, covering her too-ample body that was oddly *less-than* in one area.

"Fun, fun, fun . . ." She whispered the words over and over like some new mantra.

What had one of the surgery nurses told her as she'd

fought back tears, struggling to dress herself after her mastectomy? Some kind of don't-let-life-get-you-down quote.

"Life's challenges are not supposed to paralyze you; they're supposed to help you discover who you are."

What was she going to discover today as she bared herself—literally—in front of a stranger? She could either put her clothes back on and say, "I changed my mind" or tough out the embarrassment. Deal with who she was, what her body looked like, and find some kind of fun . . . humor . . . in her first-time-last-time wedding dress shopping experience.

"All ready in there, Jillian?"

"As ready as I'll ever be." Jillian forced enthusiasm into her words. "I can't wait to see what you picked out."

Brigitte's arms overflowed with dresses encased in plastic. "I've got quite an assortment. Everybody seemed to have different ideas. I even picked a short dress like one of your sisters suggested."

"Oh, Payton was only trying to mess with Johanna—"

"I have an older sister, too. I know what it's like." Brigitte began unzipping the protective coverings. "So which one do you want to try on first?"

"Is there a lace one in there? Like my mom suggested?"

"Yes."

"Let's do that first."

As Jillian slipped out of her robe, Brigitte removed the dress, coming to stand beside her, chewing her bottom lip.

"Brigitte."

The other woman jumped. "Yes?"

"Have you ever helped a woman who's had a mastectomy before?"

"No . . . I'm sorry. I haven't."

"It's okay. No need to apologize. My sister is right. I should have said something before the appointment." Jillian took a deep breath. "I'm just like any other bride-to-be, except I have only one breast. And I'm wearing a prosthesis, which is just a fake breast, so I don't look lopsided."

Brigitte gave a short laugh. "Well, that's one way to put it."

"It's the truth. Might as well say it straight up. I won't have reconstructive surgery before my wedding because we're doing chemo and radiation. And I may be bald by April, so I'm not sure about the whole veil option because I don't know if I'm doing a wig or not. It's not your problem. It's mine."

"I understand."

"All right then. We'll just go with what I have." She needed to stop talking so much. "Sorry. That was not a joke, believe me. Maybe it's best if we get me into the first dress, okay?"

Eight dresses later, what little hope she'd conjured up about finding a wedding dress had faded. She hadn't discovered a stronger, better version of herself as she faced today's challenge. She wasn't paralyzed, but merely going through the motions of putting on dresses, displaying herself to Harper and Geoff's mom and her family, and retreating behind the curtains to remove the dresses. Facing her reflection in the mirror again. And again. And again.

She was still overweight. Too hippy. Too short-waisted. Fleshy arms. And two breasts—one real, one fake—that made finding the right kind of bodice an absolute impossibility. Her mother liked her in ivory. Geoff's mother preferred white. Harper gave a swift thumbs-down to the empire-waist gown Johanna said was perfect. And Payton . . . Payton sat in her chair, more and more quiet as the session went on.

Brigitte hung the last dress on the hanger, preparing to go search for more.

"I think I'm done for today, Brigitte."

"Are you sure? I can go find some other styles."

"Thank you, but no. I just haven't seen anything yet. And to be honest, I'm tired."

"Oh, I'm so sorry. I didn't even think about that—"

"No, no. I'm just normal tired." Jillian twisted the end of the belt between her fingers. "Nothing more. You've been great."

Silence greeted her when she appeared in her regular clothes. "So that's all the wedding gown shopping for today."

Johanna set aside her phone. "What? You've only tried on a few dresses."

"Eight. I've tried on eight. And I'm done."

"But I think we should—"

"I'll tell you what I'd like to do."

"What's that, Jill?" Harper jumped in.

"I'd really like you all to browse the dresses for possible styles to wear for the ceremony. Even you, Mrs. Hennessey, and you, Mom. I talked with Brigitte—" she motioned to the saleswoman standing behind her—"and she said that's fine because another woman canceled her appointment."

"That's not the plan." Johanna remained seated.

"I realize that. But it's what I'd like to do. Okay?"

Payton jumped up from her chair. "The bride's in charge. Let's go look at some dresses."

Could I make my escape while Johanna and Harper and the two mothers-in-law-to-be browsed the racks crowded with dresses, organized by color in extended fabric rainbows? No. I wasn't abandoning Jillian in her hour of need. I couldn't do anything about her cancer, but I could stiffen my spine, bite my tongue, and shop for dresses. It was one day. One day. And then I could retreat into my world of planning other people's parties.

I turned my back on the red-and-white Exit sign over the door leading to the parking lot. Ignored every other person in the shop. Geoff's mother had paired off with my mom, Johanna had allowed Jillian to wander into the small section of the store devoted to an eclectic assortment of bridal shoes, and Harper was nowhere in sight.

Now to find a dress or two we could all agree on—or that we could all compromise on. But what to choose first? Design or color? And would Jillian want short, mid-length, or long?

The chime of my cell phone interrupted my musing as I shifted hangers along the metal rack. I snugged my phone between my ear and my shoulder and kept browsing. "Payton Thatcher."

"Payton, it's Nash."

My fingers clutched the satiny fuchsia material of one dress. *Nash*. We hadn't talked since our breakup, thanks to my refusal to answer his repeated calls or texts the following week.

"Don't hang up. Please." His voice was low, but calm, not desperate. "I'm not going to harass you. Scout's honor."

Okay. "I don't recall you ever mentioning you were a Boy Scout."

His laugh was tinged with relief. "True, but I am honorable, Payton. I'm just calling to see how you're doing. That's all."

I kept my voice down. "I'm fine. Thank you for asking."

"I'm glad to hear that. Care to tell me why you're almost whispering?"

"I'm with Jillian and some other people at a bridal salon. Jillian's looking for her wedding gown."

"I can only imagine how much you're enjoying that."

The man knew me well, but then, we had dated for the better part of a year.

"I wanted to ask about Jillian, too. How's she doing?"

This was the Nash I remembered from the early days of our romance. Easygoing. Considerate.

"It's been rough. Harder than she lets on, I think." The crack in my voice forced me to stop talking.

"Has she started chemo?"

"Her first treatment is this Monday. That's why we're shopping for dresses today. Once the next stage of treatment

186

starts, she's not sure what she's going to be up to from one day to the next."

"I'm sorry, Payton."

"Thanks, Nash. I appreciate you calling."

"Listen, I just wanted to say—"

"Nash, please . . ."

"No pressure. If you could see me, I've got my hand up in the whole 'Scout's honor' position."

His words defused the situation as I laughed. "Sure, sure, Mr. Boy Scout. I forgot."

"Anyway, I'd love to meet up for coffee one day. Or a drink. Again, no pressure. Just to catch up."

"No hidden agenda, right?"

"Right. Not even dinner. You can call, 'Time' when you're done."

And just like that, he made me laugh again, something I'd appreciated about him when we'd first started dating. Before he'd gone all "Let's live together" serious on me. "So I get to bring both a penalty flag and a stopwatch?"

"Absolutely."

"Let me think about it?"

"Sure."

"Who are you talking to?" Johanna's voice sliced through the air like a teacher who'd caught her star pupil cheating on a final exam.

I stayed facing away from her. "Thanks for calling. I've got to go now."

"Johanna show up?"

Nash knew my family so well. "Yes. We'll talk again soon."

"Take care, Payton. Coffee whenever you're ready."

I faced Johanna once I'd ended the call.

"Who was that?"

"Really? And you expect to monitor my calls because . . . ?"

"Don't pick a fight with me every time I say something, Payton." Johanna carried several long gowns. "You didn't find anything to try on?"

I pulled several random dresses from among the selection. Were they even my size? "Just a couple. Let's go."

But Johanna stood where she was. "I told you that Jillian wasn't up to doing this, which is exactly why she needs to plan something sooner. Something simpler."

"Just because she got tired and didn't find a dress today doesn't mean she should do what you want and change the date of her wedding." I brushed past my older sister, the scent of Coco perfume, her signature fragrance, assaulting me. "How many times are we going to argue about this? If you're lucky, maybe she'll choose the style you like for the bridesmaid dresses."

"This is not about me getting my way!" Johanna spoke through gritted teeth.

"Really, Johanna? It's been about you getting your way for years." I slowed my steps, refusing to argue in front of Jillian and my mother. "Does Beckett know you're a control freak? Or have you managed to hide that character trait from him until after you're married?"

Johanna stopped in the middle of the store, her face going

white. Had I finally managed to silence my sister? But wait . . . was she blinking back tears? Had my words been too harsh in an attempt to gain the upper hand?

"I shouldn't have said that. . . ."

Johanna waved my words away. "You always say exactly what you mean, little sister. I learned that a long time ago."

Me? What about Johanna, who left the ring with her arms raised in victory more times than not?

But what else did I expect? This was our normal. Put me in the same room with Johanna for any length of time and we fought. Sincere apologies were few and far between. Usually time . . . well, time didn't heal our wounds, but it eased the effects of the verbal blows. Unlike actual boxers, we weren't limited to using our fists. Johanna and I had gone hundreds of rounds in the ring by now. Endless rounds. Alternate winners. Some knockouts. And too little time spent in neutral corners.

Prizefighters leave the ring, their wounds visible to one and all. A bloodied lip. A black eye. But then there are the fights that leave injuries no one else ever sees. Emotional lacerations that made it hard to breathe as I struggled not to cry. That could almost bring me to my knees, even as I questioned the definition of *sisters*.

Because sisters, true sisters, didn't act like this, did they?

Had I ever wanted something different? Long ago, maybe. But some things can't be changed. I could only keep moving forward.

Mom and Geoff's mother stood in front of the mirrors that had, only a short while ago, reflected Jillian in different wedding gowns. Each woman wore a classic mother-of-the-bride or -groom dress. Mom's was all lace with three-quarter sleeves, while Geoff's mom's style flowed from a gauzy jacket down to a handkerchief hemline. Everyone approved of both options, agreeing the moms didn't have to match, merely complement one another.

"Why don't Johanna and Harper try on their picks next while Mom and Mrs. Hennessey change?" I slid the two random dresses I'd selected onto one of the chairs.

When Johanna and Harper appeared again, it was apparent they had completely opposite tastes in dresses, too.

Johanna wore an elegant, no-frills mauve A-line dress. Harper had gone the party-girl route, appearing in a short, off-the-shoulder turquoise number.

Harper twirled in front of the mirror. "It is a spring wedding, after all."

"Springtime in the Rockies." Johanna smoothed the front of her gown. "It could snow on Jillian's wedding day."

"I like them both." Jillian was already appeasing both sides. "And I promise never to say, 'You can wear it again,' no matter what dress we choose."

"Because that never happens." Even Johanna smiled at the comment.

"Which is why I'm not going to say it."

"Have you decided on your colors?" Harper moved away from the mirror.

"Geoff's favorite color is blue. I was thinking either a royal blue or maybe a cornflower blue."

"Oh, Pepper would have loved the off-the-shoulder style, wouldn't she, Payton?" Mom's words caused everyone's attention to turn to me. "And the blue, too."

The question faded into the silence as I struggled to answer. My throat seemed to be closing up, my mouth dry, making it difficult to swallow, much less formulate a reply. It was as if Mom had invited Pepper's ghost into the group . . . or shoved me back into one of my unwanted dreams. I closed my eyes. Was I going to see Pepper walking through the bridal salon?

"Payton?"

As Jillian touched my arm, I jerked away. "Yes. Of course. Pepper would have loved the dress. And the color. Our . . . our club volleyball jerseys were blue . . ."

Everyone seemed to wait for me to say something else. But the one thing I wanted to say, needed to say, was buried so deep inside me I didn't know how to exhume the truth and bring it to light.

"Not sleeping, Payton?"

I stared at the ceiling of the hospital room as the nurse adjusted my covers. "No."

"Dr. Langley left a prescription for a sleep aid. It's not a sleeping pill, just something to help you doze off."

"No."

When I blinked, my eyelids seemed to scrape against hot, dry eyes, although I knew I had oceans of tears somewhere inside me.

"Is there something on your mind? I'd be happy to listen if you want to talk about anything worrying you." The nurse paused at the foot of my bed, standing half in the shadows.

Anything worrying me?

Just how to tell the truth to my parents. How to explain to them that my words, careless words, had caused Pepper's death. That I might as well have been driving the other snowmobile, not Zach Gaines.

"No."

"Payton?" Mom's voice bore the weight of unshed tears.

"No."

"No what, dear?"

"Nothing. I—I've got to go."

"What?" Jillian stepped forward. "Why?"

"I'm not feeling well. . . . I'm sorry, Jillian." I gave my sister a brief hug. I wasn't lying, not really, what with the way my fingers tingled and how the faint odor of ammonia unsettled my stomach. "We'll talk soon . . . about the bridal shower . . . and the . . . the . . ."

Johanna grabbed my wrist. "Sit down. Don't go anywhere until you're feeling better."

My sister's words were sharp, not offering comfort. I would not fall apart in front of Johanna. Not again.

I pulled away from her grasp and half ran to the exit, the Colorado air a welcome relief.

Please, please, please, no one follow me.

Key in the ignition. Jam the gearshift into reverse. Exit the parking lot as if everyone in the store had chased me to my car.

Careen into traffic and cut off not one but two cars. Cling to the steering wheel with hands that shook. Ignore the honking horns. The shouts. The glares from the drivers of other cars.

Exit traffic again. Pull up behind a building. Park beside a Dumpster. Slam the gearshift into park. Turn the car off.

And then I crawled into the backseat of my car, curled my knees up to my chest, and shook. Sun streamed in through the windows, but I shivered as if I were outside in a blizzard. My vision blurred as I gasped for breath, rubbing the heel of my hand against the pain building in my chest.

Was I having a heart attack? Would I die here, alone, in my car?

Some people said you could die from a broken heart. I'd been dying a slow, torturous death for years.

Even as I fought against the waves of panic, I wasn't afraid of dying.

Let it be so.

What was there to be afraid of? *Anything* had to be better than this.

PEOPLE WERE LAUGHING. And talking—their words fast and loud, ricocheting against the windows of my car.

My car?

What was I doing in my car?

When I forced my eyes open and stared at the dim interior of my Subaru sedan, twilight was being dispersed by the glow of a nearby streetlight. I rolled from my side onto my back, my feet colliding with the door when I tried to stretch out my legs.

What time was it? How long had I slept in the back of my car?

With a groan, I pulled myself to a sitting position, shoving hair out of my eyes. The laughter stopped.

"There's someone in that car—"

"I'm getting out of here!" One of the teens disappeared around the building.

The other stared at me, then approached, rapping on my window. "Hey, lady. You okay?"

I nodded, unable to find my voice.

"You sure? I can call somebody for you—a cop or something."

"I'm fine." I raised my voice. "Fine. I wasn't feeling well and, um, pulled over here until I could drive."

"Okay. Sure you don't want me to call—?"

"I can drive myself home now. Thanks."

As my teenage Good Samaritan waved and followed after his friend, I escaped from the backseat to the outside, bending over, hands on my knees, and sucking in deep breaths. My muscles protested their cramped position. At least the sharp ache in my chest had subsided. And my hands no longer shook. My fingers no longer tingled. The air was scented with the aroma of Chinese food, not the pungent odor of ammonia.

Time to go home. I'd live to see another day . . . and the upcoming night.

But the closer I got to my neighborhood, the tighter my chest got. I gripped the steering wheel. I was not a coward. I was going home. Once I parked the car, the engine running, I stared out into the darkness, my hands still wrapped around the steering wheel.

This was ridiculous.

"I am a grown woman. I am going into my house. I'm sleeping in my bed."

Who was I talking to?

"Stop bothering me."

Pepper.

"Do you hear me?" I pounded a fist against the steering wheel. "Leave me alone, Pepper. No more showing up in my dreams. No more talking about telling the truth. I can't do it. I can't."

Despite my defiant words to my sister, I collapsed into the seat, covering my face with my hands. She wasn't listening to me. Pepper had been displaying her independence . . . her unwillingness to listen to me, to what I wanted, in the months before she died.

I could be independent, too. After all, what had I been doing for the last ten years?

I turned my car off. Yanked the keys out of the ignition. Gathered my purse and ran into my house.

Once inside, I turned on every light downstairs, repeating the process as I went upstairs and changed into black leggings and a loose-fitting top. Then I turned my back on my bed and went downstairs, searching through my DVDs until I found *Gone with the Wind* and *Pearl Harbor*, not because I wanted to watch movies about war, but simply because both movies were over three hours long.

I'd fill the house with noise. Walk around. Maybe I'd even clean—forget the dishwasher and wash dishes by hand. Anything to stay awake.

But by the time Rhett walked away from a stunned Scarlett, all I wanted to do was lie down on the couch, cover myself with a quilt, and give in to sleep's demand.

I couldn't ... *would not* ... stay here. I put on my coat and grabbed my car keys, not bothering to turn out any lights.

Minutes later, I put my car in reverse and put my home in the rearview mirror. I didn't know where I was going, but I wasn't sleeping in my bed. Not tonight.

Cold coffee was better than no coffee.

Sometimes.

If you were sleep-deprived. Calorie-deprived. And parked on the side of the road, at the last place you ever thought you'd be.

I was all of these things. The only thing fueling my body was fast-food coffee that I'd picked up along the way as I'd driven to Winter Park. Gas stations were not known for being vegan friendly.

How did I even find my way here? Ten years ago, I'd been huddled in the backseat of some unknown adult's car, following the ambulance transporting Pepper to the local emergency clinic. The flashing lights and the siren's wail echoed the words I'd sobbed over and over.

"Don't die, Pepper. Don't die, Pepper."

Of all places I could have gone, why had I chosen to come here? I'd warred with my emotions for hours, pacing back and forth between my living room and kitchen, determined to stay awake. Then I'd gotten in my car, at first uncertain where I was going. Once I'd realized my destination, I tried talking myself out of the decision. I pulled off the highway again and again for another cup of coffee, telling myself to turn the car around and head back home to North Denver.

But I didn't.

It was the same struggle I fought whenever I went to see my family. Wanting to turn the car around. To head in the opposite direction. But I kept driving toward where I didn't want to be even as the questions *Why am I doing this? Why am I spending time with these people?* ran around and around in my head like the crazy cats in those YouTube videos Bianca liked to watch during her lunch breaks. I had no good answers—except I had to go. Family obligation counted for something, right?

But there was no obligation that led me here. No "have to." After all these years, my connection to Zach Gaines was tenuous at best, despite its being steeped in tragedy.

A truck rumbled into view, coming down the driveway that had been paved sometime during the past decade. An ornamental wrought-iron archway with the name *Gaines* had been installed, too. As the battered old Ford drew closer, I recognized Zach in the driver's seat.

What was he doing up here? His family had used the cabin as a weekend getaway when he was back in high school. Was he continuing the tradition? Were his parents here, too?

Zach turned onto the road and would pass right by my

car. I pressed back against the seat, resisting the urge to slink lower. Turn my face away. Most likely he would drive on by.

As I started to exhale, Zach's truck slowed. Stopped. Reversed and parked on the shoulder of the road in front of my car. The driver's door opened, and Zach stepped out, pausing near my door with his hands on his hips.

Okay, imagining that Zach would pass by my car had been wishful thinking on my part.

I half opened my car door but remained seated, unable to find the strength to stand and meet him.

He rested his crossed forearms on the top of the door, leaning back to make eye contact with me. "Payton? What are you doing here?"

"I can explain."

Only I couldn't.

There was no reasonable justification for my being here.

And this was how I'd felt whenever Pepper and I got caught playing our harmless version of "trading places" when we were younger. Caught in the act. In the wrong place, at the wrong time. But those little escapades had all been in good fun. And people always laughed. There was nothing fun about Zach discovering me sitting at the end of the driveway leading to his family's cabin.

A poor excuse for a laugh escaped my lips. "I, um, didn't plan to come here."

Zach quirked his eyebrow but stayed silent.

"Yesterday was a . . . a rough day. I had a . . . I couldn't sleep. Ended up driving around for a while." No matter what Zach thought, I was telling him the truth. Or at least, most of the truth. "I, um, I guess I drove a lot farther than I ever intended."

As I talked, the clean scent of the surrounding pine trees wafted into the car, gentling my emotions. I hadn't been in the mountains in years. I always found an excuse to decline an invitation to go skiing. Or hiking. Or snowshoeing. And then people stopped asking me.

"Have you eaten?"

"I'm fine—"

"If you've been up all night, you must be hungry." Zach's gaze scanned the interior of my car. Two insulated coffee cups perched in cup holders. Others littered the floor in front of the passenger seat. "Well-caffeinated, but hungry."

"If you'll recommend a decent place for breakfast—"

"I can make you breakfast, Payton."

What? "There's no need for you to do that."

"My cabin's right up the road. It's not a problem."

"Weren't you heading somewhere?"

"I'll call and tell them I'll be late. Follow me." Zach stepped away, shutting the door.

Looked like I could either drive off or take the man up on his offer of breakfast.

I directed my car behind Zach's truck. His mention of calling someone caused me to check my phone. I should respond to some of the voice mails or texts. Sometime.

After the way I'd treated him, why was Zach Gaines being nice to me? Pity, maybe? *Poor little Payton.* Zach got religion and pulled his life back together. And me? I was a mess who fell apart in front of some of our high school classmates because I thought I saw my dead sister walking around.

Yeah. *I see dead people.*

Well, only one person.

This was what too little sleep and too much caffeine did to me—turned my sense of humor macabre.

As we approached the cabin, I caught a glimpse of the open field behind the building—wide and long, with a few trees at one end. Perfect for snowmobile races. I averted my gaze from even such a quick look, pulling my car alongside Zach's truck.

A large black dog ran toward us the minute Zach opened the cabin door, low woofs not quite convincing me that he—or she—was dangerous.

"Stop, Laz!" Zach snapped his fingers and the dog skidded to a stop in front of him, panting. He scratched the dog's ears. "I'm sorry. I forgot to warn you about Laz."

"Laz?"

"Short for Lazarus. He's harmless, just a little over friendly. I'll put him outside for now."

"It's not a problem. He can stay inside." I patted Lazarus on his head. "What kind of dog is he?"

"Just a mutt. I found him wandering the property about a year ago—not much more than a puppy. I think someone had dropped him off."

"That's awful."

"Happens quite a lot in remote areas." With another quick

command, the dog settled in front of a large stone fireplace. "He'll behave now."

"He's well-trained."

"If you're going to have a big dog, you've got to train him or live to regret it."

A bank of floor-to-ceiling windows in the great room showcased the field in the back. A closed door probably led to a bedroom or study and stairs led upstairs to a loft. After hanging our coats on a wrought-iron rack by the door, Zach granted me a reprieve from looking out at the field by leading us into the kitchen off the living room.

"Do your parents still like to come up here on the weekends?" I asked.

"Not so much anymore."

"No?"

"They live in California now. My dad got a job transfer there about six years ago. And besides, I live here year-round."

"You do?"

"Yeah. I don't really care for the city. I pay my folks rent and keep the place up for them. It works for all of us."

Zach surveyed the contents of his fridge. "I had chipped beef on toast this morning. How about if I reheat the leftovers for you? Sound good?"

"Um, I'm vegan. Sorry."

"Well, that rules out chipped beef. Why don't you come on over and take a look and tell me what you can eat?"

"I don't want to be any trouble—"

"It's not any trouble, Payton. I'm just not sure what to serve you."

He offered to make me breakfast and now I had to ransack his fridge. Perfect. "Do you have any fruit?"

Zach stepped aside. "I think there's an orange in there and maybe an apple."

"*An* orange? *An* apple?"

"What can I say? I need to go grocery shopping." Zach's smile was reminiscent of the teenage boy who could charm both students and teachers. "Don't you need some protein?"

"Yes. I can do nuts or tofu." I couldn't hold back a laugh at Zach's expression. I could have just told him I ate dirt or bugs. "I guess I won't find any tofu in here."

"Nope. Never. I'm not a tofu guy. And I don't apologize for that."

"No apologies needed." I retrieved the lone orange and apple from the recesses of his fridge. "I noticed you had peanut butter. I can have that on toast. Great source of protein."

"I'll make the toast."

"You don't need to—"

"I'm making the toast."

"Hmm. Both hospitable and bossy. Interesting combination."

"All my lady friends find it irresistible."

Another laugh escaped. "Lady friends?"

Zach reached around me and retrieved the jar of peanut butter. "Two slices okay?"

"Yes, please."

"Do you want me to make coffee?"

"No, thanks. After all the coffee I've had, water sounds good. Do you have a cutting board?"

As I prepped the fruit, Zach set the table with stoneware dishes. After placing water glasses on the table, he sat across from me.

"You're not going to eat?"

He raised his glass in a salute. "Already did."

"You really like living here?"

"It's quiet, but yeah, I do. After I stopped drinking, I figured it would be smart to get away from my normal routine. Start over in some ways. The cabin was sitting empty, so I talked to my parents about living here, and they liked the plan."

"And you said you do upkeep."

"And some bigger projects."

"Like . . . ?"

Zach motioned around the room. "I upgraded the kitchen."

While small, the kitchen boasted high-end appliances and countertops, as well as a copper farmhouse sink and rustic, well-built cabinets.

"Really? This is fabulous. I love the cabinets."

Zach grinned. "Thanks. I did those, too."

"You installed them?"

"Well, yes. I also designed them."

Unable to resist a closer look, I abandoned my half-eaten breakfast to run my palm across the surface of a cabinet door. "These are beautiful, Zach. I can't imagine the time and effort this took."

"I enjoy it. Some people hate their jobs. I'm one of the lucky people who can't wait to go to work every day."

"So when you told me you worked for a custom wood-working company, this is what you meant?"

"Yes. Although working at 3:17 Cabinets, I've learned it all, including installation."

"3:17?" I sat back down at the table. "Does that have something to do with measurements?"

"No. It's based on a verse, Ephesians 3:17, about being rooted and grounded in love."

Did everything in his life have something to do with God?

Zach seemed oblivious to my skepticism. "I'm taking college classes when I can. My goal is to become a master cabinetmaker. Maybe start my own business one day. But I'm satisfied with where I am right now."

"Well, there are advantages to being the boss, you know."

"I'm sure." Zach finished his water. "I have to admit I never saw you as a party planner."

"Me, either." I took a bite of my toast, waiting for the inevitable question.

"So how did you get involved with Festivities?"

"My freshman year was a bit of a bust. I dropped half my classes. I wasn't as ready for college as I thought. I took summer classes so I could still graduate on time."

"You were never a quitter, Payton."

I moved the slices of fruit around on my plate. How was I supposed to respond to a compliment from Zach Gaines? And why was I even telling him all of this? He'd asked about

Festivities—nothing more. But then again, this was better than awkward silence.

"I roomed with Kimberlee during my sophomore year of college. She'd transferred in and I, well, I wanted a do-over." More like I needed a do-over. "What I didn't realize was Kimberlee was a party girl—in the nicest sense of the phrase. If she heard about someone's birthday, she celebrated it. Banners on doors. Special cupcakes she made in the common-area kitchen. Photo collages on Facebook. Pretty soon, people were asking her to help plan surprise parties for their friends. And then campus groups started calling her to see if she'd coordinate events."

"I still don't see what got you into the business."

"I said yes."

"You said yes . . . to what?"

"Kimberlee got in over her head helping plan a surprise party for one of the girls in a sorority, and she asked for my help—just that one time, of course. We realized we worked well together. She's this mad genius when it comes to party themes and all the fun, fun, fun—"

"And you?"

"I'm the behind-the-scenes part of the team. I coordinate our commitments, manage our bank account, our social media . . . that sort of thing. When she got started, Kimberlee was having so much fun, she ignored the business side of things."

"Sounds like the perfect combination."

"So far. When she decided to start a business after graduation, she asked me to join her. I decided 'Why not?'"

"But you didn't go to college planning to start a small business."

"No. I ended up switching my major to business management." I placed my dishes on the counter.

"Just leave those. I'll take care of them later." Zach rested his elbows on the table, chin on his hands. "You said you couldn't sleep because you had a rough day yesterday. Can I ask why?"

I faced Zach again, leaning back against the kitchen counter, thankful he'd remained seated at the table. For some reason, his question wasn't invasive. "It was a culmination of a lot of things. The high school thing stressed me out—obviously. And then . . . my sister Jillian was diagnosed with cancer about two months ago."

"I'm sorry to hear that. How bad is it?"

"Worse than we thought." I gripped the edge of the counter. "She's planning her wedding and facing chemo and radiation."

"She's got to be scared."

"Yeah. I think we all are. And it . . . it brought up memories of Pepper's death for my mom, which made it even harder."

"I can only imagine."

"Yeah." I tugged at the ends of my hair. I must look awful. No sleep. No shower. No makeup. "Listen, I should head out. Let you get to wherever you were headed."

"Wait." Zach rose from the chair. "Before you go, would you want to see the bench I made? For Pepper?"

Oh.

Zach must have taken my silence for assent. "We can walk there in less than ten minutes. If it's okay with you, I'll bring Laz along—"

"No."

"No?" Zach stopped. "Okay, we don't have to bring Laz."

"No. I mean, no, I don't want to see the bench." I pressed my fingertips against my temples. "I need to go."

"Whoa. Slow down, Payton." Zach raised his hands as if he were surrendering. "I'm sorry if my suggestion was out of line. I thought you might want to see the bench, that's all."

"I can't . . . I really think I should just leave—"

Zach took two strides and faced me as I moved toward the front door. "Payton, stop for a minute. You've been up all night. It's an hour-and-a-half drive back to North Denver. Why don't you rest here for a few hours and then head home?"

I stiffened. "Stay here?"

"Yes. I've got some things to do. Just take a nap. I can put Laz outside or leave him here, whichever you prefer. I'd feel better knowing you had some sleep before you drove again."

"Why are you being so nice to me, Zach?" His eyes were pewter gray and a faint scent of soap lingered on his clothes. We were too close. "I'm not going to change my mind about you talking to my parents."

"I know." Zach shrugged. "I'm not going to ask you about that again. I just don't think you should be driving right now. That's all."

Once again, Zach was acting like we were friends—but

we weren't. I wasn't about to curl up on his couch and take a nap. I was a big girl and I could take care of myself.

I preferred to take care of myself.

I sidestepped around him. "I appreciate your concern, but I'll be fine. Thanks for breakfast. If I could use the bathroom, then I'll get out of your way."

"You're sure?"

"Yes."

I was more than sure.

"Well then, would you do me a favor and text me to let me know you made it home safely?"

Who did Zach Gaines think he was, my father? I agreed—knowing I wouldn't text him—and traded cell phone numbers with him.

But as I drove away, I still couldn't figure out why I'd driven all the way to Winter Park. To Zach's cabin. Maybe even though I'd said no to his invitation to see the bench, there was a part of me that had wanted to say yes. A very small part. It was like sitting on a swing at the park and pushing into the ground with the balls of my bare feet so that my legs were straight. Swaying back . . . but then I stayed frozen, refusing to lift my feet off the ground, tuck them underneath myself, so that I could lift off into the air.

Not yet. Not yet.

If I crossed the field . . . walked alongside Zach to see the bench he'd made . . . went back to that spot . . . to that night . . . If I told the truth that Pepper died instead of me, it would be like swinging higher and higher and then jumping off into the unknown. Falling, falling . . .

And who would catch me?

⌐

He'd missed church. No big deal. He could still catch up with his friends for lunch if he wanted to.

Zach rested his hands on top of the bench, closing his eyes. He'd been so close. When he'd spotted Payton parked alongside the road, he'd thought God had answered his prayer so much sooner than he'd anticipated. She'd looked as exhausted as he used to feel after a cross-country meet. But maybe fatigue, not divine intervention, had lowered her defenses and allowed her to say yes to his offer to make her breakfast.

They'd been comfortable for a while. And then she'd shut him out the moment he mentioned going to see Pepper's bench.

Zach shifted, hands gripping the rough wood of the bench. "Here I am again, God. Am I rushing her? Did I hear You wrong?"

He waited in the stillness, Laz stretched out on the ground by his feet. Maybe the time with Payton hadn't gone the way he'd hoped, but then, he hadn't anticipated seeing her at all today. He had to remember that things not going exactly the way he wanted them to go didn't mean he was a failure.

His time with Payton wasn't wasted.

She'd talked to him. Told him about her life—not just

facts, but personal details. And now that he knew about Jillian's cancer, he'd start praying for her, too.

His life was proof that prayer changed things. Changed people.

Zach rotated his left arm, pushing back the sleeve of his jacket and then doing the same with the sleeve of his flannel shirt, revealing the tattoo etched into his forearm—this one created by a professional. A grayscale image of pine trees that started above his wrist and covered the inside of his arm. The foremost tree was smaller and lighter in color than all the rest.

If someone looked close enough, they would notice the word *REDEMPTION* and *Ephesians 1:7* written along the bottom of the tattoo. A reminder that God had forgiven all of his mistakes—even the mistake that wove his life together with the Thatcher family.

Three lives—his, Payton's, and Pepper's—intersected one winter night by a trio of choices. God could resurrect—redeem—anything. Anyone. He could only hope Pepper was in heaven. And he would continue to pray for Payton, the sister still on earth.

On so many nights when his choice to be sober . . . to stay sober . . . flooded his mind with images he'd rather forget, he'd sit on the edge of his bed and trace the outline of the tattoo. Turn his thoughts into a broken prayer for himself . . . for the Thatcher family . . . for Payton.

God was the author and finisher of his faith. His story wasn't done yet. And neither was Payton's.

MONDAY MORNING. And here I was walking in not one, not two, but three hours late.

In the past month, I'd wrecked my reputation of being the first one to arrive at work and the last one to leave. I just never realized how proud I was of the self-appointed honor.

It wasn't like Kimberlee and I competed against one another. Festivities was based on trust, not rivalry. But my work ethic was part of being a team player—doing my part to make Festivities successful. Unlike Kimberlee, I wasn't a party waiting to happen. I wasn't able to pull off blue highlights and a multitude of rings and also be comfortable with wealthy socialites or eighty-year-old matriarchs or twentysomethings planning a wedding with an exorbitant budget and too many ideas for how to spend it. But I could ensure things ran smoothly behind the scenes both at the office and at our events. I could make Kimberlee's life easier. After all, she'd rescued me when my life had run off the rails—as useless as a middle attending a summer volleyball camp with a broken ankle.

If this had been high school volleyball practice and I'd shown up late, I'd know just what to do. Offer no excuses. Suit up. Run a mile's worth of laps around the gym perimeter and then join the team in whatever drill they were working through. But this was Kimberlee, not Coach Sydney.

"Sorry I'm late." I tossed my purse on my desk, digging through it in search of my makeup bag.

"I'm not your mother. Or your boss." Kimberlee set a mug of coffee on my desk. "This is for you. You'll need to add more sugar. It was for me, but you look like you need it more than I do."

"I didn't put on any makeup yet." I spilled the contents of the clear plastic bag onto my desk. Mascara, foundation, several compacts of eye shadow, an eyelash curler.

"I could say something like you're going to need an extra layer—"

"But friends don't say things like that, do they, *Kimmie*?"

"And friends don't call their friends *Kimmie*, either, do they?"

"Sleep deprivation does funny things to a girl." Humor, however slight, was better than feeling exposed.

For the moment, I ignored the much-needed makeup on my desk and cradled the coffee mug in both hands, the better to hide the ever-present tremor in my fingers. Maybe I'd skip the eyeliner today.

"What's going on, Payton?"

I set aside the mug, thankful for the warmth that had seeped into my skin for those brief seconds, and selected a neutral shade of eye shadow. Opened the compact, swiped the brush through the powder. "I'm just having a rough time sleeping lately."

"Okay. But why?" Kimberlee perched on the edge of my desk. "I know we're business partners, but I thought we were friends, too. Good friends. You've stood by me through everything from bad haircuts to breakups."

I tossed the brush aside. No makeup was better than poorly applied makeup, no matter how haggard I looked. Poor Kimberlee and Bianca would just have to put up with looking at me au naturel all day. I, on the other hand, could avoid mirrors.

"Payton?"

Fine. Kimberlee wanted me to talk? I'd talk.

"I broke up with Nash—"

"Oh, come on! This is not about Nash." Kimberlee snorted. "I've seen you break up with plenty of guys and you never lost sleep over any of them. Don't try to convince me that you were so in love with Nash that it's keeping you awake at night. Not buying it."

If only all this upheaval was about breaking up with

Nash. But it wasn't, and Kimberlee had seen right through my diversionary tactic. Why couldn't the sleepless nights, the loss of appetite, the inability to focus be caused by something as simple as breaking up with a guy?

The daily to-do list sat on my desk—the one I always prepared. Bianca must have printed it out. She was doing both her job and mine. Maybe I needed to find a pen and add, *Tell my family the truth* to the list.

"I . . . I've been having these odd dreams." The admission was a flat whisper.

"What kind of dreams?"

"My twin sister, Pepper, shows up and, um, talks to me."

I had to give Kimberlee credit. She didn't freak out.

"What does she talk about?"

"Different things." I leaned back in my chair. "She asks about me. My family. She wanted to know why I wasn't playing volleyball—"

"Volleyball? Because you played together in high school?"

"No. I mean, yeah. But we'd also made plans after we graduated. Pepper would have gotten a college scholarship. And I'd thought about volleyball, too."

"You never told me this."

"Well, those dreams got wrecked."

"Why?"

I didn't answer.

How could I explain something I'd never said out loud before? It had all made sense to me ten years ago—an emotional cause and effect. My actions caused Pepper's death. No amount of medication or time or space or penance erased that truth. Why should I get what I wanted out of life when Pepper didn't? When I was the reason Pepper didn't?

And my family still didn't know the truth.

"Payton?"

"Sorry." I took a long sip of the coffee, savoring the warmth. "So, yeah. I'm not sleeping well. And the dreams make me anxious."

"Anxious how?"

Now Kimberlee sounded like the psychologist who used to lead group sessions at the hospital. At first, I was quiet during the sessions. Let everyone else talk. Answer the "How are you feeling today?" and "Why do you think you feel that way?" questions. But then I learned that if I wanted to get out of the hospital—if I wanted everyone to think I was fine, that I was getting over Pepper's death—I had to talk.

"How are you feeling today, Payton?"

"Better."

"Why do you think that is?"

Because that's what you want me to say. *"It's helping me to listen to other people talk."*

"How does that help you?"

Because then I don't have to talk. *"I realize I feel sad. And angry. And that I can find different ways to process my emotions."*

For once, the guy made eye contact with me. Had my answer sounded too rote? If nothing else, I was a fast learner.

I rubbed the heel of my hand against my sternum. "Talking eases some of the tightness in my chest."

"I'm glad to hear that, Payton. I hope you'll participate more in the group in the future."

"I'll try." Anything to get out of here.

"When you stare off into space like that, I'm not sure what to do." Kimberlee's voice pulled me back to the present. "Let you stay where you are or bring you back."

"I'm sorry." I held the empty mug close. "Just shake me or something."

"Right."

Kimberlee wasn't some unwelcome stranger prying into my life, jotting notes in a chart whenever I said something— notes that I never got to see. What had they written about me, anyway? Did a group of them sit around later and read over all the different scribbles?

"Maybe you should ask Pepper why she's showing up in your dreams."

"What does that mean?"

"I know it sounds a little crazy, but haven't you ever read about how powerful dreams can be? Symbolic? And you keep dreaming about Pepper. Isn't it true that twins have this special, almost-magical connection? Maybe that's still there, even though Pepper's gone."

Pepper and me. The identical, powerful Double Trouble.

"It's true, Pepper and I were close." How much of this did I want to remember? "My parents even said we had our own language when we were toddlers. Nobody else understood what we were saying, but we understood each other perfectly—or so they said."

But no relationship is perfect. And people change. And twin relationships aren't magical.

"You know what? I appreciate you listening. I really do." I eased past Kimberlee so I could rinse my empty cup and then insert a fresh pod into the Keurig. Time for caffeine, round two. "But don't you think it's time to table this 'Let's analyze Payton' discussion and get to work?"

"Why do I get the feeling you're not telling me something?"

I faced away from my friend. She was persistent. And right. I poured water into the top of the Keurig. Why not tell her the truth? Someone not involved? Kind of like a trial run. If I stumbled over my words, so be it.

As I turned, Bianca stepped through the doorway. "The Engessers are here."

"The Engessers?"

"Yes. They made an appointment to discuss their daughter's baby shower. She's having twins, remember?" Bianca held up a floral folder. "I pulled their file."

Twins. How ironic.

"Right."

"After that, Kimberlee has an appointment with the Toppers to finalize plans for their annual Christmas party."

"Right."

Decision made. Today was not the day for any truth-telling practice. I ran my fingers through my hair. The contents of my makeup bag remained spilled out across my desk. Kimberlee and Bianca—not to mention any clients—would have to put up with me going makeup-free today.

Kimberlee rose from my desk. "Tell them we'll be right with them, Bianca."

"Okay."

"And see if they want coffee—"

"Already done."

I added the last sugar to my mug. "Thanks for listening, Kimberlee."

"I can take this myself if you need some time—"

"I'm good. I mean, if you're okay with me appearing looking like this in front of the clients."

"You are a professional with or without eye shadow and mascara."

"Thanks for that. Well, let's go wow them, shall we?"

"You and me—we've got this." Kimberlee linked her arm through mine. "And remember, I'm always here to listen if you need to talk."

"I'll remember. Now let's go do what we do best and plan a party."

Jillian perched on the edge of her bed, tugging at the cuff of her cotton jacket. On a regular Monday morning, she'd be in work clothes—dress pants, a blouse and sweater, low-heeled pumps. She touched the simple gold necklace she'd added to her casual outfit. She probably didn't need that. No sense in wearing something that might interfere with today's procedure.

Her fingertips skimmed the area just below her right

collarbone, where they'd be inserting the chemotherapy port beneath her skin. About the size of a fifty-cent piece, it was supposed to make the process easier—no repeated injections. No worrying about her veins rolling or collapsing. Just one more thing to do today. One more way this wasn't a typical Monday.

She was dressed and ready to go. Now all that was left was to wait for Geoff to pick her up.

Nice of him to make time to take her to her first chemo appointment.

Jillian pressed the palms of her hands against her closed eyes. That was no way to think—and it certainly didn't fall within Harper's guidelines of positive thoughts only. Geoff wasn't avoiding her. She knew that. His work demanded long hours—and her cancer diagnosis didn't change that. If she was going to get through today, then she couldn't be mentally questioning what Geoff was or wasn't doing.

She wasn't nervous exactly, not like she'd been for her first date with Geoff. She'd paced her apartment for two hours before he'd arrived. Would he call and cancel? Would they run out of things to talk about halfway through dinner? Would he try to kiss her? Did she want him to kiss her? And what would he think if she told him she was thirty-one years old and had never been kissed?

Now Geoff was taking her to her first chemo appointment. Dr. Williamson had talked her through what to expect, but Jillian fought the urge to call the surgeon and say, "Can you explain it to me one more time?"

A wig sat on the left side of her dresser on a faceless white Styrofoam stand. The color was a little darker than her natural hair, but it was close enough. Some articles she'd read had recommended taking it to her salon and having her stylist cut it to resemble her regular hairstyle. But "thin and straight" wasn't exactly that difficult to re-create—and she wasn't even sure she'd wear the wig if . . . when she lost her hair.

Another unknown. Shouldn't she be more prepared? More decisive?

Jillian brushed her hair back from her face. She'd complained for years that it was too thin. Wished she was a towheaded blonde. Or a redhead. Or that her hair was curlier. And now that cancer was stealing it from her, she'd do anything to keep her thin, straight hair.

If she let herself stop and think about the enemy lurking inside her . . . about the ways her body might react to the chemo . . . how it might not conquer the cancer cells . . . she'd open the door to fear. But she couldn't allow dread any access to her life. She knew it waited, silent, for any opportunity to take her down. Sometimes she woke in the middle of the night, the room dark, knowing something was wrong. Terribly wrong. But for a moment she couldn't remember what it was. She rolled onto her side, her breathing shallow, blankets drawn up to her chin. And then memory returned, and with it barely controlled panic—until she sat up, turned on the lights, and found all the positive thoughts taped to her mirror.

Attitude is a little thing that makes a big difference.

Pessimism leads to weakness, optimism to power.

Don't think about what might go wrong; think about what might go right.

This too shall pass.

They didn't make her feel any braver, but they filled the silence.

When her cell phone rang, Jillian expected it to be Geoff telling her that he was here, but instead, Johanna greeted her.

"You start your chemotherapy today, don't you?"

"Yes. I'm waiting for Geoff to pick me up."

"Good. I'm glad I caught you before you left." Johanna seemed ready to dive into a lengthy conversation.

"Geoff could be here any minute. . . ." And she didn't want to rehash the idea of moving up the wedding. Not today. Besides, it was too late to do that now.

"I understand. I wanted to let you know Beckett and I were talking about some practical ways to help you the next few months while you're dealing with chemo. I know you're going to be tired, so I hired a cleaning company for you."

"You what?"

"I hired a cleaning company. I did some research and found a reputable company. They'll be calling you to figure out what day of the week you want them to come. I hope it's okay that I gave them your cell phone number, but I didn't want to make that decision for you. It's all set up for them to come in twice a month for the next four months."

"Johanna, I don't know what to say—"

"You don't have to say anything. Like I said, it's all set up.

I'll text you the info. I'm at work, so I've got to go. Make sure to let me know how today goes, okay?"

"I will."

After her sister hung up, Jillian stared at her phone. What had just happened? No *"Hello"* and *"How are you?"* No asking if she even wanted a cleaning service. Just Johanna, calling to tell her about an unexpected act of kindness that left her feeling ungrateful.

The threat of tears tightened her throat and burned the backs of her eyes. Why weren't there kinder, gentler moments like those between them? Conversations that started with a simple "Hello, how are you?" Where they talked about the latest movie they'd seen or a favorite restaurant? Times when they called each other and talked about nothing at all . . . or maybe risked talking about something troubling them, without fear of being analyzed or judged or fixed? Was growing apart just the natural result of growing up?

Jillian huddled in her bed, clutching her blankets around her. If only the room wasn't so dark. If only she could run to Mom's room. If only—

"Are you crying?" Johanna's voice whispered through the darkness.

"Ye-es."

"Why?"

"I had a bad dream."

"It was just a dream. Go back to sleep."

"I can't. I'm scared."

Her sister's sigh sounded across the room. And then Johanna slid out of her bed, crossed the room, and climbed into bed with Jillian. "Move over."

"Okay."

Her sister's arms slipped around her. "You better now?"

"Yeah."

"There's no reason to be scared. It was just a dream. Think about something nice."

"Like what?"

"Like when Dad makes us root beer floats."

"Or when we get to go shopping with Mom?"

"Yeah. Stuff like that."

Jillian shook off the memory. She and Johanna weren't little girls anymore, facing nightmares that disappeared with the morning light. Bad things didn't go away by thinking about something nice. People changed. Relationships changed. But she could accept Johanna's gift for what it was—an expression of care and concern.

On the way to the clinic, Geoff held her hand as he steered the car. "You're awfully quiet."

"Just thinking."

"About the chemo?"

"Yes . . . and no. It's hard to imagine something I've never experienced. I mean, I looked at articles and videos online, but until I actually get through the first session, I won't know what to expect."

"We'll get through this, Jillian." Geoff concentrated on the traffic. "What else is on your mind?"

"Johanna called."

Geoff stiffened. "Did she talk to you about changing the wedding date again?"

"No. She told me that she hired a cleaning service for me."

"Johanna?"

"Yes, *Johanna*." Jillian shifted in the seat. "I admit to being as surprised as you sound. But it reminded me that we used to be close . . . and it made me wonder what happened. I mean, she's not all bad."

"No, she's just all bossy, like my aunt Ro."

"Aunt Ro?"

"My mother's sister. She died when I was in college, so you'll never meet her. But what Aunt Ro said, we did."

"Do you think she's right?"

"My aunt Ro?"

"No. Johanna—is she right about needing to change the wedding date?"

"Honey, we've talked about this. We can't move the wedding. You're just starting your chemo. We're not sure how you'll feel. How tired you'll be. And you haven't found your dress yet."

She might not ever find a dress.

Maybe it wasn't about moving the wedding up. Maybe they needed to *postpone* the wedding. Maybe she wasn't going to be up to any of this. And after the chemo, she'd be facing radiation.

"What are you thinking?" Geoff squeezed her hand.

"Nothing. You're right."

Why was she thinking about postponing the wedding—

talking herself out of the one thing she'd always wanted? It wasn't that she didn't want to marry Geoff. She did.

Just not like this.

She was fighting for her life by trusting in doctors and chemicals and positive thoughts, all while her dream-come-true wedding slipped away from her. While she faded into the background.

19

THIS WAS A MISTAKE.

But I also had no choice. After what happened at the awards ceremony for Pepper—and all the other honorees— I owed Sydney for failing to come through on our agreement. Of course, if I thought about all the hours she'd coached me during high school, I'd never be able to repay her, but right now I was only thinking about the debacle eleven days ago. I didn't even know what happened after I walked out, chasing a figment of my overemotional imagination.

I didn't want to know.

"I was calling to see if you'd like to drop by and watch one of Club Brio's practices. The fourteens and sixteens teams practice on Mondays and Wednesdays. What do you think?"

I'd replayed Sydney's voice mail several times before calling her back and agreeing to come to a practice.

One.

Right after I hung up with Sydney, I wanted to call her back. Ask why she called me. What her ulterior motive was.

I should have said a polite "No, thank you" and changed the subject. Asked about her husband. Or her kids. Instead, I said, "Sounds fun."

I hadn't touched a volleyball since Pepper died. My grief had kept me from finishing out our club season. I didn't even bother to try out my senior year. I went to school, attended classes, and went home. And then I graduated, survived my last summer at home, and left for college as soon as I could.

Now, here I was, standing just inside the doorway of a rec center gym, dressed in navy sweatpants, a T-shirt, and an old pair of tennis shoes I found in the back of my closet that I'd bought the last time I decided I needed to work out.

Two volleyball nets were set up in the center of the gym, each surrounded on both sides by a group of girls in typical volleyball garb—an assortment of club T-shirts, spandex shorts, and athletic shoes, their long hair braided or pulled back in ponytails or piled on top of their heads in messy buns. The far team—the fourteens—was doing run-throughs while Sydney ran the sixteens through the "W" drill.

How many hundreds of hours had Pepper and I spent in a gym just like this one after starting club ball when we were thirteen? Conditioning, running through drills, scrimmaging with other teams. Celebrating our victories and bemoaning our defeats. Watching videos of our games so we could figure out what worked and what didn't. Celebrating team birthdays with cupcakes or cookies after practice.

Some coaches suggested to my parents that Pepper and I should split up—try playing on separate teams. But we insisted we were a duo—an identically matched set—and that we played volleyball together or not at all.

Together. Or not at all.

"Payton! You came." Sydney waved and ran over from the court to hug me.

"Of course. Thanks for the invite."

"I'm hoping you'll do more than watch tonight. I need some help."

"You need me to shag balls for you?"

"Actually, my assistant coach can't make it. Her car broke down. I was hoping you'd stand in for her."

"I don't know. I haven't played volleyball in years—"

"I'm not asking you to scrimmage with the girls." Sydney looped her arm through mine, tugging me toward the court. "I just need help running them through some drills. No matter how long it's been, you don't forget stuff like that."

No, there are some things you never forget . . . and all of this was so familiar. The sound of the girls' voices blending together. Laughter mixed with shouts of "Three, three, three!" or "I've got it!" The repeated thump of volleyballs hitting the court. The sharp squeak of skin against wood as a girl dove for a ball and slammed her body onto the floor.

Even as the word *no* formed in my mind, the word *sure* came out of my mouth. "I guess I can run some drills for you."

"Great. I thought I'd have you work with my middles."

"Okay." I ran my fingers through my hair, wishing for a headband. Or a bottle of water. Or the chance to run outside and hide in my car. "What do you want me to do?"

"Let me introduce you to my middles. They haven't been getting out to the block in time. Can you work on some of the footwork with them?"

"Sure." The real question was, would I remember the steps? "Let me, um, run to the bathroom and I'll be right back."

I fast-walked down the hall, muttering to myself, "Footwork. Footwork. What did we do?"

Once in the bathroom, I stood at one end of the elongated mirror, pretending that it was a volleyball net and that my reflection was an opponent.

Without analyzing my movements, I crossed over to the middle of the invisible "net," pushing up to block an imaginary volleyball coming across the top. I did it again, and then I slowed my steps, reciting, "Open, cross, plant, up . . ."

Just as I went up, my hands over my head, a girl wearing a Club Brio T-shirt walked into the bathroom. Our eyes met in the mirror as I landed on my feet. Neither of us said a word. She entered a stall. I exited the bathroom.

Enough practice. Time to act like I knew what I was doing.

Sydney waited with a trio of girls. I couldn't tell if they were bored or curious. "Payton, meet Jody, Katelyn, and

Tiffany. Girls, this is Payton Thatcher. She and her sister were two of the best middles I ever coached."

Huh. Nice of her to include me when she said that.

"I asked her to work with you tonight since Coach Alex couldn't make it. Pay attention. Got it?" Sydney stepped back. "I'll take the defenders to the other side of the court and slam some balls at them while you work with these guys. Sound good?"

"Perfect."

Seconds later, I faced three girls. What happened next was up to me.

What would Pepper do?

"So tell me your names again. I figure if I'm working you hard tonight, which I will—" I grinned—"I ought to remember your names."

The girls chorused their names at me, smiles on their faces.

"You and your sister played volleyball?" The tallest girl—Jody—asked the question.

"Yeah. My twin sister, Pepper."

"You have a twin sister?"

"Yes." I knew what the next question would be. "We're identical twins."

"You still play?"

"No."

"Does she?" Katelyn rearranged her ponytail as she talked.

"No—we don't."

"Why not?"

The conversation had gotten too personal too fast. Time to be the coach.

"Listen, we could stand around and talk, but I think Coach wants me to work you guys. So line up, okay? Jody, you first, then Katelyn, and then Tiffany. Let's talk about footwork. You've got one second to get to the outside. Your footwork needs to be . . ." I replayed the movements I'd practiced in the bathroom. "Open—you face the hitter. Cross—start planting your feet. Plant—anchor both feet and bend your knees to prepare to go up. Up—push off and jump."

I ran the girls through the moves several times before emphasizing their hand position—reminding them that at "open" they framed the hitter with their hands and that at "cross" and "plant" their hands lowered to provide momentum to push up when they jumped and blocked the opposing hitter.

"Your hands always stay above your head at the net." I demonstrated the position. "Okay, let's switch and do this from the right side of the net, and then we'll grab some volleyballs."

Coaching was easier than I expected. Despite being away from the sport for a decade, the skills were second nature. Good old muscle memory kicked in. Helping the girls improve their abilities reminded me of all the different coaches who had made a difference in my life.

"Tiffany, if you jump like that, you're falling into your right side. Make sure you don't float when you block. Plant that right foot and go straight up."

As they practiced the drill while holding on to a volleyball—moving in front of the net to jump and press the ball over the net before dropping it over to the other side—part of me wanted to join them. Just to feel a volleyball in my hands again. But I kept my feet on the ground and fisted my hands on my hips. I wasn't a player. I was a coach—and a very temporary one, at that.

"If you're doing this drill correctly—penetrating the net— you're engaging your core and squeezing your shoulders. You'll know you did it right if your abs are sore tomorrow."

"Thanks for that." Jody ran past me as she retrieved a stray ball.

"My pleasure."

Just then, the lights dimmed in the gym. The universal warning sign for the end of practice.

"All right, girls. Good job tonight. Go ahead and take down the nets."

I retrieved the rolling cart, depositing volleyballs in it as my contribution to cleanup. This was familiar, too. The post-workout wind-down. Girls from both teams took down the black-and-white nets, while others gathered up stray balls and disassembled the mats and poles. Sweatpants and jackets and boots covered workout gear as the noise level in the gym decreased and the girls headed for their homes—and proba-bly a late-night snack of some sort while they did homework.

"Thanks for helping out tonight, Payton." Sydney and I stood just inside the doorway, car lights sweeping across the parking lot.

"It was . . . fun."

"More fun than you expected?" Sydney slipped into her coat, pulling her long hair out so that it fell across her shoulders.

"To be honest, yes."

"Would you consider coming back?"

"Maybe." I pulled on my lightweight gloves. "I'd have to think about it. See what my work schedule is like."

"Just know you're welcome anytime. You did a great job with those girls. You're a natural."

"I was afraid I'd forgotten everything I ever knew—"

"Not gonna happen."

I shoved open the door, the cool air hitting me in the face like a jolt of reality. "I should let you get home to your family."

"You've got my number," Sydney called after me. "Call before you come—or just show up."

She was assuming I'd come back.

Maybe I would. I hadn't realized how much I missed the sport. All of it. Entering a gym full of teen girls walking, talking, *playing* volleyball. Their backpacks stitched with the Club Brio logo, their water bottles tossed alongside. The easy camaraderie. Jokes. Laughter. Pats on the back. Competition as the teams divided and lined up on either side of the net, girls rotating from back row to front row. Even the parents sitting on the metal bleachers, cheering their daughters on when they made a good serve or block.

So familiar. I almost heard the echo of Pepper's voice follow me to my car. *Great practice tonight, Pay! I can't wait for the tournament this weekend.*

With a shake of my head, I dispelled the thoughts. What had I been thinking? I had no right to visit Sydney's club tonight. To help out. To have so much fun with those three girls as I ran them through the drills.

No right to want to go back.

⌒

"You have fun tonight?"

Pepper—asking the very question I dreaded. But where was she? I couldn't see her in the all-encompassing blackness, so I stood still.

"Did you?"

"Are we having this conversation in the dark?"

The lights came up and there she was, facing away from me, at the back of a court, next to a cart filled with white-and-blue volleyballs. She could have been a Club Brio member in her white T-shirt and navy-blue spandex, her hair in its familiar long braid. She picked up a ball, balanced it on her palm, turning it around in her hands. Raised it up and then, in one fluid movement, jumped and served it over the net.

"Yes. I had a good time."

Pepper ignored my answer. Picked up another ball. Took her time and launched another serve. "I always knew you'd be a good coach."

"I'm not a coach." I retrieved a ball, lining up on the other side of the cart. I used to have a killer serve—even better than Pepper's.

"You wanted to be. What happened?"

Pepper was asking me that?

My palm slammed against the ball so that it skimmed across the top of the net and banged into the opposite wall.

"Too hard, Pay. That would have been out."

My second serve hit the wall again.

"Why aren't you coaching?"

"I quit volleyball after . . . after you died."

"Why?"

My serve went wide.

"Pepper, you know why." *My voice broke.* "You're dead because of me."

"That's not true—"

"Yes, it is. I was the one who was supposed to race that night—not you."

"It was my choice, Payton."

"It's my fault."

"So I died . . . and you stopped living, too?"

I picked up another volleyball, ready to send it across the net.

"That's crazy thinking. You might as well have been on the snowmobile with me."

"I wish I had been."

"Don't say that. That's not how it works."

"Don't tell me how things work!" *I dropped the volleyball, and it bounced a few feet away.* "Nothing's worked since you died, Pepper. I don't know how to do me without you. . . . Don't you get it?"

"You start by telling the truth."

"What?"

"Tell the truth."

The lights went out in the gym.

I jolted awake. My laptop lay at my feet on the couch. So much for my plan to stay awake.

"Tell the truth." After ten years of hiding everything from my parents, how was I supposed to tell them what had happened the night Pepper died? For all these years, it seemed easier to bear the weight of the secret myself. No matter how much I wanted to confess how I had caused Pepper's death, I couldn't figure out how to start the conversation. How to revisit that night.

But I wasn't the only one who knew what had happened. The reality was like a slow-burning fuse in the back of my mind. Zach Gaines knew what I'd done. Maybe not the entire story—all the whys and hows—but he knew Pepper had pretended to be me. He'd thought I was the one injured in the crash . . . until I'd come running across the field, fallen to my knees, and screamed my sister's name.

20

ZACH LEANED BACK in his chair, studying the 3-D rendering of the built-in bookshelves surrounding a fireplace in a family room. Did he continue working with the existing fireplace or suggest a new design to complement the overall flow of the shelves? It was the first week of October—how much did he want to mess with the project timeline?

The light on the phone on his desk lit up, indicating an incoming call. Decision postponed for the moment.

"3:17 Cabinets, this is Zach Gaines."

"That was very professional, Mr. Gaines."

"Payton?" Zach straightened, righting his chair.

A brief muffled laugh came through the phone. "I'm

sorry. I just haven't ever heard you sound so businesslike before."

"Well, thank you, I guess." Zach opted to keep this lighthearted tone going. This was a new version of Payton. "What can I help you with, Miss Thatcher? Were you so impressed with my skills that you decided to redo your kitchen?"

Even as he waited for her answer, he glimpsed the edge of his tattoo beneath his shirtsleeve and breathed a silent prayer. Payton might sound cheerful, but they were the merest of friends. Who knew why she was calling?

"I kept thinking about your offer when I was at your cabin—" Payton's words were rushed—"to go see the bench you made for Pepper . . ."

He couldn't have been more surprised if she had asked him to build her cabinets. "Yes?"

"And I'd like to come see it . . . please."

Silence. Try as he might, he couldn't think of anything to say.

"Are you still there?"

"Yes. I'm just surprised."

"I can understand that, considering how less than two weeks ago I refused when you asked if I wanted to see the bench." Payton paused. "But now . . ."

"I'd love for you to see the bench. When were you thinking of coming up?"

"Would tomorrow work for you?"

"Tomorrow?" She kept surprising him. "Saturday?"

"Yes. Is that too soon? You're probably busy—"

"No. I'm not busy." And even if he was, he'd cancel anything he was doing. "Tomorrow is fine."

Their conversation was as awkward as if this were their first dance together. They kept trying to avoid tripping over one another's virtual toes, not sure who was leading and who was following.

Was there something else Payton wanted to talk about?

The question rose in his mind. Hovered. But Zach pressed his lips together and waited. All she'd asked to do was to see the bench. Nothing more. He wouldn't presume. Wouldn't pressure her.

"Why don't you come up midmorning?"

"That's fine. And then you don't have to worry about feeding me breakfast."

"I should warn you that I still don't have any tofu in the house if you get hungry."

"Do you want me to pick up any on my way?"

"Don't bother. Really."

With a laugh, they hung up. Tapping his fingers on the desk beside his keyboard, Zach stared at the computer screen but saw Payton Thatcher's face.

What was that about?

For requesting something so serious, Payton had been almost too upbeat. When he'd asked her to go see the bench the first time, she'd flinched.

"I can't . . . I really think I should just leave—"

He swiped his hand across his face and eased out of his

chair, heading toward his friend's office. Maybe Colin could help him figure this out, as he'd done so many other things.

With a sharp rap, Zach half opened the door. "Hey, do you have a minute?"

Colin pushed back from his desk, a welcoming smile on his face. "Absolutely. Come on in."

"Thanks." Zach couldn't help but take a moment to admire the view of the aspens turning color outside the office, backed up by snowcapped mountain peaks.

"Is this about work?" Colin twirled a pen between his fingers like a mini baton.

"No." Zach forced his attention back to his waiting coworker. "It's about Payton Thatcher."

"Oh?"

Zach had to give Colin credit for his understated reaction, but it wasn't as if they hadn't talked about her. "She just called and asked to see the bench I made—the one you helped me with."

"In honor of her twin sister, right?"

"Yes. Remember how I told you that she showed up at my cabin almost two weeks ago?" When his friend nodded, Zach continued, pacing back and forth in front of Colin's desk. "And when I invited her to go see the bench, she said no—and almost ran to her car. Now she wants to see it."

"So?"

"What do you think is going on?"

"Why do you think something is going on? Maybe she wasn't ready the first time you asked her and now she is."

"But she didn't sound like herself."

"Meaning?"

"She was almost . . . friendly. That woman does not want to be my friend."

"Okay. Or maybe something is going on . . ."

"Why is it I can never get a straight answer from you?"

"I did give you a straight answer—two of them. Look, maybe Payton Thatcher suddenly decided to be your friend."

"Right."

"Or maybe she decided she wants to see the bench . . . and she's nervous. And she's covering that up by going all friendly on you. It's as simple as that." Colin stood, coming to stand in front of Zach. "Enough pacing. How about I pray for you?"

"That would be great."

Colin rested his hand on Zach's shoulder. And as he had so many times before, he talked to God in a quiet, sure voice as if He were standing in the room with them.

"You know why Payton called Zach today, God. Help him to be the friend she needs. May her heart find healing and hope. Amen."

The closer I got to Winter Park, the faster and thicker the snowflakes fell from the gray sky overhead. The wipers beat a steady rhythm against the windshield, the scenery fading to white as I sipped coffee and let Keith Urban sing about boys getting a truck.

Of course, I'd left Denver that morning, not once thinking that it might snow in the mountains.

I slowed down, other cars passing me by and tossing dirty snow onto my windshield. Bad weather or not, I was going to see Pepper's bench. Confront the past. Find a way to tell the truth.

But what would be gained when I did so? What would be lost?

When I arrived and parked alongside Zach's truck, Laz greeted me by running around in circles. Zach shook his head at my sleeveless down vest and low boots, leading me into the cabin, despite my protests that I was fine.

"You must be the only person living in Colorado who doesn't check the weather report." Zach's voice was muffled as he dug through the hall closet.

"Very funny."

"Here." Zach offered me an oversize winter jacket, a pair of gloves, and a knit cap. "This should keep you warm enough. My mom always kept spare things up here, and I never got around to cleaning out the closet."

"Thanks." I slid the coat over my vest, pulling the hat over my ears. "You're sure I'm not keeping you from anything?"

"Yep. I try not to work on projects on the weekend unless I absolutely have to." Zach zipped up his coat, pulling a pair of gloves out of one of the pockets. "What about you? No events this weekend?"

"Kimberlee is doing some prep today for a celebration

tomorrow. Bianca—she's our receptionist—is helping her. We'll talk tonight about what else needs to be done."

"You two are a good team."

"It's a good arrangement."

Zach held open the cabin door. "You about ready?"

Ready? No. Determined? "Yes."

Laz ran ahead of us the moment we stepped outside, barking and kicking up little puffs of snow.

"We're heading that way." Zach motioned toward the cluster of trees at the far end of the field behind the cabin.

"Right."

If Zach was hoping for me to chat, he'd be disappointed. This was like my dream . . . the one where I was searching for Pepper. Only it wasn't dark. No. Instead, I was outside in the Colorado mountains, snow falling all around me. Zach Gaines walking alongside me. And I wasn't looking for Pepper.

I was looking for some way to face my past so I could face my family.

My steps slowed the closer we got to our destination. It was as if something . . . the truth, maybe . . . weighed me down. My chest hurt, and I struggled to take a deep breath.

Zach matched his steps to mine. "You okay, Payton?"

"Yes."

I'd come this far. I wasn't turning back. Wasn't escaping to my car. Wasn't going back to what I'd lived like for the past ten years. No more dodging memories. Or closing my eyes, my heart, to what had happened. Maybe . . . maybe if

I returned to the scene of my crime, I could—what? Absolve myself of my sins?

My steps faltered . . . stopped.

Something was different. What was it?

The stretch of trees ended abruptly in a staggered row of severed trunks. In front of the stumps, facing away from the cabin and toward the expanse of the Rocky Mountains, stood the bench Zach had made for Pepper.

"What happened to the trees?"

"I . . . I chopped them down." Zach stared at the horizon. "It was a type of physical therapy. Or a whole new form of anger management. I spent five years dulling my emotions with alcohol. Once I stopped drinking, I had to figure out how to deal with the memories. My anger. My regret. You spend all day swinging an ax, you don't have any energy left except to eat whatever's in the fridge, take a shower—maybe—and go to sleep."

"What did you do with the wood?"

"I burned most of it in the fireplace." Zach moved forward and rested his hands on the back of the bench. "And I used some of it to make this."

Zach had transformed the tree into a bench. Pepper's bench. My knees buckled and I stumbled forward, allowing Zach to guide me. He brushed a layer of snow from the seat, helping me sit before I fell to my knees.

When Zach said he'd made a bench to commemorate Pepper, I'd envisioned some sedate bench with wooden slats and wrought-iron arms—the kind of thing I'd seen hundreds of times set near a park lake, creating an idyllic scene.

But this . . . this bench was part tree, part memorial, with its rough edges and polished surfaces. The inner veins of the tree glistened gold, umber, and brown on the back and the seat, while two pieces of the trunk held the bench in place.

I removed my gloves, my fingertips finding a few stray snowflakes as I traced the design of the wood. "This isn't what I expected. . . ."

Zach sat beside me, leaving space between us. "I'm sorry if you don't like it—"

"No. No, I didn't say that. I think it's perfect."

Neither of us said anything for a few moments, snowflakes falling around us, until Zach broke the silence. "Why did you decide to come up here today, Payton?"

"I'm trying . . . trying to tell the truth. To *finally* tell the truth."

"The truth?"

"About what happened that night. All these years I've struggled with wanting to forget . . . and needing to remember. . . ."

Where was Pepper? Not at the hot chocolate station set up behind the cabin. Not watching the snowmobile races. And not among the group of kids circled around the bonfire. Shaking my head, I exhaled a breath that appeared in the air as a small white cloud. I didn't come to Zach Gaines's spring break party to spend my time looking for my twin.

One last "Have you seen my sister?" directed me inside the cabin, where she sat talking with several other girls, including Tari—one of her new friends. She was laughing. Relaxed. When was the last time she and I had sat around and talked like that?

But when I waited at one end of the brown cloth couch so Pepper could see me, she ignored me. What was going on? Pepper was nice to everyone, saying hi to people she barely knew. Being my twin didn't give her the right to act like I was invisible.

"Pepper." I raised my voice. "Can I talk to you for a minute?"

"Now?"

"Yes, now. I just need a minute."

Pepper smiled at her friends. "I'll be right back."

A moment later, we stood in the small kitchen decorated with rooster statues and graphics, Pepper leaning against the counter while I paced the room. "If you want to sit around talking, you could have stayed home."

"What do you care if I hang with friends and play a board game?"

"You can do that at home, too."

"Did you find me so you could criticize what I'm doing tonight?"

I needed to calm down—especially if I was going to talk my sister into my plan. "No. It's just, I'm signed up to do one of the snowmobile races, against Zach Gaines, but I don't want to do it now. Take my place, okay?"

"What? No." Pepper emphasized her words with a quick shake of her head. "Do your own race."

"Oh, come on, Pepper. They're doing a contest of some sort, or

I'd forfeit. It's one race. We haven't switched places in years—and no one will even know."

"We're not little kids anymore. . . ."

What was wrong with her? We used to have fun together, and now she wouldn't do this one little thing? The whole time we were talking, she kept glancing back at her friends.

"I know we're not kids anymore, Pepper."

"Besides, it's not honest."

"Are you kidding me?"

"Don't shout."

"I'm not shouting." I lowered my voice to a rough whisper. "I'm asking you to race for me, not rob a bank or vandalize property."

"You know what I mean."

"No, I don't. And sometimes I don't know . . ." I stopped. "Never mind."

"Sometimes you don't know what?"

"I'm not getting into this here. Would you please—" my teeth were clenched—"switch places with me for one snowmobile race so I could go to the bonfire?"

"Payton—"

"You've had a chance to be with your friends for a while. Why can't I hang out with mine?"

"Your friends . . . or Brice?"

"It's a bonfire. And he might be there."

"I don't like to race. . . ."

The person I was talking to looked like my twin sister. She even sounded like my twin sister—at least her voice did. But the Pepper I knew was always up for a joke or a good time.

THINGS I NEVER TOLD YOU

"Go slow. Don't win."

"Right. Then people will really think it's you."

"Just do the race."

"I thought you were asking me."

I turned my back on Pepper, only stopping when she sighed and agreed. Asked for my coat to pull off the switch. There was no camaraderie. No "This is going to be so fun" moment. No shared laughter and hug.

And I never shared anything with Pepper ever again.

Someone was shaking me.

Zach gripped my arms, his face close to mine. "Payton. Payton. Come on. Snap out of it."

"What?"

"You were quiet at first . . . and then you started talking about the night Pepper died." Zach released me, half-turning away and swiping his hand down his face. "At least, you were telling me about switching places—"

I dropped my face into my hands, my skin heating at the thought that I'd said any of that out loud. I couldn't look at him. Any minute now, he'd get up and walk away from me. I'd spilled out the ugly truth—at least part of it—while seated on a bench made from the tree Pepper had collided with.

"It's my fault Pepper died." I lowered my voice, afraid my words would turn into a scream. "I never told my family about switching places with Pepper—about why. Or about how we argued. They met us at the emergency clinic, and by that time . . . by that time, she was already dead . . ."

My voice faded. Laz had returned, sitting at my feet, nuzzling my hand until I buried my fingers in the soft fur at his throat. Zach's silence was an invisible barrier between us. He probably hated me. My immature actions—wanting to spend time with a stupid guy, hoping he would kiss me—had killed my sister . . . and derailed Zach's life, too, for a time.

⁓

Laz moved closer to Payton, resting his furry black head dusted with snow on her knee as she rubbed his fur. His body leaned against her legs. How many times had the dog instinctively sought Zach out, sitting beside him in silence, when darkness had descended in his mind?

Only when Payton's other hand pressed against her face, her fingers trembling, did Zach realize she was crying. Oh, he understood that kind of pain. The torment that could keep you awake at night. Stop you from attending family gatherings . . . birthdays and holidays . . . Always providing an excuse to avoid going home and hearing the unspoken words that echoed with even more unanswered questions and unmet expectations.

"Payton, I know what it's like to disappoint your parents." He stopped. Cleared his throat. Started again, hoping she was listening. "My parents . . . my dad was so proud I earned a full-ride scholarship. And then when I spiraled out of control after what happened during spring break and partied it all away . . . flunked out of my college classes . . . lost the scholarship . . ."

"You didn't kill your sister."

Her words brought him up short. Payton was listening, all right, but she was having none of it.

"No. But I wrecked the relationship between me and my dad. Between me and my mom. She's caught between the two of us. She loves my dad. Still loves me. Although I don't know why." He switched tactics. "Besides, if I'd watched out for you that night, things might have been different."

"Watched out for me? You wanted the volleyball team to come to the party because you liked Bailey Davis, from what I'd heard. You weren't responsible for me."

Zach said nothing, but he could still hear Brice warning him to steer clear of Payton. "No. Brice invited the team—and I knew he was, um, interested in you."

"So? It wasn't your job to babysit me." Payton leaned forward, staring at the ground.

"Well, I shouldn't have been drinking. None of us should have been." He leaned forward too, elbows on his knees, hands clasped. "Back then I thought a couple of beers was no big deal."

"Why did your parents let you drink that night?"

"They didn't know—not until after the accident."

"But they covered for you?"

"Yeah. It was all about the scholarship."

"How stupid can you be, Zach? You're going to lose everything you worked so hard for!"

Did his dad even care about what—who—the Thatchers had lost?

He'd kept his dad happy. Kept his scholarship . . . for a time.

Zach clenched his jaw and then inhaled, exhaling a small white puff of air, trying to release the pressure building up inside him.

No root of bitterness. So often pastors preached about not letting bitterness toward another person grow in your heart. But he'd had to learn not to become embittered toward himself. His own actions. He'd spent months digging up the resentment and anger that had wrapped around his heart, strangling hope and peace and the ability to forgive himself.

Zach faced Payton on the bench, sliding closer, daring to rest his gloved hand on hers, ignoring how she flinched. "Payton, your sister's death wasn't your fault. Everyone made choices that night. Each one had consequences. Yes, you told Pepper to take your place, but Pepper could have said no. And maybe you're better at racing, but it's not like Pepper had never been on a snowmobile before. Did you know the police said they don't think her helmet was fastened properly?"

Payton's eyes widened at his question.

"And I was stupid, too. I know I'd only had a couple of beers, and I probably scared Pepper because I was going faster than I needed to—"

"Because you thought it was me—"

"No. Because I raced fast. All the time."

Some people believed the eyes were the window to a person's soul. When she looked at him, Payton's eyes were blank, her soul starving for truth. He knew what truth she needed.

But she also needed forgiveness. Hope. How was he going to reach her? He needed to go slow. Choose the right words. Temper grace with caution.

Zach rubbed his arm where his tattoo was. Whenever he considered a special woodworking project, like the table he was making for the living room in the cabin, he examined the piece of wood. Studied the grain, trying to imagine what he'd discover as he worked with the wood, staining it, polishing it . . . always considering the finished piece.

Payton Thatcher was so much more valuable than any woodworking project—and God wasn't finished with her yet. She just didn't realize it.

"Payton, you are not more powerful than God. You don't hold life and death in your hands. He decides when people are born and when they die—"

"You're saying God killed my sister?"

"No, that's not what I'm saying." At least, that's not what he meant for it to sound like. "Pepper's death was an accident, brought on by people's choices. Yours. Mine. Pepper's. But you're still here, Payton, and that's because God has a plan for your life—"

Payton shook her head. "Zach, I told you I don't do God."

"But I do." Zach paused. His hand still rested on Payton's. "If you were honest with yourself right now, you'd admit that you're miserable. That nothing's been right for a long time. But that was probably true even before Pepper died—"

Payton gasped, pulling her hand away. "Why would you say that?"

"Because life is always out of balance until we realize we need God. You haven't been living your life since Pepper died. How much have you given up? Avoided?"

"Stop talking about all this, Zach."

"You're not going to find any peace until you do two things."

"And what do you think I have to do?" She asked the question, but her voice dared him to answer.

"Tell your family the truth."

She must have accepted his answer. "And what's the second thing?"

"Do you think, after all these years, that you have the strength to tell your family the truth?"

"Are you offering to come with me?"

"I would, if I thought it would help." Zach waited until Payton made eye contact with him. "Take a good long look at who God is and decide what you believe about Him."

"Oh, so God's going to help me tell my family?"

"He will if you ask Him to."

"I don't think God, if there is a god, would listen to me, Zach."

"He will. Talk to Him."

"Right. Me, talk to God. I barely talk to my family. I'm not sure I want to take on some all-powerful, invisible force I don't believe in—"

"Payton. God is powerful. But He also loves you. He created you. He offers you grace that erases your guilt. I'd still be wallowing in alcohol and regret if I hadn't come face-to-face with God."

"Face-to-face with God, huh?" Payton's words mocked him. "Just how did you do that?"

"Someone told me his story—how God changed him. And I wanted change, too. He said—"

Payton shook her head, holding up her hand. "I'm sorry, but I'm not up to any stories today."

"I wasn't trying to push you." Colin had prayed for Zach to be the kind of friend Payton needed. Today he needed to listen, not talk. "I knew coming here would be hard."

"My sister would have loved this bench, Zach. Thank you." Payton's shoulders shifted as she sighed. "Can I ask you something?"

"Sure."

"Do you miss running cross-country?"

Why was she asking him that? "Competitively? No. I still run for the fun of it." Maybe answering her question earned him the right to ask one. Should he risk it? "Do you miss volleyball?"

She stood, indicating she was ready to head back to the cabin. "If you'd asked me a week ago, I would have said no. But that was before . . ."

"Before?"

"Before I helped my high school volleyball coach run a club practice. And don't ask how that happened. All I can say is I showed up to watch, and the next thing I knew, I was putting three middles through their paces."

"And after that you realized you missed volleyball?"

"Yes. When I played in high school, I'd thought about

coaching, but . . . but I gave that up." Her boots scuffed through the snow. "It's not that I don't like my job. I do."

"Could you get back into coaching now?"

"I don't know. But Sydney—my coach—told me to come back to practice anytime I wanted."

"Will you?"

"Maybe. If I have time."

Payton seemed willing to talk as long as the topic remained casual. Fine. He'd follow her lead.

Once they were back at her car, she declined his invitation to come inside.

"It's a long drive home and we both have other things to do." Payton opened the car door, slipping behind it. "Thank you for showing me the bench."

"You're welcome. Feel free to come back up anytime."

"Thanks."

"Drive safely."

She gazed up at the sky, where blue patches were appearing between the clouds. "It's stopped snowing, so the drive back will be nicer than the drive here."

"Just be careful." He stepped away, hoping he didn't sound like a parent.

"Wait. I need to give you your gloves . . . the coat . . ."

He waved her back into the car. "Stay warm. I'll be seeing you again, right?"

"Right." Her answer was hesitant. "Sure. Take care, Zach."

"You, too, Payton." He lowered his voice to a whisper as she closed the door. "I'll be praying for you."

21

ALL THE SNOW reported in the mountains a week ago—and here in the Springs, nothing. The roads had been clear. Dry. And still no hint of any snow to come. The sun shone bright, dappling the autumn leaves in the trees lining the streets leading to Jillian's parents' house.

How fun it would have been to run away and see snow. Drive up to Breckenridge or even Aspen.

Wishful thinking. She had a wedding to plan. And her second chemo appointment tomorrow.

"You told your parents that I was making chili, right?"

Geoff's question cut through Jillian's thoughts. "I'm sorry, what?"

"Chili. You let them know we were bringing chili . . . ?"

When exactly had she stopped listening to him? Let her thoughts wander to other things? Like snow in the mountains. Their wedding. And chemotherapy.

"Jill?"

"Yes?"

"Is there something on your mind?"

"I'm sorry. I was just thinking . . ."

"About?"

"I was thinking we should postpone the wedding."

"What?" Geoff, ever calm, never slowed the car. Kept driving to her parents', his voice even as if she'd asked about going for a drive up into the mountains. "Why? The nausea was minimal from your first chemo treatment—"

"Yes, but things are likely to get worse as time goes on. Johanna called and reminded me of all the possible side effects."

Lack of appetite.

Mouth sores.

Headaches.

Skin sensitivity.

And those were the less serious ones—she didn't want to think about the conversation with the oncologist.

"Sometimes your older sister ticks me off." Geoff's voice was tight.

"She meant well."

"Right." Geoff cleared his throat. "No matter what, you're going to get through this—"

"I'm going to need radiation once I'm done with chemo." Reciting positive thoughts had failed to soften the blow of that pronouncement. "And I . . . I just can't handle one more thing."

Cancer had reduced her wedding to *one more thing*.

"When do you want to postpone it to? The summer?"

"I was thinking later than that." Jillian tried to keep her tone casual. As if postponing their wedding was no big deal.

"The fall?"

This was so like Geoff. Nothing discouraged him. *"We'll get through this. You can do this."* He kept working. She kept working. And now she was suggesting they postpone their wedding and he took it all in stride. So loyal—dogging her heels no matter what she did or said that should deter him.

"Why does he keep calling me?" Her question came in the middle of a regular Girls' Night after she and Geoff had been dating for two months.

"Are you asking me why Geoff Hennessey keeps asking you out?" Harper paused the DVD they'd been watching. "Duh. He likes you."

"But why? There are other women he could ask out. Cuter women. Women who are—"

"Stop right there. If you say he could ask out women who are skinnier than you, I swear I will toss this bowl of popcorn in your lap." Harper raised the container high over her head.

"There are."

"Geoff keeps calling you because he likes you. A lot. You just have to believe it."

After a while, she had believed it. But now, the doubt had crept back in. Why was he staying through all of this? It didn't make sense. If she could duck and run, she'd leave herself, but she had no choice. Geoff did. Was love keeping him by her side, or was he staying because he was so faithful that he wouldn't leave her during chemo treatments? Didn't he realize she'd rather he leave her now, than stick around, celebrating her survival—if they did get to celebrate it—and then leaving?

"Jill?"

"Yes . . . yes, I think we should postpone the wedding until the fall." She twisted her engagement ring around her finger.

"Do you want to pick another date?"

"We're almost to my parents', so what if we look at the calendar later?"

"That's fine. Once we do, I can call the vendors—"

"We'll figure it out."

She'd suggested they postpone the wedding, and Geoff agreed—almost too easily. Was he agreeable . . . or relieved?

As they parked in her parents' driveway, Jillian gathered her strength. She needed to find a way to smile and assure her mother she was doing okay. To pay attention to the Broncos game. At least she wouldn't have to worry about her sisters bickering. Payton hadn't shown up for a family football Sunday in years.

The house looked the same. White paint. Black shutters anchoring the windows. The front door was decorated with a new fall wreath of red-and-orange leaves dotted with small black berries, which meant Johanna had decided it was time to update the old one.

The aroma of one of her mother's favorite eucalyptus candles greeted them, along with the background noise of commentators discussing the upcoming game.

Her mother met them just inside the doorway and hugged her, smiling at Geoff as he carried in the Crock-Pot of chili.

Geoff nodded at her mother. "I'll put this in the kitchen for later."

"How are you feeling?" Jillian's mother pulled away from her, holding on to her shoulders.

"I'm fine."

"You can rest if you need to—"

"I'm fine, really. Ready for tomorrow."

Johanna appeared in the hallway. "Oh, good. You're here. You know how Dad likes everyone to be here before the kickoff."

Jillian followed her mother and Johanna into the family room. "I don't suppose Beckett made it down this weekend, did he?"

"No. But I'm planning to go visit him for Thanksgiving and then he'll come here for Christmas."

"That'll be nice for you two to see each other for both holidays."

"Yes, he's planning on staying through New Year's."

Jillian picked the love seat, knowing Geoff would settle on the floor in front of her and get caught up in the football game, right along with her father. She could fade into the background. No one would be surprised if she dozed off before the end of the first quarter. The important thing was that she was here, upholding—enjoying—the family tradition.

⌒

I couldn't remember the last time I'd been home for a family football Sunday.

Wait. Yes, I could. I'd bowed out the year I went away for college. I didn't need to invent any excuses, thanks to classes and studying and "things." And from then on, I made certain "things" always interfered with any plans to make it home to cheer on the Broncos and eat grilled burgers or brats or one of my mom's homemade soups.

Which was exactly what I walked in on—my family sitting in front of the TV, the aroma of spicy chili filling the air.

The Broncos made it all the way down to the red zone before anyone noticed me standing in the back of the family room.

"Payton!" Mom jumped from her seat and rushed over to hug me as if I'd disappear before she had the chance to wrap me in her arms. "When did you get here?"

"Payton?" Jillian turned, a smile curving her lips. She looked good. "How wonderful to see you."

For just a moment, I allowed myself to rest in Mom's arms instead of short-circuiting her attempt to hold me. Cherished the welcome in Dad's voice. After years of avoidance, my parents thought I was here to watch football. They might wonder why . . . but they thought all I wanted to do was spend the afternoon rooting for the Broncos with my family. Well, once I made my confession, my mea culpa, I wouldn't be welcome back for another football game . . . or Thanksgiving . . . or Christmas . . . or possibly ever again.

Would Mom want to hug me—would she be able to touch me?

I had to do this. Telling everyone the truth was the reason I'd come today. Not for burgers or chili. Not because I cared if our favorite football team won. Not for any familial togetherness, which had been missing for so long.

"Do you want something to eat? Geoff made chili." My arrival had managed to pull Dad away from the game.

"That's not part of her diet anymore, Dad." Johanna stood off to one side. "Coffee?"

"That'd be great."

"I'll bring the sugar bowl, too. I know you'll want to sweeten it the way you like."

I could see Johanna's offer as a gibe—or as a simple offer, nothing more. Today was not about bickering with Johanna over how many sugars I tossed into my coffee. I accepted Jillian's invitation to sit on the love seat next to her, Geoff shifting on the floor to sit closer to her.

"We're almost to halftime."

In other words, no talking until then.

It had been a week—eight long days—since I'd visited Zach. Seen the bench he'd made for Pepper. Unburied the memories of the night she died. Convinced myself that, at last, I would tell my family the truth. Each day I'd battled the soft yet insistent voice urging me to stay quiet. But if I did, the truth would be silenced forever.

My heartbeat seemed in sync with the play clock, starting and stopping with the referee's whistle.

25 . . . 24 . . . 23 . . . 22 . . .

Time-out.

Say. It. Say. It.

Wait.

I'd held on to the secret for so long, how was I supposed to release it now? It was as if I'd spent years leaning against a door, using all my weight to hold it shut, refusing to let the door open and the light shine inside. Let the truth be known. And now I was supposed to step away from the door? Stop exerting so much energy to hide what had happened?

Halftime came. The sportscasters began evaluating the game. And I remained silent, letting Johanna talk about work, Dad and Geoff discuss plays, Mom offer seconds of the chili. Jillian joined me in the silence zone.

"You start by telling the truth."

I jerked as if everyone else in the room had heard my sister's words. Pepper's whisper jolted me into action.

"I, um, actually came over today because I wanted to talk to you—all of you—about something." With everyone now looking at me, I pressed my fingertips against my lips, trying to swallow the lump in my throat.

"Payton, if this is about what happened at the awards cere-mony—" Mom reached out to touch my arm, but I leaned away, raising my hand to stop her from saying anything else. From offering words of comfort.

"No. No, it's not about that." I paused again. I'd started something and I had to finish it. "It's about Pepper . . . and the night she died."

No matter what my family had expected me to say, they hadn't expected me to mention Pepper. I never talked about my twin sister.

Dad muted the TV. "Go on, Payton. We're listening."

"That night, I was supposed to be racing the snowmobile, not Pepper. But I convinced her to . . . to trade places with me because . . . because there was this boy I liked. I wanted to hang out with him." I stared straight ahead, unable to look at my parents' faces, the image of football replays on the TV screen blurring. "So even though I knew she didn't like racing . . . even though she didn't want to at first . . . we switched coats. She raced. Instead of me. It's my fault Pepper was killed. . . . I should have been on the snowmobile, not Pepper."

With every word I spoke, it was as if time slowed down more and more. In some ways, this was worse than a flashback. This was here. Now.

And I couldn't escape the fact I'd confessed to my family that my actions had killed my sister.

Silence reigned in the room. So similar to the silence that greeted me in the house—in my bedroom— for months after Pepper died. Jillian and Johanna had gone back to their apartments, to their lives. Dad was at work, Mom in her room—resting. The only thing that greeted me when I came home from school every day was silence. And the unalterable truth of what I'd done.

What had I expected my parents, my sisters, to do? To say? I didn't deserve anything else from my family.

"Payton . . ." My name was a whispered gasp on Mom's lips. "Payton . . . you've held on to this for all these years?"

I stared at my clenched fists.

"Pepper's death . . . it was an accident." Dad's voice overrode Mom's. "Listen to me, Payton. It was an *accident*."

"Dad, it's my fault—"

He spoke again. "I could just as easily say it was my fault because I let you and your sister go away with the volleyball team for spring break. Do you know how many nights I used to lie awake in bed and think, if only I'd said no when you two asked to go? If only I'd made you and Pepper stay home and play board games?"

His words chipped away at the condemnation I'd carried for the past decade. "What?"

"All this time I felt like I lost two daughters that night." Dad shook his head. "I just thought you were brokenhearted about Pepper. . . . I never thought you *blamed* yourself."

"You didn't know—"

Mom reached for me again. "No. No, but now we do. And I'm thankful you told us. . . . I just wished we'd known sooner." She moved from her chair and drew me closer. "I know it won't ever be the same without Pepper, but maybe, maybe we can figure out what our family looks like now."

This time I relaxed into Mom's embrace. Her hand caressed my back in a slow circular motion, her tears wetting the shoulder of my blouse. How long had it been since I let myself rest in her arms instead of allowing myself only a partial hug before backing away?

"I'm sorry, Mom. . . ."

"Shhh, baby, shhh . . ."

Tears stung my eyes, but instead of blinking them away, I let them fall. For me. For Pepper. For everything we lost the night she died. For everything my secret had stolen from our family.

White crystals descended from the sky, sparkling in the moonlight and dusting the ground. A perfect way to end the day. The day that offered me a chance to begin again.

With one last wave to Geoff as he helped Jillian into his car, I stepped onto my parents' front lawn. Tilted my face up to the night sky, welcoming the whisper of tiny snowflakes floating down against my skin. Like a small child, I stuck out my tongue, tasting the wet, cold flakes as I flung my arms open wide.

If I believed in supernatural forgiveness, would it feel like this hushed silence finding its way into my heart like a heavenly benediction?

Behind me, the front door opened. Closed.

"You're telling secrets now." Johanna's voice shattered the

stillness. "Are you going to share all your secrets with the family?"

I sought my sister where she stood on the front steps, overshadowed by the porch. "What . . . what are you talking about?"

"Oh, come on, Payton, don't act like that with me." Johanna's eyes glittered in the porch light. "You know what I'm talking about. You're not the only one who knows your deepest, darkest secret."

Why was she talking like this?

"Johanna, you're not making any sense."

Out of the corner of my eye, the taillights of Geoff's car disappeared around the corner. If only I'd left sooner, instead of chasing some imaginary sense of blessing, I would have avoided this confrontation with my oldest sister. But this was what Johanna did best. She always found a reason to bait me.

Not tonight. Tonight I was going home and sleeping a sweet, dreamless sleep. I'd done what Pepper had demanded of me.

I was free.

"You want me to say it? Fine." Johanna stepped out of the shadows. "I read your journal, Payton."

Any lingering sense of consecration evaporated. "What did you say?"

"The journal you kept in high school? I read it." Step by step, Johanna came closer. "I know you were going to kill yourself after Pepper died."

Johanna's declaration seared through my mind. "You had no right—"

"I had every right! Mom and Dad were distraught over losing Pepper—one of their precious twin daughters. Was I just supposed to let you kill yourself and completely tear this family apart?"

I sucked in a cold, sharp breath, trying to comprehend the depth of Johanna's transgression. This wasn't my big sister taking charge of the remote control and what TV shows we watched. Or bossing me around about my sugar addiction. Or questioning my decision to become vegan. *No.* Johanna thought it was her right to invade my privacy . . . delve into my innermost thoughts. To play God and control my life and death.

"I told Mom and Dad that you weren't doing as well as they thought after Pepper died. As well as you were pretending to do. I'd researched several options and they decided to send you to that adolescent mental health facility for inpatient care. It was the best decision."

"The best decision? *For who?* For you? For Mom and Dad?" I clenched my fists by my sides. "What about me, Johanna? One day I come home from school and I'm told I'm going to a mental hospital. . . . Nobody asks me . . ."

The last day of school was over—and I had no one to celebrate with. No one to make plans with for the summer.

No Pepper.

I shut the front door behind me. Leaned against the hard

wood, closing my eyes. Dropped my backpack to the floor, where it landed with a dull thud.

No more stares. No more unspoken questions.

Yes, the house was too quiet, but I preferred the silence to the school hallways filled with students who didn't know me but had heard rumors . . . or who did know and whose glances slid away from me as I passed by.

Quiet. And then . . .

"Payton?"

I straightened, moving away from the door. "Dad? What are you doing home this early?"

"Why don't you come into the living room?" Dad nodded toward the left, then moved out of view.

Okay.

The curtains were closed, blocking out the late May sunshine. Mom sat in the wingback chair, her legs curled beneath her, hands clasped together in her lap. Dad stood behind her. Johanna and Jillian sat side by side on the couch.

Why were they here?

"What's going on?"

"Payton, we've all been worried about you since Pepper died." Dad's words were evenly paced as if he'd practiced what he was going to say. "We know, in some ways, losing her is harder for you than the rest of us."

"I'm fine." For a moment, no one said a word, but Dad and Johanna exchanged a glance. "I'm fine."

"Payton, really——" Johanna spoke up.

"Johanna." Dad raised his hand. "I said I would handle this."

My oldest sister closed her mouth, crossing her arms, Jillian a silent, red-eyed sentinel beside her.

"Your grades suffered the end of this semester. You're barely eating or sleeping. We talked to our family physician and he recommended an inpatient facility for you—"

"What does that mean?"

"There will be . . . doctors and counselors there to help you process how you're feeling. . . ." Dad chose his words with care.

"What? Is this some sort of psych ward?" A chill coursed through my body. "I'm not crazy!"

"We didn't say that. You're grieving—" At last Mom said something.

Dad squeezed Mom's shoulder, causing her to stop. Look away. "It's just for a short while. A month, maybe."

"A month? Or maybe longer?" I scanned the room, trying to understand what was happening. Who were these people?

Next to the coffee table was a suitcase. My suitcase—the one I used whenever Pepper and I traveled for club volleyball games.

"What is my suitcase doing here?"

"It was recommended that we have things ready to take you tonight." For just a moment, Dad's voice seemed to waver.

Tonight. Meaning now.

"Mom, please . . . don't send me away." Tears filled my eyes, blurring my vision.

"It's for the best, Payton."

"It's for the best . . ." Had they really believed that—even as I sobbed my way to the car, collapsing in the backseat? Refused to look at anyone. To say good-bye.

Johanna's voice pulled me from the memory.

"It wasn't your choice, Payton. You lost that choice when you started talking about killing yourself."

I closed the space between us. "I wasn't talking to anyone about that—"

"No, but you were hoarding pills." At my gasp, Johanna smiled, almost a grin of triumph. "Oh yes, I found the pills, too. You were just going to do it and let Mom or Dad or me or Jillian find you—"

"Shut up! Shut *up*!" I lashed out, the palm of my hand connecting with Johanna's cheek. She jerked back, her breath hissing through clenched teeth.

Johanna's fingers wrapped around my wrist, and she held my arm suspended between us. "Feel better?"

My hand burned and I fought to catch my breath. Everything she'd done—reading my journal, convincing my parents to send me away—this wasn't about Johanna trying to help me because she cared about me. Because she was afraid of losing me. No, her actions were about being right.

It was always about Johanna being right.

"I'd just buried my sister, Johanna. My twin sister." I choked back a sob. "Did you ever think I needed to be home? Not in some medical facility?"

"Not if you were going to kill yourself."

"You could have tried to talk to me."

"You would have denied it."

"Denied it? You had my journal! How could I deny it?" I twisted my arm, pulling out of her hold, fighting to maintain some sort of mental foothold . . . some sense of stability as I battled my sister. But the louder I got, the quieter Johanna became.

"Maybe we can figure out what our family looks like now."

Mom's words mocked me. Johanna and me? Family—in some sort of loving, caring, honor-neutral-corners way?

No. Never. How could I ever trust someone who'd seen me at my weakest . . . and abandoned me?

"Stay away from me, Johanna." I half turned, wanting nothing more than to put as much distance between us as possible.

"Always so dramatic, Payton."

I whirled around. "I mean it. We may be family, but you stay away from me. You think you're some kind of heroine because you stopped me from killing myself after Pepper died? You might as well have shoved those pills down my throat yourself."

22

JILLIAN ALLOWED HER HEAD to rest against Geoff's shoulder, closing her eyes and inhaling the familiar lemon and bergamot scent of his aftershave. For such a laid-back guy, the man liked his cologne.

Even after all these months, Jillian still couldn't decide what she liked most about Geoff. Was it his smile that so often morphed into a bit of a goofy grin when he told one of his jokes? Or was it his hazel eyes with golden flecks and the way they warmed whenever he looked at her? Or the way his brown hair always looked as if he was in need of a haircut—and how soft it was when she ran her fingers through it while she kissed him?

Her last thought caused a small smile to curve her lips. Oh yes, she most definitely liked kissing Geoff, but that wasn't why she fell in love with him.

Geoff's work demands had lessened enough to allow for a Friday night in, thanks to her not being up for much else. Geoff had picked up their favorite MOD pizza—and eaten most of it himself. Now they sat curled up together on her couch, watching *National Treasure*, which Geoff had found as he'd searched for something on TV. The Nicolas Cage adventure always seemed to be available on some channel any hour of the day or night.

Three more days until Monday. Three more days until her third round of chemo. Jillian swallowed against the tightening in her throat. How would she feel in five days? In two weeks? Her hands were already more sensitive to hot and cold. Would the nausea linger longer than it had last time?

Jillian touched the pink piece of paper she'd slipped into the pocket of her sweatpants when she got home. The positive thought for today.

Perseverance is not a long race; it is many short races one after the other.

If she looked at her chemotherapy sessions as individual races, then come Monday night she'd be halfway through her competition against cancer.

"You okay?" Geoff's gaze moved from the TV screen to her. "Not interested in watching any more of this?"

"I'm fine." She'd become quite an adept liar in the past few weeks.

How was she feeling? Fine. *Lie.* No, how was she really? Good. *Lie.* Anything bothering her? No.

Lie. Lie. Lie.

She shifted, curling her feet beneath her. "Can we talk?"

"Sure." Geoff muted the TV. "What's up?"

He was always so agreeable—and had become even more so after her cancer diagnosis. Agreeable—but distant. Was it just because he was so busy with work? How was she supposed to know if he was staying with her because she had cancer . . . or because he still loved her?

He hadn't changed. He was the same hardworking, joking guy she'd fallen in love with. But she wasn't the woman he'd proposed to. No, she'd changed in ways they'd never imagined. And Geoff was nothing if not loyal. He'd never walk away from her, no matter how his feelings might have changed.

She'd thought about this decision night after night, lying awake in the dark. She needed to do what was right and give him the freedom he deserved. She couldn't spend the rest of her life wondering if he married her out of love or out of some sort of unfailing allegiance or, worse, pity.

Jillian tucked one of her hands beneath the soft blanket on her lap, unable to let go of Geoff's other hand, even knowing what she was about to do. "I've been thinking about the wedding—"

"Great." Geoff's smile caught her heart off guard for a moment. "Did you decide when you want to reschedule it?"

"I don't want to reschedule it, Geoff."

"What?" A crease appeared between his eyebrows.

"I . . . I want to cancel the wedding." Even though she'd known what she was going to say, hearing the words out loud pained her, like the initial sting of a needle when they drew her blood for lab tests. She always tried to prepare herself, to believe the tech who said, "This won't hurt that much," but somehow every poke and prod was magnified now.

"Cancel the wedding? For how long?"

"This isn't about postponing the wedding, Geoff. . . . I don't want to get married anymore."

That was the biggest lie of all.

Because she did want to marry him. She did.

But she wouldn't marry him. Not now. Not ever. Not like this. And there was no undoing *this*.

Geoff twisted to face her. "I don't understand."

"There's nothing to understand. We just need to call off the wedding. That's it."

"Jillian, I know you're halfway through your chemo. I know you're tired. More emotional. But you're going to beat this. I'm not scared—"

"Stop, Geoff. Stop." He was saying all the right, understanding things he'd said before. And he'd keep on saying them. That was who he was. "You don't have to prove anything to me. I get it. You'll stick by me. But I . . . I don't want you to. I don't want to get married."

No matter how her words made Geoff feel, he'd never know how saying them cut deep into her heart. How bits and pieces of her were disappearing, day by day. The mastectomy was only the beginning.

She was finally losing weight. How ironic that cancer caused the scale to move downward like she'd always wanted it to.

And she didn't care.

By December, she'd lose her hair. She'd already talked to Harper, asking her to help shave her head when her hair started to thin out. It was just hair. No big deal.

"Take control of the situation," the almighty "they" said. *"Shave your head instead of watching it fall out because of the chemo."*

Fine. She'd be brave. She'd take control.

Now her words were separating her from the one man she'd ever loved . . . the one man who'd ever looked past all the things she wasn't and seen *her*. Loved her.

Despite her declaration, they still held hands. Jillian had always enjoyed the sight of their fingers intertwined— a small, everyday representation of their closeness. She'd imagined them being that old married couple, walking along side by side, holding hands. Imagined people seeing them and smiling, wondering how long they'd been married.

She released Geoff's hand, tucking her other hand beneath the blanket, too.

"Jill, honey . . . I understand you're overwhelmed right now." Geoff leaned closer as if trying to maintain some sort of connection. "We're heading into the holidays and you're still trying to keep up with work. And I know Payton's conversation with your family was hard on you, too."

"Geoff—"

"We'll just postpone the wedding until this is all behind you and you're not so tired."

"This is not about me being tired. This is about me having cancer. I'll get over being tired some day . . . but cancer . . . who knows how long I'll be fighting this?"

"You're going to beat this—"

"Stop saying that!" Her outburst startled Geoff into silence. "You don't know that. No one knows that. Maybe . . . maybe I win. Maybe the cancer wins. The truth is even if I win, I won't be the same."

"I don't care. I love you, Jillian."

Before she realized his intent, he leaned over and pressed his lips to hers. He braced himself with one hand on the back of the couch, the other on the edge of the cushion beside her. The kiss was gentle, almost tentative. Only their lips touched. Geoff was so careful not to allow the weight of his body to overwhelm her—to hurt her in any way.

But even as she treasured the tenderness of his kiss, Jillian couldn't respond. Not when she knew all too well what she lacked. A breast. A certain future of any kind.

And then there was the port. The scar. Her overly sensitive skin.

And cancer.

For a second longer, she tasted Geoff's kiss before turning her head away, pressing her hand against his chest. "No."

"Jill—"

"You need to leave. Please." She kept her eyes closed.

And just like always, Geoff did what she asked of him . . . and left.

After the door closed, signaling that Geoff was gone, Jillian sat in the silence of her apartment, broken only by the sound of her breathing. Inhale. Exhale. Inhale. Exhale. For the moment, she'd do the minimum required of her.

She reached over and turned off the TV. Sometimes good didn't conquer evil.

At last, Geoff had stopped fighting her.

This was her normal. This was the life everyone expected her to have. Not breast cancer. No. But being alone.

Well, hadn't she fooled them all—at least for a while? Fooled herself, too?

As she threw aside the blanket, her engagement ring sparkled in the light. Jillian pressed her fingertips against her eyelids. How could she have forgotten to give Geoff the ring? Lowering her hands, she twisted it around and around her finger.

"That's the ring you like?" From the trio arranged on stands in front of them, Geoff selected the square-cut diamond set in a white gold band intertwined with a band of smaller diamonds.

"Yes." Jillian held her breath, not quite able to believe they were looking at engagement rings.

Geoff took her hand. "Let's have another look, shall we?" He stepped closer and slid the ring on her finger. "What do you think?"

"I think it's perfect." She caught herself. "I mean, we're just looking—"

"I've found what I've been looking for—who I've been look-
ing for my whole life, Jillian."

Their gazes entangled.

"I know a jewelry store isn't the most romantic place to pro-
pose, but I'd like for you to leave the shop wearing this ring—
if that's possible." Geoff turned to the salesman, who nodded.
"Jillian, will you marry me?"

She needed to take the ring off. She had no right to wear it.

The ring slipped off with almost no effort, thanks to her
recent weight loss, falling into the palm of her other hand,
where she covered it with her fist.

Funny how doing the right thing broke her heart at the
same time.

23

THREE DAYS since she'd broken off her engagement . . . and today hadn't been too bad.

Jillian's mother had agreed to take her to her chemo appointment, accepting her explanation that Geoff needed to work. Which was true. She'd skipped the Sunday football get-together, saying she was tired.

Not a lie. And staying home meant she didn't have to lie to her family about why Geoff wasn't there—or tell the truth. She'd tell them about the breakup soon.

She knew some of the staff by name now, and they knew that she'd talk about the Broncos game. And then they left her alone while the medicinal "cocktail" did its job. She'd even convinced her mother to go run some errands, telling her that she'd most likely doze off during the treatment.

But now her apartment was too quiet. She'd never realized how waiting for someone filled both time and space. With anticipation—almost as if the waiting for someone was an invisible presence, sitting with her in the stillness so that she wasn't alone or lonely until Geoff showed up, with his smile and his laughter. His love.

Maybe it was time to get a cat. Or a dog. So that when she came home at night, something was waiting for her, needing attention and love.

She could spend the evening browsing rescue sites instead of reruns on TV. But first, hydration. If Geoff were here, he'd remind her to drink lots of water.

There was no sense in feeling sorry for herself. This was her choice. The right choice. For both of them.

Pounding on the front door stopped Jillian midway between her living room and kitchen. Could that be Geoff? No. Pounding on doors wasn't his style.

Sure enough, Harper, not her ex-fiancé, stared at her when she opened the door.

"Um, hello?" Jillian leaned against the doorjamb. "I thought we agreed no Girls' Nights when I had chemotherapy."

"Oh, believe me, I am not here for a Girls' Night." Harper handed Jillian a smoothie, brushing past her. "I don't know whether to hug you and let you cry on my shoulder or knock you upside your sweet little head."

"What?" Jillian pivoted, trying to keep up with the one-sided conversation.

"Do you want to explain to me why you called off your wedding?"

"You talked to Geoff."

"Yes. I talked to Geoff. He came by the bank today and told me you broke off your engagement. He looked so awful at first I thought . . . well, I'm just going to say it: I thought you'd died."

Ouch. Her friend wasn't pulling any punches. Jillian sipped on the smoothie. Triple berry. Her favorite. Just like Harper—she was mad at her and still taking care of her. Jillian hadn't seen her best friend this conflicted since Trent walked out. That night she'd alternated between throwing all his clothes into big black trash bags and picking up different framed photos from around their house, reminiscing about favorite memories.

Harper rounded on her again, hands lifted. "Why did you do it, Jill?"

Before she could answer, Jillian stopped. Narrowed her eyes. Focused on her friend.

"Where's your wedding ring?"

Harper tucked her hands behind her back like a little girl caught playing with her mother's nail polish. "That is not the topic of conversation for tonight."

"It is now. Why aren't you wearing your wedding ring?"

"Because I was stupid enough to call Trent and ask him if

he wanted to spend Thanksgiving or Christmas—he could take his pick—together."

"What happened?"

"Some woman answered the phone." A weak laugh followed her statement. "Silly me. Why would he want to see me during the holidays, when he's going skiing with Lana?"

"Oh, Harper—"

"I shouldn't be surprised. But it was the first time she answered his phone. A reality check, you know?" Her friend swallowed. Shook her head. "Happy Thanksgiving and merry Christmas to me. And happy New Year's, too."

Jillian wasn't the only one grieving the loss of a relationship. She'd been so caught up in her own heartbreak, she hadn't been paying attention to her best friend's. When was the last time she'd asked how Harper was doing, instead of letting their conversation center on her? Her cancer?

No more. Things needed to change.

Harper put her hands on her hips. "I didn't come here to talk about me and Trent. I'm worried about you and Geoff."

"I know you are. But you can't do anything to fix this."

"That man loves you something crazy—"

"And I love him." It was the truth. She might as well admit it.

She'd found one of his jackets after he'd left last Friday—who knows how long ago he'd left it at her apartment. Since then, she'd hugged the coat against her body every night as she fell asleep, inhaling the scent of his cologne. Did Harper do that with Trent's shirts?

"Then why?"

"Because . . . cancer messed up our relationship." She'd had the same conversation with herself over and over again. Maybe saying it out loud to Harper would help. "I don't know why he loves me anymore. Does he love *me* or does he love me because I have cancer?"

As her friend's eyes filled with tears, Jillian wrapped her in a hug, careful to hold the smoothie away from Harper's back. "I promise not to dump this on you."

That earned her a small laugh.

"I'm so sorry about what Trent did—"

"Tonight is not about me."

"But I want to talk about you. Life's not just about me, you know. We're both going through tough times."

Harper hugged her. Hard. "But it's not the same—"

"Friendship isn't a comparison game so that whoever is having the hardest time gets to monopolize the conversation." Jillian adopted a stern tone. "And this is a Girls' Night—plural—so it's not all about me. Okay?"

"Okay."

Jillian held on to her friend for a few seconds longer. If only her relationships with her sisters were more like her relationship with Harper. She never felt lost in the life shuffle with her best friend. Never felt assigned to a certain position—the middle—and left there.

Jillian stepped away. "Do you think we can have an abbreviated Girls' Night?"

"Meaning?"

"Meaning, I'll drink my smoothie—thank you for this, by the way—and you can break into the stash of chocolate you left here. We can skip the rom-com and go for a mystery or something with really good car chases—"

"And if you nod off, I'll tuck you in bed before I leave."

Jillian looped their arms together. "You're a good friend, Harper Adams."

"So are you, Jillian Thatcher."

They'd avoided a showdown. Declared a truce. She'd be drinking a smoothie while Harper indulged in chocolate. But the best of friendships went through all sorts of phases and survived.

And the next Girls' Night, she'd ask how Harper was doing first.

⌒

I dropped my pen on top of the lined sheet of paper, resisting the urge to crumple it and toss it in the trash can. I prided myself on being such a good list maker. Make the list. Accomplish the task. Efficient. Effective.

Well, I'd made my list. Labeled it *Christmas Shopping*. Written down everyone's names: *Mom, Dad, Jillian and Geoff, Johanna and Beckett*—although I wasn't certain my sister would accept anything from me after our last showdown— *Kimberlee, Bianca*.

I'd even added Sydney's name with a small question mark beside it. I'd only been back to the gym once since the first time I'd attended a volleyball practice. I was still undecided if I would show up for another practice or not.

So why was her name on my gift list?

Not that it mattered. A list of names with no gifts written next to them, no check marks denoting "mission accomplished"—well, that was just another thing that wasn't going to be crossed off my bigger to-do list.

So many lists. So little accomplished.

"I don't know how to do this."

Kimberlee looked up from her desk. "Do what?"

"Christmas shop for my family."

"You've never done it before?"

"Very funny." I swiveled my chair around to face her. "Of course I've done it before. I just haven't cared about what I bought them in years. This year I care, so the gifts have to mean something."

I hadn't realized I'd care more about things when I told the truth. Care more about people. My family . . . well, most of my family. After the last confrontation with Johanna, the only question was, who was down for the count and who had retreated to the neutral corner?

Maybe I should buy her boxing gloves. Or a mouth guard.

It had been just over three weeks since I'd shown up for football Sunday. And while there was open space between my family and me instead of No Trespassing lines drawn by fear and deception, we all seemed unsure of how to proceed. What, if anything, would change? Maybe there would be a new sense of closeness in a few weeks at Thanksgiving, instead of the facade of a happy family holiday against the backdrop of nonstop football games.

In some ways, my confession was like walking into a long-ignored room. Pulling back the curtains and opening the windows so light could dispel the darkness. But how would we fill the space?

"You've been messing with that list for the past twenty minutes." Kimberlee came and stood beside my desk, picking up the paper. "What do you have so far?"

"People's names."

"It's a start. Oh, look! There I am." She retrieved the pen. "I can definitely help you with that. You know how much I love rings."

"You, my friend, have a ring addiction—" I stopped midjoke.

The faint scent of ammonia lingered in the air. What was going on? That only happened when a panic attack lurked around the corner. I was over those. I'd confessed, and my family hadn't disowned me. What more was there to do? Penance?

No. Zach might think I had to decide what I believed about God. But that wasn't the question that had haunted me for the past ten years. All I needed to do—according to Pepper—was tell the truth.

The ping of a text message distracted me. Geoff.

"Huh."

"What?"

"My sister's fiancé texted, asking if I was at work. He

wants to talk." I texted back yes. "He's waiting outside the office."

"What is it with men showing up at the office wanting to talk with you?"

"Geoff is engaged to my sister! He probably wants to do something to surprise her for Christmas."

"Well, I'm going home. Call me later if you want help with your gift list." Kimberlee gathered up her purse. "Go ahead and talk. Ask him if they've figured out a date for their bridal shower. The calendar is starting to fill up for next year."

Geoff waited on the other side of the glass doors labeled with the word *Festivities* in white cursive. He was an impromptu kind of guy, but it didn't seem like he was happy to be here. No. He looked more tired than I did after a run of sleepless nights, thanks to Pepper showing up in my dreams.

I needed to unlock the doors. To let him in the office. But what if he wasn't here to talk about some fun surprise for my sister? What if he was going to tell me something about Jillian? What if . . . what if I needed to brace myself for the loss of another sister when I was just coming to terms with Pepper's death?

No matter how tired he was, no matter what his reason for being here, Geoff was also a hugger, wrapping his arms around me almost before he got through the doors.

"Hey, Geoff."

"Payton." Geoff stepped back, running a hand through his hair. "I'm glad you're still here."

I motioned toward the back room. "Just working. Nothing that can't wait. Can I get you some coffee?"

"That'd be great. So this is your office, huh?"

"Yes. Not much to brag about. And believe me, the front office is much more organized than where Kimberlee and I sit." I opened the door, waving him toward the table in the middle of the room. "It works as our base of operations and the break room. We did manage to find a separate location for storage, but the truth is, we've outgrown this space."

"Looking to move?"

"It's up for discussion after the holidays."

The idle chatter faded as I handed Geoff a mug of coffee. "Go ahead and sit down. My coffee will only take a moment. So what's on your mind? Planning some sort of fun Christmas present for Jillian?"

"No." Geoff stared into the depths of his mug.

The way Geoff sounded, I braced myself for bad news, even as I avoided it. "Have you two talked about dates for the bridal shower—?"

Geoff locked eyes with me. "There's not going to be a bridal shower."

"What? Why not?"

"Because Jillian called off the wedding."

I couldn't have heard him right. "That's an awful joke. Jillian would never—"

"Do you really think I would joke about this, Payton?" Geoff slammed the mug down. "I was at her apartment four nights ago. She told me that she doesn't want to marry me."

I set my coffee cup down on the counter, shaking my head. "That doesn't make any sense. She loves you. I've never seen Jillian as happy as she is with you."

"I don't understand it either." Geoff sat with his elbows on the table, his hands clasped. "I mean, at first I didn't. But I've thought about it and I keep coming back to something Jillian said . . . about not being the same, even if she beats the cancer diagnosis. Do you think maybe she believes I can't love her because of her mastectomy and because she'll lose her hair and because . . . because . . . ?"

Was I supposed to say the words he couldn't say?

"Because she might die?"

"I know I joke around a lot, Payton. And I admit work's been busy . . . and maybe . . . maybe I like how it distracted me a bit from what was happening with Jillian." Geoff's eyes filled with tears. "But I understand how serious this all is . . . how *life-and-death* serious it is. I lie awake at night because I'm afraid Jillian might die. But the thought of losing her instead of growing old with her makes me want to marry her sooner—not walk away from her."

Why would Jillian not want to marry someone like Geoff Hennessey?

"What are you going to do now?" I sat down beside him, wishing I could fix things for him. For my sister.

"I was hoping you'd talk to her."

I couldn't have heard him right. "Me?"

"Yes. She won't answer my calls or texts." He pulled his phone from his pocket as if to prove it to me. "I thought about showing up at her apartment, but then I realized she'd probably listen to you sooner than she'd listen to me. Would you talk to her, Payton? Please? Tell her that I love her? That I still want to marry her?"

What? I wasn't the one to step up and intercede for Geoff. I reveal a decade-old secret and suddenly I'm the family relationship guru? That's not how things worked. Confession didn't magically heal relationships or change people or span the distance created by years of silence and misunderstanding.

All he needed to do was ask Johanna.

"I think you're the one to do that, Geoff. Not me." I wrapped my hands around the ceramic coffee mug to still their trembling.

My hands were shaking. And now the odor of ammonia was even stronger. Was I on the verge of another panic attack? Wasn't doing the right thing—confessing the truth—some sort of guarantee that my life would get easier? That the pressure would ease up?

Geoff covered one of my hands with his. "Would you just think about going to see her? Check on how she's doing?"

Why was I surprised that someone else wanted something from me?

Just go to the awards ceremony, Payton.

Just tell the truth to the family, Payton.

Just check on Jillian, Payton.

I could only imagine how this would turn out. My sister would figure out in no time that Geoff had sent me. But did I have a choice?

"Yes. I'll go check on her." I held my hand up to shake his as if sealing a business deal. "And I'll see if I can manage to get her to talk about you and the wedding and what's going on—"

Geoff stood and pulled me into another rib-crunching hug. "Thank you, Payton. Thank you. I knew I could count on you."

I'd never been to Jillian's office. I'd never called my sister and asked, "Do you want to meet for lunch?" or "How about drinks after work today?"

I could blame it on the geographical distance between her work and mine—North Denver to Colorado Springs. Or I could be honest—a still-new thing for me—and blame it on the emotional distance between us.

A series of six framed watercolor hearts lined the wall behind her desk. Was the artwork standard issue from the bank? Not likely. Which meant my sister liked watercolors. And hearts. Why? Several award certificates hung over the bookshelf sitting to the left of her desk. No reason to be surprised by them or the fact that Jillian had never mentioned them—at least, not to me.

Jillian came around from behind her desk, her smile forced. "Payton, this is a surprise. Applying for a loan?"

Her attempt at humor did little to defuse the tension in the room. "I was hoping I could convince you to have lunch with me—if you're not too busy."

"You want to take me to lunch?"

"Is that so surprising?"

"Actually, it is, since we've never been those kinds of sisters." Jillian returned to her chair, placing her cherrywood desk between us. "Is this because you want to have lunch with me—or because Geoff told you that I broke off our engagement?"

My sister might as well have said, "Loan declined," shown me out of her office, and slammed the door in my face. But Jillian was too kind for that sort of brute-squad tactic. No, that was more Johanna's style. But even her innate kindness didn't keep Jillian from being candid.

For just a moment, time reversed, and it seemed as if I'd wandered into the forbidden territory of my older sisters' bedroom instead of showing up at the bank where Jillian worked. The age difference between us had loomed so large when I was younger—eight years and six years. Johanna and Jillian, busy with school and their friends, had no time for Pepper and me. But Pepper and I had each other. That was enough. At least for most of our lives we were enough for each other.

I shook off the shadow of the memory. I was here to stop Jillian from walking away from her future, not to get snared in the past. There was no easing into this over lunch with chitchat and pleasantries. I could confess the ruse and retreat or stand my ground and plead Geoff's case.

"Fine. Geoff came by yesterday and asked me to check on you. But it is lunchtime, so why don't we—?"

"Save your breath, Payton." My sister clasped her hands on top of her desk as if she were discussing a loan application. "If you're hoping to try and convince me to still marry Geoff, that's not going to happen."

"He loves you, Jillian. He doesn't care that you have cancer."

"Of course he's going to say that."

"You don't believe him."

"I believe him—and I think he believes it, too. But will he feel that way a month from now? A year from now? Call me old-fashioned, but I believe marriage is a forever commitment."

"And Geoff doesn't?"

"Cancer changes . . . things." As she talked, Jillian shuffled the papers on her desk, not meeting my eyes.

It took me a moment to realize she wasn't wearing her engagement ring. She'd loved that ring.

"Isn't it beautiful? It's the perfect ring. The jeweler didn't even have to resize it." The entire time she spoke, Jillian moved her hand this way and that, never taking her eyes off the ring. And the entire time she talked, Geoff never took his eyes off her.

This was no time to retreat. I'd promised Geoff. I just needed to figure out how to talk sense to my normally level-headed sister.

"I know you love Geoff—"

"I'm not the woman he proposed to, Payton." Jillian leaned back in her chair. "And I'm not talking about being perfect. I have no pretenses about that. But it's one thing for

THINGS I NEVER TOLD YOU

Geoff to propose to a woman who is forty pounds overweight and has no aspirations of being a runway model. He didn't sign up to marry someone with cancer."

So many questions ran through my head, but all I said was "Is this about you losing your hair?"

Jillian's brief laugh had the echo of a sob in it. "I wish it was. My hair will grow back. It may be curlier or a different color, but I'm told I will have hair again. But my breast? That's gone. And I may lose the other one by the time this is all over. I don't know. That's the problem. I can't see the future. If I could, I would have never said yes when Geoff proposed to me."

"You don't mean that."

"Yes, I do. We're not married—just engaged. There's no 'for better, for worse, in sickness and in health' vow holding him to me. He's got an out—and I'm making sure he takes it."

For all her bravado, I recognized myself in Jillian—the person I was after Pepper died. My sister was hurting. Scared. Unsure of what was ahead and how to face her future.

She was committing emotional suicide. Destroying her hopes and dreams with her bare hands because the thought of losing them was too painful to bear in light of all she'd lost already.

Jillian sat there, her already-thinning hair brushed into place. What she needed was a mask to disguise the emotions flitting across her face. Fear. Grief. Anger.

Years ago, I'd needed someone to rescue me from myself.

Was that what Johanna thought she was doing after Pepper had died—stopping me from making a horrible mistake? The questions snarled in my head, tangling together with memories of nights spent alone, separated from what was left of my family.

I couldn't think about that now.

How could I reach my sister? Stop her before she inflicted any more damage to her dreams?

I could only hope Geoff would forgive me for what I was about to say.

"Fine. Don't marry Geoff."

If possible, Jillian's face got even whiter. "What?"

"I said, don't marry Geoff." I leaned forward. "But you need to decide if you're going to fight for your life."

"What are you talking about? I'm doing everything the doctors have told me to do—"

I snorted. "Doing what the doctors tell you to do is the bare minimum. It's like warming up for a marathon. Do you even think your life is worth fighting for?"

"What kind of question is that?"

"It's the most important question of your life, Jillian. One you need to answer."

And now I sounded more like a shrink than a party planner. I didn't even know where that question came from, but Jillian's response proved her actions were fueled by more than just "Geoff deserves more than this." And the fact that she still kept a photo of the two of them on her desk was a not-so-subtle clue that Jillian wasn't moving on.

"I really don't want to argue with you. Geoff loves you—"
I picked up the silver photo frame, taking a moment to enjoy
the image of the two of them laughing together before placing it front and center on her desk—"and this little photo-
graphic Freudian slip tells me that you still love him, too."

"Payton—"

"After Pepper died, I pushed the family away for years. I
was wrong to do it because I needed all of you. Don't make
the same mistake and push away the man you love because
you're afraid. And right now, it looks like Geoff loves you
more than you love yourself."

"Is that all you want to say?"

"Yes."

Jillian stood. Walked around her desk and opened the
door leading out of her office. "Well then, thank you for
the invitation to lunch, but I'm only working half days right
now, so I have a lot of work to do. I'll have to take a rain
check."

Was this how Zach Gaines felt after the first time he tried
to talk to me? As if he'd wasted both his words and his time?

But he hadn't. He just didn't know that at the time. All
I could do was hope something I said made a difference in
Jillian's life. And if I'd been accustomed to praying—if I
knew who to pray to—I'd do that.

Maybe the next time I talked to Zach, I could ask him to
pray for Jillian.

Was I even planning on some sort of next time with Zach?

Snowflakes tumbled from the sky around my car. Pure

white flakes falling to the dingy asphalt, forever changed. Tainted.

I sat in my car, the engine running, the wipers clearing the windshield of the blanket of snow. Outside, the process happened over and over again. Sparkles of white falling to earth. Sullied over and over again.

Now there's a question I would like to ask Zach. How did forgiveness work? The divine interacting with the less-than of mankind? How did the supposed goodness of God not get overpowered by the world's darkness?

24

THE NETS, POLES, pads, antennas, and ever-elusive crank were put away in the storage room until the first postholiday practice. With a wave good-bye and a laugh from Chandler, the team's setter, the gym quieted.

I tugged at the bottom of my damp T-shirt, which clung to my skin. The last two hours had gone by so fast, something I hadn't experienced since high school. Being on the court and scrimmaging with a group of girls. Laughing and encouraging one another. Being part of a team, even if it was only for tonight.

Sydney shrugged into her coat. "What were you and Katelyn talking about after practice?"

"She was frustrated because she felt like she hadn't played

as well as she wanted to the last couple of practices—like she was missing too many blocks."

"So what did you tell her?"

"I told her I remember feeling the same way. That everybody has off days. And that you just have to work through them. Keep showing up. That she's a good volleyball player."

"You're doing a great job with the girls, Payton."

"Just telling them what you told us." I dug my car keys out of my purse as Sydney tried to juggle the multiple cards and gifts the girls had given her when practice ended. "Do you need any help with all of that?"

"Thanks, but I can manage." Sydney set the bags on the metal bleachers and stuffed the cards into her purse.

Why did the days after Thanksgiving and leading up to Christmas always seem to be in fast-forward? While Christmas Day loomed too close, Thanksgiving was the flash of a memory, the scaled-down dinner with just my parents and Jillian squeezed in between Festivities events. Johanna had spent the long weekend with Beckett in Wyoming. My oldest sister's absence meant a reprieve from our emotional standoff. Geoff's absence meant no running string of jokes punctuated by bursts of laughter.

With a quick shake of my head, I returned to my conversation with Sydney. "I remember Christmas seasons with the team. The annual party—"

"Those are always fun. We're going out of town this year to visit my husband's family, so we're going to do a team party after the New Year. You're invited, you know."

"Thanks." I nodded toward the pile of gifts. "I would assume you're restocked on your gift cards for the next few months."

"I hope so."

"Pepper and I usually opted for Starbucks." The small memory from our former volleyball years was pleasant, not painful.

"Believe me, I appreciated every single one of those gift cards."

"This looks a lot like the gifts I've gotten for my family."

Sydney's eyes widened. "This? What do you mean?"

"Gift cards. All gift cards."

With a loud metallic click, the lights in the gym shut off, dousing Sydney and me in darkness and signaling us to move to the rec center lobby.

Sydney picked up the conversation again. "Is work so busy you don't have time to go Christmas shopping?"

I wasn't about to go into the long, drawn-out why. "Yes, but also I'm just not a good shopper."

"It's not that hard. I mean, shopping does take time, of course."

"Agreed."

"Have a little fun with me here." Sydney dumped her armload of bags and her purse on the lobby counter.

"How, exactly?" I rubbed at the stiff muscle in my right shoulder. How many times had I served the volleyball?

"Tell me something about your dad. What does he do? What does he like?"

"My dad? He likes to grill out. And he's a die-hard Broncos fan."

"Then you buy him a chef's apron with a funny saying. Or a Broncos T-shirt." She cut me off when I started to say something. "Doesn't matter how many T-shirts he has. Football fans can always use one more. Did you ever count up how many volleyball T-shirts you had?"

"Good point."

"What about your mom?"

That was easy. "She collects carnival glass. And she likes to bake."

"Easy again. A nice piece of carnival glass. Or a cookbook."

"I don't suppose it matters that she has a gazillion cookbooks."

"Nope—kind of like T-shirts. Buy her a bestseller. Sisters?"

There was no need to mention Johanna wasn't speaking to me. "My oldest sister likes vintage jewelry. A bracelet or earrings?"

"See? You're catching on."

I paused, envisioning Jillian's office. "I just found out Jillian likes watercolors. She had a collection of abstract hearts in her office at work."

"That's unusual. Check out Etsy online."

"I'm familiar with Etsy. Kimberlee and I use it for some of our parties."

Sydney tried her best not to look shocked. "Then why are we even having this conversation?"

"Because I didn't make the connection between Etsy and Christmas shopping?"

Sydney accepted my more than lame excuse. "Well, now you have."

For years, Sydney had coached me about volleyball. And now she was coaching me on gift giving. I was twenty-six years old. I should be capable of buying my family Christmas gifts.

"That reminds me . . ." I pulled a red envelope out of my purse. "This is for you."

Sydney laughed as she tucked it in among the other envelopes. "Starbucks?"

"If I tell you, it's as good as you peeking at a gift before Christmas."

"True. I just figured you were consistent."

"Well, maybe I surprised you and went with a Chick-fil-A gift card."

"I happen to love Chick-fil-A."

"Who doesn't?"

The lights in the lobby dimmed, and Sydney regathered her things to lead us outside. The winter air fingered the damp hair on my neck. The dark sky overhead sparkled with hundreds of tiny white stars. But instead of heading to her car, Sydney matched me step for step to mine.

"I wanted to ask you a question."

"Go ahead."

"Just promise me that you'll think about it for a few days before you give me an answer."

"Fine. I'll think about it. And the question is?"

"You know club season starts in a couple of weeks. I was

wondering if you'd consider being a backup assistant coach for the sixteens team."

"What? Did Alex quit or something?" Even as I asked, my chest tightened.

It was just a question. I could say yes. Or no. Sydney couldn't force me to say yes. There was no reason to struggle to catch my breath.

"No, she didn't quit. But it looks like she'll be traveling with her job this spring, so she's not sure how many games she'll be able to get to. We've been talking, and we thought you could come to practices and be another assistant coach."

I leaned back against my car and gripped the door handle, the metal cold against my fingers. "But I've only come to a few practices . . . and I haven't really done volleyball in years. . . ."

"The girls like you, Payton. And you know volleyball. And remember, you promised to think about it." Sydney paused. "You okay?"

I had promised to consider her question. Which meant, as much as I wanted to say, *No, absolutely not*, I couldn't. I had to wait at least one day before telling Sydney no.

"Yes. Just hungry. I probably needed to eat and drink a little more before I came tonight."

"Well, you didn't know I was going to throw you into the scrimmage against the other team. I'll let you go. . . . You'll think about what I said?"

"Yes." As Sydney wrapped her arms around me, I hugged her back. "Merry Christmas."

"Merry Christmas, Payton. I'm so glad we've reconnected."

"Me, too." And as I said the words, I realized just how much I meant them.

As much as Sydney said the girls liked me, the truth was, I liked them, too. Walking into the gym and onto a volleyball court with a bunch of enthusiastic teen girls was almost like time traveling. For two hours, I went back ten years to high school, when my life was all volleyball, all the time.

I allowed myself to embrace something I'd walked away from . . . something that, even now, I was afraid to admit I missed. Something I still wanted to be a part of my life.

25

"Merry Christmas, Pay."

"Merry Christmas, Pepper."

Christmas morning. My sister and I sit in front of the family Christmas tree, the multicolored lights causing all the ornaments to glimmer and glow among the branches. We wear matching pajamas—soft-gray bottoms with coordinating red tops, not unlike the matchy-matchy pj's my parents gave us every Christmas. When we were younger, we'd find them waiting on our beds when we woke up, exchanging the old for the new before running downstairs to ransack the presents waiting for us under the tree.

I fingered the soft flannel fabric of my sleeve. Where did these pajamas come from?

"What's wrong?" Pepper's question was a normal one. Nothing probing about my life choices.

"You don't think this—" I motioned back and forth between us—"is a little weird?"

"What? It is Christmas . . ."

"No. You. Me. Wearing identical pajamas."

"We always used to do this when we were kids."

"But we're older now."

"You're older. You're even older than me. Now that's weird. We always thought we'd be the same age. But you're twenty-six and I'm . . . not."

"Things are so different than we ever expected. I tried to help Jillian and probably made things worse . . . and I told the truth and now Johanna isn't talking to me. . . ."

Pepper selected a present and handed it to me. "Sometimes you just have to forget all the other stuff and remember we're sisters."

I tossed and turned, pulling myself from the dream, my heart pounding in my chest. My pillow was on the floor, my blankets tangled around my legs.

Why? Why was Pepper still showing up? I'd done what I needed to do. What Pepper asked of me. I'd confessed the truth to my family.

My heart rate slowed to a dull thud. For a few years after Pepper had died—before I'd turned my back on that part of my life—I'd wanted to see my sister again . . . to find some way to connect with Pepper. And now all I wanted was for her to go away. To stop appearing in my dreams. To stop asking questions. To disappear.

For someone to tell me what more I was supposed to do so Pepper would stop haunting me.

Christmas Day stretched ahead of me and I was already exhausted. I needed to shower. Get dressed. Drive down to my parents' house, after declining their invitation to stay overnight on Christmas Eve.

My improved pile of gifts sat on the couch, next to my purse. Gone were the tiny foil bags containing impersonal gift cards. Everyone would now receive a more personalized gift, as well as the original gift card. *Thank you, Sydney. Thank you, Etsy.* Even Beckett, who was making a rare appearance for Christmas, would receive a custom pen made from California redwood. I'd tucked something extra into Johanna's bag. Whether she'd accept it or toss it back in my face . . . well, I wouldn't know until later.

There was no white Christmas for Colorado this year. I skipped the Christmas music as I drove south on I-25 to my parents' house, the highway mostly deserted. One of the few cars I passed was decorated to look like a Rudolph, complete with two brown antlers and a big red nose centered over the front grill.

Why didn't the holiday feel different this year? Why wasn't I looking forward to spending time with my family, now that everything was out in the open? The truth should grant me some measure of freedom, right? But I was no happier than any other Christmas since Pepper had died. Granted, Johanna and I were at an emotional standoff, but I was hoping to change that.

The sound of my phone ringing startled me, but I welcomed the interruption, activating my Bluetooth.

"Merry Christmas, Payton."

Zach.

"Merry Christmas."

"I hope it's okay that I called. I don't want to interrupt you if you're with your family—"

"No, you're fine. I'm driving down to my parents' house right now."

"Are you having a good day? I imagine Christmas might be hard for you."

"Thanks. It's going to be different . . . I think."

"Okay. Should I ask what that means?"

"Why not? You're partly to blame."

That didn't come out the way I meant it to.

"Let me start over." I flexed my fingers on the steering wheel. Made sure I was driving the speed limit. "After I told you about what happened the night my sister died—how I talked her into switching places with me—I realized it was time to tell my family the truth too. And I did—back in October."

"That's fantastic." When I didn't respond, Zach lowered his voice. "Isn't it?"

"Yes. And no. I mean, my parents and Jillian were amazing. They responded better than I ever imagined. But Johanna—"

"Your oldest sister, right?"

"Yes. She . . . didn't understand." Did I say more? Go into all the details of our argument?

"I'm sorry. Maybe you just need to give her time."

"Maybe. Although Johanna and I have never been close, so things may never change no matter what I do."

I stopped. This was an intense conversation when all Zach had done was call to say, "Merry Christmas." Time to back-pedal a bit. "Are you having a good day?"

He took the change in topic well. "I'm at the airport."

"The airport? On Christmas Day?"

"Yep. At the gate, waiting to board my plane."

"Are you going to see your parents?"

"For a few days. I'll be back before New Year's Eve. Don't want to leave Laz for too long."

"Is he in a kennel?"

"No, a friend is watching him for me. Kelsey loves taking care of Laz."

Kelsey. Why had it never occurred to me that Zach probably had a girlfriend? I bet she was some cute, Christian girl—just perfect for him. Why did it matter to me, anyway?

"Sounds like fun." And that comment made no sense at all. What sounded like fun? Kelsey watching Laz? "I'm almost at the exit for my parents' house."

"I'll let you go then. Merry Christmas."

"You, too."

"Talk to you soon—and maybe we can do coffee or something when I get back."

"Sure. Great."

Now on top of everything I had to untangle myself from an unexpected, and unnecessary, snarl of jealousy toward Zach and some woman named Kelsey.

Could I just go back to bed and push restart on this day? Or skip it altogether?

As my parents' house came into view, expectations burdened my heart again. I wanted more for my family. But maybe that was a bit like asking for a Christmas miracle, not unlike Frosty the Snowman coming to life and dancing through the town.

Mom's "maybe" seemed to linger as I entered the house.

"Maybe, maybe we can figure out what our family looks like now."

But how could we do that without changing? Without acknowledging that we were different—that what had happened changed us?

After Pepper died, we'd maintained our traditions. The same music my parents had played for years in the background, a mixture heavy on classic Frank Sinatra and Bing Crosby and light on more contemporary songs. Brunch, complete with Mom's eggs Benedict and mimosas and continual rounds of coffee. With the silence continuing between Johanna and me, maybe she wouldn't comment on my sugar addiction. My parents seemed oblivious to the underlying tension threaded throughout the day. It was as if we'd been pulled into the holiday movie where toys were outlawed and everything was tinted gray.

My new and improved collection of presents tucked a warm sense of contentment inside me—each one was a sign that I was trying. Opening gifts waited until after brunch, everyone settling around the room, the packages piled beneath the tree. But before my parents could begin to distribute the gifts, Johanna stood and moved to the center of the room.

"Can we break with tradition today—just a little bit?" She scanned the family, her gaze settling on Jillian. "I know we usually open presents youngest to oldest, but I thought we could just give each other our presents. And I'd like to start with Jillian."

If anyone was going to break a family custom, it would be Johanna.

And of course, she didn't wait for approval from anyone. She was holding a card in a bright-red envelope, ready to present it to Jillian. The palm of one of her hands rubbed against the back of her other hand.

Just like our father did when he was nervous.

How had I never noticed that before?

Johanna sat beside Jillian, who now wore a knit cap to cover her bare head. She clung to her corner of the couch like she was stranded on a desert island, waiting for someone—Geoff, maybe?—to come rescue her. But he was absent—and so were his easygoing manner, his corny jokes, and his boisterous laugh. We all missed him, but the loss had erased any hint of joy from my sister.

A tiny smile curved Johanna's lips as Jillian opened the

card. Removed a small plastic bag. Held it up, turning it around.

Jillian's brow furrowed. "What is this?"

"It's a piece of my hair. You need to read the note that comes with it." Johanna undid her chignon. Her hair, which used to fall almost to her waist, skimmed her shoulders. "Merry Christmas, Jilly. I donated my hair to Locks of Love in your name."

"You what?" Jillian covered her mouth with her hand. "No . . . you can't do that—"

Johanna ran both hands through her hair, shaking her head. "It's done. And I don't regret cutting it at all."

My oldest sister donated her hair to charity? That was like Rapunzel cutting her own hair—and if I was honest, I often considered Johanna more like the evil not-really-Rapunzel's-mother in the Disney remake.

A small chill coursed through me. Here I was hoping for my relationship with Johanna to improve and I was still thinking such awful things about her. Where was my Christmas spirit?

Jillian wrapped her arms around Johanna, pulling her close, and Johanna held on, tears streaming down both their faces.

The two of them had always been close, just like Pepper and I had been close. We were like a four-legged stool. Johanna and Jillian. Pepper and Payton. And then Pepper died and the Thatcher sisters were knocked off-kilter.

As Johanna leaned away from Jillian, a smile softened her features. A true smile, reaching all the way to her eyes.

Would I ever experience that kind of smile from my oldest sister?

When my turn came to give my gifts to the family, I tried to rein in my expectations. I wasn't competing with Johanna. I was only trying to do more than I had in years past. But I couldn't help but hold my breath when Johanna opened the Christmas card I'd added to her gift bag.

She glanced at the words inside. Closed the card. Slipped it back into the gift bag and thanked me for the bracelet and the gift card to Sephora.

I shouldn't be surprised. Some relationships are set in emotional stone.

My vaulting act of honesty didn't erase the strain from the family relationships. Johanna had ruled the day, setting the table, organizing the cleanup, and even establishing a new gift-giving tradition. And all the while, Beckett—the so-often Invisible Man now become visible—lingered on the edges of the activity.

I excused myself, claiming I needed some water, and retreated to the kitchen.

As Mom entered the kitchen, I retrieved a glass from the cabinet, aware of how much more I'd wanted for this day.

"Jillian's going to lie down for a little while in the guest bedroom."

"That's understandable. I thought she was going to fall asleep during brunch."

"Johanna and Beckett and your dad and I are going to play Sheriff of Nottingham. Do you want to join us?"

"No, thanks." I filled my glass with ice and water. "I think I'll find a quiet corner in the house and kick back for a bit."

It wasn't until I was standing outside my bedroom door that I realized my unspoken intention. I wrapped my fingers around the smooth brass doorknob. I hadn't been inside this room in years—not since I'd left for college. Was I ready to breach the barrier?

I eased the door open a few inches. It was just a room. Four walls, a floor, a ceiling. Nothing more.

When I turned on the overhead light, I half expected Pepper to be sitting on the bed, waiting for me.

Absurd.

The room wasn't untouched, left as some sort of sacred shrine to my sister. The walls were bare of all the items Pepper and I had decorated them with during high school. Our sports photos. Team pictures. A collage of news articles. Our full-length mirror was gone, our single beds replaced by a simple queen-size bed. The walls were painted a soft powder blue, not the vivid turquoise Pepper and I had begged for in an attempt to match our eyes. Over the desk that occupied one corner was a selection of family photos. A closer look revealed photos of Pepper and me from kindergarten up until our junior year. A small framed copy of my graduation photo ended the montage.

Did my parents ever come in here? Did they ever stand

and look at these photos of their twin daughters, torn apart so unexpectedly by my stupidity?

What had Mom done with all our clothes? I'd never asked her. Hadn't cared.

I pulled open the closet door. Once it had overflowed with a jumble of shirts, pants, dresses, shoes, and boots. Now one side was empty, while the other side held . . . what? I pulled out a hanger and stared at my old volleyball jersey. Number 13. Pulled out another hanger. Another jersey, this one number 11. Hanger after hanger held either my jerseys or Pepper's—from our club seasons from sixth grade until our junior year. And at the very back of the closet were our crimson-and-white high school letter jackets.

Of everything we owned, my parents kept our volleyball jerseys?

I pulled my jacket from the hanger, slipping it on, the weight of it falling onto my shoulders. For just a moment, the years faded away and I was sixteen again, walking down the school hallway next to Pepper, my hair loose and cascading down my back. Pepper and I waving hello to teammates. Talking about upcoming games.

I slid my hands into the pockets, my fingertips finding something smooth and metallic in one of them.

What was that?

I pulled out my hand, a small key resting in my palm. It wasn't on a key chain. Didn't look like a car key. What was a key doing in the pocket of my letter jacket?

I returned the key to the pocket, taking off the coat and folding it over my arms. This was going home with me. If I thought about it long enough, I'd remember what the key was for.

Voices drifted up from the foyer as I came downstairs.

"Is this your warped idea of a Christmas present?" Johanna stood with her arms crossed, her back rigid.

"Johanna, be reasonable. I had to tell you sometime—"

"You decide to say, 'Merry Christmas, Johanna. I'm not deploying for a year like we talked about. I'm taking another assignment even farther away from Colorado.'"

"Going to a year's postgraduate study has advantages over going remote. And I said I haven't made a final decision yet."

"And now you're lying to me. I know you, Beckett. You've already made up your mind."

"Let's get married this summer. Then you can come with me to Alabama."

"We've talked about this over and over again. I've got a good job here. You agreed to the plan we talked about so we could get married and live here."

"It always comes back to your job. There are plenty of hospitals that need a top-notch clinical pharmacist like you—" Beckett stopped as if he sensed my presence at the top of the stairs.

"Sorry to interrupt." The poor guy looked like he'd been backed into a corner.

"You're not interrupting anything." Johanna didn't even glance my way. "Beckett has to leave."

"Johanna, we're not done talking about this." Beckett sounded ready to take my sister on. I had to believe the man hadn't dated her for seven years without learning how to deal with her strong personality.

Beckett reached for her arm, but Johanna shrugged him off. "I am not talking about this. Not on Christmas."

"Walk me out to my car." Beckett's words were a statement, not a question.

A few minutes later, Johanna found me in the family room saying good-bye to my parents.

"What's that, Payton?" Mom asked.

"I found my letter jacket in the closet upstairs." I held up my arm. "Is it okay if I take it home with me?"

"Absolutely. You don't need to ask."

Johanna followed me into the foyer again. I ignored her, gathering my coat, purse, letter jacket, and the reusable plastic bag that contained my gifts.

"I suppose you enjoyed watching that."

"You and Beckett arguing? No, not really." I buttoned my coat. "I'm sure you two will figure it out."

"We will."

If nothing else, witnessing my sister's argument with her fiancé had gotten her to talk to me again. For all her bravado, was she bothered by her long-term, long-distance relationship with Beckett? Then why didn't she just marry the guy?

Halfway home, as the sun set behind the Rocky Mountains off to the west, Geoff called.

"Merry Christmas, Payton."

"Merry Christmas, Geoff. How are you?"

"Lonely. I saw my parents last night and now I'm eating Chinese takeout and having a Lord of the Rings movie marathon. How's Jillian?"

"When I left my parents', she was asleep in the guest bedroom. I think she's planning on spending the night." I eased my car over into the right lane. "How are you doing?"

"I miss her. I'm waiting for her to miss me." Geoff cleared his throat. "But I'm afraid that's not going to happen. That she's not going to change her mind."

"You may be right—" I stopped. It was cruel to tell a man to stop hoping, especially on Christmas Day.

"Don't say that, Payton. I can wait however long it takes."

"You haven't talked to her at all since she broke off the engagement?"

"No. She ignored my texts and voice mails. So I stopped."

Should I offer him any reason to hang on? "I can tell you that she looks tired, but you know that. She's quiet. She also looks sad. I can't help but believe she misses you."

Was I even saying the right thing? What was I doing, trying to be the go-between for Geoff and my sister? Trying to be someone I wasn't—a woman who could fix things that were broken when I still didn't feel completely mended?

"The next time you talk to her, will you tell her I called, please?"

"Sure."

It was the least I could do for the guy. As I exited the highway, lyrics from the traditional Christmas song wandered through my mind: *"It's the most wonderful time of the year . . ."*

What a huge expectation to put on a single day of the year. To decide that this day, this season, was the most wonderful of every other time of the year. Children counted down the days to Christmas. Parents overloaded their credit cards to make the day perfect and regretted it for months later. We dressed it up with lights and tinsel and stars and festive *fa-la-la*, determined to ignore whatever pain or heartache we were experiencing because, well, Christmas was wonderful.

Or so everyone said and sang. And hoped and demanded.

When had Christmas been wonderful? The day came again and again after Pepper died, but I'd never recaptured any sense of joy, no matter how many years separated me from the loss of my sister. There was no "wonderful" in Geoff's Christmas. Or Jillian's. And if Johanna was honest, she'd admit to some disappointment woven through her Christmas expectations, too.

Maybe wonder-filled Christmases were only for children . . . whose hearts hadn't been broken by life.

26

"Is Bianca going to join us for lunch?" I ladled another scoop of the fragrant butternut squash soup from the Crock-Pot into my bowl.

"She was finishing up a phone call." Kimberlee set a basket of rolls on the table in the back room.

"If she doesn't hurry up and get back here, there may not be any soup left."

Kimberlee laughed and placed three bottles of water on the table. "That's your first bowl."

"I'm just saying." I sat at the table, selecting a roll. "You know, if you ever want to stop being a party planner, you could always open a restaurant featuring bread and rolls and soups."

"No, thank you. I'm very happy helping other people celebrate their birthdays and weddings. I cook to relax."

"That's like saying you clean house to relax." I tasted the soup. "This is just as good as it smells."

"Thank you very much."

"We have a delivery." Bianca entered the room carrying a colorful bouquet of flowers.

"For Festivities?" Kimberlee clapped her hands. "From a client?"

"I don't know who it's from—" Bianca placed the bouquet on my desk—"but I do know it's for Payton."

"Me?" I almost choked on my spoonful of soup.

"Oooh. Now this is much more interesting than a client sending us flowers." Kimberlee grinned. "Who sent you flowers?"

"I have no idea." I ignored my lunch to get a closer view of the bouquet, which was a fragrant arrangement of white roses and purple irises.

"Nash?" Bianca came to stand beside me.

"No. Nash and I are over. He's fine with being friends now. He wouldn't be sending me flowers."

No one should be sending me flowers. I was unattached and I wasn't looking to get involved—even if the thought of Zach Gaines distracted me every once in a while.

Thinking about the guy didn't mean I was interested in him.

"You're sure?"

"Yes." I brushed my fingertips against the soft petals of one still-unopened rose. "How am I supposed to figure out who these are from if there's no card?"

"Yes, there is." Bianca held up a white envelope. "The delivery guy also gave me this."

I tapped the card against my palm. "What is this, some kind of floral riddle?"

"Come on and get some soup, Bianca." Kimberlee tugged her toward the counter. "Let Payton read the card in peace."

"But I want to know who—"

"And so does she. Eat your lunch."

My name appeared on the front of the envelope, the stamped address of the florist on the back flap. I couldn't decide if the handwriting was familiar or not. The only way to solve the mystery was to read the card.

On the front of the card was a black-and-white sketch of waves washing against the sand, tiny little sandpipers running amid the ripples. I opened the card and found the signature.

Johanna.

Johanna sent me flowers?

Payton:
    I've read and reread your card from Christmas.
    I want you to know that I appreciate your apology.
    I understand now how what I did after Pepper died could seem wrong to you. My intent wasn't to hurt you. I was thinking of Mom and Dad. Of our family—and that includes you.
    I hope we can somehow put this behind us.
                         Johanna

I read the note once. Twice. And then I placed it on my desk.

How like my oldest sister to be straight and to the point. She sent me flowers, but there was nothing flowery about her note. Did a part of me want more?

No.

This was enough. This was a start.

I traced the outline of the waves on the front of the card. A beach scene. Did Johanna still remember our long-ago family vacation? Was it a good memory for her, too?

"So?" Kimberlee's voice interrupted my musings.

"Believe it or not, Johanna sent me the flowers."

Kimberlee's eyes widened. "Your sister Johanna?"

"Yes, my sister Johanna."

"Why would she send you flowers?"

"It's a long story—"

"I like long stories," Bianca chimed in, resting her chin on her upturned palm.

"Me, too."

I returned the card to its envelope and moved the flowers to the middle of the lunch table. "It's a long, complicated story. I'll just say Johanna and I had a major blowup a couple months ago . . . and I apologized . . . and she accepts my apology."

"That isn't a story—that's a miracle." Kimberlee stared at me as if I'd announced the card contained a marriage proposal from a stranger.

"Can we eat lunch now?" I added fresh soup to my bowl.

"Are you going to call Johanna and thank her?"

"Right now I'm going to eat lunch if that's okay with you."

Should I call Johanna? My sister hadn't called me. Of course, that didn't devalue the significance of the flowers and the card. Or the words written inside the card, which were even more unexpected.

Navigating a new relationship with Johanna was like trying to glue together two jagged pieces of a broken vase. The pieces refused to fit . . . to align . . . and then, with a little patience and a little shifting, they came together. The vase was no longer perfect . . . but it could still be beautiful from certain angles.

Maybe my relationship with Johanna wasn't set in stone after all.

27

JILLIAN INSERTED THE KEY in her lock, pushed the door open, and dropped her purse to the floor, three steps inside. Half days were wonderful things. She'd change her clothes—starting with taking off the knit cap on her head—crawl into bed for a nap, and worry about eating later.

Shutting the door, she sagged against it. She used to love to go to work. Going in early wasn't a problem. Staying late? She'd do that, too. But that was before cancer stole her stamina. Her mental ability.

Her future with Geoff.

No sense in standing here and thinking of the life she could have had.

"What in the world?" She managed to stop short before she fell over her bright-yellow hard-sided suitcase sitting just inside her living room.

How did that get there?

"Sorry." Geoff's voice caused her to stumble back a step. "I should have said something sooner." He rose to his feet from where he'd been sitting on the arm of the couch.

"Wh-what are you doing here?"

"I'm waiting for you."

Jillian shook her head, her gaze flitting between him and the suitcase. "And why is this here?"

"I packed it for you."

"You packed it?" The man came to her apartment and packed her suitcase? "I'm not going anywhere."

"I hope to change your mind about that."

Her world seemed tilted off center. Was this some kind of joke? Yet Geoff hadn't sounded this serious since the day Dr. Williamson told her . . . them . . . the cancer was worse than they'd expected.

Geoff paced the small space between Jillian and the living room. He never paced. Oh, how she wanted to tell him to stop. To stand still. To hold her so she could find the rest that had eluded her since she'd sent him away.

She squared her shoulders. This was not the time to run back to Geoff. To start thinking she could still have what she'd lost.

"You need to leave. And please give me the key to my apartment."

"Not until I say what I came to say." Geoff stopped pacing, facing off with her, hands on his hips. "I listened to all the reasons you called off our wedding. And I've thought about every one of them over and over again."

"If you'd listened, then you wouldn't be here—"

Geoff raised one hand like a police officer halting traffic. "You had your say. Now it's my turn."

Jillian swallowed the rest of her sentence. Closed her mouth, pressing her lips together.

"You're scared, Jillian."

She waited half a beat to see if Geoff was going to say anything else before speaking. "I am not scared. I'm thinking of you, Geoff."

"No, you're not. You're running scared." He exhaled, his eyes meeting hers. "And I get it. I really do. I'm scared, too."

Right. "All I ever got from you was 'You can beat this, Jillian. Everything is going to be okay, Jillian.' And then you'd go off to work—"

"I admit it. I got caught up in work. Yes, I had that crazy project, but the truth is, keeping busy helped me not think about what was happening to you—it helped me not be so scared." Geoff took a step forward. Stopped. "I wanted to fix what was happening . . . but I couldn't . . . and without realizing it, I pulled away. I'm sorry."

His admission, the pleading tone of his voice, tempted her to weaken. But she couldn't.

"Fine. You're scared. I'm scared." Even as she said the words, she steeled her heart. "But I'm not changing my mind."

Now Geoff would leave—and she could collapse. But he remained where he was, looking even more determined.

"There's just one thing."

"What's that?" Her question wavered. Just the smallest bit. Had Geoff heard?

"You never said you didn't love me, Jillian." Geoff's tone softened. "You're afraid I'm going to stop loving you because you have cancer. Let me prove you're wrong."

"How?"

"Marry me. You want 'for better, for worse, in sickness and in health'? I do, too. Let's forget about the big wedding. All the other people. They don't matter to me. You do."

"Geoff, I'm not the woman—"

Geoff took three strides, pulling her into his arms. "I don't care, Jillian. I don't care that you're bald. Wear the wig or don't wear it."

"It's more . . . more than that."

Geoff held her so close their bodies pressed together. With the back of his hand, he caressed her face, her neck, his hand trailing to her collarbone before he stopped. "I'm sorry you lost a breast. So, so sorry. But I still want you, Jillian, in every way a man wants a woman. I'll wait until you're ready, but know that I do want you."

He bent his head, watching her. She should move away. Turn her face from his. But instead, Jillian slipped her arms around his neck, tugging him closer, his name escaping her parted lips on a sigh right before he kissed her.

So not fair. It wasn't fair for Geoff to kiss her. She'd missed his voice. His laugh. His tenderness. But his kiss undid her, crumbling her defenses and igniting a longing for this man. There was no denying she still loved him. When Geoff held her, she was still a desirable woman, no matter how her body failed her.

Geoff ended the kiss. Whispered in her ear, "Will you marry me?"

"Yes. Yes, I will." Her words eased an ache in her chest.

"You said yes." Geoff held her away from him.

"You're a very persuasive man, Mr. Hennessey."

"I should have come and kissed some sense into you sooner."

Laughter bubbled up inside Jillian and spilled out, but she stopped as Geoff pulled her engagement ring out of his pant pocket and slipped it on her finger. "You had my ring with you? You were that confident I'd say yes?"

"I've kept this ring with me ever since you left it in my desk drawer at work."

"I'm sorry I did that." Jillian refused to look away, even knowing the happiness in Geoff's eyes would be shadowed by hurt. "I couldn't keep the ring, not after we'd broken up . . . but I couldn't face you again, either."

"I understand." Geoff pulled her close again. "You won't believe how many times I've sat in my car outside your apartment and talked myself out of coming up here."

"What changed your mind?"

A grin stole across his face. "Because today I've got it all planned out."

"What do you mean?"

"I want to marry you, Jillian. Today."

"Today?" It was her turn to pull away. "We can't get married today."

"Yes, we can." Geoff sounded like he'd just won the Super Bowl and was going to Disney World. "I told you that I have a plan. We need to go get a license, but that's doable. And a friend of mine's mother is a judge. She's agreed to marry us this evening in her chambers."

"You've already asked her?"

"Yes." He held up his phone. "She's on standby."

"You, me, and a judge?"

"It can't be a whole lot simpler than that."

"And then what?" Heat coursed through her body even as she asked the next question. "We flip a coin to see whether we come back here or go to your house for our wedding night?"

"I did make some plans for our honeymoon—"

"What if I'd said no?"

"But you didn't." Geoff reached for her suitcase. "You ready to go?"

"Can I change into a dress? Something a little more festive than my work clothes?"

"Sure. But we are on a bit of a schedule."

"I realize that. Call the judge." Jillian hesitated. "You're not going to surprise me by having my family there or anything, are you?"

"No. It will be you, me, and Judge Estrada. A brief ceremony—and then a short honeymoon before we have to go back to work."

"Did you even tell my family?"

"No. Now no more questions." Geoff put his hands on her shoulders and directed her toward her bedroom. "Go pick your wedding dress, please. I'll load your suitcase in the car. We can talk more on the way to get the marriage license."

A moment later, Jillian stood in front of her bedroom closet, her arms wrapped around her waist. Memories of the disastrous day she'd gone wedding dress shopping flooded her mind.

And then a smile curved her lips. That day—with all its challenges and uncomfortable moments and the shock of Payton disappearing—held one unexpected benefit. A benefit that would be perfect for tonight.

Jillian shoved the hangers in the closet to one side, reaching for the dress she'd hidden in the deepest corner. Even covered in the clear bag, the soft lavender chiffon dress seemed to shimmer in the light.

No one—not her mother, not Johanna, not even Harper—knew she'd gone back to the bridal shop to try on this dress after noticing it while the two mothers were trying on their dresses. And certainly no one knew she'd bought it for a reception dress, back when she still believed her wedding would happen.

Now, of course, there would be no white gown. No long-dreamed-of April wedding. No reception, where family and

THINGS I NEVER TOLD YOU

friends watched her dance with Geoff—their first dance as husband and wife.

The truth was, the months ahead held so many more questions than certainties.

But it didn't matter.

She and Geoff would be together.

And tonight . . . tonight she would wear this dress. She would feel beautiful. And she would stand beside the man she loved—the man who never stopped loving her—and say, "I do" to facing the future together.

28

THE FLICKER OF THE GYM LIGHTS caught me off guard. Practice was over already? That couldn't be right. I swallowed a laugh, realizing that I'd lost track of the time—again—as I'd worked with my middles.

Wait a minute. *My* middles? This was Sydney's team. These were Sydney's girls. I'd agreed to be a backup assistant coach—nothing more. I'd help out at practices sometimes as a favor to my former coach. Come to games when I could.

And yes, there was a part of me that was excited about being involved in volleyball again.

"Thanks, Coach." Katelyn ran past me as she dumped a ball in the rolling mesh bucket cart. "It was fun tonight."

Coach? "You had a great practice tonight. If you want to come about a half hour early next time, we can work on your hitting."

A grin lit her face. "That'd be great!"

"Okay. You can get my number from Sydney if there's a problem."

"Thanks."

Jody stopped beside me. "Coach Sydney was your coach, too, right?"

"Yeah, when I was in high school." I tossed a ball over the net. "My sister and I both played on varsity."

"Did you play in college?"

"No."

"Neither of you? Why not? I thought Coach said you were good."

It was a straight-up question. Jody didn't know how complicated the answer was. Of course, I could keep my answer straight-up, too. "Pepper—my twin sister—was killed in a snowmobile accident during spring break when we were juniors in high school."

"Oh. Wow."

This was almost like the start of tryouts, where everyone knew what was going to happen—volleyball—but didn't know the order of the specific drills. I was an adult. I knew how to have a basic conversation with other people, but I avoided talking about Pepper, about her death, for this very reason. Straight-up answer or not, telling someone your sister was dead made them uncomfortable.

Time to move the conversation on to a better topic. "Anyway, after that, I didn't want to play volleyball anymore. I own a party-planning business with a college friend."

Parents were trickling into the gym to pick up their daughters. The girls sat along the left side of the court, changing into warmer clothes and checking their phones. One dad lingered just inside the door, hands stuffed in his pockets.

Wait. That wasn't a dad. That was Zach.

He waved as we made eye contact. I offered a small wave back, my initial surprise blending with a sense of pleasure mingled with awkwardness.

Maybe my agreement to meet him for coffee after practice when he'd called late last week was a mistake.

But we were just meeting for coffee. Nothing more. I wasn't even sure why I'd said yes when he'd followed up on the suggestion he'd made on Christmas Day.

"Is that your boyfriend, Coach?" Chandler tossed the question my way.

"What? No. No, that's . . . He's a friend."

"He's cute."

"Sure, if you say so." And that sounded adolescent. "Thanks for your help taking the nets down."

Sydney and I chatted for a few minutes about the practice. "Is that guy waiting for you?"

"Yes. He's a friend. We're going to have coffee. You want to meet him?"

"Absolutely. Just a friend, huh?"

"Yes." I stopped with a couple of feet between us. "Hey,

347

Zach. Sorry to keep you waiting. Um, this is Sydney. She owns Club Brio."

"Hi, Zach."

"And Zach is my . . . I mean . . ." Why was I stumbling over this?

Zach shook hands with Sydney. "Zach Gaines. Payton and I knew each other in high school. I came to a couple of her games back then."

There. Why hadn't I just said that? We knew each other in high school. Of course Zach and I were barely friends in high school. And we were casual friends now. Nothing more, nothing less.

A small cross hung against Zach's T-shirt. Another reason there would be no "more" for Zach and me. I didn't know much about being a Christian, but I knew enough to realize I wasn't the kind of woman he was looking for. That would be someone like Kelsey.

He wasn't the kind of guy I was looking for, either.

I wasn't looking at all.

Which made it easy to decline Zach's offer to ride together over to the coffee shop. To friend-zone him and pay for my own coffee and begin dumping in sugars as I asked how his Christmas was.

"Monterey is beautiful. But I was glad to get back home to the cabin."

"And Laz?" I refused to mention Kelsey.

"Of course."

"And a few days was enough time with your parents?"

Even as I asked, I couldn't help but wonder if I'd overstepped a boundary.

"It works best for all of us. We're still trying to find our way with each other. They're still not sure what to make of the new me." His smile was brief. "Besides, my parents' holiday tradition is to head to England for New Year's."

"You weren't lonely, up in the cabin all by yourself?"

"Nope. There's a difference between loneliness and solitude." Zach still hadn't taken a drink of his coffee. "I spent a lot of my years looking for the next party. Filling my hours with people and noise and alcohol and drugs. I couldn't hear myself think and I didn't know who I was. The truth is, back then I didn't want to be alone. Christmas Day was the best one I've had with my parents in years, but I wouldn't say it was comfortable. Not yet. Being in the cabin by myself? I enjoyed every minute . . . and the fact that I was okay with that shows how much I've changed."

"You were one of the kids I always envied in high school."

"What?"

I couldn't blame the guy for being confused by such a sudden change of topic.

"You were *Zach Gaines*. The guy with all the friends. You broke all those athletic records —"

"And you were Payton Thatcher, one half of the too-cool Thatcher twins."

"The lesser half." Had I just said that out loud?

"Come on, Payton." If Zach had been drinking his coffee, he just might have spewed it on me. "You really believe that?"

"Yes. Pepper was the better athlete. Pepper was more outgoing. Pepper was—"

"Well, you can't say she was prettier."

"No, I can't. Because we looked exactly alike."

How did we get from talking about Zach's Christmas to talking about who was prettier in high school—Pepper or me? The truth was, Zach wasn't that confident teen athlete anymore—and most likely he'd struggled with insecurities back then just like me and every other kid in our high school.

Zach rubbed his right forearm through the material of his long-sleeved T-shirt. Was the guy nervous? Or had he hurt himself somehow? It didn't matter. I didn't want to be curious about Zach Gaines.

Keep it simple. Keep it safe.

Zach shifted, reaching for his coat, retrieving something from the pocket. "This is for you." He placed a small square package wrapped in bright-blue Christmas paper and topped with a gold bow on the table between us.

"What's this?"

"Just a little something . . ."

"A Christmas present?"

Zach laughed, nudging the present across the table to me. "You, Miss Thatcher, are quite astute. Yes, it's a Christmas present. You going to open it?"

Yes, I was going to open it. Once I got over the fact that Zach had given me a gift.

"Thank you."

"You haven't even seen what it is yet."

Zach wasn't one of those people who took malicious pleasure in over-taping gifts. Within seconds, I held a small wooden box, tracing the elegant lines with my fingertips. The polished wood glowed varied shades of browns and yellows.

"You made this, didn't you?"

"I did."

"It's beautiful, Zach."

"Thank you."

Such an unexpected gift—not like something you receive from a family member who is supposed to get you something, maybe even a repeat of the same-old-same-old thing they get you every year for your birthday. Like a candle in a scent you don't like. Or bath salts you regift. Or a book—and you don't read sci-fi.

Zach had made this. Maybe had even thought of me as he did. And it was one of a kind.

I turned the box over and found *ZG* intersected with a small cross.

"Is this how you sign your work?"

"Yes."

"Distinctive . . . and meaningful." My skin heated. "I'm sorry I don't have something for you—"

"It's a gift, Payton—and you get to keep it even if you didn't get me anything." Zach's smile accompanied with a soft chuckle eased my desire to apologize again. "You said you had a good Christmas?"

"It was different."

"Different, but not good?"

How was I going to explain all this to Zach? "I hoped that telling my family the truth about what happened the night Pepper died would change things."

"And it hasn't?"

"It has . . ." My voice trailed off. "I think I mentioned that my oldest sister didn't understand . . ."

"I remember you saying something like that when we talked on Christmas Day."

"We had a huge argument out in front of my parents' house." I pressed my lips together, unable to admit I'd slapped Johanna.

Zach had the strength to not look shocked. "Why?"

I twisted a strand of hair, tucking it behind my ear. "I found out something that explains why things are like they are. I was an emotional mess after Pepper died. Johanna read my journals."

"Doesn't that break some sort of sister code?"

"Johanna may not have gone about it in the right way, but I think it was her way of being the big sister, of watching out for me. Of stopping another disaster. She had to be upset over what she read. I—I was suicidal for some months." At the admission, I stared down at the table. "I don't know if I would have actually done anything . . . but I wrote about it a lot. Wanted to be dead. Couldn't imagine being alive without Pepper."

"Understandable." Zach covered my hand with his. "You had to be heartbroken."

"I was." I shook my head, refusing to be pulled back into the memories. "Johanna told my parents—not the details, she said, but that she was worried about me. She's eight years older than me, and she recommended professional help. My parents sent me to an inpatient facility for teens."

"Did they talk to you about it before?"

"No. That was the worst part. I came home the last day of school to find my suitcase packed. They told me I was going. No discussion. Nothing."

"Not to defend your sister, but she probably did what she thought was best—"

"Johanna always does what she thinks is best. And what she thinks is always right." My hand tensed beneath Zach's. "After my confession to the family, Johanna wanted to know if I was going to be honest about everything—about the fact that I was going to kill myself back then."

"But you said you weren't sure you would have gone through with it. . . ."

"It didn't matter. And then I lost my temper and slapped her . . . and we didn't talk for weeks . . ."

"I'm so sorry, Payton. I understand strained family relationships."

"Well, believe it or not, there's a bit of a happy ending to this sad tale."

"I'm listening."

Zach didn't have to say that. He'd been listening to me all along.

"I wrote an apology to Johanna. Put it in her Christmas

gift—but she didn't say anything until a few days ago when I received flowers at my office—and a note from my sister."

"Johanna apologized?"

"As best she could. She said she never meant to hurt me and that she hoped we could put this all behind us."

"That's pretty amazing, Payton."

"It is, isn't it?"

"You're pretty amazing, too." Zach squeezed my hand.

I waved away his words, even as they snuck into a thirsty part of my heart. "I failed my family—"

"Stop." Zach's voice was firm. "You told the truth. After all these years, you told the truth—and things are changing."

"I guess you're right."

"Healing relationships take time—and it's not just up to you to make it happen. Believe me, I know."

Zach's skin was rough against mine, his fingertips calloused. His touch was so unexpected. But he didn't want more from me, did he? Friends could . . . touch one another this way and still be friends, right? For just a second I fought the desire to turn my hand up so that our hands met, palm to palm. To appreciate the tenderness Zach offered.

But instead I slid my hand away.

29

No one has to tell me I'm dreaming.

The difference this time is I'm not fighting . . . I'm not afraid. When you know you're dreaming, you know whatever reality you're in will end when your alarm goes off.

I know I'm dreaming . . . and I still can't quite figure out where I am. The area looks familiar. Rocks. Scrub brush. Blue sky overhead. Familiar . . . but not familiar enough.

"I see you found the key."

Pepper speaks from behind me, causing me to spin around, stumbling just a bit as I search for my sister. The key? I have the key? I uncurl my fingers, and yes, there it is in the palm of my hand. "Do you know what it's for?"

"*Yes. And you do, too.*"

"*Tell me.*"

"*Payton, I can't do it for you.*"

"*I'm not asking you to do it for me—*"

"*Sweet sixteen and never . . . never . . . never . . . so many things, Payton. So many things.*"

"*You're not making any sense, Pepper.*" *I grip the key in my fist again.* "*But why should that surprise me? I didn't understand you at all before you died. New friends. New ideas about who you were and what you wanted to do.*"

"*I wasn't changing that much—*"

"*The only time we did the same thing was on the volleyball court—and even then I was playing catch-up.*"

"*That's not true.*"

"*Just because you say it's not true doesn't change . . .*"

"*Change what?*"

"*Never mind. It doesn't matter anymore.*"

"*It matters now more than ever.*"

"*No!*" *Did I yell that out loud? I fight to move my arms or legs, but I'm weighted down against the bed. Am I awake or still asleep?*

Wake up. Wake up. Wake up.

In painful slow motion, I forced myself to sit upright, the blankets tangled around my legs even as the last remnants of the dream were tangled around my subconscious. I bracketed my face with my hands, my hair falling against my skin.

The dreams needed to stop. But it seemed I didn't get to decide that.

It wasn't quite five o'clock Friday morning. If I got ready for work now, I'd arrive hours before Kimberlee and Bianca. But what choice did I have? There would be no going back to sleep. And I had no desire to linger in my town house either—with the shadows of Pepper's appearance.

Work it is.

I was so productive that when Kimberlee arrived hours later, I'd updated Facebook, Instagram, and Pinterest and was sitting at my desk, staring at the mystery key as if willing it to reveal its identity to me.

"You look like you spent the night here." Kimberlee set her purse on her desk, along with a plate of bran muffins.

"Thanks for that. And I took extra time with my hair this morning."

"Uh-huh. Good thing for you that you're one of those women who can pull off the whole messy-bun look." She selected a muffin and put it on my desk.

"Yeah, well, if my sister would stop interrupting my sleep . . ."

"Another dream?"

"Yes." I admitted defeat. "Another dream."

Did I really want to talk about this again? Still? So much of my life had been linked to Pepper before she died and after she died. And now my life was still about Pepper.

It's always about Pepper.

Where had that thought come from?

"What was the dream about this time?" Kimberlee replaced my empty mug with a fresh cup of coffee, motioning for me to eat my muffin. "Here—three sugars just like you like it. I figure you need it."

"Thanks." I tossed the key on my desktop. "The dream was about this."

"This?" Kimberlee picked the key up, turning it around. "This key?"

"Yes."

"What's it to?"

"I don't know. I went looking in my old bedroom closet on Christmas Day and found it in the pocket of my high school letter jacket."

"Have you googled it? You know, typed in 'different types of keys' and then clicked on Images?"

"No. It never even occurred to me to do something like that."

Kimberlee pulled up Google on my computer and began typing. "This looks like the kind of key that goes with a metal lockbox or a fireproof safe—you know, for storing important papers."

"Like passports and stuff?"

"Exactly. My parents have one. They kept their marriage certificate and passports in it for safekeeping. They gave me one when I went away to college." She clicked on the Images link. "There. Does that look familiar?"

"No. Not the fireproof safe. Let me see . . ." I typed in *lockbox* and clicked the link.

In the half second it took for the results to appear, adrenaline seemed to spill into my veins, revving up my heartbeat. It was as if I knew we were close to solving the mystery of the key. Part of me was ready, while part of me wanted to back away from the computer. Close my eyes. Not remember.

"It goes to a lockbox . . ." I whispered the words to myself.

"What?"

"The key . . . it goes to a metal lockbox. . . ."

"Let's make a time capsule!" Pepper sat on her bed and clapped her hands like a little girl.

"A what?"

"A time capsule—you know! People collect stuff and bury it in a container and then it's dug up fifty years later—"

"Fifty years? That's forever!"

"It only seems like forever. We can figure out how long we want to wait to dig it up while we collect stuff."

"What are we going to use for the time capsule?"

"What about that old lockbox out in the garage? I bet Dad will let us have it."

"Do you know where the lockbox is, Payton?" Kimberlee's question pulled me back to the present.

"Yes . . . well, if it's still where we put it."

"What do you mean?"

"It's a box Pepper and I . . ." For some reason I found myself hesitating to tell Kimberlee the complete truth. I was only just remembering it myself. "We stored stuff in it. School stuff. You know. I remember where we put it last, but I'm not sure it's still there."

"You're going to go look for it, right?"

"Yes. Sure." I closed the browser. "Okay. Mystery solved. Now we can get back to work."

But as Kimberlee moved over to her desk, I stared at the key, doubting my own words. Maybe it would be best to leave the time capsule alone—if the lockbox was still where we'd buried it a decade ago.

Pepper and I had made the time capsule together. Buried it together. Kept the secret together. Promised each other we'd come back and unseal the time capsule twenty years later—or when the first one of us got married.

Well, there'd be no "together" when it came to unsealing the time capsule. Maybe it was best that it be forgotten again.

⌒

This was the right thing to do, wasn't it?

Jillian didn't regret the decision to marry Geoff two weeks ago. Not at all. And their families had to know she and Geoff were married sometime before their first anniversary.

But deciding to invite their families over to Geoff's house to tell them all at the same time? Maybe that was a mistake.

Then again, it was a little late now to rethink how they were going to reveal their elopement, not with their parents and her sisters waiting for them to come out from the kitchen with a few requested drinks.

Jillian twisted her hands together, turning a small circle in Geoff's kitchen. *Their* kitchen. She'd been back to her apartment only three, maybe four times since they'd eloped. They were moving some of her furniture over here, replacing some of Geoff's older pieces, and opting to let the lease run its course for now. One less thing to worry about.

What if someone noticed her furniture in Geoff's place before their announcement? Why hadn't she thought about that?

She was more nervous tonight than she'd been when she and Geoff got married. Once they'd made the decision, she'd had no qualms about standing in front of a judge and saying, "I do." And then showing up at work a few days later and sharing the news with Harper had been such a fun moment punctuated with laughter and tears—and Harper's promise to keep their secret until they told their families.

But tonight was making her wish she could plead a headache or nausea—or both—and go hide in the bedroom.

"Maybe this was a bad idea." Jillian leaned closer to her husband, keeping her voice to a whisper as if anyone could hear her on the other side of the kitchen wall.

"Getting married? It's a done deal, honey." Geoff placed a swift kiss on her lips.

"No, not that. Deciding to tell everyone. Maybe we should let them think this is only a 'we're back together' party."

Geoff held up his hand. "We should have just worn our wedding bands—"

"No! Someone would have noticed before we had a chance to say anything." Jillian pressed her fingertips against her temples, closing her eyes. "I'm just not sure I'm up to their reactions."

"You don't think they're already wondering what this is all

about?" Geoff covered her hand with his own. "And what are they going to say? We're adults. We were planning on getting married. We just decided to be a bit unconventional—"

"Geoff, we went from planning a huge wedding, to postponing it, to canceling it, to getting married without telling anyone—"

"You don't have to review everything with me. I'm thankful it's behind us and we're married. Plain and simple."

"Well, there's nothing 'plain and simple' about telling everyone."

"Then I'll tell them. And then we'll break out the champagne and celebrate."

"I don't want to disappoint anyone—"

"In case you're wondering, I'm not disappointed at all." Geoff wrapped his arms around her, pulling her close.

"Are you sure?"

"Yes. I'm completely—"

Before Geoff could finish his declaration, a commotion in the other room distracted Jillian. Voices raised. Footsteps. And was that . . . barking?

"Oh no! Winston's loose!"

Sure enough, as they rushed from the kitchen to the living room, the black-and-white puppy on the run tried to streak past them—halted only by Geoff's quick reflexes. He captured the wriggling dog, cradling him in his arms as best he could while evading Winston's attempts to lick his face.

Everyone turned to stare at them. Geoff's parents. Her parents. Johanna and Payton.

"What is that?" Johanna's tone implied that Winston was half-canine, half-rodent.

"This is Winston." Jillian scratched behind the puppy's ears. "Our dog."

"You have a dog? Are you crazy?" Johanna's eyes widened. "You're not finished with your chemo yet, and then you have radiation—"

"My doctor is fine with me having a puppy." Jillian paused. Maybe this was the perfect, unexpected opening. "Geoff gave him to me as a wedding gift."

Her mother gasped. "A wedding gift? You mean the wedding is back on?"

"No, I mean Geoff and I got married January 5."

Jillian's announcement plunged the room into not-quite silence—the stillness broken by Winston's tiny whimpers and barks as he struggled to escape Geoff's hold. Was this how Payton felt when she told the truth about what happened the night Pepper died? Did she try to gauge everyone's reactions by the varied expressions on their faces?

Were her parents angry with her . . . or sad? And what did Geoff's parents think about their only son eloping?

"This is so romantic!" Payton clapped her hands before wrapping Jillian in a gentle hug. "I'm so happy for the two of you!"

"Thank you." Jillian held on for a moment longer. "Really . . . thank you."

"You two got photos, right? Did you run away to Las Vegas?"

"Hardly anything that dramatic." Jillian stepped closer to Geoff, who slipped one arm around her even as he maintained control of Winston. "We got married by a judge here in the Springs and had a brief honeymoon weekend at a bed-and-breakfast in Vail."

Geoff spoke up at last. "I take responsibility for the whole idea—"

"You didn't kidnap me—"

"No, but I was the one who suggested it." Geoff released Winston, who scampered off down the hall. "When Jillian called off the wedding, well, I couldn't accept it. And then I realized we kept trying to figure out how to make it all work—and that the most important thing was being married to Jillian. Not *how* the wedding happened—just that it happened."

Jillian allowed Geoff to talk, realizing he wasn't looking at anyone but her. In all the months since her diagnosis, even when his actions toward her changed, the way he looked at her hadn't. He always looked at her as if she were the most beautiful woman in the world.

"So I showed up at her apartment—"

"He was there when I came home from work one afternoon. He'd already packed my suitcase—"

"And I asked her to marry me. Then. That day."

"And I said yes. Because I realized I was letting the cancer—I was letting fear—control my life."

Geoff laughed. "Well, that's an abbreviated version of the conversation. We had some things to talk out. But the most important thing is, we're married."

At last, her mother moved to embrace her, and Geoff's mother stepped forward to hug her son—both fathers following behind them.

"I can't believe this." Her mother's words were woven with laughter and tears. "You're married."

"I know. Sometimes I can't believe it, either."

"You're planning some sort of reception in the future, right?" Even as Johanna hugged her, she began making plans.

Ah. The question she'd been anticipating—and had prepped for.

"We're not planning anything right now—except for me to finish the chemo and get through my course of radiation." Jillian sought out Payton again. "We did want to send out announcements, and I was hoping you, Payton, could recommend a designer and Johanna would help me figure out the wording."

Johanna nodded. "I'm sure we could design something ourselves—"

"We thought about that, but right now it's all about keeping life as simple as possible." Jillian paused as Geoff excused himself to take Winston outside. "Although I realize adopting a puppy doesn't equal 'simple.' Besides Winston, we're keeping everything else simple, which is why I hope Payton can recommend someone to design the announcements."

"Is a reception off the table completely?"

"Maybe. Maybe not. I may just do a celebration when I'm finished with my treatment, Johanna, but I can't think about it yet. Geoff and I are going to tell people that we don't expect gifts and that if they feel like sending anything, we'd rather they make a donation to the Make-A-Wish Foundation."

"I have a question." Payton spoke up.

"What?"

"Why did you name your dog Winston?"

Payton's unexpected question caused everyone to laugh.

"We found him at the homeless shelter. They told us that despite being the runt of the litter, he was scrappy and fearless. For some reason, that made me think of Winston Churchill and his whole 'never, never, never give in' quote. It seemed appropriate."

"I like it." Her younger sister hugged her again. "And you're proving to be pretty scrappy and fearless yourself."

"Thanks. It's easier . . . not being alone."

"I'm so glad you have Geoff."

Jillian couldn't remember the last time Payton had willingly hugged her—and not once, but twice. Even after Payton's confession, Jillian had been the one to embrace her sister, who seemed almost brittle, as if holding her too tight would shatter her. But tonight Payton wrapped her arms around her as if eager to connect.

Even Johanna hadn't argued with her that much. She didn't look thrilled about the unexpected announcement that Jillian and Geoff were married, but she didn't grill them about the details or list all the reasons they shouldn't have done it.

Could things be changing between her and Johanna and Payton? Shifting so they could have better—more respectful—communication? Learn to accept one another as adults, not just continue to react to each other the way they had growing up? Or was that wishful thinking?

Maybe it was, but that didn't mean it was too much to hope for. People could change. She was changing. Daring to be braver. To love without holding back in the face of a disease that threatened to take everything from her.

She could only change herself. One day at a time. One action at a time. Opening her heart up wide enough to love Geoff—no matter what the future held for them. And even choosing to adopt a puppy and name him after a British statesman . . . and keep the puppy even when he chewed her favorite high heels and demanded a spot at the foot of their bed. That was a kind of love, too. Loving the imperfect because she needed the laughter and the comfort Winston brought to her life.

"Now that everyone knows, it's time for some champagne, don't you think?" Geoff stepped away, his arm slipping down her shoulders so that he could take her hand.

"That sounds like an excellent idea!" Her father clapped his hands. "I'm going to give the first toast to my daughter and new son-in-law."

"Maybe your first official act as my father-in-law could be to help me open the champagne? Those corks are tricky."

"Absolutely."

Geoff and her father disappeared into the kitchen as Jillian found herself surrounded by the women in the room. Her mother took her hand. "And now we want a look at your wedding band."

Jillian pulled her hand away. "I'm not wearing it. I needed to wait to put them on until we told everyone."

"Well, go get your rings." Her mother nudged her toward the bedroom.

"I'll be right back. Don't start any toasts without me."

What had Harper said when she'd told her that she and Geoff had eloped?

"All's right with the world again."

Well, that was overly optimistic. There were still a lot of things wrong in the world in general . . . and in Jillian's little corner of the world, too. But she and Geoff? Yes, they were all right again.

30

I WAS TEN YEARS TOO EARLY—and I was alone.

A wool coat, scarf, and gloves shielded me from the cold air that bit at my nose and cheeks, and fallen leaves and twigs crunched beneath my boots as I made my solitary trek upward. The trail leading to the Siamese Twins rock formation was deserted, cloaked in predawn darkness. But that had been my hope all along when I'd arrived at the Garden of the Gods at five o'clock in the morning—right when the park opened.

The last time I'd walked this path lined with scrub brush, Pepper had been with me, her laughter ringing out as she led the way.

She always led the way.

"Are you sure it's okay for us to do this?"

"We're burying a small lockbox, Pay—not a dead pet or something."

"Ewww . . . gross."

"I'm just saying it's no big deal." Pepper turned and faced *me, walking backward, not seeming to worry about tripping on stones or fallen branches on the trail. "We'll bury the box out of the way, where no one else will see us."*

I shifted the camera strap on my shoulder. "How are we going to remember where we leave it?"

"I'll write it down. And you can take a picture of the location, too."

"What if somebody else finds it?"

"We'll find a good spot—far enough away from where most people wander. . . . Just stop worrying, okay?"

Pepper had it all figured out. She'd gotten Dad to give us the lockbox. Talked us through what we were going to put in the box. Asked our parents if we could borrow the car, telling them we wanted to walk through Garden of the Gods—which was the truth. Just not the entire truth.

"Think about coming back here in twenty years and finding our time capsule—"

"Twenty years is a long time, Pepper. Who knows what we'll be doing—"

"We'll still be playing volleyball in twenty years. And we'll bring our daughters with us. They'll be volleyball girls just like we are."

BETH K. VOGT

The breeze against my face was like an echo of Pepper's laughter. She'd always dreamed bigger than I did. Always invited me into those dreams.

I couldn't stop now. I wouldn't be back in another ten years to find the lockbox. It was now or never. And for Pepper's sake—for both our sakes—I needed to break the promise we'd made to keep the time capsule hidden.

But I would keep the promise to find the lockbox again.

So much had changed in ten years, but not the Siamese Twins. The two red stone columns rose up from the ground, side by side, an arch forming between them and creating a jagged oval opening in the middle. Facing west, I could see Pikes Peak off in the distance framed between the "twins."

"We'll have to wait our turn to get a picture."

"This could take forever." I didn't even bother to keep the whine out of my voice.

"Just be patient."

We stood off to one side, Pepper holding our time capsule, waiting for tourists and locals as they took their turns posing in front of the Siamese Twins.

"You want me to take your picture for you?" A middle-aged woman wearing a floral top approached, motioning to the camera I held.

"Sure." I slipped the camera strap over my head. "Thanks."

"You two are twins, aren't you?"

"Yes, ma'am."

"Identical?"

"Yes, ma'am. I'm Payton. She's Pepper."

371

"Those are cute names." The woman took the camera. "Peyton, like the football player?"

"Yes, ma'am, only spelled with an a.*"*

We settled in the center of the rock formation, side by side, arms around each other's shoulders, and smiled, the lockbox and spade at our feet.

I sat in the curved seat of the rock formation, the view of Pikes Peak behind me. All was quiet, save for the soft whisper of the breeze in the underbrush. Closing my eyes, I tried to recapture the moment, ten years ago, when my sister sat beside me, a stranger taking our picture, right before we hid the time capsule.

Now where had we hidden it?

"Let's not make this too complicated. We're facing away from Pikes Peak. Let's head downhill . . . south . . . and see what we find."

There was nothing magical about my search. No sense of Pepper's presence or of her leading me to the location. But it was easier finding the hiding place than I expected—probably because I was looking for an outcropping of rocks with a small mound of various-size rocks we'd covered the lockbox with, after only partially burying it in the hard red dirt.

I leaned back on my heels, setting the box on my knees, brushing the dirt from the surface. My fingertips tingled, trembled, as I pushed to my feet, searching for a place to sit where I could open the container.

Should I wait until I was home? Hike back to my car?

But holding the lockbox, I couldn't wait.

I settled on a larger rock that had overshadowed the lockbox's hiding place, the box in my lap, and removed my gloves. Inserting the key into the lock, I mentally rehearsed what I'd find inside. Pepper had been so decisive about what belonged in the time capsule and what didn't. I held my breath, bracing myself to view the treasured mementos we'd hidden away as idealistic sixteen-year-olds—unaware of what the future held in just nine months, much less twenty years.

⁓

"Hey, Laz! Come on inside, boy!" Zach whistled, searching the area for the rambunctious dog. He could always leave Laz outside while he was at work, but with snow predicted, it would be wiser to leave the dog lounging inside.

Laz's barks sounded from around the side of the house. Why wasn't he obeying the command to come when called? Had he cornered an animal by the woodpile? Zach strode toward the sound, stopping short at the sight of Payton's car parked next to his truck. Laz paced back and forth beside the Subaru, occasionally offering several sharp barks as if to alert Zach to Payton's presence.

How long had she been here? And why was she here?

Quickening his pace, Zach approached the car, peering inside the window that was obscured with haze. "Payton? You okay?"

She sat hunched forward in the driver's seat. When she didn't move, Zach rapped on the window. "Hey, Payton! Open the door!"

She startled at the sound of his knuckles hitting the glass, turning almost in slow motion, her gaze searching for his face. "Zach?"

What on earth? Didn't she know where she was? He grabbed the handle, yanking the door open. "Payton, what's wrong? Are you sick?"

As he leaned down to peer into the car, Payton jerked, stumbling out, catching him off guard and off-balance. He anchored his boots in the ground, determined to keep them both upright as she wrapped her arms around his waist, buried her face against his chest, her body shaking uncontrollably.

"I shouldn't . . . shouldn't have looked . . ." Payton's words were muffled, broken up by half sobs.

What? Shouldn't have looked at what?

"I thought . . . knew what was in it. . . . I didn't . . ." Payton's body shook harder.

"Okay . . ."

"I don't want it . . . I don't . . . Why would she . . . ?" With those words, Payton broke down completely, wrenching sobs almost choking her, a torrent of tears soaking his shirt.

Laz paced at their feet, whining, nudging Zach's legs. Zach didn't know what Payton was talking about . . . *who* she was talking about, but they couldn't stay out in this cold, not with the wind whipping across the land. He lifted her into his arms, cradling her against his chest, praying for wisdom. She didn't resist—just continued to sob while he carried her into the house.

"I'm going to set you on the couch, okay?"

"Don't leave me. Please."

Her plea caused an ache in his chest. "I'm not going to leave you. It's just you're cold and I want to get a blanket for you. You need to get warm."

No reply.

How long had Payton been sitting in her car?

He settled her in a corner of the couch, managing to snag a knit comforter to wrap around her before pulling her back into his arms.

Payton wasn't the first woman he'd ever seen cry—but he'd never seen one this broken. It was as if her sobs were tearing her apart . . . as if they would expose her heart . . . or some hidden wound that had been buried deep inside for years.

She'd always been so strong. Careful to maintain a distance between them, even the day she told him the truth about the night Pepper died. But now she burrowed into his embrace like a small child seeking both safety and solace, choking back her tears until she silenced them. But still her body trembled against his.

"I'm sorry." Her words were fragile as if she skated on a thin surface of ice covering her emotions.

"You don't need to apologize." Zach continued to hold her. "And you don't need to explain, either."

Silence settled between them. Her breathing evened out, and she relaxed against him. Somehow even Laz, ever a barometer of the emotions around him, knew to stop his pacing and lie down at Zach's feet. Within minutes, it was evident that Payton was asleep.

Zach ignored the questions running through his mind and continued to hold Payton as he prayed. For God to comfort her. For healing. For peace. For the Spirit to wrap around her like an invisible blanket—a spiritual comforter—and let Payton know she was safe.

At last he dared to ease her from his arms, shifting her onto the couch, still wrapped in the blanket, positioning one of the cushions beneath her head. She never stirred.

Was the car door still open?

Motioning for Laz to stay, Zach left the house to check. Sure enough, the driver's-side door stood ajar. Zach leaned inside, thankful to find the keys weren't in the ignition. Her purse sat in the passenger seat, and next to it was a tan lockbox.

Checking that Payton's keys were in her purse, he gathered both the purse and the lockbox, then shut the car door before returning to the house. Laz cocked his head and then, with a soft groan, stretched his body out on the floor. Payton didn't move.

Time to text Colin and ask him to pray. And then he'd pray some more. The best thing he could do was wait—maybe do some preliminary design work on a new project. Let Payton sleep. Be there when she woke up—and listen if she was ready to talk.

Three hours later, things were still quiet in the living room. Should he check on her?

Zach pushed away from the desk, stood, stretching his arms over his head, and made his way to the other room.

Empty.

The comforter was piled in a corner of the couch. No sign of Payton—or his dog. Her purse still sat on the coffee table, so she couldn't have gone far—and she'd taken the lockbox with her.

Pepper's bench.

She had to be there.

~

Zach made no attempt to sneak up on me, his boots crunching against the remnants of fallen snow, underbrush, sticks, and rocks. Laz heralded his approach with a bark but chose to remain sitting at my feet.

"I thought I'd find you here—" Zach stopped a few feet in front of me—"after initially being scared to death when you weren't still asleep on the couch."

"I'm sorry. I didn't think about that—"

"It's okay, Payton." Zach remained standing, the wind shifting his hair against his forehead.

I moved the metal lockbox into my lap. "You can sit down."

"Thanks."

He settled on the bench, leaning forward onto his knees, leaving space between us. Memories of collapsing against him, sobbing, kept me silent. I wanted to apologize . . . and at the same time, I wanted to forget how undone I'd been.

"How are you feeling?"

I guessed there was no ignoring what had happened earlier.

"Calmer than I was when you found me in my car."

Nothing like stating the obvious. But maybe I also reassured him that I wasn't going to dissolve into tears again.

"Do you want to talk about anything?"

No. Yes.

I traced the edges of the lockbox with my fingertips. "I drove up here because I thought . . . I hoped you could make sense of something for me. But now I realize I was being irrational. And unfair to you. This has nothing to do with you . . ."

"Sometimes it helps to have a friend be an objective person."

Just another thing I couldn't figure out. Had Zach and I become friends since he showed up at my office months ago, wanting to talk about Pepper? To make things right?

Things couldn't be more wrong.

"I've never tried to talk to anyone about this before. . . ."

Zach shifted, turning to face me but still leaving space between us. "I assume this has something to do with Pepper?"

"Yes." Instead of bringing any relief, the admission weighed on me, making it hard to draw a breath. And now I struggled with the thought of another panic attack.

Zach touched my arm. "It's okay . . ."

I gathered a breath. And another. "I thought if I came out here, sat on the bench . . . that I could finally figure everything out."

"Because you'd feel closer to her?"

I nodded, closing my eyes for a moment. "I haven't felt close to my sister in years—"

"That's understandable—"

"No. You don't understand." How could I say this out loud? "The problem between us . . . it started before Pepper died."

"Is that so unusual? I mean, sisters don't always get along, right?"

"Not me and Pepper. Never me and Pepper. We were 'the twins.' We looked alike. Sounded alike. We liked the same things. Reading. Cartoons. Fishing and football, thanks to our dad. And volleyball. Always, always volleyball."

Zach nodded. "What happened?"

It was only fair for Zach to ask the question, but I couldn't answer him. Not yet. Instead, I tapped the lockbox on my knees. "So, this."

"The lockbox."

"It's not just a lockbox."

"It's not?"

"It's a time capsule."

I had to give Zach credit for not laughing. "O-kay. I've never seen a time capsule before."

"It was Pepper's idea to make a time capsule right after our sixteenth birthday." I focused on opening the box, tucking the key back into my coat pocket. Ignored Zach, who slid closer, causing our shoulders and knees to touch. "We hid it near the Siamese Twins in Garden of the Gods. We were going to come back and open it twenty years later. After . . . after Pepper died, I forgot about it until I found the key on Christmas Day."

"And you decided not to wait to go find it."

"There was no point."

"What did you and Pepper put in your time capsule?"

I pulled out various items. "Our team photos from that year—varsity and club. You can tell us apart because she was always number 11 and I was number 13. A newspaper article. It's mostly about Pepper, but I'm mentioned because we were Double Trouble. Our learners' permits."

"All fun things."

"We also wrote out our dreams. Our goals." I'd kept the lists, written on notebook paper, folded. I still hadn't read those.

Zach was smart enough not to ask what they were. It wasn't necessary to say none of those had come true.

When I'd opened the time capsule, I wasn't surprised to see those things I'd shown Zach. But one item remained. Something Pepper must have put in the lockbox when I wasn't looking.

"Anything else?"

Instead of answering his question, I stared off into the distance. "When our junior year started, Pepper made some new friends."

"You mean she got mixed up with a bad group of kids?"

"Hardly." It was my turn to laugh, the sound short. Sharp. "She'd been hanging out with another girl on the varsity team some during the summer. This girl—Tari—invited Pepper to a Bible study after school, and Pepper went. She liked it, liked the other girls, so she went again. When I asked her about it, Pepper said she wanted to learn more about God."

"Okay." If Zach was surprised, he hid it well.

"The more she went, the more she changed. She got a Bible—I don't know if someone gave it to her or if she bought it—and started reading it. Memorizing Scripture verses she taped up on our dresser mirror. I tried to talk to her—to tell her to stop fooling around. That's when she said she was serious. That she was a Christian. Our family didn't—doesn't—do God, Zach."

At last I faced Zach, not quite meeting his eyes.

"Did she ever invite you to the Bible study?"

"Of course she did. All you Christians are the same! Share the . . . the 'good news,' right?" I bracketed the two words with air quotes. "We fought about that. And about how different she was. Then we stopped talking about pretty much anything except volleyball. Why did she have to change? She wasn't my sister anymore. Why did she have to get new friends? Be all about God? I could never keep up with her anyway . . . and then she had to do that?"

All these years later, I still couldn't understand what had happened. How was Zach supposed to explain it?

"She wasn't choosing between you and God, not really—"

"It felt like she did. I mean, I figured a guy might come between us . . . but God? How do you deal with that?" I was tempted to close the lockbox. But I'd gone this far with the story. I needed to finish it. "On our sixteenth birthday, our grandparents gave each of us five hundred dollars."

Zach took the change of topic well. "Nice."

"I used my money to buy a new cell phone. I'd been

begging my parents for one. I couldn't figure out why Pepper didn't do it, too. I figured she just put her money in the bank."

Now, all these years later, I knew what Pepper did with her money.

I took the white envelope from the time capsule. My name was written on the front in Pepper's handwriting—all loops and curlicues. First I removed the note inside. Then I slipped my fingers between the delicate gold links of the necklace, allowing the small diamond cross to fall against my palm.

Zach touched the cross. "That's beautiful, Payton."

"Pepper bought it for me. The note . . . the note says, 'For when you know Jesus like I do.'"

I clenched the symbol between my fingers, pressing it into my palm. "Why would my sister do this? Waste her birthday money—hundreds of dollars—on something I would never wear?"

"She hoped you would eventually believe in God, too—"

"But I don't. I won't. Twenty years . . . we're supposed to open the time capsule and find . . . this? What was she thinking?"

Zach's hand covered mine, his bare fingers cold against my skin. "Payton, listen to me. We're not talking about what you and your sister originally planned for the future. None of us controls life. Or death. You need to look at this necklace—today—for what it is."

"And what is that?"

"It's a gift from your sister. No strings attached."

"Oh, there are strings, Zach. There are always strings with something like this. I can only wear it if I believe what she did . . . but I don't. . . ."

"Then don't wear the necklace. Put it somewhere in your house where you can see it and remember your sister. Or put it away in your jewelry box. But remember you loved her and she loved you, too—no matter what kind of distance there was between you. Her faith was important to her, and she wanted you to have that same kind of faith because she loved you. Can you accept that much?"

"Before she died, there was no talking to her unless I agreed with her—"

"I get that. New believers . . . we're just plain stupid sometimes. We're excited. Eager to talk about something that has made such a difference to us. Something that has brought us peace. Comfort. Cut Pepper some slack." Zach's tone was so earnest. "Maybe she didn't do it all right. Maybe she said things wrong. But can you think about it with ten years of perspective and realize you were both sixteen . . . that you both got things wrong . . . and that you still loved each other?"

"I don't know. I don't know." I returned the necklace to the envelope. "It doesn't change anything."

"It will change you, Payton—who you are today. And it will help you tomorrow, too."

Zach believed what he said, but did I? Could the imperfect love between my sister and me span the past, present, and the future . . . and somehow heal the grief I was only beginning to face?

⌒

"Why do you believe in God, Zach?"

Of all the things Payton Thatcher could have said next, he hadn't expected that. But since she'd asked the question, he'd tell her.

"Have you ever heard the phrase, 'coming to the end of yourself'?"

"Yeah. I guess so."

"That happened to me. I'd messed things up pretty badly because of my choices. Doing drugs and drinking. Lost my scholarship. Strained my relationship with my parents. Still haven't fixed that yet. I messed up things with my college girlfriend too." He paused. How much did he need to share about the mistakes he'd made before and after settling things with God? "Anyway, after she kicked me out of our apartment, I found myself sitting in my car with no place to go, about ten bucks in my wallet, and that was it."

"What did you do?"

"I cried like a baby. I wanted to go home, but I knew I couldn't do that. My parents had told me they'd given up on me the last time I came home drunk for my mom's birthday." Zach stared straight ahead as he talked. "There was only one person who'd ever believed in me."

"Who?"

"Mr. Welkins—you probably remember the high school cross-country coach? He taught history, too." The memory eased some of the regrets surrounding him. "I drove to his house and knocked on the door. His wife answered, took one look at me, and called for Coach. Honestly, I don't know why she didn't shut the door in my face. But they took me in, fed me, let me stay in their basement bedroom—"

"For free?"

"Oh no. That's not how Coach Welkins does things. I was welcome to stay, but not freeload. At first I did yard work for him—and by that I mean I painted his deck and repaired his fence—after I got sober. That was the other condition—no alcohol and no drugs. That wasn't easy . . . or pretty. After a while, I got a job and paid rent."

"So where does God come in?"

"I'd heard about God on and off during my life—"

"You haven't always been religious?"

"No. My family was the kind that went to church for Christmas and Easter." He twisted to face her. "I had to decide what I believed about God—if I even believed in God—for myself."

"And?"

The answer was obvious, wasn't it? So Payton had to be asking more. What was her original question?

"Why do you believe in God, Zach?"

"Once I was sober . . . I could listen when Coach talked about God. He told me his story . . . and I realized I needed God—"

"Like a crutch—"

"No. Like the One who knows me best because He created me. The One who offers me more grace than I offer others . . . more grace than I offer myself. The One who forgave me of things I still struggle to forgive myself for. That's why I believe in God, Payton."

There was so much more he could say to her, but Zach forced himself to wait to see if Payton had any more comments. Any more questions. He'd learned it was better to be ready with an answer than to rush ahead, assuming someone else wanted to hear what he had to say.

She shifted on the bench, and for a moment, he thought she'd pull her hand away. But she didn't.

"No one's ever talked to me about God like that before." Payton made brief eye contact with him. "Thank you, Zach."

He wasn't sure what she was thanking him for. "You're welcome."

"And thank you for being my friend."

"I'm glad we're friends, Payton."

There was a moment's pause before she replied. "Me, too, Zach. Me, too."

31

Two PIECES of unfolded white notebook paper lay side by side on my breakfast nook table, the kind of paper Pepper and I used to take class notes on for English and history and Spanish. Both papers were labeled *MY DREAMS* in big block letters with a blue Sharpie, but other than that, they were completely different. One list was familiar because I'd written it out ten years ago. The other I recognized because it was written in Pepper's still-familiar, more elaborate handwriting.

When people make lists of dreams and goals in their youth, do they ever turn out?

That was a ridiculous question. Just because I was staring at my adolescent list of hopes and expectations—and had veered so far from any of them—that didn't mean no one else achieved their dreams.

Look at Johanna. Four years of college. Four years of pharmacy school. Dream job. A long-term, one-day-they-would-get-married relationship with Beckett. Was all of that what she'd daydreamed about back when she was a teenager? Did Johanna even allow herself time to daydream?

And Jillian . . . well, Jillian never said much about her dreams. She was everyone else's cheerleader. Did she go to college because she wanted to or because that's what you did after high school? Was working at the bank a dream come true—or just a good job because she'd always liked math? And cancer . . . I was certain that hadn't been on Jillian's goals as a grown-up. But she hadn't let that stop her from marrying Geoff, even if they'd skipped the traditional wedding and reception.

Kimberlee was living her dream and had invited me along.

My list of teenage dreams sat open on the table in front of me. Numbered. Plain print letters. And each one somehow had to do with volleyball.

1. Major in kinesiology in college.
2. Play volleyball.
3. Help coach a club team during the spring and summer.
4. Start a club with Pepper.

None of that had come true.

When I'd read through Pepper's list of dreams and goals—twice—it didn't make any sense to me.

She hadn't dreamed big like I thought she would back then. No, if anything, her dreams were small.

1. Get a scholarship.

Yes, that was at the top of her list. But I didn't recognize any of the colleges she'd listed. When I'd searched for them online, I discovered they were private Christian colleges, which had only confused me more.

2. Go on a mission trip.

First Christian colleges? Then she'd wanted to go on some kind of religious trip to Africa?

3. Get married. Have a family.

Okay, fine. But only after she'd had an amazing college volleyball career, right?

4. Get closer to my mom, dad, and sisters. Keep praying for them.

There were multiple hand-drawn stars on either side of these sentences, and they were underlined three times. It was easy to see that was important to my sister. I understood the whole "keep praying for them" part. Probably her newfound friends were telling her to do that. But what did she mean about getting closer to her parents and sisters? We were fine before she died. Mostly.

That was it. Short . . . some people would even say simple, but it made my sister all the more complicated.

None of Pepper's dreams and goals had come true, either.

Could I rescue my teen self that had dreamed of a different life? Could I rediscover a part of my heart that I'd neglected for years? Were any of these adolescent dreams ones I should have held on to, despite the heartbreak of Pepper's death?

My throat ached at the thought of what I'd lost. What Pepper had lost. Each other. Our dreams. Even if I didn't understand the dreams Pepper had written down, she'd still deserved the chance to pursue them.

I'd assumed I'd known what my twin sister wanted.

And I'd been wrong.

Pepper had never had the chance to go after what she wanted.

Me? I'd had chances. I just hadn't taken them.

Why should I have my dreams when Pepper didn't get hers?

The belief, buried deep within my heart, didn't surprise me. I'd lived bound by the unspoken "I can't" for so long, letting it guide my choices, my decisions. Pepper died. I lived. But I would live differently . . . live *less than* I'd hoped for because my actions had stolen my sister's future from her.

It was only fair. Some sort of sisterly "eye for an eye."

An unlived life for an unlived life.

Maybe someone else would have lived bigger, lived better. Tried to be more, or even be the person Pepper would have been. But identical looks, identical voices, identical laughs didn't mean identical abilities. I couldn't be Pepper just because our height, our weight, our eye color, and our preference for hamburgers with mustard and onions were the same.

But there was more holding me back than the lie I'd lived as a truth for so many years.

I stared at the two lists, our handwriting so different—another indication that despite having the same birthday, the same DNA, Pepper and I were not the same people. Given time, we would have grown up, changed. Maybe even gone to different colleges.

Given time.

And that's why I was so angry with my sister.

Yes, I was upset, confused about her faith.

But I was more upset . . . hurt . . . that Pepper was changing . . . excluding me . . . leaving me behind . . . and I wasn't ready. I couldn't find the common ground between us when she chose to believe in God and I didn't.

There was no common ground.

Given time, could I have learned to be okay with the change—the distance between us? Would we have agreed to disagree? Or would her faith have created an insurmountable barrier between us as the months passed?

There was no answering those questions now.

How do you reconcile with someone when she doesn't

even know you're angry with her? How do you reconcile with someone when she's gone?

"Can we talk about something before we both dive into the day?"

I turned my chair to face Kimberlee. "Calling a middle-of-the-week meeting?"

"You could say that."

"That was a joke. What's on your mind, partner?"

"The truth is we probably need to schedule more regular meetings, now that things are getting busier." Kimberlee leaned back in her chair, putting her booted feet up on her desk. "I know you've been having a rough go of it lately, but I need to talk to you about something."

"And I appreciate how understanding you've been. I promise things are going to settle down."

"That's what I wanted to talk to you about. Things aren't going to settle down—at least not for the business." She pointed to her computer screen. "I had Bianca make a spreadsheet for our spring events and into the summer. This is going to be our busiest year ever."

"I knew last year was good. I haven't been paying close attention to what this year looks like."

"Understandable. You've had a lot going on outside of work—"

"There's no denying that."

"Word of mouth has paid off and we're finally getting the

kind of attention—and the kind of clients—we've always dreamed of." Kimberlee paused. "And I need to know if you're with me in this, if you're going to be around for the future of Festivities."

I leaned forward, resisting the urge to jump to my feet. "What kind of question is that? Why wouldn't I be around—?"

Kimberlee held up her hand. "Don't say yes because that's the expected answer, Payton. We both know Festivities was my dream back in college. I've always been thankful you joined me. Not that you're not good at what you do. You are. We wouldn't be where we are now without your skills, especially with social media. But this next year could be a huge leap for the company. That's why I need to know if you're all in."

Kimberlee was being honest with me. She deserved for me to be just as honest with her.

"If you'd asked me this question a week ago, I would have automatically said yes." I paused, not sure how to explain that my hesitancy was caused by a list of dreams I'd written back when I was all of sixteen. "Festivities was your dream— and it's been fun being business partners, but . . ."

"Like you said, this business was my dream, not yours. What was your dream, Payton?"

I didn't hesitate. "Volleyball."

Kimberlee smiled. "I can't say I'm surprised."

"But I stopped thinking about that dream a long time ago."

"Why?"

It seemed as if telling one truth led to more and more

truth telling in my life. But was I ready to confess out loud to my friend why I'd followed in her footsteps instead of forging my own path?

"I guess . . . I guess I believed if Pepper couldn't have her dreams, then I didn't deserve to have mine."

"Oh, Payton, that's no way to live your life."

I couldn't hold back a laugh that mocked Kimberlee's words. "Well, that's where you're wrong. I've lived that way for ten years. And I've been successful at it—*we've* been successful. What I'm just beginning to realize is that living like this was easier than fighting through the grief—and even the anger—caused by Pepper's death."

Don't dream. Take the easy way out.

"Maybe it's time to revisit your dreams again." Kimberlee stood, crossing over to my desk. "You let grief keep you from them for too long. Don't let fear stop you now."

"I hear what you're saying. But you asked me a question. I just want time to think about it. I love what we do—"

"Be honest, Payton. No, you don't. You're good at being the planner part of the business. But you don't love Festivities like I do." Kimberlee tilted her head, narrowing her eyes. "What did you want to do when you graduated from high school? What did you want to major in?"

"What are you, some sort of guidance counselor?"

"No. I'm just asking the question. Were you always a business major?"

"It doesn't matter. We're not in college anymore, remember?"

"You're twenty-six, Payton. You've helped me achieve my

dream. It's not too late for you to go for yours. And if it means leaving Festivities, I understand. I'll miss you, but I understand."

I know Kimberlee meant to encourage me with her words. To offer me freedom to choose a new path. A different future. But instead, it was as if she'd backed me into a corner with no way out.

"Are you firing me?"

"We're partners. Partners don't fire each other. We talk and figure out the future. Our future. The company's future."

"What about you, Kimberlee? I mean, personally?"

"Personally?" She tossed me a grin. "Who's got time for a personal life when her dream is coming true?"

Could I abandon Kimberlee now? "What would you say if I wanted a couple of days to think about the future— whether I stay with Festivities or not?"

"I'd say fine. And what would you say if I started looking online at résumés? Because no matter what, we're going to need extra help. Maybe see if Bianca is interested in moving up from being a receptionist, too?"

"I already know the answer to that question. Just don't replace me right away."

"Deal." Kimberlee offered me her hand.

"I'll let you know within a week what I'm going to do. Fair?"

"That's fair." We both shook hands in agreement and then Kimberlee backed away. "Good talk?"

"Yes. Good talk."

It left my future undecided . . . but it was still a good talk.

32

Maybe this was not the best time to be contemplating my future.

Not when Sydney hadn't told me how mentally exhausting it would be to stand on the sidelines and help coach the sixteens team—all day long. And my voice? Almost nonexistent from cheering them on, my throat so raw it sounded as if I had a bad cold.

Granted, it was only seven o'clock at night. And I'd showered and changed into sweatpants and an old sweatshirt—certified comfy clothes. It was still early and I needed to do some research. Answer some questions.

But I'd also forgotten all the choices that came with going

to college. I hadn't even decided if I was really going back to school or not, and I was already overwhelmed with questions.

Full-time or part-time?

Online or classroom?

University or junior college?

My breakfast nook table was cluttered with my laptop, highlighters, and a legal pad scrawled with notes.

I grabbed my coffee mug, collapsing against the chair and taking a sip, choking on the cold liquid. While I sat there daydreaming—wondering if this crazy idea of going back to college could become a reality—my coffee had cooled.

Why was I allowing a ten-year-old list to spark long-forgotten ambitions? I should put it back in the lockbox with everything else and forget about it—not leave it tacked up on the bulletin board in my kitchen, next to my latest grocery list.

That's just what I'd do.

A loud knock at my front door interrupted my decision. *What on earth?*

Zach stood on my front porch holding two insulated cups of coffee. What was it with this guy showing up with coffee?

"I hope one of those is for me."

"Um . . . hello to you, too." Zach's smile had become familiar. "Yes, one of these is yours. If you'd answered your phone, you would have known I was going to drop by."

I motioned Zach inside. "You called me?"

"Yes. I don't make it a habit to just show up on my friends' doorsteps." Zach handed me one of the cups. "I was in the area and I remembered you mentioning during one of our conversations that you lived around here . . . so I did a White Pages search, and here I am."

Here he was. Bringing me coffee. Something a friend would do. I guess Zach and I were friends after all. Friends with the most unlikely of beginnings.

I had to admit I liked the idea of being his friend, but I didn't have to say it out loud—or think too long about how appealing his smile was. He wasn't as polished as Nash. Some women probably would think Nash was more handsome, but . . .

And that kind of thinking about Zach had to stop. Right now.

"You called? Because I didn't hear my phone ring—" I set the coffee aside and scrabbled through the mess on the table in search of my phone. "Aha! And . . . two missed calls."

"And a text or two, I think." Zach's smile widened into a grin as he settled in a chair across from me. "What is all this?"

"Would you believe I'm thinking about going back to college?"

"Tell me more."

"Don't laugh. I'm serious."

"And I'm not laughing. That was a seriously interested question."

I sipped my coffee, which was hot and sweet, just the way I liked it. "Thank you for this, by the way."

"One thing I've learned about you, Payton, is you're a woman who likes her coffee. Now, what's this about college?"

"It's the lockbox again and my list of goals and dreams. Oddly enough, being a party planner is nowhere on that list."

"What is?"

"Volleyball. Lots of stuff having to do with volleyball. I used to think about being a coach. Or starting a club." I ran my fingers through my hair, thankful I'd at least showered after I'd come home from the tournament. "But I gave that all up after Pepper died. I didn't think I deserved to have my dreams."

"And now you do?"

"I realize I did the best I could do back then. I made decisions that weren't great, even if they were understandable. And I can make different ones today. But I keep thinking it's too late for me to go back to college."

"Remember who you're talking to."

"Right. A college kid."

Zach laughed. "You're twenty-six, Payton. Some people go back to college in their seventies."

"Well, when you put it that way . . ."

"What are you thinking of studying?" Zach leaned forward and moved some of the catalogs. "Wait. What's this?"

Caught.

"It's just a book that I'm skimming."

"You're *skimming* C. S. Lewis's *Mere Christianity*?"

"Ye-es. Don't make a big deal about it, Zach. I was curious, I guess."

"Hmmm." Zach flipped through the first few pages.

"I googled 'books about Christianity' and the image for this book was second."

"Okay—what was number one?"

"Something to do with apologetics."

"Hmmmm."

"Again with the 'hmmmm.' I'm just curious about why Pepper believed in all of this."

"College. Books about God . . ."

"*A* book. One." Even as I corrected him, I laughed.

"Fine. Just be careful."

"What?"

"You might end up wearing that necklace Pepper bought you."

"Zachary Gaines! I can't believe you'd joke about something like that."

"I never joke about things I'm praying for, Payton."

And just like that, he turned the conversation serious. His voice dropped low, almost a whisper.

Zach was praying for me?

Weeks ago, I would have shoved him away. I had shoved him away. But he'd never stopped pursuing me, no matter how badly I behaved toward him. No matter what I said. He brought me coffee. Held me when I cried over my sister's death. Crafted a work of art in her memory.

And he prayed for me.

Had anyone ever prayed for me?

Pepper had . . .

"Payton? Did I lose you?"

Zach's voice had me blinking tears from my eyes. "Yes . . . sorry. Just for a moment there I thought about Pepper . . ."

"I'm sorry—"

"No. You made me realize Pepper probably prayed for me, too."

"I'm sure she did."

"I wish I could go back and change things . . ."

"She'd want you to focus on the changes you can make today, don't you think?"

"You're right."

"Which reminds me why I'm here." Even as he sat back, hooking his arm over the back of the chair, Zach sounded nervous.

"Oh, really?"

"I, uh, wanted to invite you to go on a hike with Laz and me on Saturday. It looks like the weather is going to be gorgeous."

"A hike?"

"Yep. We can enjoy the outdoors, talk about books . . ."

"Books, huh?"

"I'm reading a great military thriller right now."

I rolled my eyes and Zach's laugh rang out, seeming to draw me—or my heart—a bit closer. This was where I usually backed away. Put up virtual Do Not Cross This Line tape. But Zach wasn't pushing me. I could say yes or no, decide if I wanted to go.

"It sounds like fun, but I haven't been hiking in a while—"

"It's not speed-hiking, Payton. It's about enjoying the scenery and each other's company."

"I guess I could do that." I couldn't resist teasing him. "You're talking about Laz, right?"

"Ouch. I deserved that."

"Yes, you did."

"We won't go any faster than you want, okay?"

"Promise?"

"I promise. You can trust me, Payton."

"I do."

Were we even talking about hiking on Saturday anymore? There seemed to be a weight behind our words that went beyond Zach's initial invitation. But I refused to analyze every little thing the man said to me. And I wasn't going to ask about Kelsey, either. He'd said she was a friend and left it at that. Fine. We weren't even close to a "define the relationship" conversation. He'd said the hike was about enjoying the scenery and each other's company—so be it.

As friends. Going slow. Most definitely going slow.

33

THERE ARE CERTAIN THINGS you need to do yourself. Yes, this was my parents' house. And yes, our relationship had improved in recent months. But I was dealing with my childhood bedroom closet. Alone.

"Are you sure I can't help you, Payton?"

Mom's question stopped me halfway up the stairs—almost to the room Pepper and I had shared for so many years. As I half turned to face her, I gripped the wooden rail, bracing myself against the eager tone in Mom's voice. "I'm good. Honestly, I'd rather do this by myself."

"Do you need any boxes? Markers?"

"No. I brought some clear plastic containers." I motioned toward the hallway, where they waited outside the room, my letter jacket resting in the crook of my other arm.

"Fine. Decide what you want to keep and then Dad and I'll deal with whatever's left."

"Okay." As I continued toward the room, Mom's voice stopped me again. "Want me to bring you some coffee?"

"No, thanks. I don't think it will take that long."

And she didn't need to know I'd already consumed three cups before I got here.

"Let me know if you need anything—"

"I will."

But once I started, I wasn't leaving until I was finished.

I paused outside the door, one hand resting on the brass knob. I flashed back to the night of Jillian's engagement party, when I'd passed by this room, unable to enter. And then, months later, I'd discovered my letter jacket. The key to the time capsule . . . and so much else.

It was time to deal with whatever my parents had left in the closet. I rested my forehead against the door, inhaling and holding my breath for one . . . two . . . three heartbeats.

I could do this. I *wanted* to do this. There was nothing to be afraid of. I was looking through stuff. Boxing it up. Maybe taking a few things to my house.

Maybe.

Opening the door, I switched on the light, tossing my letter jacket onto the bed. Picked up the stack of containers and carried them into the room, lining them up against the far wall below the window before removing the lids and setting them on top of the queen bed.

The assortment of photos above the desk snagged my attention again. Our lives captured in freeze-frame moments.

We looked happy.

We had been happy.

I didn't have any photos of Pepper in my house. Should I disturb the montage and take one or two?

No. Maybe I'd look through family photos some other day. And maybe in doing so, I'd recapture more of the closeness I'd shared with Pepper.

Today was only about clearing out the closet.

It was easy to remove Pepper's letter jacket from its hanger. To hold it close for a few seconds before folding it and placing it in a container and then placing my matching crimson-and-white letter jacket on top of it.

Why was I keeping them? People didn't wear their letter jackets after they graduated from high school—or did they? Maybe some people dug them out of storage for class reunions. But I didn't know if I'd be attending any of those. Maybe one day, if I got married and had children, they'd find these . . . and I could tell them stories about playing volleyball with their aunt Pepper.

I traced the outline of the white cloth letter stitched to the front of Pepper's jacket. For the first time, I was thinking about my future, even if my thoughts were still tagged with *maybe*. And for the first time, my sister was a part of my future.

Did I ache when I thought about what might or might not happen years from now? Yes. But Pepper had been such an important part of my yesterdays. I wanted her to be a part of my tomorrows, too.

Six years of club ball—twenty-four jerseys between the two of us—remained in the closet. We'd claimed the numbers 11 and 13 early on and managed to keep them through every season. I gathered an armful of jerseys, each with the name of our club—*Endurance*—written across the back, and transported them to the bed, repeating the process until a messy pile of blue and white covered it.

With the closet cleared, I noticed a black CD player that had been pushed to the back. What was that doing in here?

Picking it up, I shoved aside the jerseys, the plastic hangers rattling, and sat on the bed, clicking the CD player open. Sure enough, inside was a CD labeled *Practice Playlist*.

Setting the player on top of the desk, I knelt and searched for an outlet. Would this even work? My fingers trembled as I pushed the Play button and sat on the edge of the bed again.

Within seconds the first song filled the room.

"These are great songs, Pay!" Pepper lay across her bed, her eyes closed, a smile stretching across her face.

"Why wouldn't they be? Everybody on the team picked two. All I did was put the CD together."

"But the order of the songs makes a big difference. I can't wait to play this over the school's speakers in the gym!"

We'd listened to these songs over and over during our varsity season junior year. I knew every word to every single song on this CD. Sometimes we'd danced on the court with our teammates. Sometimes we'd have a quick sing-off with the girl on the opposite side of the net while we waited for a teammate to serve the ball. Oh, how Pepper loved to crank the music up loud if we were having an off night. . . .

Oh, how my sister loved volleyball.

How I loved her.

"I miss you, Pepper. . . ."

My whispered admission cracked something open inside me. It was as if I'd tried to defend against a giant outside hitter, but instead, the volleyball slammed into my chest and knocked the air out of my lungs. I slipped from the bed to my knees, jerseys falling around me, rubbing my fist against my sternum as my entire body shook with a decade of repressed emotion. Tears streamed down my face, each one a testament to my loss. I bent over, my face to the floor, hoping the carpet would muffle my sobs.

Surely the weight of all this would suffocate me. . . .

And yet, somehow, I wasn't alone. Pepper seemed to sit beside me. Mourning with me.

We'd lost each other too soon . . . lost the chance to grow and change together . . . to understand one another . . . to accept one another.

When we were sixteen, I'd expressed confusion and hurt as anger. But I never stopped loving Pepper. And she never stopped loving me. We just hadn't been able to talk it all out together.

But I could say the truth out loud now. And doing so could change things. It could change me.

THE AROMA OF MOM'S BEEF STEW lingered in the kitchen. She probably had just enough left over for my father and her to have it for dinner again tomorrow night, what with all of us having seconds—and Geoff having thirds.

Johanna, Jillian, and I had made quick work of cleanup after dinner, and we'd all agreed to a game of Scotland Yard.

If anyone glanced in the bay window that bordered the breakfast nook, they'd probably see nothing more than a trio of sisters sitting at the table, talking on a mid-February evening—never imagining what a monumental event this was.

Johanna. Jillian. Me. All sitting together. Talking. For more than five minutes. And so far, no arguing.

I was certain Geoff and my parents were waiting for the

three of us to join them in the family room, but they would have to continue to wait. We were in no rush to exchange our conversation for a board game.

"Anybody want more coffee?" I stood at the island, prepping the coffeemaker.

"Sounds good." Johanna nodded. "Just black."

"None for me, thanks." Jillian tugged her purple sweater closer around her body.

"Johanna, how's work going?" I could only hope I didn't sound like a desperate TV interviewer, trying to avoid the dreaded dead air in front of thousands of viewers.

Me, trying to engage my oldest sister in a conversation. How different from a few months ago, when all I wanted her to do was leave me alone so I could set desserts out for Jillian's engagement party.

None of us imagined how life-changing that night would be.

"Pretty well. We're training a new pharmacy technician— and you know what that's like."

No, I didn't know what that was like, but for the sake of continuing a pleasant conversation, I wasn't going to say that. "Challenging, I would imagine."

"Just getting her used to the routine, helping her learn the way around the hospital. The whole crawling-up-the-learning-curve thing."

"Right. How's Beckett?"

"He just got orders to Alabama this summer."

Jillian took a sip from her water bottle. "He took the new assignment after all?"

"Yes. We talked about our options and decided post-graduate school was the right thing for him to do."

There was no reason to ask my sister if that was really the way things went after her showdown with Beckett on Christmas Day. This was her story—a mutually agreed-upon decision—and she'd stick to it.

Although none of us liked talking about Jillian's cancer, I still had to ask the question. To let my sister know I cared. "How are you doing with your radiation therapy, Jillian?"

"Managing. I'm tired, but there's an end in sight."

"You still like having a puppy?"

Johanna's question, asked without a trace of skepticism, was almost not worth asking. Geoff and Jillian took Winston with them everywhere. Right now, the puppy was probably snoozing in Geoff's lap—or my dad's.

"Winston is part comic relief, part comfort, and part constant aggravation. I'm focusing on the first two and reminding myself that he will outgrow the third one."

"Dad certainly likes the little guy. Makes me wonder if he's going to talk Mom into a dog."

We all laughed over the thought. If only someone could capture the moment—the three of us smiling and laughing.

We'd get back to normal soon enough. Occasional rounds in the ring between Johanna and me. Jillian taking up her position in the middle, forever and ever, amen.

I had to be realistic. Even with truth . . . with confession . . . some things were destined to remain the same.

"Sometimes you just have to forget all the other stuff and remember we're sisters."

The truth of Pepper's words no longer seemed to remind me of what was lacking in my relationship with my sisters. Instead, they drew me closer to Johanna and Jillian—and Pepper—and made me grateful for the good.

"You know, I've been thinking about Pepper a lot lately."

My comment was met with surprised silence. Johanna stared at me and Jillian glanced back and forth between the two of us as if uncertain what to say.

"I think . . . I think maybe this year was tough, what with it being ten years since she died. Or maybe I just made it tougher on myself. Tougher for everyone else, too." I swallowed the salty taste of unshed tears. "I'm learning how to live without her . . . letting myself miss her."

"I miss her, too." Jillian reached across the table to touch my hand.

"We all do." Johanna's agreement united us.

I had to clear my throat before I could say the next words. "I have to tell you both something Pepper said. Something we all need to remember."

And as I spoke the words, I heard the echo of Pepper's voice with mine.

ACKNOWLEDGMENTS

WHENEVER I WRITE A BOOK, I expect challenges. And challenges did happen while writing *Things I Never Told You* . . . some that brought me to tears and also drove me to my knees in prayer—again and again—as I faced some ongoing health issues and also wrestled with my beliefs about family and yes, sisters.

If a book strengthens my faith, then it's worth it. I learned over and over again that God is faithful and His mercies are new every morning (Lamentations 3:22-23). And I also was encouraged by the love and prayers of family and friends who walked alongside me. Every page of this book was prayed over as I wrote. I pray God blessed you in some way as you read it.

I do want to mention the different people who supported me through the months as *Things I Never Told You* went from just an idea to a real book:

My family: Writing a book disrupts life—mine and my family's. But my husband, Rob, and my children—Josh,

Katie Beth and Nate, Amy and David, Christa, and my two GRANDgirls—accept and love me for who I am: a *creative*. They adapt to conversations about imaginary characters, deadlines, and impromptu "What do you think about this?" discussions.

Special thanks to my physician-husband, Rob, who also moonlights as my "doctor on call" when I decide to weave a medical angle into a book.

Special thanks also to my youngest daughter, Christa, who was my sports consultant for *Things I Never Told You*. I'm not an athlete, but Christa is, and she's a very good one, too. When I needed volleyball information, I went to my favorite volleyball player, an unconventional left-handed middle.

Advance readers: Angie, Casey, Jeanne, and Shari—I like to think I'm a good writer, but *Things I Never Told You* is all the better because of your insights.

Rachel Hauck and Susie May Warren: Here's to another December Meet-Up where we talk story, brainstorm our upcoming books, laugh, relax, and remember the value of good friends. You two mean the world to me.

Rachelle Gardner: How did we get here? Oh yes. You believed in me and this change of direction along the writing road. Lots of conversations and e-mails. Prayer. Thank you for being the best of agents . . . and for being my trusted friend.

Casey Herringshaw: *"Casey, would you . . . ?"* Every busy writer—and yes, every writer is busy—needs a virtual assistant (VA). But I have dibs on Casey Herringshaw. Why? Because she keeps me sane—and keeps my to-do list under control.

Tyndale House, including Jan Stob (acquisitions director), Sarah Rische (editor), Sharon Leavitt (senior author relations manager), Julie Chen (senior designer), and Emily Bonga and the marketing team: I was told by other authors that I would love being with Tyndale House Publishers. I didn't doubt them—but it's wonderful experiencing being part of Tyndale for myself. Thank you for believing in me and for all your expertise while I worked on *Things I Never Told You*.

My Dream Team: The group changes a little with every book. But the purpose is always the same: These people support my dream . . . and I support theirs. And it's always fun and life-giving.

ABOUT THE AUTHOR

BETH K. VOGT is a nonfiction author and editor who said she'd never write fiction. She's the wife of an Air Force family physician (now in solo practice) who said she'd never marry a doctor—or anyone in the military. She's a mom of four who said she'd never have kids. Now Beth believes God's best often waits behind doors marked *Never*. *Things I Never Told You* is the first novel in her women's fiction series with Tyndale.

Beth is a 2016 Christy Award winner, a 2016 ACFW Carol Award winner, and a 2015 RITA finalist. Her 2014 novel, *Somebody Like You*, was one of *Publishers Weekly*'s Best Books of 2014. *A November Bride* was part of the Year of Wedding series published by Zondervan. Having authored nine contemporary romance novels or novellas, Beth believes there's more to happily ever after than the fairy tales tell us.

An established magazine writer and former editor of the leadership magazine for MOPS International, Beth blogs for Novel Rocket and also enjoys speaking to writers' groups and mentoring other writers. She lives in Colorado with her husband, Rob, who has adjusted to discussing the lives of imaginary people, and their youngest daughter, Christa, who loves to play volleyball and enjoys writing her own stories. Connect with Beth at www.bethvogt.com.

DISCUSSION QUESTIONS

1. Which sister did you most identify with in *Things I Never Told You*: Payton, Pepper, Jillian, or Johanna? Why? If you have a sister or sisters, how would you describe your relationship(s): supportive or competitive—or a blend of both?

2. Were you an athlete in high school or college or part of another group or organization that influenced your identity? Did you have a coach, teacher, or other mentor who had a significant impact on your life? How did those experiences shape who you are today?

3. If you've ever grieved the death of a family member or close friend, what helped you deal with the pain? Was there something—a book or a Scripture verse or a song—that ministered to you?

4. Jillian is closer to Harper than she is to her sisters, Johanna and Payton. How has a good friend made a difference in your life when you've faced a trial?

5. What did you think of the "positive thoughts" jar that Harper made for Jillian? Would something like that be helpful to you during a tough time? What thought would you add to the jar?

6. Payton and Jillian both see examples of times when Johanna means well but causes hurt in the way she tries to take charge or impose her own solutions. How do you handle a loved one—a friend, a sister, or other relative—who is more strong-willed or opinionated than you and, while attempting to help, hurts you or overlooks your feelings or desires? Have you ever been a "Johanna" to someone? What was the result?

7. After Pepper's death, Payton gave up many of her goals for the future and chose a different path for her life. What dreams did you have when you were younger that changed or were lost along the way? If you had the chance, would you pursue those dreams now? Why or why not?

8. Zach Gaines struggles to share his faith with Payton. How and when do you talk to others about what you

believe about God? When someone talks to you about their faith, how does that make you feel?

9. Payton kept a secret from her family for ten years. How do you feel about secrets—are they necessary or are they destructive? When do you think a person should keep a secret?

10. As identical twins, Payton and Pepper shared a unique bond, but they began to grow apart when Pepper started exploring ideas of God and faith. Have you ever felt betrayed, as Payton did, by a change in someone you love? Were you able to navigate that change to keep the relationship? If so, what helped you?

Keep an eye out for the next Thatcher Sisters novel.

VISIT WWW.BETHVOGT.COM FOR UPDATES.